Mountains Join The Sea

By
Cyndi Banister Wilson

Mountains Join The Sea

Copyright © 2015 Cyndi Banister Wilson

All rights reserved. No part of this publication may be reproduced, stored in a retrieval system or transmitted in any form by any means, electronic, mechanical, photocopy, recording or any other—except for brief quotations in critical reviews or articles—without prior written permission of the publisher, except as provided by USA copyright law.

ISBN 978-1-482548-35-8 (Print edition)
ASIN: B012BJAAKW (Ebook)

Book Design by AE Books, AEB Graphics, Denver, CO.

First Printing, 2015 Tattered Cover Press, Denver, CO.

To my Loving Husband, Mom, Daddy, and all my Friends and Family who encouraged me, supported me and believed in me. Without all of you this would not have been possible.
If someone in the book reminds you of yourself, well hopefully I did you justice.

Chapter One

The music played softly on the radio. Every once and awhile, the signal would be lost for a short time. The mountains occasionally wreaked havoc on the airwaves, creating an irritating static. Not that he noticed much. Instead, he marveled at the beauty that surrounded him, and let nature fill in the missing beats of the music.

The oldies station that Austin was listening to started playing John Denver's "Rocky Mountain High". He thought of how ironic it was that that song happened to be playing as his midnight blue, newly restored '52 Chevy pickup rambled down off of Rabbit Ears pass into the Yampa Valley.

Austin instinctively knew that this was the place for him, and that he'd made the right choice. This beautiful country was unlike anything he'd ever experienced. He was fulfilling his life-long dream of owning a working cattle ranch as well as coaching the high school football team.

Even growing up and living on the West Coast, Austin hadn't had the opportunity to experience the beautiful landscape of Colorado. During his professional football career, he hadn't had the chance to play here.

The valley intoxicated his senses with the mixture of aspen and pine trees. Some of them were beginning to change color at the top of the pass.

The smell in this part of the country was sensual. The cool air smelled fresh and of nature itself, with no competition. No traffic jams or crowded streets to contend with- only the wide-open spaces and the majestic mountains that commanded your attention.

Yes, this was the place. Austin was the proud owner of utopia in two of the most beautiful places on earth. The other was the perfect tropical place, quiet and serene. In that tropical paradise, he had made the decision to follow his dreams.

This was truly God's country, and he was glad to be a part of this beautiful place.

Austin knew that he would spend the rest of his life here, and that this is where he was meant to be. Good things were going to happen to him in this valley.

~ ~ ~

CeCe finished mixing the dough for her final batch of cookies. She punched at the dough to release some of her anger, toward the hiring board for the football-coaching job.

"How dare they tell me I don't have enough experience for the coaching job", she muttered under her breath.

Why, she knew more about football than anyone else who had applied from the surrounding area!

There was a rumor floating around that they had hired some ex-pro player, but that didn't mean he would know anything about coaching high school ball.

Oh well, she would still support the team. The thought of her sitting and calculating her play calling against any one they put into the position made her relax a little. CeCe put the cookies in the oven and began her clean up.

Her little coffee shop was the local gathering place in a rural town in the Rocky Mountains of Colorado.

A small group of kids barged in the door. They hoped to raise money for the band members' trip to the Super Dome in New Orleans to perform in a high school competition. A few raffle tickets remained to be sold, and then they could be on their way to do whatever it was that kids did nowadays.

A senior named Mandy approached the counter. "How about a raffle ticket, CeCe?" she asked.

"What's the prize?" CeCe asked in return, knowing that she would buy a ticket regardless.

Mandy waved the tickets in the air announcing, "A trip to Hawaii. There's an added bonus. Two islands, Maui and Kauai."

CeCe had always wanted to go somewhere tropical, but had never been much further than Denver. She knew how much the trip meant to the band, and besides, what was there to lose?

"How much is the ticket?" CeCe asked.

"We're selling them $5 for one or $15 for four," Mandy replied.

CeCe went to the register and handed Mandy $15. "I might as well try for the big one."

"Wow, thanks, CeCe, you took the last of my tickets! I can go meet Scott earlier than I thought."

CeCe filled out the stub and off they went. Absent-mindlessly, she laid the raffle tickets on the edge of the register.

The morning had already wound down close to closing time for the shop. CeCe always looked forward to this time that she got to spend with her best friend since childhood. Reece and CeCe were as close as sisters. Their similarities and differences had always complimented them both.

Reece was elegant and beautiful. She was tall, thin and had fiery red hair to match her personality. Her features were almost aristocratic, and her eyes were the color of rich dark chocolate. Reece was the owner, editor, and reporter combined of the local newspaper.

CeCe, on the other hand, was petite; her hair was the color of wheat and she had a little bit of everything in all the right places. Her features were soft with huge blue eyes; they often reminded people of the deep blue sea. All of this coupled with her olive colored skin made for a beautiful package.

Both CeCe and Reece had an array of men vying for their attention.

Each of the women enjoyed the outdoors. CeCe was cautious and loved sports. She dragged Reece to all the high school football games. CeCe rarely accepted the offers for dates that she attracted at these events. CeCe knew that eventually the right man would come along. When that happened she would just know.

The bell rang and CeCe looked up, expecting Reece, but instead in walked the most handsome, muscular man she had ever laid eyes on. He was tall- around 6'2". Dark, curly hair sprouted from under the ball cap he wore. And the way the jeans fit his body sent a shiver up CeCe's back.

"Can I help you?" CeCe asked.

"I just drove into town and really need a cup of coffee. The sign out front says you serve the best coffee and cookies in the West- is that true?" The man asked.

"Well, I guess you'll have to find out for yourself. Have a seat and I'll bring you some," CeCe felt an unfamiliar stirring in her stomach as she moved to get this handsome stranger his coffee.

Austin was reluctant to sit after his long drive, so he walked around the small room looking at the pictures on the wall, while watching CeCe pour his coffee out of the corner of his eye.

"Are you just passing through?" CeCe asked conversationally.

"No, I've bought the Olsen place lock, stock, and barrel. I'll also be coaching football at the high school".

So this is the guy they gave the job to, CeCe thought. She wanted to know more about him.

"That's a big undertaking. What do you plan on doing with the Olsen place?"

"I thought I'd keep the ranch hands on and run about 1000 head of cattle. The house needs some work, though."

"I'd heard the place sold, but I didn't know to whom. Why such a big project if you're going to be coaching football?"

"I've always wanted to own a ranch, but I can't seem to give up the game of football. I played for the University of Hawaii, and then went pro with the San Francisco 49er's. I was injured my fifth year in the NFL and that pretty much ended my career."

With a shock of recognition, CeCe exclaimed, "You're Austin Carter, aren't you!"

"The one and, thank God, only. How did you know my name?" Austin asked, surprised that he was recognized.

"I'm a huge football fan. I'd have played the game myself if they'd have let females play when I was in school. I'm CeCe Wellington". CeCe extended her hand. "What happened to you after your injury?"

"I returned to Hawaii. I bought a small place where I could think, and decided I wanted to be in ranch country. I thought I'd try my hand, and the Olsen place was very attractive to me. The football coaching job was available, and well, here we are."

"I watched you play on TV. I thought you were a great wide receiver, but pushed off too often."

"Oh, no, here we go, the great football critic. There's always one in the crowd."

Just as CeCe was about to let him have a piece of her mind, the bell rang again and in came Reece.

Reece stepped in, talking loudly, "Wait 'til you hear about …".

She stopped dead in her tracks. "Well, good morning, or is it afternoon?" Reece strolled to where the two of them stood. "Let me introduce myself: I'm Reece Landon. And you are…?"

Austin was taken off guard, but figured that Reece was talking to him, since he was the only other person in the coffee shop.

CeCe reached over and grabbed Reece's arm. "Reece, this is Austin Carter, he bought the Olsen place, and is also the new football coach for the high school. He just got in town and stopped in for some coffee."

Reece raised her eyebrows and said, "Nice to meet you. How does your family feel about living in such a rural place? Or are you used to small-town life?"

Austin rested a long leg on one of the stools as he leaned forward to talk to Reece. "I'm by myself, and yes, I've lived in a place where the population is small. I actually much prefer intimate towns to the big city." Austin's mind flashed to his place in Kauai.

As Austin spoke, his eyes sparkled. His deeply tanned skin showed off a few attractive wrinkles around his eyes. Every time he moved, the muscles under his T-shirt rippled. CeCe didn't want to take her eyes off of him, but she couldn't stand and stare. She had never had this reaction to a man before, and she told herself that she certainly wasn't interested in this one.

Reece thought he was cute and wanted to talk to him more, but she had to tell CeCe about the letter she had received in the mail.

"Mr. Carter, nice to meet you. I'm sure we'll see you often. CeCe never misses a football game. As a matter of fact, she applied for the coaching job that you got."

CeCe couldn't believe what she was hearing- her best friend spouting off to the man who got the job, telling him about her applying and being turned down. She stepped between Reece and Austin.

"The coffee shop is closing, but if you'd like a great lunch you should try the Alpine Café around the corner."

"I'll take my check now please."

"The coffee is on the house today," CeCe said.

As Austin stood at the register, he saw the raffle tickets sitting there, proudly stating the grand prize.

"Grand prize: a trip to Hawaii," he read. "Hmmm. Well, if you win, I'd be happy to tell you about some of my favorite places and sights to see. Thanks for the coffee and the cookies. They really hold up their claim. You know, I'm sure you would like Hawaiian coffee, and some macadamia nuts would put those cookies out of this world. Next time I go to my place in Kauai I'll bring you some, or better yet, you just might get lucky and win that prize."

~ ~ ~

As the door shut behind Austin, his thoughts were on the women he left behind. He thought they were two of the most beautiful women he had ever met. That was a pretty bold thought, seeing as how he had been surrounded by beautiful cheerleaders in San Francisco and on the island of Kauai, the women wore their bikinis so skimpy it left very little to the imagination.

The minute he walked in the door and saw CeCe's curvy blonde figure, he felt a swelling in his jeans. She was feisty as hell. He didn't know if he had ever seen a more desirable mouth, and the way she filled out her clothes, she should be arrested. Austin walked to his truck and looked back.

CeCe would be a challenge to him, and they would have to wait and see as to how much she knew about football. How dare she say that he "pushed off", although she was right. That's how he got to the ball and broke away so often. Thank goodness the referees weren't as observant as she was.

To think she applied for the football coaching job. Well, they'd see how much she knew about the game. He planned on spending a considerable amount of time in the coffee shop. Austin smiled and drove away.

~ ~ ~

As soon as the door closed behind Austin, Reece waved her hand in front of her face. "Did you get a load of that body? He's one fine specimen of the male species, isn't he?"

CeCe rolled her eyes. "You think anything in a pair of jeans is a fine specimen, Reece. Now what were you so excited about when you walked in the door, before your hormones got in the way?"

Reece reached in her overly large handbag and pulled out a letter. "Wait 'til you hear this. I don't know if I've ever read anything like this before." Reece handed the envelope to CeCe.

"What's this?"

"Just read. Then tell me what you think."

CeCe opened the envelope and unfolded the page. It was evident that although the letter was typed, it hadn't come from a printer. The words were written on what appeared to be handmade paper. It had uneven edges with the wood grain and earthy colors showing through. The words flowed as smoothly as the stream that ran behind her own little cottage. They were like nothing CeCe had ever read before.

> *As I sit and watch the sun setting I can only think of having you by my side. The fire in the sky reminds me of the colors in your hair. The sound of your voice is like wind chimes blowing in a gentle breeze. Your scent to me is that of being in a field of wild flowers. As you pass by, I'm intoxicated and my mind is clouded. I can only watch from afar for now, but soon hope to hold you close and feel the warmth I can only now imagine. Love for now, Me!!*

CeCe held the letter close to her chest, "Where did you get this? This is somebody who has some pretty deep feelings for someone."

"The letter came to the newspaper addressed to me. I'm not quite sure if someone wanted the prose printed in the paper or if this was meant for me."

"What are you going to do with this?" CeCe asked her.

"I plan to hold on to the letter and see if there's any follow-up. Now, tell me more about the coach."

CeCe put her hands on her slim hips and said, "What the hell was that all about anyway, telling a stranger, and the one who got the job I might add, that I applied for the position of football coach?"

Reece shrugged and smiled slightly, "I just thought that Austin would like to know that you two have a lot in common."

"He came in here for some coffee and cookies and wanted to know if they stood up to their claim. We got to talking, and he told me he bought the Olsen place and that he's the new coach. I recognized Austin from when he played professional ball. He was a good player, sometimes brilliant, but he had a bad habit of cheating. Then, he called me a football critic, and I was just about to let him have a piece of my mind when you walked in the door. There's no doubt that if you didn't come in when you did, well, let's just say he was going to get an earful."

CeCe pulled out the cash drawer as she finished giving Reece the low down on her brief encounter with Austin Carter. Her cheeks felt flushed.

Reece picked up the raffle ticket and said, "I see some of the kids talked you into buying a few of these tickets."

"Why not? The money goes for a good cause, and wouldn't a trip to someplace tropical be fun? If you behave yourself, I might even take you with me if I win. Who knows, we could meet the men of our dreams on a trip like that."

Reece tipped her head to the side and smiled. "I thought I heard Coach say he had a place in Kauai. Wouldn't that be something if you win and he's the man of your dreams? I think there's some kind of omen or something like that going on here. He's the right height for you, too, CeCe; you two would be so cute together. Just think what you could teach your children about football. They'd all be very successful, not to mention beautiful."

CeCe threw a cloth at Reece. "Cut that out. You're something else! You already have me married and producing a whole football team, when I don't even like him! Although, I have to admit he isn't too bad to look at."

"Are you ready to go?" Reece stood. "I have to run off the breakfast I ate this morning. I had to go to the town council meeting and you know the type of breakfast they have...a pound of cholesterol here and a pound of fat there."

As the two of them were walking out the door, the phone rang. "Just a minute Reece, I need to get that"

CeCe pulled the key out of the door and raced to the phone.

"Good Afternoon, CeCe's, can I help you?"

"Yes, you can." The male voice answered.

"Oh, hello, Dr. Baldwin. I was on my way out for a run with Reece."

"Reece is one of my favorite ladies on earth, besides you, that is. How's the beautiful editor today?"

"She's great, but I'm sure that you didn't call me about Reece." CeCe rolled her eyes.

Dr. Baldwin chuckled. "No, but I bet you above all people could get me on her good side. I called to remind you of your appointment tomorrow for Nitro at 3:00 pm."

"Thanks for the reminder, but I'd never forget about Nitro."

"I'll see you tomorrow then, and tell Reece that Dr. Baldwin said hello, would you?"

"I'll make sure I do that. See you tomorrow". CeCe hung up the phone.

Dr. Baldwin was the very handsome but thrice married and divorced veterinarian. He was excellent at his profession, but his personal life could use some help.

He'd been after Reece since he came back to town and opened his practice. CeCe was grateful for the wonderful care he gave her full time companion and only bed mate Nitro.

Nitro was the love of her life. The 65 lb. black lab would greet her at the door every day when she returned home. They would play for hours on end. Nitro never tired of the time they spent together, hence his name. He was named Nitro for the color of night, and for his explosive energy.

CeCe had found Nitro in the parking lot of the local public library. He was the last of a litter that one of the local ranchers set out to find good homes for.

CeCe had been on her way out of the library, her arms filled with books, when she felt the cold wet nose on her ankle. She was startled, and dropped a few of the books. The owner called to the puppy as CeCe reached down to pet him and gather her books. She fell in love instantly when the pup licked her whole face in one sloppy swoop.

That was two years ago, and CeCe still felt like she'd gotten the best deal of her life that bright sunny day. Someone to give her unconditional love and depend on her love in return.

As CeCe replaced the phone, she turned to Reece to see a thoughtful look on her face.

"Dr. Baldwin. Hmmm. I wonder if he could have sent me the letter."

"Do you really think that he could write from the heart like that and have been married three times?"

"I suspect that if he wrote those words, that's the way he hooked numbers two and three." Reece laughed as they walked out of the tiny shop.

Chapter Two

He placed the paper in the typewriter. The feel of the unique paper made his heart pound- the anticipation of what he wanted to write was almost too much to bear.

He knew that most folks now used a computer, but to him, the sound of the keys tapping as his fingers flew across the keyboard was like artfully carving out the words rather than just processing them.

He didn't know how else to express his feelings to Reece. He knew that she had many men to choose from, but he was the right one for her. Only a short time need pass for her to realize that he was her prince, and then they could be together forever. He imagined how it would be: he would not have to write the words; instead he'd be able to let them flow openly, as they'd settle in for the evening. The letter began.

*Today I watched you walk gracefully by. The way you move is amazing. You don't just walk from one place to another, you glide. The fall leaves remind me of you, so brilliant in their beauty, yet fragile and still full of life. The kindness you show others is an inspiration. I only hope that soon I can be by your side, holding your hand, and giving you strength to forge on with your quests. I picture you in my mind every hour of every day. When I get a glimpse of you, my days are filled with joy. The little acts of kindness you do for so many people do not go unnoticed. I see as well as others. Never change! Stay the same as you are: **loving, caring, and beautiful inside and out.***

~ ~ ~

After a few errands, Austin drove out to the ranch. He was still amazed that all of this belonged to him.

The log home had been built in the early 1900's and was still full of charm. However, he had his work cut out for him. There were major repairs that needed to be done. Austin knew that he could hire someone, but he really enjoyed doing that sort of work himself.

The ranch had a few other dwellings that housed some of the ranch hands, and, of course, the foreman's quarters. The ranch foreman, Tucker Johnson, had been around for a long time. He handled all of the working parts of the ranch. Tucker had a vast amount of knowledge that Austin couldn't wait to tap into.

Austin planned on getting involved in all aspects of the ranch; he had a lot to learn and was excited to get started.

As he drove his pickup truck into the drive, Ruth stepped out onto the porch. Austin had met most of the staff that had worked for old man Olsen when he came for the closing.

Ruth was a real character. She didn't let anybody get away with anything, no matter who you were. Her primary job was to cook the meals for the ranch hands, but Ruth also kept the place spotless and acted like a mother hen. Austin liked her.

Ruth waved a dishtowel in the air as dust blew up on to the porch. "Why do you think you have to drive so fast as to stir up all that dust? Why, you'd think we're having one of those tornadoes they have in the panhandle. Make sure you wipe those boots before you walk into this house."

"Well, nice to see you again too, Ruth." Austin smiled as he walked onto the porch and gave her matronly figure a tight squeeze.

"Don't think you can come in here and butter me up just like that, young man. I've seen your type, with your silky words and million dollar smiles. You need only to follow a few rules and we'll get along just fine."

"Do you know where I might find Tucker? He and I need to

hash out some things."

Ruth rested her hands on her round hips and said, "Well, seeing we're darn near suppertime, give him a few minutes and he'll show up."

As Ruth finished talking, Tucker walked around the corner brushing dust from his jeans. "Hey there, Austin, I thought you might be around this evening. How's bout we talk over some coffee and some of Ruth's famous apple pie? She's one of the best cooks in the surrounding counties. Lucky for me, she's been my bride some 45 years," said Tucker.

Austin smiled. "Well, there must be something in the air. I stopped in CeCe's coffee shop today and had some outrageous cookies."

Tucker crossed his arms over his chest and said, "Well, you met Ms. CeCe today. Isn't she something? I can't figure out why she hasn't been scooped up by some lucky man yet. There ain't nothing like her anywhere- why she can out-cook and out-play anybody. Matter of fact, I heard tell that she wanted to coach that there football team you'll be coaching. She knows the game better than most of the men around. She has the face of an angel, and the body of one of those playboy models, not that I ever get a chance to look at them, Ruth there would hog tie me and wash my mouth out with soap if she heard me talking like that." Tucker shook his head.

After dinner Austin and Tucker sat in the great room of the main house. Austin asked Tucker, "What things need to be done to get ready for the winter?"

Tucker settled into his favorite chair. "We need to put up the hay and check the fences. Not much, which is probably good for you since you have the football team to get ready."

Austin was ready for that challenge, though he'd not been involved with the game for a couple of years. He still had his contacts around the league; maybe he'd call his old roommate who played for the Denver Broncos. He had been traded there after leaving the

'Niners. It would be fun to drive in for a game and catch up on the goings-on in the league.

After their conversation, Tucker and Ruth headed off to retire for the evening.

Austin walked outside and stood, watching the sun setting on the mountains.

He now understood those words in the song 'America the Beautiful', when it described purple mountains' majesty. The mountains were set aglow with the rays of the sun. He thought how beautiful the colors were that played against the mountains; a flaming mix of pink, orange and purple.

The temperature sure was different here than in Hawaii. He could already feel a chill in the air. In Kauai, the temperature didn't change much more than about five degrees or so between the summer and winter months.

Austin couldn't help feeling proud that he owned property in two of the most beautiful places on earth. He couldn't imagine living anywhere else besides here or Kauai, or how his life could get any better. Of course, he hadn't thought about having someone like CeCe in his life. He'd have to see if he could persuade her to let him get to know her better.

Reece walked into her house and set the mail on the table. The article that she needed to write for the newspaper about the upcoming football season occupied her mind. This would give her a good opportunity to introduce the coach, what was his name? Oh yeah, Austin Carter. Remembering his name made her smile.

She had felt something in the air between he and CeCe today. Reece really would like for CeCe to find a special someone. She deserved to be happy.

Reece decided that she'd call CeCe and ask her some technical questions about football so the article wouldn't sound as if she didn't know anything about the game (which she didn't). No one else needed to know that though.

Reece saw the now familiar letter sticking out of the pile of mail on the table. She touched the envelope and breathed in the scent of the paper. Reece read the contents, and then again more slowly.

The words were beautiful, but a bit scary. There seemed to be a dark side to them. She told herself she was being silly, folded the letter and tossed it to the side.

The phone rang. "Hello," Reece answered.

"Hi Reece! I was wondering if you wanted to go to the movies with me tonight. I hear there's a great chick-flick playing," said CeCe.

Reece rubbed her temples as she spoke. "I really would love to go, but I have to work on this article about the football season. So, if you promise to help give me some pointers tomorrow afternoon, I can go tonight. You know so much about the game that I'm sure you won't mind helping me. Besides, I want to introduce Coach to the rest of the town. I'm thinking of asking him to let me put his picture in the paper along with the article. What do you think?"

CeCe laughed, "I knew you would find a way to talk to him again. And of course I'll help you with the article."

Reece quickly responded, "I have no interest in him for myself. Don't think I don't find him attractive, but there were some major sparks flying when I walked in on you two. Austin's definitely interested in you. He couldn't take his eyes off of you."

"The sparks that you saw flying were from me and they didn't have anything to do with us hitting it off. On the contrary, I was just about to tell him what I thought about his arrogant attitude. He's very attractive though, I must admit. I did feel my heart flutter when he leaned over and smiled. He's kept in great shape since he played ball."

"See, I told you. What time will you get here?" asked Reece.

"I'll come by at 7:15. Be ready so we can take our time walking over to the theater."

"Okay, I'll be on time for a change. See you in an hour." Reece hung up the phone and went to change her clothes.

~ ~ ~

After a few hard weeks of training, Austin felt he had his team ready to play. There were some talented players on the team.

The quarterback had good arm strength for a junior, and the weight-training program that Austin had implemented would help all of the kids.

Austin was, of course, partial to the offense but couldn't believe the way the defense practiced. He had high hopes that they would play that hard in their first game.

The weather was perfect for football; there was already that delicious crispness in the air. The team would all be together at 5:30 this evening to get ready for the Hornets.

Austin arrived at the coffee shop at 6:30 am. The aroma that was emitting onto the street was amazing; his stomach grumbled hungrily in response. As he opened the door, the bell rang and a few heads turned. He was surprised to see so many people in the shop. He'd always come later in the morning.

He was searching for CeCe, anxious to invite her to the game.

"Good morning, Austin," CeCe said as she wiped her flour covered hands on the crisp white apron that covered her wonderful bottom.

"Good morning in return. You ought to be arrested for having such sinful aromas coming from your place. You could make a man go crazy." Austin thought that wasn't the only thing in this place that could cause a man to lose his mind.

"What can I get for you?" CeCe smiled at his compliment.

"I need some coffee and one of those cinnamon buns you just took out of the oven," Austin said, as he took a seat at the counter.

CeCe did an amazing job of running the shop. She knew everyone and almost always knew what they wanted. She sat the coffee and roll in front of Austin. "How's the team coming along? I know tonight is the first game. The Hornets are a good team. They've won the state championship the last four years. They always seem to give the Wildcats some problems."

Austin fumbled with his napkin, which he hoped his team didn't do with the ball in the game tonight. "The team's doing great. The kids have worked hard and I implemented a new weight training program for them, which I believe will make them stronger and better."

Austin took a deep breath; he felt like one of the high school boys. "I came in to ask if you were going to the game tonight, and if you'd like to stand on the sidelines with me." Austin wanted to show her how well he had prepared the team and to let her see that when they gave him the job they had made the right choice. He also wanted to have CeCe next to him.

"I never miss a game, Austin. I'd love to come down and give you a few pointers if you find yourself in need. Would you mind if Reece joined us?" CeCe smiled and showcased the deep dimples at the corners of her mouth.

How dare she think he would need pointers? Austin furrowed his brow as he thought, and then said with a little smirk, "Sure, Reece can come if she can find her own way home afterward. I was wondering if you had plans for dinner after the game? I thought we could get something to eat. I never liked to eat before a game when I was playing, and I still have the same habits."

"That would be great. Where shall we go? I hope someplace casual since we'll be dressed for the cool weather."

Austin finished his breakfast and stood to pay the bill. CeCe felt the flutter in her stomach as she watched him reach into his faded jean pocket to pull out some money. Her face flushed and she tingled all over. What was wrong with her?

As Austin paid the bill, he said, "Ruth is expecting me for a late dinner. I'll just tell her there will be the two of us. She's an incredible cook."

"She certainly is! Ruth has filled in for me a time or two, and I was always half afraid that no one would want anything I made afterward, seeing as how artful she is in the kitchen. You better watch out, or she'll put enough pounds on you that you could be one of those defensive linemen in the future."

Austin laughed, "You're right about that. I'll see you outside of the locker room at 6:15 tonight then."

"Great, see you then!"

After Austin walked out of the door, Tom Dancer, the local Ferrier, came to the register to pay his bill.

CeCe was never sure how she felt about Tom. He was tall and had a slight frame. He didn't speak to many people, as he had a slight stutter.

Mostly, Tom smelled of stale liquor, as he spent many evenings in the local bar and was never without his flask in his hip pocket. Tom was, however, excellent at his trade. He worked on most of the ranches.

Tom claimed that he used corrective shoeing methods that would alleviate hoof wall stress, and that he could align the hooves and support the tendons of the leg. Tom was not a veterinarian, but he knew everything that one could about horse's legs.

Tom handed CeCe his money and asked, "W-who is that g-guy?"

CeCe made change, "That's Austin Carter. He owns the old Olsen ranch, and he's the football coach for the high school. He used to play professional football."

"Oh, t-that's who he is. I am s-supposed to g-g-go out to the r-ranch and meet him this w-w-weekend."

"I would imagine he has some work for you. Take care now, Tom. Hope you're able to help Austin out."

"The c-coffee was sp-special today Ms. C-ceCe. Have f-fun tonight and tell Ms. R-r-Reece hello f-for me. See you s-soon."

CeCe sat waiting for Reece to come so they could go for a run.

Reece walked in the door out of breath like she usually did. "Sorry I'm late, but here I am. Are you ready to go?"

"Let's hit it. I have something special to tell you. Austin came in this morning and invited us to be on the sidelines with him at the game, and then he asked me out to dinner at his place afterward."

"You mean he invited you to be on the sidelines and out to dinner. What's this we stuff?"

"Well, he did ask if you could find your way home after the game. He said you could be on the sidelines. I think you might be able to learn more about the game if you're right in the middle of the action. Besides, I may need you to referee. If I start to tell him what plays to call, he may tackle me right there in front of everyone."

"Oh I think he'll save the tackling for after dinner, when the watchful Ruth has retired." Reece laughingly ducked out of the way of CeCe's shove.

~ ~ ~

Reece went back to the newspaper after her run with CeCe and sat at her desk to finish some work. She started to sort through the mail and recognized the unique envelope instantly. Carefully, she picked up the rough-edged envelope. Reece removed the letter and breathed in the earthy fragrance of the paper. She began to read.

This was really strange. Now there were letters and the envelopes were clearly addressed to her. She racked her brain to think who this could be. Most of the men she went out with never had a problem telling or showing her what they wanted. Certainly none of them had spoken to her like this. The whole thing was a puzzle to her.

Maybe CeCe could help. She saw all kinds of people in her shop and perhaps somebody had spoken in this poetic manner to her. Reece decided that she would take this letter with her to the game tonight for CeCe to read.

~ ~ ~

CeCe was excited for the beginning of the football season and to be Austin's guest at the game. She would mentally track her play calling against his, and then they would see who was better at this coaching thing.

Carefully, CeCe chose what clothes she would wear. She had to remember that it would be chilly at the game, but she needed to be comfortable afterward on the ranch. She chose a pair of stone-washed jeans with a short powder-blue cashmere sweater, both of which showed off her curvy figure.

Nitro wanted to play, so CeCe took him out and threw the ball for about an hour. When they came back inside, CeCe decided to take a long hot bath. The water and bubbles were so soothing that she soon nodded off.

She woke to someone pounding on the door. CeCe hurriedly got out and put on her robe, only to find Reece standing at the door.

"What's going on? Is there someone here? Am I interrupting something?" Reece was babbling questions at CeCe.

CeCe grabbed hold of Reece and pulled her inside as she said, "You know better than that. I am saving myself for the man I marry. We'll have a storybook wedding and live happily ever after."

"Oh brother, not that again. CeCe you don't know what you are missing. Why I could tell you….."

"Stop that Reece, don't go any further. I don't need you to get me in any more a tizzy than I already am. Let me get dressed and we'll be on our way."

"I want you to read this. I got another one of those letters in the mail. Who do you think is sending them, and why to me?"

CeCe took the letter and read. "I don't know who's sending

them, but from the sound of this, I'm pretty sure they're meant for you. Can I hold onto it? Maybe if I reread the letter I might be able to see if anybody comes to mind?"

"Go ahead. There's something about them that kind of makes me feel weird. Now go and get dressed, or you'll be late meeting Coach."

CeCe padded off to the bedroom with Nitro at her heels.

Chapter Three

There was great excitement in the air. The school was starting a brand new season, and everyone in the community supported the football team. The team had been good in the past, but never good enough to win the state championship. Everyone had high hopes this year. Reece and CeCe arrived at the field around 5:30.

Reece turned to CeCe and said, "Now, don't let on that I don't know very much about the game. I really do want to learn, but it'll take time. I do wish we were watching a professional game; then I could concentrate on the male bodies a little more. These are just kids. When I've seen some of the games on TV, I think, how do those bodies get created? CeCe, have you ever been to a professional football game? Wouldn't it be fun?"

CeCe took hold of Reece's shoulders and said. "Reece how can your mind be on sex all the time? If you really want to learn about the game, I'll teach you. But you must remember that these are only kids. And to answer your question, no, I haven't been to a pro game, but I'd love to go. Those bodies you see are the product of a lot of hard work. They spend hours in the weight room working on strengthening. Look, here comes Austin."

Austin walked over to CeCe and Reece. Boy was he handsome. What a shame Austin had to quit playing ball, but then again, CeCe might not have met him.

"Hello ladies. I see you made it on time. The kids are ready to play ball, and I'm anxious to have this first game under my belt."

"Well, it's certainly football weather. I'm excited to be here on the sidelines; maybe the kids will hear me rooting for them." CeCe smiled.

Austin winked at Reece and said, "Are you ready for this? I understand you're going get a football lesson tonight"

Reece glared at CeCe and said, "Oh you would be surprised at what I know I know that the game is played by men, coached by men, refereed by men, and watched mostly by men, with the exception of a few women."

"Enjoy the game ladies. I'll see you in a few minutes." Austin laughed as he walked back to the locker room.

The game was a good one; Austin did have the team pumped up and ready to go. The Wildcats were only down by four points near the end of the fourth quarter.

Austin looked at his playbook to determine what play to call. The Wildcats had the ball on their own thirty two-yard line with a third down and two to go for the first down. They hadn't been able to run the ball very effectively all night, and the Hornets were putting on a fierce pass rush. They had to score. There were only two minutes left in the game.

Austin spoke with the quarterback during the two-minute warning. "What do you think, Jason? Do we try the run, or do you think the offensive line can hold them off long enough for you to get the pass off to the sideline?"

"Well, Coach, I don't think we will have enough time to get in the end zone if we try the run play and Andy doesn't get out of bounds. I think we need to try the pass play," replied Jason.

CeCe said, "Why don't you try a 'flea flicker'? I've been watching all evening, and the left side seems to be open. The safety keeps cheating toward the line and I think you can pull it off."

Austin couldn't believe what he was hearing. CeCe didn't know what she was talking about. It was easy to call that play, but it very rarely worked. When he was playing for the Niners, they tried it a few times and the quarterback either got sacked or the toss went bad, or something along those lines. The play wouldn't work.

"I think we should try….." Austin began telling Jason another idea when Jason broke in.

"Come on, Coach, we tried the play in practice and we executed it perfectly. How about letting us try it- what do we have to lose?"

"The game is what we have to lose, but we might be able to catch them off guard. They will be expecting the pass play. Okay, Jason, if you feel comfortable, go ahead and try it." Austin thought that he must be crazy, listening to a woman's play calling. He only hoped that it worked.

Reece turned to CeCe and said, "What the heck is a flea flicker, and what does it have to do with football? It sounds like something Dr. Baldwin should be dealing with."

CeCe grinned and thought about how funny it was, the way that Reece processed things. "It's when the quarterback takes the snap and hands off the ball to the running back. Then he fakes the run and tosses the ball back to the quarterback, who throws it to the wide receiver. It's a fun play when it works."

Reece frowned, "What happens when it doesn't work?"

"Let's hope that doesn't happen," replied CeCe.

The play clock had clicked down to five seconds by the time the ball was snapped back- it all seemed to be happening in slow motion. Jason handed the ball to Andy, he then back-peddled as Andy faked right, turned and threw the ball to Jason; Jason could see Scott wide open on the left side just as CeCe had said. He threw the ball. Scott went up and caught it; he broke a few tackles and ran into the end zone carrying the safety on his back. Touchdown!

Everyone was on their feet, screaming and yelling. Austin grabbed hold of CeCe, picked her up, and swung her around. He lifted her high in the air, and when he put her down, Austin gave CeCe a kiss right there on the field.

Austin ran over to congratulate the team. They had done a wonderful job, and to think, it was CeCe's idea. He may have to have her on the sidelines all the time. Maybe she was a good luck charm.

CeCe was excited that the play had worked; she had been right about that left side. She was more overwhelmed with Austin's reaction. CeCe felt like she was flying, and when he put her down on the ground and kissed her, she felt like she was suspended in air. His touch made her body tingle all over. CeCe's face was flushed from the heat she felt within, and she hoped that everyone else thought the high color in her cheeks was from a combination of the cold and the excitement of the Wildcats winning. The rest of the game was a blur- not that there was much time left.

All kinds of people came by to congratulate Austin and the team: Tucker and Ruth, Tom Dancer, all of the faculty, and Dr. Baldwin.

Austin reminded Ruth that he and CeCe would be at the ranch later for dinner.

Ruth, of course, never forgot things like that and she told Austin the same. "Austin, what makes you think I have scrambled eggs for brains? I hope you're a gentleman to Ms. CeCe. She deserves to have someone wait on her for a change."

Austin smiled at that and said, "Don't you worry Ruth, I'll treat her right. Matter of fact, everyone should be congratulating CeCe since she's the one who called the winning play."

Tucker's voice boomed. "I told you so, that she knew the game better than most men. Maybe you two should work together on the game plan from now on."

They all laughed as Tucker hooked his arm in Ruth's and said, "Let's get on home. I need a warm fire and some of that dessert you made". At that, the two strolled off into the night.

Tom walked over to CeCe, Reece, and Austin, and said, "N-nice game, Coach.

R-Reece, I didn't know y-y-you were interested in f-football. I guess we w-will see your article in the newspaper t-tomorrow."

Reece backed away; the smell of alcohol was strong on Tom's breath. "I like the game, and you get a better perspective of it from the sidelines. I certainly will write some good things in the paper tomorrow, nice to see you, Tom."

Reece pulled at CeCe's arm so they could get away from the crowd.

As they were walking away, Dr. Baldwin walked over and said, "Two of the most beautiful women in the state. Why, you two could brighten a dark room with your smiles. Can I invite you both to dinner?"

CeCe quickly answered, "I have plans, but as far as I know Reece is free."

"Is that so, Reece?" asked Dr. Baldwin.

"Well, I am kind of hungry, so if you're inviting, then I guess so. I'll see you tomorrow, CeCe, and I want a full account of this evening's activities." Reece waved good-bye as she walked off toward the parking lot.

Austin came over to CeCe, and asked her if she would mind waiting a while longer while he talked to the team.

"Go ahead- I'll get myself a cup of tea while I wait."

"It didn't take Reece long to find a date," Austin commented.

"It never does. She has a long list she can choose from. Matter of fact, she seems to have someone very smitten with her. She's been receiving letters of sorts. Reece isn't sure if they are for her, but it sounds like it to me."

"What do you mean, letters of sort?"

"Well, they're almost poetic. The words are beautiful. She gave me the latest one to read more carefully, in case something might jog my mind as to who might be writing them."

"Are the letters coming to her home or work?" asked Austin.

"They're coming to the paper, but they're addressed to Reece. I'll show you the letter later, you need to go and talk to the team. Besides, I'm starving and can't wait to see what wonders Ruth has cooked up."

Austin gave CeCe a little hug and went into the locker room.

CeCe hadn't been in the Olsen place for a long time. There was work to be done, but overall the place was still grand. The log structure looked sound, and the overly large fireplace kept the house nice and cozy.

The dinner Ruth had prepared was wonderful, but now CeCe needed to walk off some of those calories.

Austin asked, "Would you like to take a walk before we have some coffee and dessert?"

CeCe stood and moved toward the door. "I'd love to take a walk, then we'll see if there's room for any dessert."

"Let me get your jacket- there's a chill in the air out there tonight."

Austin helped CeCe into her jacket. He put his own on and they walked out onto the porch and then around the ranch.

"Are you enjoying life on the ranch and in Colorado?"

"I love it here. I'd have a hard time choosing which place I love the most, here or my place in Kauai. They're different, but not that much. A short distance from my home in Kauai, the mountains meet the sea. I love both of these places so much that I couldn't think of choosing between them. Here I have another love, football. Coaching the team is good. I didn't realize how much I missed the game. Tonight was special, having that first win under my belt, and I have you partly to thank. But I do think there was luck on your side with that play."

CeCe threw her head back and laughed, "I knew you wouldn't be able to accept my play calling, especially if I made a good call. You can't always be so conservative in your play calling. Sometimes you have to let your hair down and take a chance. That's what the game is all about. You above all people should know that. You took that chance every time you pushed off. Look where a little bit of cheating got you. You were one of the best wide receivers in the game."

Austin was stirred as he watched the moonlight dance on CeCe's hair as she tossed her head back. He loved to watch her mouth as she talked. He could only think of how wonderful she'd felt in his arms tonight when he picked her up after the touchdown. And her lips were so soft and giving. He wanted to kiss her again right here.

All of a sudden, CeCe tripped and fell forward, almost hitting the ground. Austin was quick to catch her. "Are you all right?"

"I twisted my ankle a bit, and it hurts pretty badly."

"Can you walk?"

CeCe tried it out. "I can't put too much pressure on the damned thing."

"Let me carry you back to the house." Before she could protest, Austin lifted CeCe off her feet and into his arms. He carried her inside and sat her on the sofa next to the fire. "Let me get some ice for that."

CeCe sat back and waited for Austin to return. She had felt the muscles under his clothing as he carried her back to the house. When her skin touched his there was a spark of electricity that went through her body. She didn't know if she would be able to control herself.

Austin returned with the ice and another glass of wine.

"I thought this might take the edge off the pain." He sat down beside her. "Lean up against me, and you can put your ankle on the pillow at the edge of the sofa."

CeCe did as he said.

As a few hours passed, CeCe could feel the effects of the wine and the warmth of the fire. Austin and she had talked about so many things. She felt like she knew Kauai personally from his descriptions of the beautiful island. She would have to go there herself sometime, even if she didn't win the raffle. Austin had been touching her hair as they talked, and when CeCe turned to ask him something, Austin cupped her face in his hands and kissed her softly at first, then more deeply.

CeCe couldn't help but return the kiss; she opened her mouth willingly to let his exploring tongue in. CeCe had never experienced such wonderful feelings before. Every inch of her body was alive. She could feel the stirring deep within her. Just as she was turning toward Austin to meet him fully, her foot fell off the pillow and dropped to the sofa, which brought her back to reality. "Ouch!" CeCe cried.

Austin, unaware of what had happened, asked, "Are you all right? Did I hurt you?"

"No, but my ankle is killing me. I think I better go home and have it looked at in the morning."

Austin reluctantly agreed. "I'll carry you out to the truck. Just wait here while I get your coat and warm it up."

CeCe thought to herself while Austin was gone, how could she have been so stupid and fallen in that hole? And if her foot hadn't fallen off the pillow, who knows what position she would be in now.

Austin drove CeCe home. The light glowed from within the little cottage that CeCe lived in, which made her home look very inviting.

Austin pulled his truck to a gentle stop, got out and went around to open the door. CeCe was already trying to get out.

"You shouldn't put any weight on that foot until you have it looked at. Are you sure you wouldn't like me to take you to the emergency room now?"

CeCe scoffed at his suggestion and said, "The pain is better since we put the ice on. I'm sure my ankle will be okay."

CeCe stepped down out of the truck on her good foot and tried to put her weight on the one she hurt. Her ankle wouldn't support her, pain shot up her leg and she had to lean up against Austin to keep from falling. Austin lifted her like she was a bag of feathers. Darn him for being so strong, thought CeCe.

Austin carried her to the door and asked, "Where's the key?"

"I never lock the door, except at night when I am asleep."

"You can tell you've never lived in the city." Austin opened the door and stepped in. Just as he did Nitro came bounding out of the bedroom to greet them.

"What the heck…!" Instantly, Nitro jumped on Austin. He almost knocked them over.

"Austin, meet Nitro- Nitro, meet Austin."

"No wonder you don't lock the door."

"Oh, he won't hurt you, he's nothing but a big teddy bear."

Austin said, "Let me guess -the bedroom is over there."

"Austin, you can set me down on the sofa. I'll be able to make my way into the bedroom later."

Austin reluctantly sat her down.

"Nice place you have here. How quaint. This cottage suits you very well," Austin commented.

"Are you saying I'm quaint?" CeCe asked with a grin.

"Of course not. I was just commenting on your place. The setting is not unlike my place in Kauai. I prefer a small place to a bigger one."

"The cottage has been in the family for a long time. I lived here with my grandmother for a time before she passed on. I love this place. The stream outside the bedroom window lulls me to sleep at night. I even have a garden that I try to grow things in."

"I like this place," Austin said as he sat on the edge of the sofa. Nitro jumped onto his lap.

"He thinks he's a lap dog. He loves people."

Nitro jumped off Austin's lap, but not until he gave him a big sloppy kiss. He came running back with a ball for Austin to throw.

"He seems to like you. Nitro, it's too late for us to play. We'll play tomorrow." Nitro lay on the floor with the ball under his paws and looked up with his dark brown eyes. "He knows how to make me feel guilty," CeCe said. Austin petted Nitro and he rolled over for a tummy rub.

Nitro had forgotten all about the fact that he wanted to play. Having his tummy rubbed was another of his favorite things.

Austin stood and said; "I should be going. Can I get you anything before I leave? I'll come by in the morning to take you to get that looked at if you call me."

"I'll be all right. I need to open the shop in the morning and if my ankle's still hurting I'll call Reece and she'll take me in." replied CeCe.

Austin leaned over and said, "I had a really good time this evening. I hope we can get together again soon."

CeCe smiled and said, "I'd be happy to help you win some more games. Ask my opinion any time."

Austin laughed, as he kissed the top of her head lightly. "You take care of that ankle now. I'll stop by and see you tomorrow."

"Good night, Austin, and thank you for a good time. Tell Ruth she out-did herself on dinner."

Austin let himself out of the door. All he could think of was the wonderful feel of her in his arms. The perfume that she wore was light and delicious. The scent made him think of those cinnamon rolls she had been baking that morning.

He'd had different plans for the walk they were taking when she fell in that damn hole. He'd have to fix it tomorrow so no one else would do the same.

Where would the evening have gone if she hadn't hurt herself? CeCe tripping did give him the opportunity to touch her most of the evening, however.

The kiss they had shared was intense. He didn't just imagine that she willingly kissed him back.

He could feel the blood rush through his body the minute he put his hands on her face. The glow of the fire on her hair was too much for him- he just had to kiss her. He wanted more of her, but things would have to move forward on her terms. This was different than anything he had ever experienced. He had dated many other women, but not one had made him feel this way. She was intoxicating.

Reece came into the shop first thing in the morning. She had to know how the evening went.

When she saw CeCe hopping around she went to her side and said, "What the heck happened? Did you two play tackle football or what? Maybe I should've been there to referee."

CeCe laughed as she hopped to the counter. "We had a wonderful evening, until I stepped in a hole after dinner and twisted my ankle."

Reece grabbed CeCe by the arm and sat her down. "You can't do this by yourself. Where's an apron? I'll help."

"Oh, no, you don't. You're like a bull in a china shop when it comes to the kitchen. Do you know how many weeks I'd have to search to find things after you'd been in my kitchen?"

"You're right, CeCe. But there must be something I can do to help."

"You could clean off the tables, if you don't mind. I am afraid it will be awhile before we can go on our daily run, though."

"I don't mind helping, and my body could use a rest. Let me get an apron and start cleaning up, and you can fill me in on your date."

"You can do the same."

Austin had a full day, but he wanted to go to the coffee shop to see how CeCe was doing. He met with Tucker first thing in the morning about filling in the hole.

Tucker was feeling pretty bad about the fact that CeCe had stepped in the fence hole. He'd told one of the hands to take care of that. They must have missed a few.

Austin had an appointment with the Ferrier, Tom Dancer, at 9:00. All of the horses needed to be shod.

Everyone said that Tom was the best at his trade. However, he was about ten minutes late; Austin had a thing for promptness. If Tom wanted to work for him he'd have to be on time. Austin could see the dust coming up the drive. That must be him.

Tom stopped his truck right outside the corral. He could see Austin waiting for him.

"I-I'm Tom Dancer. I saw you in the c-coffee shop a while back and again l-last night. That was a g-g-good game, Mr. Carter."

Austin extended his hand to Tom, "Nice to meet you. I hear you know your trade well. I have some work here if you're interested."

"T-t-that is what I do b-best," replied Tom.

Austin thought that from the smell of him, work wasn't the only thing he did best. He reeked of alcohol. "Let me show you where to get started," Austin said as they walked over to the horses. "They're all yours. I'll pay you when you're finished. How long do you think it will take you?"

Tom scratched his head and said, "I'll need to m-m-make some special s-shoes, so I i-imagine 'round about a w-week."

"I'll tell Ruth you'll be around so she can count on you for lunch."

"T-that would be very nice of y-you, Mr. Carter. Thank you." Austin turned toward the house as Tom walked to the truck to get the things he needed to get started. Tom was a strange man, Austin thought.

Chapter Four

After the morning rush, CeCe and Reece sat down to talk. CeCe told Reece about her wonderful evening. CeCe left out the parts about how she was already feeling about Austin, but nothing got by Reece. To change the subject, CeCe encouraged Reece to tell her about her evening with Dr. Baldwin.

Reece told CeCe they went out to a local bar where there was a dance band. Gino Caparzio, who they had gone to school with, was playing there.

He wrote songs and said one day he'd hit the big one. The band was doing well, but hadn't recorded anything professionally. He had asked her out when they were in school together, but Reece didn't think he was her type.

CeCe listened to Reece as she got up to refill her coffee cup. When she accidentally put weight on the twisted ankle, CeCe winced in pain.

Reece said, "That's it- we're taking you in to see what you've done to yourself. You can't just nurse away the pain by yourself."

CeCe didn't argue because her ankle didn't seem to be getting any better. Reece helped CeCe out to her car, and they drove to the emergency room.

CeCe had a few ex-rays taken, and they determined that she had a bad sprain. She would need to use crutches for a while and keep her ankle elevated as much as possible.

While they were at the emergency room, Reece met yet another young, handsome, and available man. Dr. Mason Albright had just arrived a few weeks ago.

He used the excuse that he didn't know his way around town very well to ask Reece out on a date. Reece never passed up an opportunity to show an available male around.

By the time they left the emergency room they had a date all set up, and you would have thought they had known each other for years.

Reece helped CeCe into the car. She was bubbling over about Mason. "Isn't he the cutest thing you've ever seen, CeCe? And he's so polite. I think this could lead to something."

CeCe responded to Reece, "It won't be long before you get bored with him. He isn't enough of a challenge for you. Someday you'll meet the right man, and he'll sweep you off of your feet. That feeling will be like nothing you've never experienced before."

Reece grinned at CeCe and said, "This is coming from a woman who knows what she's talking about. Have you been swept off your feet, CeCe?"

CeCe ignored her and said, "Let's get home. The weather is turning bad and the lightning is starting to look fierce."

As Reece and CeCe pulled around the bend in the road before her cottage, they could see and smell the smoke.

The volunteer fire department was hard at work trying to control the blaze. Lighting had struck the back part of CeCe's cottage. The bedroom was ablaze. That's where Nitro slept during the day when she was gone. She had to get in and get him out.

The fireman wouldn't let her near the place. CeCe was beside herself; she sat and waited while the fireman got the blaze under control. They were able to contain it to the bedroom area- the rest of the cottage would just need some clean up from the smoke damage. CeCe still was not allowed in the cottage, and she desperately wanted to get in and find Nitro.

Reece wanted to take CeCe back to her house right away, but CeCe insisted on waiting until the fire was under control so she could go and look for her dog.

"I need you to go and pick up a few things for me at the department store. I won't be able to wear anything in there." CeCe was sobbing as she spoke to Reece.

Reece was arguing with her about staying there by herself. "I don't want to leave you. We can go and pick up the stuff when you're ready to leave."

"No, Reece, please go. I need to be alone for a while. I won't be able to go anywhere. I'll be here when you get back. Now, go, please."

Reece left reluctantly, promising to return as quickly as she could.

The fire chief, Jeff Kirkwood, came over and comforted CeCe. "He must've been overcome by the smoke. I'm really sorry you lost him. We'll go in early in the morning and search the place. You need to get off that ankle of yours. Would you like me to take you somewhere?"

"Reece will be back shortly. I think I'll just wait for her. I'll be fine. Thanks for your help in keeping the fire contained."

"We'll come back in the morning then. You take care now," replied Jeff.

CeCe sat on the little knoll outside the cottage and began crying again. Nitro was everything to her. How could this have happened to him? She would never forgive herself for leaving him alone. CeCe wept as she watched the sun setting.

She would need to stay with Reece for a while so she could get the bedroom rebuilt and the smoke damage taken care of.

CeCe sat there reflecting on the short time she had with Nitro. There was a noise behind her. CeCe rose and steadied herself on her crutches. She was shielding her eyes from the sun when she saw the figure coming toward her.

CeCe screamed, "Nitro, how did you get out! I thought you were gone." Nitro limped toward CeCe holding his right paw in the air. His paw was bleeding and looked to have been burnt.

She buried her face in his fur and cried tears of joy. Nitro needed to go to the vet, but she was unable to pick him up while she was on the crutches.

CeCe reached in her bag for her phone and called Reece. She

wasn't answering- her phone must have been turned off.

CeCe thought about whom she could call. Austin came to mind, and she dialed the ranch.

Ruth answered the phone.

"Ruth, is Austin there? I need some help. I came home from the emergency room this afternoon, and my house had been struck by lightning and it caused a fire. I'm okay, but Nitro was missing. We thought he was inside the house, but he must've jumped through the window, and he's injured. He needs to see Dr. Baldwin." CeCe never took a breath while she was talking to Ruth.

Ruth cried out, "Are you all right, darlin'? You must've been scared to death. We all know how much your cottage and Nitro mean to you. Let me get Austin for you, and if he can't come Tucker and I will be right there."

Ruth laid the phone down and hurried out to where Tucker and Austin were talking. "Ms. CeCe is on the phone, her place was struck by lightning this afternoon and caught on fire. She thought that Nitro was inside the house, but he came home and is injured. She needs some-one's help to get him to Dr. Baldwin. Do you want to talk....?"

Austin hollered over his shoulder as he was hopping in the truck, "Tell her I'm on my way."

Austin drove as fast as he could. He hoped she and Nitro were all right. He didn't think to ask how bad the fire had damaged the cottage, and if CeCe had been inside when the fire started. She must've been beside herself about Nitro.

The drive seemed to take forever. Austin could see the two of them sitting on the knoll as he pulled the truck to a stop.

"Are you okay?"

CeCe's face was streaked with tears. "I'm fine. It's Nitro that needs attention. Thank you for coming. I can't lift him."

"As long as you are both all right, that's all that matters. Here, let me take him."

Austin loaded Nitro into the truck and then helped CeCe in.

They met Dr. Baldwin at the animal hospital. Nitro was going to be okay. With some loving care and rest, his paw would heal. There was a nasty gash and a burn, but overall he was a lucky dog. Thank goodness he didn't cut a major artery.

Austin took CeCe and Nitro home with some instructions on limited activity. CeCe turned to Nitro and said "Well, buddy, we're two of a kind. We're both lame. At least we can comfort one another."

Austin offered to let CeCe and Nitro stay on the ranch; he had an extra cottage available. CeCe declined, "I 'm looking forward to Reece and I getting to spend some time together".

Austin drove CeCe to Reece's place. Reece ran out of the house when she saw them drive up. She was jumping up and down and clapping her hands in joy.

"I went by to pick you up and you weren't there. I was frantic; I didn't know where you could have gone. Where did you find Nitro?" Reece asked as she reached into the truck to pet him.

"I was just sitting there reflecting on how little time I had with him, and how much I was going to miss him, when I heard a noise behind me. I stood to look, but the sun was setting and I couldn't see too well. Then I saw him coming towards me. At first, I thought he was a figment of my imagination. I tried to call you here, but you must have been at the department store. Then I called Austin. I knew someone at the ranch would be able to come out and take us to see Dr. Baldwin. He said Nitro would be all right, just to keep his activity to a minimum. With Nitro, that isn't going to be an easy task"

Austin spoke up as he was carrying Nitro into the house, "About as easy as keeping you down, CeCe. I think that maybe there was divine intervention there when that lighting struck your place. Everyone knows that you won't take much help and that you try to do too much. I'm surprised that you weren't out there trying to run today."

Austin took Nitro into the house and returned for CeCe. "I can do this myself. I'm getting pretty good on these things. Watch me."

Austin and Reece watched CeCe climb out of the truck. She used the crutches to support herself and walked to the stairs.

"I haven't had to use them on the stairs, however," CeCe said ruefully, as she attempted the climb.

Austin stood behind her. "I'll stand behind you as you try and walk up the stairs. It's always easier to go up the stairs rather than down."

"You should know." CeCe struggled up the stairs. Reece walked ahead to open the door.

"You amaze me with the things you can do. Now, I would have just let this nice strong handsome coach carry me up those stairs."

"How am I supposed to be able to do things on my own if I call a man every time I need something?"

CeCe felt the heat rising in her face at the thought of Austin carrying her up the stairs. She remembered the other times he'd touched her. The thought made her feel warm and wonderful.

She thought that he was being nice to her by helping her through this injury. She would have to heal, and then they'd see how much touching would go on.

Chapter Five

The football game had been good, but he was more interested in the beautiful Reece on the sidelines. He watched her every move all evening. God, she was something.

He began to think that she might know who he was by the letters he was sending. She didn't see him, though. He had to find a way for her to see him for what he was.

He'd write to her again. He placed the special paper in the typewriter, and began:

The weather is changing, yet my feelings for you have not. Reece, I'm enthralled by you. I think of you night and day.

We could be so good for one another – we are both artists in our own ways. You, with your ability to touch people's hearts with your kindness and words you write every day, and me, I'm an artist too. Just in a different way.

My body aches at the thought of holding you and seeing your lovely body lying next to mine. Your body has been sculpted from the finest artists' hands. I wish that artist to be me, to mold your body myself.

The thought of touching you excites me immensely. You don't see me for what I am. You look through me and see not what the future could hold for us. The birds would sing, and there would never be an ugly word spoken. See not what appears to be perfect, but what is real. Come to me, my love, and I'll take you on a journey you'll never forget. I'll conquer your love; it's only a matter of time. Soon you will gratefully give yourself to me fully.

Love, Me

CeCe, Reece, and Nitro were adapting to living under one roof. Nitro missed his time to run and play, but he still had some more recovery time to go. Both he and CeCe were healing well.

CeCe was able to walk without the crutches, but needed to wear a splint, this kept her from being clumsy and twisting her ankle again.

It was Friday night, time for homecoming, and excitement resounded throughout town. The team had won a few and let a few slip by. Of course, CeCe felt like she could have helped if she had been on the sidelines helping to call the plays.

Reece and CeCe had worked all morning and into the afternoon, baking cookies, cakes, and cinnamon rolls for the bake sale. The money would go to the band, who'd worked hard to gather the funds for their trip. They were almost there, and the sale should put them over the top.

CeCe asked Reece, "Do you have everything? I know this is going to be a great night. The football team will win and the kids will get the money they need for the trip."

"Not to mention one of us might win that trip to Hawaii," replied Reece.

CeCe dreamed of taking a trip like that. She could see the cool blue water and the lush green mountains jutting out of the sea. She felt that she knew Hawaii intimately from Austin's descriptions. Hawaii must be a very special place. Austin spoke of his place magically.

"I would love to win that prize and be able to see the place for myself, how wonderful to get away in the dead of winter."

"CeCe, if you want something to keep you warm, I know a certain coach who would love to have the honor."

CeCe tossed a look at Reece. "I'm not interested in what "coach" has to offer romantically. He's become a nice friend. We can talk about football and he knows where I'm coming from. But it would be fun to go to Hawaii the same time he was there, so he could act as a guide. A personal guide to the sights and sounds of Kauai… now that would be fun."

"I don't believe for a minute that you live in denial. Why, it's blatantly obvious that you two have the hots for one another. Just the other day I was in the bank and ……"

CeCe broke in "Reece, let's go so I don't have to listen to you babble on about how wonderful my life would be with someone like Austin. How about you? You have how many men waiting in the wings? Dr. Baldwin, Dr. Mason Albright, why even Gino Caparizo has come out of the dust to court you."

"Okay, CeCe, we won't discuss either one of our love lives for now. Let's go."

CeCe and Reece loaded the last of the baked goods into the back of the Jeep and headed to the football field.

The bake sale was a huge success. This was the catalyst that the kids needed to send them over the top.

CeCe and Reece hadn't finished cleaning up at half time, but CeCe wanted to see who was going to be crowned homecoming king and queen. They were beginning the announcements. Mandy and Scott were her personal choice.

Reece went onto the field to get pictures of the court for the paper.

The announcer said, "We present to you the Homecoming Court. The Homecoming queen is… Mandy Schmidt!" A little squeal came from the group on the field. The announcer said, "This year's King is our own wide receiver, Scott Gregory!"

CeCe was happy- they made such a cute couple and were really good kids. They reminded her of her friend, Shaw Corbin and his wife, Lisa. They were as close as two peas in a pod all through school and still were as far as she knew. They'd moved to the Roaring Fork Valley after college and owned a fly fishing shop.

CeCe would have to make a point of seeing them soon. She remembered the good times she had with Shaw and Gino. They both were great at tying flies. They taught her everything she knew. Maybe she would have to make a trip over there to go fly-fishing on the Frying Pan River up by the Rudi Dam. She hadn't gone fishing in a long time. Once Nitro and she were both healed, CeCe would arrange the trip.

After the hoopla over the crowing of the Homecoming King and Queen, the announcer broke in again. "Now, we have what a lot of you have been anxiously awaiting the last couple of weeks: the drawing for the grand prize. The students have decided to let Coach Carter choose the lucky winner.

"Coach, are you ready?"

Austin reached into the large pile and pulled out a ticket stub. He was handing the winning ticket to the announcer when he glanced at the name. He couldn't believe what he saw. Was it fate that made him choose that piece of paper? No, it had to be a coincidence.

"The winner is… can we have a drum roll please? CeCe Wellington!" A loud round of applause erupted as the announcer asked CeCe to come onto the field to collect her travel documents.

CeCe couldn't believe her ears, had she really heard right? Reece was jumping up and down, and people were congratulating her, so she must've heard right.

CeCe was so dazed that she couldn't move. She'd wanted to win this trip and it had actually happened. CeCe walked slowly to the field with everyone cheering and congratulating her.

CeCe walked up to the announcer. Austin had a big grin on his face as he handed CeCe the envelope. "I guess I'll have to make good on my promise to tell you which sights to see when you're there. Congratulations, CeCe."

CeCe took the envelope and waved it in the air. Reece came over and snapped a couple of pictures during the hand-off and of CeCe waving to the crowd.

The announcer handed CeCe the microphone and said, "Say a few words."

CeCe took the microphone "I'll come back with some special things for the shop and lots of pictures so all of you can feel like you went along with me." CeCe handed back the microphone and turned to walk away.

Austin grabbed her arm and walked her off the field. "I need to get back to the team to finish this game, any suggestions?" He asked, smiling.

"I have a whole lot of them, but you never seem to like my play calling. I think I'll sit back and watch this time, and see how you come out on your own."

"Congratulations, CeCe, you'll love Hawaii. Maybe if the timing is right, I'll be in Kauai when you go and can show you the sights."

CeCe flushed. Had he read her mind? She was thinking that same thing a while ago. "Thanks, Austin, now go and win that game."

Reece stood waiting for CeCe. "Have I been good enough of a girl to go with you? You said if I behaved myself you might take me. Well, CeCe, what do you say?"

Reece was like a child on Christmas morning, excited and not able to wait for an answer.

"Now who else would I take with me? Nitro can't go. I will have to ask Ruth and Tucker if they'll watch him when I go away. Reece, we're going to have so much fun. All that's left is to decide when we should go."

The game was about to begin. CeCe wanted to watch the second half, but she found it hard to concentrate. She kept looking at Austin, thinking about seeing his tan body on a beach.

The cool weather was the only thing keeping CeCe from taking her jacket off; she flushed at the thought of him. She would never be able to take her eyes off him in a tropical climate. She would have to control herself. This was not a normal reaction for CeCe.

The game was finished. The score was close, but the Wildcats pulled off the win. They had won their homecoming game, and CeCe had won the Hawaiian vacation. What a great night!

CeCe had offered to chaperone the dance and Reece was taking pictures, so they headed over to the gym.

The party was in full swing, and the band had taken a break. CeCe thought that this would be a good time to talk to Gino and ask how Shaw and Lisa were doing. CeCe walked over to Gino and patted him on the back. "You still have it, Gino!"

Gino turned around. "CeCe, that was great that you won the trip. Who are you taking with you? You wouldn't like to take me, would you?"

"Gino, you know I couldn't go without Reece. She's so excited."

"I've seen her lately with Dr. Baldwin. Are they a couple?"

"No, she just went out to dinner with him after the first football game."

"She sure doesn't see me. I'd love to go with you two to Hawaii- just think of the fun we would have."

"Gino, you know that isn't going to happen. I did want to ask you about the Corbin's. How are they, and are they still in the same place?"

"Yes, they're good. I wish I could find a good woman to love me like Shaw's found."

"Gino, it'll be only a matter of time. You'll make a good husband and look how talented you are. I better let you go for now. We'll talk again soon."

"Tell Reece I said hello." Gino walked back to the stage to begin playing for the kids.

CeCe was standing off to the side talking with one of the other chaperones, when Austin walked in the door. Her heart leaped into her throat and was pounding so hard she knew that others could hear. This had to stop. Austin had such an effect on her.

Austin was looking around the room when he saw her and nodded his head. He made his way over to her.

The Homecoming dance was nearing the end.

Gino took the microphone. "This is a song we wrote for someone special. This will be the last song of the evening. So, if you can bring that special someone out onto the dance floor, now's the time."

The dance floor filled in anticipation of the last dance.

Austin walked over to CeCe. "May I have this dance?"

"I'm a chaperone. How can I dance and chaperone?"

"My lady, this is the last dance and you worked very hard to make this a special night for the kids. I think you are entitled to one dance. Let's go, shall we?"

CeCe couldn't argue with him. She hadn't danced in a long time, and she loved to dance. "Okay, Austin, but only because you pulled that win out tonight"

"I wasn't the only one to pull out a win," Austin said as he pulled CeCe into his arms.

The music was wonderfully slow and rhythmic. The words Gino wrote were beautiful. Austin wasn't thinking about them, he was thinking about CeCe being in his arms.

When he held her before it was because she needed his attention for her ankle. But this was different. She willingly came out on to the dance floor with him. She smelled sweet again, like vanilla in the coffee shop when she was baking. Didn't she know that scent could drive a man crazy?

Her body felt warm and firm under his touch. He'd love to see her in one of those tiny bikinis that the woman wore on the beaches of Kauai.

"Hmm," Austin murmured, daydreaming.

"Austin, did you hear what I said?"

Austin was brought back from paradise by CeCe's voice. "I'm sorry, I was enjoying the music and dancing, and then I guess I was somewhere else." Boy was I, thought Austin, and on dangerous ground.

"I said, I think we might take the trip in February. Is the weather good then?"

"It's beautiful, about five degrees cooler than in the summer months. The whales come back during the winter and you can see them daily. If you've never seen them, then that would be a great time to go. I was thinking of going around that time myself."

CeCe looked up at Austin with her huge blue eyes. "That would be great; we could use you as our personal guide, at least on Kauai."

"I've invited my old roommate to come to my place after the football season is over, and he really wants to spend some time relaxing. That's the perfect time for him and the way he's playing he may already be in Honolulu. That's if he gets selected to play in the Pro Bowl."

"Who is this friend and who does he play for? You said your old roommate, is he with the 49'ers?"

Austin pulled CeCe a little closer. "He plays for the Denver Broncos now, and his name is Michael D'Angelo or Angie for short."

CeCe giggled. "I should've known who that was, why, he plays just like you played. Only he's a little more subtle with the pushing off."

The music stopped. The crowd turned and clapped for Gino and the band. CeCe and Austin walked back over to the refreshment table.

"I thought I might call Angie and go to see him play. Would you like to go to a game in Denver?"

CeCe stopped what she was doing. "I'd love to go, but I promised Reece that I'd take her to a professional football game the first time I went."

"Are you kidding me? You've never been to a professional game? Why? I would have thought you'd have been to many."

"No, I haven't had the chance to go. Tickets are hard to come by here in Colorado."

"If you want to go and take Reece along, that would be fine with me. Anyway, I could introduce Angie to Reece- he could use someone to keep him in line."

"Just what my friend Reece needs, yet another man, or the whole team who'll be falling all over her. I'm kidding, I'd love to go, and maybe introducing Reece to somebody else who knows so much about football would be good. She really is interested in learning more about the game."

Austin folded the chairs as he thought to himself; it wouldn't be Reece that the whole team would be falling over. Maybe he should think this over more. CeCe might find someone who really interested her. He'd have to take that chance. He wanted her to meet Angie. And the way she looked when he mentioned the game, how could he back out now?

He'd call Angie tomorrow night after the Broncos game was over. Hopefully they'd win, that way Angie would be in a good mood and up for having company.

"I'll call Angie tomorrow night and see when a good time would be for the three of us to head to Denver. I know they play the Raiders on Monday night two weeks from now. That would be a great game to go to. They always play tough with one another."

CeCe was excited, and it showed when she spoke. "That would be great, but we would need to stay overnight. I'll see if Ruth will take care of the shop and Nitro, so it would be nice to know this far in advance. The Brown Palace is a great place to stay. It's right downtown and close to where the team hangs out after they play. If you get the tickets, I'll make the room reservations. Deal?"

"Deal," replied Austin.

Reece came over to Austin and CeCe and said, "What are the two of you cooking up over here? You're grinning like the kids who got away with the whole cookie jar."

CeCe smiled, "We're talking about going to a Denver Bronco's game, and Austin would like to introduce us to a friend of his who plays on the team. Would you like to go if he can get the tickets?"

Reece shivered in anticipation. "Are you kidding? I would never pass up an opportunity to go to Denver, let alone watch all those gorgeous bodies on those football players."

"Reece, do you always have to make this into something to do with men?"

Austin laughed, "You two are great together, you argue like sisters. I'll let you know about the tickets as soon as I find out."

"Thanks, Austin, I think it'll be fun. My ankle is stiffening up a bit, must be time to go home. Besides, Nitro has been cooped up quite a while today, he'll be glad to see us. We'll wait to hear from you, then."

Austin helped finish cleaning up and they turned off the lights. They walked to the parking lot; Austin thought he might be heading in the right direction with CeCe. She seemed to be more receptive to him than she was before. He hoped that his instinct was right.

"Goodnight ladies, I'll see you soon. Say hello to Nitro for me," Austin said as he opened the door to the truck.

"You say the same to Tucker and Ruth," replied CeCe.

Chapter Six

His heart pounded as he walked by Reece tonight. He had the letter close to his heart. The need for her to read his latest feelings was all most too much. Her bag was sitting there taunting him to place the letter inside.

The opportunity came when Reece went to the field to take pictures. She left her camera bag on the table where she and CeCe had been cleaning up. He walked by. When CeCe's name came over the speakers, the opportunity he hoped for was presented to him.

CeCe walked towards the field, and he slipped the envelope out of his jacket into the bag. He could detect Reece's scent on the bag, even in the cool air. She was one of the most beautiful women he had ever seen. He was so close to her tonight, within touching distance. The time was not right. He'd wait for her reaction to the letter he wrote.

When would she see that they were right for each other? All those others could never love her the way he did. He ached to have her near him. To feel her breath on his skin. She was so alive, but distant.

The letters would make her see him. He was confident of that.

He needed to move on now; CeCe and Coach Carter were coming off the field toward him. He mustn't let them see him so close to Reece's bag. Slowly he turned and walked back to the stands to watch the rest of the game, but most of all Reece.

The evening was late when they got back to Reece's place. Nitro was glad to see them. He almost opened the door himself.

CeCe told Reece she was going to take Nitro for a walk. Nitro was full of energy and wanted to play, but her watch glowed 12:15 and CeCe just wanted to crawl in bed.

She pacified Nitro with a brisk walk and talking to him "Nitro, what's going on with me? I find myself searching for Austin whenever I know he might be around. He makes me feel warm and special. The way his mouth turns up when he talks about football, or Hawaii for that fact. Oh, I forgot to tell you I won Nitro, I won the trip to Hawaii. I wish you could go with me, but they put animals in quarantine for six months. You'll have to stay with Grandma Ruth. She'll spoil you rotten. Come on, we should go back."

As CeCe and Nitro approached the door, they saw Reece standing there. She unlocked the chain as they walked up the stairs.

"Reece, what's up with you? What's with the chain?"

"I was going through my camera bag organizing the film that I took at the game, and look what I found." Reece held up what appeared to be a letter like the other two. "This really is for me. Look my name is here. This says I'm an artist and whoever is writing these, they're an artist too. The author thinks about me lying next to him and our future together. What do you think? Who do you think is writing these letters?"

CeCe took the letter from Reece. She thought hard as to who could put words together in such a rhythmic order.

"Reece, I don't know who could be writing these, but you're right the letters are for you. I don't know what to think of them; certainly great care has been taken to write them. The paper is beautiful. And look, you can see the imprint of the typewriter. Who uses a typewriter anymore, anyway? Actually… this paper is beautiful and unique, maybe we could check at the stationary store to see if they carry this type of paper there? The words certainly flow from within this person. He obviously thinks that the two of you should be together and fantasizes about that. Think hard Reece, about who this might be."

Reece was sitting on the edge of the chair wringing her hands. "I'm trying to think who could be writing to me. But no one comes to mind. This isn't that large of a town that I shouldn't be able to pick this person out. Do you think I should be concerned? I mean, is this like a stalker?"

CeCe replied, "I don't know much about stalking. I'm glad Nitro and I are staying with you for a while. Nitro will protect us. Are you going to be okay?"

Reece got up from the chair. "Of course I am, and I'm not going to let some words on paper get me down. Besides, I have some chocolate almond ice cream in the fridge and sorbet as well. We can sit here and eat while we make plans to go see all those beautiful bodies at the football game. Do you think we might get to go into the locker room? I'd love to do an interview in there, you know for the paper and all."

CeCe shook her head, "Oh brother, I can tell you're going to be a handful. You don't want them all to get a bad impression of us, do you?"

"CeCe, I don't think they would have a bad impression, quite the contrary. Men love women who are willing to play on their level. And I don't mean football. Although, that could be fun too I guess."

"You get the goodies and I'm going to change my clothes, then we'll talk about this trip to Denver and the Hawaii trip. I asked Austin what it was like in February. He said it was a good time to go and that he may be there with his friend Angie at that time." "Angie? What the heck? He has a girlfriend already, and I could've sworn he was stuck on you."

CeCe laughed, "Angie is his football player friend in Denver. His name is Michael D'Angelo. If you think Austin is cute, Angie is like a cookie cutter of him."

"That'll be okay. We can have two guides. I can deal with that. Hurry up so we can talk about this."

CeCe went off to the bedroom to change her clothes.

~ ~ ~

He'd been standing outside the house and watched as CeCe and Nitro walked away.

He thought about going to the door and ringing the bell so he could actually hold her as she read the letter. He changed his mind. She had to want him, and the more he wrote to her, the more she'd learn to love not only his words but also the real him. He was able to watch as she opened the letter and read. She looked around, could she feel him close by? Was she looking for him to tell him that she knew how he felt and that she felt the same?

She got up and hurried to the door. He could see her put the chain across the latch. CeCe was still out. Did she forget? God, Reece was beautiful.

He thought about watching her as she went to the bedroom to change her clothes, but she checked the lock and pulled the shade. That was all right, he could wait to see her beautiful skin. Looking through the glass was like looking at the animals at the zoo. If you can't get close enough to touch, smell, and breathe the scent of them, then what was the sense? No, he'd wait.

She touched the paper lovingly. Yes, she'd come around soon. He'd have an opportunity to be near her again. He was patient. And she was worth the wait.

Chapter Seven

The morning had been a busy one. Dr. Baldwin stopped by to ask about Nitro, but CeCe knew that wasn't the real reason he stopped in.

Dr. Baldwin made small talk about Nitro and his wonderful recovery, and then he got to the real reason he was there.

"Are you still staying with Reece? I was wondering if you would tell her I said hello, and that I really enjoyed our evening together. I'd like to do it again soon. Before you two go off to that tropical paradise and find some local guys to sweep you off your feet. You know that some of those tropical flowers are intoxicating."

CeCe laughed, "Why Dr. Baldwin, I have never known you to be so shy. Why don't you just call Reece and ask her out? I know she had a good time."

"I'm not shy, I just can't take rejection. Why do you think I work with animals? Animals love us unconditionally- that's what I haven't been able to do with the other women I've been involved with."

"Maybe wanting unconditional love from more than one woman at a time is what got you into trouble." CeCe laughed as she gave Dr. Baldwin his change. "I'll tell Reece you said hello and to expect a call from you."

"Thanks- see you and Nitro in a week."

Gino came to the counter right after Dr. Baldwin. "I thought you told me those two weren't an item, sounds to me like they might be. I'd love to ask Reece out- do you think she might go with me if I ask."

CeCe really liked Gino; he was a tall, good-looking Italian man. He didn't have those extra pounds on him that the rest of his family carried. He took care of himself. She'd like to see him find someone to make him happy. He just didn't have the confidence in himself that he needed.

"Why don't you try? All she can do is say no."

"That's what I am afraid of. I asked her out when we were in school and she turned me down flat."

"That was a long time ago. Things have changed. You should get up the courage and ask her out. I think I'm going to change the name of the place from CeCe's Coffee Shop to Reece's Dating Shop. You're the second one to ask me about Reece going on a date, what about me?"

"I would love to take you out, but from what I hear there's a certain "Coach" who already has you in his sights."

CeCe blushed as Gino spoke about her and Austin in that manner. Why, they hadn't even gone out on an official date. The dinner they had at his place wasn't a date, was it? Anyway, they were all wrong.

"Gino, don't listen to everything you hear out there. You'd be better served if you just did as your heart tells you to do. If you want to go out with Reece, ask."

Gino paid the bill and said, "I'll give her a little more time to think. But if you to put in a good word for me I'm sure she would listen to you. Take care- I hope to see you the next time we play. We have some new songs we're hoping to record next month. Talk to you soon."

The fire had only happened a few weeks ago, and CeCe was in the midst of repairs. The structure had been finished and someone came in to take care of the smoke damage.

Her bedroom expanded to two levels. A few steps took you down into where the bed was, and she'd always wanted a railing along the edge and down the stairs. This was her opportunity to make the changes.

She'd seen some of the work that Tom Dancer had done on a couple of the ranches, and she was thinking about asking him to give her an estimate on the work.

From what she saw and heard, his work was excellent. He did

amazing things with a piece of metal. The design she wanted was aspen leaves. She had many aspen trees on her property; incorporating them into the railing would be like bringing them into her bedroom.

Tom was sitting on a chair by the window gazing off into the street. CeCe approached him. "Tom, would you like some more coffee?" The odor of alcohol was very strong today. Tom sure could use coffee to help sober him up. "N-no, thank you, Miss C-ceCe. The banana b-bread sure was good today. I have a j-job to do out at R-r-randle's ranch. I should g-get g-going'."

"Tom, I was wondering if you would have time to stop by my place some afternoon soon to look at an area that I would like to put up a iron railing? I have a design in mind, and I've seen your work. I think a piece of your work is just what the room needs to complete the decorating."

Tom wiped his mouth with the napkin and reached in his back pocket to pull out his can of chew. His flask slipped out of his pocket onto the floor. CeCe reached down, but he was much faster than she was.

Tom picked up the flask and shoved it quickly into his pocket. He took some chew out of the tin. As he was placing it in his mouth, he looked up at CeCe. "I'll f-f-finish this job day after t-t-tomorrow. Will that w-work for you?"

CeCe backed away to let Tom stand as she replied. "That will be fine Tom, I won't be able to leave here until after I close, and I'll tell Reece that we won't be going to work out. Why don't you stop by here around noon?"

Tom rose and said, "D-don't let me k-keep you from going with Miss R-r-reece. I can come by h-her p-place and g-go over the details with you, or here f-for that matter."

"That's Okay, Tom, we can just leave from here. I want you to see where I want to put it and get your input as to what design you think will work. You come here, and we'll drive out there together.

The coffee and bread were on the house today, Tom. I'll see you then."

"T-thank you, Miss C-ceCe. I will c-create a m-masterpiece for you."

Tom walked out the door. CeCe thought to herself that Tom was wonderfully talented; it was a shame he wasted his life away drinking all the time. She wondered what things he did in the evening to entertain himself. He didn't seem to have too many friends.

Just as Tom was walking out of the shop, Austin walked in.

"H-hello, Mr. C-carter"

"Hello, Tom. Why don't you just call me Austin? Everybody else does. The shodding you did on the horses seems to be just what they needed. Especially the Paint, she seems to be moving around a lot better with the corrective measures you put in her shoe. Thanks again, Tom, you do nice work."

As Austin was talking to Tom, he was scanning the small shop for CeCe.

"I l-like a challenge and s-she was one of them. Let m-me know if you need any m-more work done. L-looks like Miss C-ceCe wants me to do s-some work on her house. I will s-see you around A-a-austin. Thanks for the c-compliment."

Tom walked out of the shop.

Austin spotted CeCe in the corner clearing one of the tables. It was hard for him to concentrate whenever he saw her. They would be spending a little more time together next weekend when they went to the Bronco's game, which is what he came to tell her.

Angie was anxious to see him again, and was always up for meeting beautiful women. Austin thought that he and Reece might hit it off just right.

"Hello, CeCe," Austin said as he took a seat at the counter. He liked sitting at the counter so he could watch CeCe move around the small kitchen area. She moved so gracefully in her shop; almost like a ballerina.

"Good morning, Austin. Are you getting a late start today?" inquired CeCe.

"I came in to give you some good news, and this is what I get, grief?" Austin was smiling as he said this to CeCe. "I spoke with my friend Angie this morning, and he is excited to have us as his guest. I thought we could leave early Monday morning, that way we could get all settled in. What do you think?"

"Austin, that's great! I was counting on you to get it all arranged. I've already asked Ruth to work the shop and take care of Nitro. She was willing as ever. She said Tucker gets under her feet, so it will do her good to get out away from him for a while. I did go ahead and make the room reservations as well. I was afraid they wouldn't have anything left if I waited too long." CeCe was so excited as she spoke.

"Well aren't you little Miss Arrangements. Will we have goodies to take along with us in a picnic basket?"

"I don't know about the picnic basket, but we will certainly have enough to keep us going till we get to Denver. I know some great restaurants."

Austin got up from his seat at the counter and paid for the coffee. "I just spoke with Tom Dancer. He said that you were going to have him do some work for you. I didn't know you had horses?"

CeCe laughed, "Tom does beautiful work with iron. I'm going to have him make a railing for the bedroom. I always wanted one but never got around to it. The remodeling kind of pushed me into the decision. I think the ironwork will look good in the house. How did Tom work out for you?"

"He did a great job. One of the horses needed some special work, and he was able to correct the problem. If he's half as good with the iron work, then you should have something special."

"I'm sure that he will do a wonderful job. I know that Reece is thinking about having him do a fence and gate in her garden area, but she wants to see what he does with my design first."

"I hope you get the perfect railing for the bedroom- then maybe you will be willing to show it to me." Austin grinned as he spoke to CeCe; all the while his heart was pounding thinking about being in CeCe's bedroom with her.

"Would you like me to drive on Monday?" Austin asked, changing the subject.

"I think Reece will drive her Jeep, it will be a little more comfortable than your pickup. If that's okay with you?"

"That will be fine with me, CeCe."

"What time do you want to leave? I'll tell Reece so we can stop by the Ranch and drop off Nitro."

"We can leave around 9:00. That will give me enough time to make sure everything is done at the ranch. Tucker has everything under control, but I don't like to leave it all to him to do. Besides, this was my life-long dream. I need to start living it."

"We will be there around 9:00 then, let me know if we need to do anything else. I'm really excited to go to the game. I'm sure it's a lot more intense being there in the stadium than watching it on television."

"It certainly is. Take it from someone who has been in the nitty- gritty of it all. Sometimes you can't even hear yourself think. You'll enjoy it. Make sure you bring plenty of warm clothes along. I'll see you on Monday morning, then. Take care."

Austin walked out of the shop. He would see her before Monday, it was difficult to come into town and not go and see her. She was something else.

Maybe they could go dancing when they were in Denver. That would be nice. He could hold her close to him again. He would ask Angie if there was someplace they could go out after the game.

CeCe looked out the window after Austin. Snow was just beginning to fall from the sky. She wondered if they would have some time to shop while in Denver. It was a passion of both hers and Reece's.

The snow always put CeCe in the mood for Christmas. This would be a good time to get some of her shopping done.

She liked the memories she had of growing up with her grandmother and the trips they would take into Denver around Christmas time. They usually went to see a musical or play. After the three-hour trip they would settle into the hotel before going out.

CeCe always felt like she was all grown up when they would go and have Tea at the Brown Palace. What a special treat that was. She would wear her best clothes, and her grandmother taught her how to act like a lady. The little sandwiches and fancy French pastry were enough to make your stomach rumble. She and Reece never had the opportunity to have tea during their trips to Denver. This is something they would have to do, if not this trip then another time.

The city was always so bright and decorative this time of year. CeCe thought about whom she needed to find gifts for.

She mentally checked them off in her mind. CeCe wondered to herself if she should buy a gift for Austin.

She always bought for Ruth and Tucker, so it wouldn't be unusual if she bought a gift for him. But what could she give him that wouldn't be too personal? This would take some thought. Maybe she could just make him some cinnamon rolls and cookies.

She would try and find some of those macadamia nuts to put in the cookies. That would work. But she still needed to find gifts for others on her list. This would probably be her only trip into Denver before Christmas, so there was her excuse to shop. As if she needed one.

Shopping in the city was a special treat for her. The sounds of Christmas were all around them. Sometimes CeCe swore she could hear the snow falling out of the sky. The skating rink was filled with families laughing and skating together, with Christmas carols playing in the background.

After shopping all day and being out in the cold, hot chocolate was one of those things she looked forward to. The smell of it always set off those memories, the steaming hot mug with marshmallows and whipped cream overflowing from the top of the mug. Mmmm… she was making herself hungry thinking about it.

Instead of thinking about ingesting all of those calories, she needed to think about ways to burn them off. She would have to go skating on the lake soon. She always felt like skating worked off the calories, and she had fun doing it.

CeCe wondered if Austin liked to ice skate. She always had a hard time getting Reece to go with her. She would have to ask Austin- it would be fun.

The lake needed a little more time to freeze over solid, so it would be awhile before she could go. This would give her time to find out if Austin liked to skate and if he would enjoy going one evening.

The phone rang and jarred CeCe back from her thoughts.

"Good morning, CeCe's, can I help you?" She answered.

"CeCe, it's me. I was wondering if you were going to the gym today, or do you want to go cross-country skiing? I'm up for either. It's your call."

Reece was anxious to get out and do something. She hadn't been sleeping well lately. She was racking her brain as to who could be writing to her. "I need to tire myself out. And I am off caffeine for the time being. I'm counting on you to watch me. You know that I can't stay away from it on my own."

"Reece, you can too do it on your own. You are one of the most determined people I know. Are you worried about the letters? Is that what is keeping you awake? I've heard you up roaming around at night."

"I would just like to know where they're coming from. I'm always looking over my shoulder to see if someone is there. It's kind of creepy; yet very flattering that someone seems so interested in me. I just need to get into my winter workout routine and I'll be just fine. So what do you say- outdoors or in?"

"I would love to go out cross country skiing, especially since it is starting to snow and we can make some fresh tracks."

"Then outdoors it is. Shall I meet you at the house?"

"That would be great, that way I can get Nitro and he can go with us. He needs the exercise too. How about 1:00?"

"I'll be there. See you then.

Chapter Eight

He had been thinking about Reece all morning. He had watched her walk up the stairs and into the office.

Her office window faced the park where he liked to sit. This afforded him the best view of her.

It had been awhile since he had written to her. The inspiration came after watching her and the beginning of the snowfall. As he walked back to his truck for the drive home, the words were already forming in his head.

It didn't take him long to get home. The place was cold- he needed to build a fire, but first he had to write the letter. Besides the fire that was burning within him was enough to keep him warm till he was finished.

Every time he opened the box of paper he would touch it softly and gently as though he were holding her in his arms. The paper rolled into the typewriter it was waiting for his words to fill the page.

The snow is just beginning to fall. It is cool and beautiful, glistening as it lands on the pavement. The flakes fall gently out of the sky, they are, as you are, a single work of art. The mountaintops capped by the snow are regal in beauty, but to you they cannot compare. For you are the most beautiful thing on this earth. Believe me, I shall tell you the truth. I think about us walking through the snow hand in hand. The flakes falling on your lovely hair. When they melt they look like gems sparkling there. Have you thought of who I am and how good we will be for one another? I do every minute of every day. The warmth we would create would be enough to melt glaciers and warm the coldest of hearts. You are my everything. I will win your love in time. Just keep listening and watching for me, my darling

Reece. I want you to go and sleep in peace and dream of us. I am watching and caring for you. Love, Me

He couldn't wait to mail the letter- he wanted to take it to her house. He put the letter in the envelope and sealed it. He would take it to her place and slip it under the door. He wanted her to have it right away. Then, Reece could feel the love that he felt for her.

When she read it and watched the snow falling, she would see the beauty of the two of them together. Yes, this was the way to deliver the letter. He must hurry, before she came home to find him there.

~ ~ ~

CeCe finished up in the shop and headed to Reece's house. Nitro would enjoy going out with them.

This would be the first time they had gone out cross-country skiing this year. The snow had been falling for a while, but the base just now getting good. CeCe wanted to make some hot tea to take along. She would pack them a light snack.

CeCe had made Nitro a special treat today. He loved peanut butter cookies. This was her personal recipe made just for him. It didn't contain sugar or any of the other things humans had to have in their baked goods. It was a good natural treat for him and he would smell it the minute she walked into the house.

The walk in the snow was very relaxing to CeCe; she let her mind wander to other places. Every time she did that Austin came into her thoughts.

She was sure that it was just because she was going to the game with him on Monday and because he would be in Kauai when she and Reece were there. The thoughts were wonderful and warming.

She could feel the glow on her face; thinking about seeing his body half-clad on the beautiful white sands.

CeCe turned the corner; she thought she saw a figure moving into the trees behind Reeces' house. She must have been mistaken, there shouldn't be anyone there. She was lost in thought and must have just been seeing things.

CeCe opened the door to the bounding Nitro. "Well, hello, buddy, I expected to find you asleep. You must have smelled the goodies coming." Nitro was pushing his nose into CeCe's bag. "You need to wait awhile Nitro; we are going out to get some exercise. I'll let you out the back, while I go and change my clothes."

CeCe walked to the back door and looked at the letter lying on the floor. There were footprints from the stairs leading back to the trees where she thought she saw someone.

She wondered if it was the person writing the letters. It had to be, didn't it? How else would the letter have gotten there? Reece didn't say anything about a new one, and she would have told CeCe. If only she were a few minutes earlier. She could have been here to see them. Then CeCe would know who it was.

She would have to give the letter to Reece, but CeCe knew that Reece would be upset that whoever it was had been this close to the house and worse, inside it. They would have to make sure they locked the doors when they were not there.

CeCe thought she should call the sheriff's department to see if there was anything they could do about the situation. Surely when someone starts coming in your house there was something they could do to help find out who it was.

It was probably some lovesick high school kid. She would call and try and find out what they should do about this.

~ ~ ~

His heart was pounding. He had parked his truck several blocks away. He thought he was being very safe. He walked his way around the trees and waited for a while to make sure there was no one around.

Reece's house was set back and secluded from the others near her. Yet he wanted to be safe. As he sat waiting, the anticipation of opening the door and being in her home was almost too much for him. He had to slow himself down. He could feel his heart pounding in his ears.

He also needed to think about CeCe's dog, Nitro. He had been around the dog and had seen him out with her- he always seemed friendly, but this was different. This was in Reece's house. He needed to use his skills to make sure the dog allowed him in the house.

He knew he could do it, but he so much wanted to go all the way in the house and touch her pillow. It would be the perfect place to put the letter. He would have to see how it went.

After a few minutes, he felt comfortable with walking toward the house. If someone saw him there, he had his story all ready as to why he was there. It was the perfect lie; no one would question his presence when he told them the story he had concocted. He moved slowly at first, then a little quicker.

As he approached the stairs, he called out Reece's name in case someone was in the house. This would fall in line with his story. There was no answer.

With each step up he could feel his heart pounding louder. He was beginning to sweat now. How was that possible when it was cold and snowing out?

He reached for the doorknob and turned it slowly. "Nitro?" he called out. The large black dog came running toward him.

He held out the treat he had brought along. The dog wagged his tail as he sniffed the air and smelled the food. Nitro came over to him and took the treat. He reached his hands down and rubbed the dog's ears, speaking in a soft tone was comforting to Nitro.

The dog ran away to retrieve a toy to play with. He bounded back into the room and dropped the toy in front of him. He picked the toy up and threw it for him. Nitro went running after the toy, but stopped dead in his tracks. He stood at the front door wagging his tail and whining.

He had seen this before; someone must be coming. He had to get out of there, and quickly.

He wouldn't have time to go into the bedroom. He would have to just leave it on the windowsill by the door. He placed the letter down lovingly and turned to leave.

When he closed the door, he saw the letter fall to the floor, but there was no time to pick it up and put it back. He stepped down the stairs two at a time.

Again, he had to walk slowly in case he was seen and recognized. This is why he wore different clothes than he would normally wear. No one would recognize them. They had been put away in the closet for a long time. He thought to himself, he must have put them there for just this occasion.

He was nearing the trees now and stole a glance backwards; yes, he had been right. It looked to be CeCe walking down the street toward the house. He had left just in time. It was a good thing he could read animals the way he did.

He was feeling the excitement of being so close to Reece. When he opened the door he could smell her perfume lingering in the air. It would have been a great triumph if he could have been in her bedroom. He would have to wait for another time.

He accomplished part of his goal, getting the letter into the house. But that had been a close call, and it wouldn't be a good idea for him to wait around for Reece to read the letter. He needed to get back to his truck and move it before someone thought it strange it was parked there.

Chapter Nine

CeCe picked up the telephone and dialed the sheriffs' office. The phone rang twice before it was picked up on the other end.

"Good afternoon, Sheriff's office, is your call an emergency?" CeCe replied, "No."

"How can I help you?"

"Good afternoon, this is CeCe Wellington. I have a different kind of situation here, and I don't know if your office can help or not. My friend, Reece Landon, has been receiving letters over the past two months or so. At first, the letters were coming to her at work, and she didn't even know if they were for her. Then she received one about a month ago in her bag while she was away from it. Today I came home and found one inside the door of the house. Is there anything you can do to try and find out who is writing the letters?"

The voice on the other end of the phone asked "Are you concerned for your safety?"

CeCe replied, "Not really, but this is a little unnerving. It's scary when you come home and someone has been in your house."

"How did they gain entry, was it forced?"

"We don't lock the doors; it's never been a problem"

"We can't call it breaking and entering then. I will send over an officer to talk with you. What is your address?" CeCe gave the address to the dispatcher and went to wait for Reece to get home.

Reece came around the corner to see the sheriff's car in the drive. She hurried down the road and came running into the house.

"CeCe, where are you? Is everything all right?"

CeCe came over to Reece. "I'm fine; I called the sheriff's office about the letters."

"About the letters?"

"Yes, I came home a little while ago, and I thought I saw a

figure moving toward the trees. It was snowing hard and I had my hood up, so I wasn't sure. When I came in the house Nitro met me at the door. I thought that was a bit unusual since he usually sleeps while I'm away. I went to let him out the back door when I found this on the floor."

CeCe handed the envelope to Reece. Reece opened it and read it.

"May I see that?" asked the officer. Reece handed it to him.

"Is it the same type of letter?" Reece asked CeCe.

"Yes, it's the same paper and same type of wording."

The officer read the letter and asked, "Are they all the same? Do you have them here so I can look at the others?"

Reece was retreating into her bedroom as she spoke to the officer. "Yes, they are all similar. They talk about this person's love for me. I'll get the rest of them so you can see for yourself."

Reece reached high up on the shelf and pulled out a box. She opened it and took out the other letters and walked back into the other room.

"I didn't know what to do with them. At first I wasn't sure they were for me. But as you can see, they definitely are." Reece handed the other letters to the officer.

The officer pulled out each one and read it, then replaced them in the envelope. "They are for you, I'll say. This is a difficult situation. We can't do anything unless the letters get threatening. And as I see it, they are quite the contrary. Now, another way we could do something is if someone actually broke into your home, office or car. But seeing as how the door was left unlocked, I don't see that we can do much. I suggest that you lock the door. If you see someone lurking around, you can call us and we'll come out and question the person. I'll leave you my card, and if you have any more questions or if things start getting out of control, please call me."

The officer pulled a card out of his pocket and handed it to Reece. "Make sure you don't hesitate to call. That's what we're here for- to answer your questions and help in any way we can.

Reece and CeCe walked the officer to the door. "Thank you for coming over. It's helpful to have someone else's view on this. I know that Reece and I will be more careful and lock the doors," CeCe was saying as she shook the officer's hand.

"Yes, thanks for coming," replied Reece.

The officer walked out of the door. Reece and CeCe walked into the living room and sat on the sofa.

CeCe put her arm around Reece. "Reece, I know this is nerve-racking, but the officer did say he felt the letters were non-threatening. I think it is what we were speculating about earlier: someone is very interested in you, but is not willing to come forward. They must be very shy. Nitro and I will be with you awhile longer. I am meeting Tom Dancer tomorrow to have him start work on the design of the railing. When we do move back to the house, maybe you should come with us for a while. Besides, we've gotten used to your quirky little habits. What do you say?"

Reece smiled, "Me, quirky? What about you? I think that would be a good idea, at least for a few days. Maybe I'll move back here after we come back from our trip to Hawaii. Now, what do you say? I still need that exercise, now more than ever. I need to change my clothes and it looks like you need to do the same."

"Yes, that's what I was doing when I found the letter. I will put some water on for tea to take with us. Speaking of tea, I was just thinking about having 'tea' at the Brown Palace when we go to the game on Monday. I used to do it all the time with my grandmother and it was wonderful. It makes you feel so special. I think it's something we need to put on our agenda."

"That sounds great, now go and get changed already, will you?" Reece tossed a pillow at CeCe as she was getting up.

~ ~ ~

It had been a busy morning, and CeCe had barely enough time to think about the afternoon. When Tom came walking in the door, CeCe remembered her appointment with him.

"H-hello, Miss CeCe. I will j-just sit over here and have a c-cup of coffee until you are r-ready to go," said Tom as he took a seat in the corner.

"Hi Tom, I won't be long. I just have to finish cleaning up and take the money out of the register. What kind of coffee would you like today?"

"S-s-something strong, please."

Tom looked good today. He didn't have the usual overwhelming odor of alcohol on him. CeCe wondered if his drinking had anything to do with how much work he had. If that were the case, she would have to help find him work. If he did a good job on her railing, she knew Reece would use him for the garden.

"I have just the thing for you, Tom." CeCe took the steaming cup of coffee over to him.

"Thank y-you." Tom held the coffee cup as if warming his hands.

CeCe finished cleaning up and closing out the register. She removed her apron and checked the back door.

"Are you ready, Tom?"

"I am, M-miss CeCe," replied Tom.

"Would you mind following me out there? I need to run a few errands afterward and I wouldn't want to inconvenience you."

"That will be f-fine. I have another j-job close by that I need to b-bid."

CeCe and Tom climbed into their vehicles. Tom followed CeCe to her place. As they drove up to the cottage, CeCe kept thinking about when she had last been here. She didn't like thinking about the fire and how she almost lost both the cottage and Nitro. Things had been coming along nicely. She was happy with the reconstruction and clean-up.

CeCe climbed out of the vehicle and waited for Tom. Tom was just behind her. Tom got out he walked toward CeCe.

"I have always l-loved your place, Miss CeCe. The s-setting is just beautiful. Why, all the Aspen t-trees must be like an a-artists paint p-pallet in the fall. The v-view you have of the m-mountain range is incredible. I l-love this area."

"Why, Tom, I didn't know you were so poetic. It is a wonderful setting, though, isn't it? My grandmother used to come out her and sit for hours "just watching nature", as she used to say. Let's go inside and look at the area where I would like the railing. I have an idea as to what design to use, but you will have to make the final decision."

They walked toward the door. CeCe walked over to a rock in the garden, picked it up, and removed a key.

"I'm so bad about carrying my keys with me that I need to place one outside in the hidden rock."

Tom looked at CeCe and frowned. "M-miss CeCe, you shouldn't do t-that. Someone c-could see you t-take it out and come in on you."

CeCe laughed as she opened the door. "Tom, the only time I lock the door is when I am in bed and when I go away for extended periods of time. It is just fine. Now let's get to it, shall we?"

CeCe lead Tom to the bedroom.

"This is where I would like the railing. I was thinking of incorporating the aspen leaf design inside the house. Do you think you might be able to do that, Tom?"

Tom bent down on the floor as he was taking out his tape measure.

"I think t-that would be b-beautiful. This room is like n-nature itself. I can create you a masterpiece that will be r-regal in its beauty with no other c-comparison. I just n-need to take some measurements. If you could h-help me Miss CeCe, I will b-be on my way."

"Of course Tom, how long do you think it will take to make the railing and install it?"

"About three w-weeks, there is a lot of d-detail I want to put into it. I-if that's all right with y-you? Otherwise I could be f-finished s-sooner."

"No, Tom, take your time creating the piece you want. I will be moving back in sooner than that, but that is not a huge concern of mine. It's just something I think will finish off the construction. Just like a picture. I am convinced that you were the right choice for the job."

"T-thank you, Miss CeCe, now l-let's finish these m-measurements."

Tom and CeCe finished the measurements and Tom was on his way. CeCe looked at her home more carefully. She sure would be happy to get back here. Thankfully, it would be only a few more days.

Nitro would be happy to get back to his old place as well. He had completely healed and still loved to run and play. He would also get to play at the ranch while she was gone to Denver with Reece and Austin. CeCe checked a few more things, and left to go back into town.

Chapter Ten

Reece had been trying all week to get through to some contacts in Seattle. She was in the process of writing an article on the handsome new doctor.

Dr. Mason Albright was different than the men she was used to dating. He was fresh and charming, not to mention more sophisticated.

As Reece had always done in the past, she was writing an article on the most recent newcomer to the valley. She was going to enjoy this one even more. She felt that she and Mason could get something going. Maybe she would be able to find the man of her dreams right here and settle down.

She was having trouble with finding the area that Mason said he came from. He had said it was outside of Seattle. She would have to call him and confirm the name of the place.

He specialized in treating orthopedic injuries, and had worked at a ski resort not too far from the Seattle area. She would call her good friend Claire, whom she had met in college.

Claire had gone to the Seattle area and taken a job as a television news reporter. That was the direction Reece had been headed in when her father became ill and she had to come back and make the decision to take over the newspaper.

The job that Reece had been offered in Denver was a good one as an evening anchor on one of the local network stations. She would have done a good job at it, but deep down she really loved the newspaper. It also allowed her to make a good living in the place she grew up in. No, she never regretted coming back and taking over. But this article she was writing puzzled her. She had never run into this before. Claire would be able to help, she was sure.

The phone rang and Reece reached to answer it. She glanced out the window as she did and saw Austin and CeCe walking toward her door.

"Yampa Journal, this is Reece, how may I help you?"

Austin and CeCe walked into the office talking with one another. They sure looked good together, thought Reece.

"Hello, Mrs. James, yes I did hear about the community garage sale. Yes, the article will be in the paper tomorrow. We will continue to mention it until next weekend when the event takes place."

Reece paused to let Mrs. James rattle on about her pet project. It benefited the children in the surrounding area and was a good cause. Reece and CeCe always volunteered to help out.

"Yes, CeCe and I will be there to help out. As a matter of fact, she just walked into my office. Would you like to speak to her?"

Reece smiled and placed her hand over the mouthpiece, so Mrs. James wouldn't hear her giggle. CeCe was waving her hands at Reece mouthing 'no, not now'. Reece grinned as she said, "Just a minute, Mrs. James", and handed the phone to CeCe. CeCe glared at Reece and took the phone.

"Hello Mrs. James, how are you today? Yes, I know how the damp weather can wreak havoc on your bones. Yes, both Reece and I would love to help out. I will call you and get the final details on Thursday. I promise I will look for more volunteers. As a matter of fact, I have someone in mind. I will ask him and get back to you."

CeCe grabbed hold of Austin's sleeve and pointed to him as if saying you will help with this project. "You take care now, Mrs. James. Keep yourself warm and don't over-do it. I won't forget to call you Thursday. Goodbye."

CeCe hung up the phone and reached for Reece in jest. "She is so long winded! I can never get away from her. Mrs. James does have a heart of gold, though. Austin, how would you like to help out next weekend with the community garage sale?"

"What is it, and what do I have to do?" Austin asked

"Reece, why don't you tell him about it?"

"Well, Austin, it is for a really good cause. Every year we get the whole community together and have a huge garage sale, everything from sporting equipment to furniture to clothes. The money goes to help a variety of programs helping children. You will…"

Austin broke in and said, "Say no more, just tell me when and where to be and what to do. I'll be there. Anything to do with kids is an all right project for me."

"Great!" said CeCe "Now, we came in here to ask you to go out for some lunch, are you interested?"

"Yes, I'm starved. I've been working hard on this article and keep running into dead ends."

CeCe asked, "What article is that, Reece?"

"The article on Dr. Albright, I must have the name of the town wrong. I have to call Claire in Seattle; maybe she can help me. Let's go; I need to eat. Where would you like to go?"

"How about the Alpine Café?" Austin suggested with a smile. I've eaten there a couple of times since I've been here and it's always good."

"The Alpine Café it is," said CeCe and Reece in unison.

Reece locked the door and they walked to the café. It wasn't too busy since they were later than the usual lunch crowd.

"Tell me more about this garage sale. I'm interested in how the funds are used. Growing up, I was a beneficiary of these sorts of things. Otherwise, I would have never been able to get into football and would have never gotten to where I am today."

Reece said, "I remember that from when I wrote the article on you. You came from a rough part of the city."

"Yep my old man was a drunk; all he cared about was himself. He left us with nothing. My mother had to work two jobs to make ends meet, and they barely did at that. My sister and I did as much as we could to help out, but it is difficult when you don't have much. That is why I don't have much tolerance for drunks. It can ruin your life. There are much better things to life than getting lost in a bottle."

Austin could still feel the pain of those days. 'I would get into trouble until this great guy from the youth center took me under his wing. He set me straight and got me into sports. He thought I had some talent and fought for me every inch of the way. He made me work hard and learn the system. If it weren't for him, I would never had stayed in school and gotten the scholarship. He was like a father to me."

Austin's real reason for was his wanting to help out was to be around the kids. "I really love kids, and always want to do something for them that somebody else did for me. I am a firm believer of what goes around comes around. Count me in."

CeCe asked, "Austin, where does your sister live?"

"She still lives on the West Coast. She has my mom living with her. I bought them a house to live in. She met a nice guy and they have two great kids together. I get out to see them whenever I can get away. Actually, I need to do some Christmas shopping when we're in Denver. Do you think we might be able to do that before we come back?"

Reece and CeCe laughed together. Austin looked puzzled.

CeCe touched his arm and said, "Austin, we thought we were going to have to twist your arm to let us shop. It's one of our favorite things to do, and always when we go into Denver. We can help you pick out some things. It's even more fun when you are shopping for kids."

The waitress came over and took their order, and then the trio resumed their conversation.

"Angie is excited to meet you, two. Of course, Angie never passes up a moment to meet two beautiful women. The game should be good. Both teams are playing well. I never got the opportunity to play in Denver when I was playing ball. I hear it's a great place to watch a game, especially if you're pulling for Denver. The noise is deafening. The weather while we're there is supposed to be cold with a chance of snow. We should make sure we are dressed warm." Austin looked at CeCe meaningfully. "Of course, we could just snuggle together and keep warm that way."

The thought of snuggling close with CeCe was enough to set him off. Austin was sitting close enough to her to smell her perfume. God, she smelled wonderful. She was as fresh as the snow that had just fallen.

He had to figure out a way to get her to be more interested in him. They had a good friendship going, but he wanted more. He wanted to know her more intimately.

This was an unusual position for Austin to be in. He never had trouble with getting women to want a relationship with him before; in fact, it was usually the opposite. He couldn't get them to leave him alone. This trip would be a test as to whether or not she was interested in him.

After lunch, they all said goodbye and went their separate ways. Reece was anxious to get back to work on her article, Austin needed to take care of some things with Tucker, and CeCe needed to pick up some things for Nitro before she left on their trip to Denver.

CeCe went into Dr. Baldwin's office to pick up food for Nitro. Dr. Baldwin came from one of the exam rooms to greet her. "Hello, beautiful. How is my favorite dog owner?"

"Hello, Dr. Baldwin, I'm fine. I just came to get some food for Nitro. He's going to be spending a few days with Ruth Johnson. Austin, Reece, and I are all going to the Monday night football game in Denver."

"Ahh, Reece. I have never seen a more beautiful woman, of course I mean with that color of hair. CeCe, you're just as beautiful as Reece, it's just that...."

"Dr. Baldwin, you don't need to explain to me your feelings about Reece- I already know them. Remember? You and half the town would love to have her be your one and only. Only I don't think she is ready to settle down just yet. But it can't hurt to keep asking."

"You're right, CeCe. Hey, do you think that you could use another male escort to go to the game? I would love to come along."

"I think we'll be just fine. Besides, Austin got the tickets from his friend who plays for Denver; I don't know that there would be any more available. This game, like all the others, is sold out."

"Really, who is the player that Austin knows?"

"Michael D'Angelo. He's a wide receiver. They played together when Austin was playing for the 49ers. I'm excited to go. I've never been to a professional game"

"Yes, I know him well. He is a good receiver. Denver was lucky to get him. Some guys have all the luck, talent, good looks, and friends with beautiful women friends to introduce him to. You guys have fun and tell Nitro hello for me. Here, let me give you some of these treats that he likes. He'll know they are from me. Next time you bring him in for shots, maybe he'll remember that I am the one who gives him the treats and he won't bother growling at me. Take care and tell Reece I said hello, and I won't give up calling her."

On her way out, CeCe remembered that Ruth was going to be the one bringing Nitro in on Tuesday so Dr. Baldwin could look at his paw. "I just remembered that I won't be in on Tuesday, but Ruth will bring him in. You can tell her anything I need to know and I will take care of it. Bye , Dr. Baldwin, I will make sure Nitro knows the treats are from you. Look for us at the game. I'm sure you will hear us. Maybe I can give the coach an idea or two as to what plays might work!"

CeCe laughed as she walked out of the door.

Chapter Eleven

The weekend was turning out to be a good one, with the weather cooperating. The snow was beautiful. It sat up on the mountain peaks like angel hair.

He knew that Reece was going to be out of town with CeCe and Austin. What better a surprise than to send her a letter in Denver? She would feel close to him even with the distance between them.

He had to remember which hotel they were staying in. If he sent the letter off today, it would be there on Monday when she got there.

What was the name of the hotel? 'The Denver', no that was in Glenwood. It was a famous hotel. It had been around for a long time, since the turn of the last century that was what CeCe had said. It was a color wasn't it? Yes, it was the Brown Palace.

He would call the hotel and get the address. That way he could send the letter right away. She would be very surprised and pleased. He wished he could be there to see her when she got it. She would feel very flattered. Maybe he should send flowers; no, that would be too risky. They could trace the credit card or call to him. The letter would have to do. The paper and the typewriter were waiting as usual.

The paper and the envelope were so unusual that he was sure she would recognize it immediately. There wasn't much time to waste; he needed to get it off in the mail. He dialed the phone for information. He got the address to the hotel and addressed the envelope.

The Brown Palace Hotel
321 17th Street
Denver, Colorado
% Ms. Reece Landon

He drove off to the post office to mail the letter. How much longer would he have to wait before he revealed himself to her as her one and only true love? The answer would not come today. He would know when the time was right. For now, he would have to be content with having her read how he felt. She could feel the intensity of their love. He just knew it.

~ ~ ~

Monday was a dark and gloomy day. It looked as if it might snow.

The trip would take about three hours; CeCe made sure they had plenty of supplies and snacks. She was so excited she could hardly stand it. How often had she been by the stadium and wish she could go in? Now she would have her wish.

Austin said he had never been to the stadium either. He seemed to be as excited about the game as she was. She wondered if he hadn't been to a professional game since he hurt himself, because he would miss the game so much.

He really had been a wonderful player. It would have been great to see Austin when he was playing. This had to be tough on him- he hadn't been ready to give up the game but knew that he couldn't continue with his injury.

"Good morning, Miss Daydreamer." Reece had walked up behind CeCe while she was making a pot of tea.

CeCe jumped and splashed the hot water out of the pot. "You scared the pants off me, Reece. I could have spilled this pot of hot water on you. You need to make more noise when walking up behind someone."

"I wasn't that quiet, CeCe. As a matter of fact, I was humming 'Let it snow Let it snow Let it snow' cause it sure looks as if it's going to. I love it when it snows when we go to the city. Where were you, anyway? You weren't in this kitchen. Are you already in Hawaii? What a contrast the warm weather will be to this. I can't wait!" Reece was talking to CeCe as she put a bagel in the toaster.

"I was just mentally checking off that we had everything we need. I was also thinking about the game tonight. We are going to have so much fun, Reece! I hope the weather doesn't get too nasty, so we get into the city before the roads get bad. Looks like the boys will have to play some old fashioned football. The snow will favor the Broncos."

"Why is that? I mean why will the snow favor the Broncos, because it is warmer in California?"

"Well, a little, although the players are used to playing in the cold. It can be cold in the wintertime in Oakland. No, the snow makes it harder to throw and catch the ball, and Denver has a better running game than Oakland. It could be a wild game though; sometimes the cold wet weather causes lots of turnovers."

"I take it you mean turnovers like in fumbles, not as in apple or cherry turnovers," Reece laughed at her own joke as she got plates out for their breakfast.

"Reece, you know more about the game than you let on. Sometimes I think you just pretend not to know the facts so someone will explain them to you. Are you all packed and ready to go?"

"Yes, I am. I'm very anxious to get going."

"I loaded Nitro's things in the car last night. My bag is ready, so all I need to do is finish fixing our snacks and shower. I told Austin we would be at his place around 9:00am. Ruth is anxiously waiting for Nitro- you would think he was her grandchild or something. She will spoil him rotten while we're gone. I sure am lucky to have people like her and Tucker to count on to take care of Nitro when I go away. Otherwise, I wouldn't be able to have such a good time worrying about him."

"CeCe, I don't think Ruth is the only one to spoil Nitro. I think any child you would have would have competition with him. You might want to think about having a child. Now, I could spoil that kid. Don't you think that you and Austin would have beautiful children together?"

CeCe just rolled her eyes. "Come on, Reece, I think it's time for you to feed your brain- you are obviously getting delirious. So eat and finish packing. I'm ready to get on the road."

"All right, CeCe, but you can't deny the fact that your children would be beautiful." Reece ran out of the kitchen before CeCe could toss something at her.

That's all CeCe needed to think about- having children with Austin. It was hard enough being around him; let alone thinking about making babies with him. They would be cute, though.

"Enough of that," CeCe said aloud. "Nitro, you are not allowed to tell anyone what I was thinking. Promise?"

The dog gave CeCe a quick sloppy kiss. CeCe laughed and finished packing the snacks.

~ ~ ~

Austin woke Monday morning with the same anticipation he had when he had been playing. This was the first time he had been back in a stadium since his injury. He could feel the excitement and energy surging within his body. It was a different kind of feeling on game day.

He hadn't slept well the night before, just like when he played the game. What was it that caused his body to react this way? His brain knew he wasn't going to play, why didn't the rest of his body?

He had made it a habit of keeping himself in shape. Maybe that was it, all of that lactic acid running around in his muscles. He had worked himself hard last night.

It was not going to be easy to just sit there and not be able to play. That's why the coaching job was good for him. It still kept him in the game, and he could give some of his knowledge about football to the kids.

His season had been good; they had made it to the championship game, but lost. There was always next year, and he was sure they would win it all.

Austin walked out into the kitchen; the aroma there was always so wonderful. He never knew how Tucker stayed so trim, eating Ruth's incredible meals.

"Have yourself a seat here, Austin. Tucker will be right back. He just went to check on something. You need to eat before you go on that long trip into the city. I hope you don't mind picking up the things I put on the list for you."

Ruth's round figure was gliding around the kitchen with the ease of a kite flying in the spring breeze as she spoke to Austin.

"Ruth, you know I don't like to eat breakfast on game day". Austin smiled as he hugged her tightly.

"Game day? It's not your game day. You don't have to go out there and fumble those papers around to see which play to call, you also don't have to go out there and have your bones crushed by the other team. So you just sit yourself down here and eat something. Besides, it looks as if it might snow hard and you may be grateful to me for making you eat if you get stuck on the road."

"Okay, Ruth, I'll eat some breakfast. It smells wonderful in here anyway; it would be hard to resist. What is that you're putting in the basket?"

"It is just some of my jalapeno corn bread and cranberry relish for you and the ladies to take with you. It is always good to be prepared. You never know when you will be happy to have such a thing."

"Ruth, you act as if we're going into uncharted waters here. Denver is only a three hour trip, and on good roads. Not that I mind taking your basket with me. I love your corn bread, and that relish is out of this world. You wouldn't mind if I give my friend Angie some would you?"

"Austin, I've already packed a goodie bag for your friend. I'm sure he will enjoy it. Does he have the same bad habit of yours, of not being able to eat on game day?"

"No, Angie eats anything in sight. He packs his body full of food before the game. Maybe that's why he has the extra spurt of energy and can get away from the defenders so often. He does have a strong Italian family background, where you eat everything your mother or grandmother puts on your plate. He has a good metabolism to keep the extra pounds off. If it were me, I would weigh a ton.

"Well, I guess his mama taught him well. Miss CeCe is very excited about this game. She is a huge fan of the Broncos, if you didn't already know that. She deserves to get away and have some fun. She is always working so hard."

"Yes, I know. She has asked me to help out with this annual community garage sale. It benefits children. I told her I would help out. I enjoy anything I can do for kids to try and get them a good start."

"Miss CeCe got you to volunteer, good for her. I'll be there myself. It's a huge event. Everyone shows up for this thing. It's for a great cause and you can find some good deals as well. I didn't know you liked kids so much. Why haven't you found yourself a wife and settled down, so you could start a family?"

"Ruth, I just haven't found anyone who will put up with me. And all the good ones are taken, like you. Tucker would shoot my backside full of buckshot if I took you away from him. Not that you would put up with me any more than any other woman."

"I don't know what you're wanting from me, but you ain't going to get it with that sweet talk. I told you that before. There are plenty of woman who would be good for you and you for them. Look at Miss CeCe; she's a prize just waiting to be claimed. You couldn't ask for better. She's beautiful, intelligent, self-sufficient, and knows more about football than most men. Look at the play she called in that game that you won. If it hadn't been for that Carlos guy, why…"

"Miss CeCe isn't waiting around for anyone to ask her out. I am sure she has men knocking on her door all the time. But you are right about the part of her being damn near perfect. I'm a slow mover, but once I get going, watch out! Maybe we can get something moving this weekend."

Just as Austin finished talking, Tucker walked in the kitchen.

"Well, Austin are you ready to go? I wish I were in your shoes, being escorted by two of the most beautiful woman in the surrounding area to a big Monday night football game. But Austin, remember, I have the best of both worlds. I have a beautiful woman who I can snuggle up with and watch the game in the comfort of my own home. I can even crawl in bed during the middle of the game if I want to.

Tucker smiled at Austin and gave Ruth's ample bottom a pat as he spoke.

Ruth turned toward him and said, "It must be something in the air with you boys today. Or maybe it's all that testosterone that fills the air when football is about to be played. Now just sit yourself down, Tucker, and have breakfast. You need to talk to Austin before he leaves- I don't want him to be tied up when the ladies get here. They will need to get on the road before that storm blows in."

Austin and Tucker sat and talked while Ruth finished cleaning up the kitchen. The snow was just beginning to fall with the flakes big and fluffy. Ruth thought to herself, They need to get going. This could be a good storm.

Just as she was thinking, she could see Reece's Jeep coming up the long drive.

"Here they are, Austin," Ruth sang out as she walked to the door.

The Jeep stopped, and CeCe got out and opened the door for Nitro. Nitro bounded out the door and ran up the steps.

Ruth opened the door, and Nitro jumped up and gave her a kiss. "Why, hello Nitro, nice to see you, too," Ruth said as she steadied herself against the door-frame to keep from falling over. "What did you give him this morning, CeCe? He sure is wound up."

"Good morning, Ruth," CeCe said as she was unloading Nitro's things out of the back of the Jeep. "I didn't do anything different with him- he's always excited to see people, especially ones who spoil him."

"Stop getting that stuff out of the Jeep. There are two strong men here. They'll help."

Ruth turned and hollered into the house, "We could use some help out here!"

Tucker and Austin came through the door. Austin looked so incredibly handsome; he practically filled the doorway. The way his jeans fit him, whew, thought CeCe. He looked good in anything he wore.

Austin walked over to CeCe. "Put that down, I'll get it. Besides, it's a long trip and I need to use my muscles before I get into that car and take, according to Ruth, the long adventurous trip to the far away Denver."

CeCe watched as he moved toward her. His blue eyes were crystal clear- the color of the Colorado sky on a warm summer day. He moved sleekly as if he were a wild cat. As he lifted the bag of dog food, his muscles stretched and flexed in perfect coordination.

His voice jolted her back.

"Where would you like this? Hello, did you hear me?"

"Oh, I'm sorry, Austin, I was just thinking about what I need to tell Ruth about Nitro. Ruth, where would you like us to put this stuff?" CeCe asked, as she reached into the back of the Jeep to try and cover her agitation.

Her cheeks were stained with embarrassment at the thoughts she had been thinking.

"Just put it inside the door, and Tucker and I will put it where we need it. You just get yourselves on the road." Ruth was waving her hand in the air, shooing them off.

"Ruth, the snow isn't supposed to reach Denver until later this evening," Reece said as she stepped out of the Jeep. "I am sure we will be just fine. I'm a good driver and grew up driving in the snow."

"I know, I just want you out of here so I can get started on the fun with Nitro while you all are gone." Ruth laughed

"He will give you all you can handle, I'm afraid," CeCe said. "I wouldn't trust him to be too much of a watchdog either, after him letting someone come in the house with that letter."

CeCe walked over and was hugging Nitro he was washing her face with his tongue. "You be a good boy and take care of things here. I will miss you, but I know that you won't miss me, Nitro. You won't want to come home from here the way these two spoil you."

"Did you ever find out anything about those letters?" Ruth asked with a worried look on her face.

"No, we're trying to track the paper since it is so unusual, but we haven't had any luck yet. We are locking the door when we aren't home. I don't know if they would be brave enough to break in. I think Nitro would go after them in that case. It's just a wait and see situation, according to the sheriff's department. No need to worry, we will be surrounded by lots of strong, handsome men for the next couple of days. They will protect us; I'm sure of it. Reece laughed as she, too, petted Nitro.

"You be good, Nitro," CeCe said as she stood up and brushed off her jeans.

"I will make sure he gets some exercise, Miss CeCe," Tucker said as he finished putting Nitro's stuff in the house. "He can run along with me, while I ride out and look at the fence on the north end of the ranch."

Austin watched Nitro being hugged so tightly by CeCe and thought to himself, I wouldn't mind kissing that face and neck myself. CeCe had her hair pulled up into a knot on top of her head. A few strands of hair had fallen loose and curled softly against her neck. She had a very sensuous neck, and the thought of touching it made him very excited. He needed to get his mind off of her body, get his bag, and get on the road.

"I'll just throw my bag in the back and we can go. Ruth is sending us off with some of her famous jalapeno cornbread and cranberry relish." Austin took the stairs two at a time.

"Ruth, don't you go and give any of that stuff to Nitro," CeCe warned laughingly. CeCe gave Ruth some final instructions before they were off.

As they were preparing to leave, CeCe said, "I'll sit in the back. I have the shortest legs of all of us; besides, it allows me to have the whole back seat to myself. Nitro takes up half the bed at night." CeCe laughed and waved goodbye to Ruth and Tucker as Reece drove away from the ranch.

Just a mile or so from the ranch, they passed the lake. There were a few people out skating. It was a little early, but a few diehard skaters came out each day to practice their skills.

It was best for them to come early, as the kids came after school with sticks and pucks for their on-going game of hockey. No one ever kept score; it was just a game of individual skill.

CeCe asked Austin, "Do you skate?"

"Yes, I do. I love to skate, but wasn't able to when I was playing professional ball. They were afraid that I would hurt myself and not be able to play. How ironic; it wasn't anything other than my job that caused me to get injured and not be able to play. I guess I could skate anytime I want now."

"Great, we'll have to go. I love to skate, but getting Reece to go with me is like pulling teeth. Let's plan a skating party when we get back from Denver, maybe right after the holidays. They have the bonfire going in the evening. It'll be fun."

"Sure, you say when. I will have to buy some skates. Maybe I'll do that when we're in Denver. I didn't have much use for them in Kauai. I used to be a pretty good skater as a kid, but I'm not promising anything now. The Y had an indoor rink not too far from my home. It may take me a few times to get my skating feet back. Do you promise to not leave me in a cloud of ice dust, CeCe?" Austin asked, laughing

"I promise. It will be nice to go with you. I'm not that great myself. I just enjoy going out and doing it."

"Oh, don't let her fool you, Austin, CeCe is good at just about anything she does. Okay, I will go too, if you promise to make some of that special hot chocolate of yours, CeCe," Reece said as they all laughed.

The clouds were so heavy with snow that it almost felt like evening. There was very little traffic, and would probably stay that way.

Conversation was light when CeCe asked Reece, "You seem to be spending a lot of time with Mason, how are things going there?"

"He's a really nice guy, a little on the quiet side, but fun to be with. I need to get him to open up more. He doesn't like to talk a lot about himself. I'm still having trouble with the article on him. He keeps telling me not to worry about it, and that nobody wants to know anything about him. I keep saying that it isn't true; all kinds of people are interested in the new folks in the valley. He insists I not write it."

"Well, I kind of know how he feels," Austin said. "You don't want people to get the wrong impression. Some people might think that you think you are better than them when they find out what you did and where you did it. I was unsure of it when you wrote about me. You did a good job, but still I was nervous about it. I would tell him, though, it allowed me to get to know a lot of different people. They would walk up to me and tell me that they had read the article and they felt like they knew me already."

"Thanks, Austin, for saying I did a good job. I like finding out things about people and letting others know about their accomplishments. I wish I could get inside his head a little more."

"Have you had any luck getting a hold of Claire?" asked CeCe

"Yes, she called me back and is in the middle of a big project, but she's looking into it for me when she finds the time. I think I might just write the article with the little I know about him and get it in the paper. He has been in town for a while now, and if I wait much longer he won't be a newcomer."

"That's true. Hey, Austin, do you know where the seats are and where we are supposed to pick up the tickets?" CeCe sat forward to ask the question. As she did so her jacket parted and revealed the scooped neck shirt she had on. Her breasts swelled over the bra she wore and made a deep valley between them.

As Austin turned to answer her, he saw that incredible sight,, and colored immediately at what he felt within.

He had the overwhelming desire to rest his face between her breasts. Her skin was so beautiful, and looked so soft. For now he could only imagine what she felt like there, and how she would fill his palms with her wonderful breasts.

He thought about the creamy white skin and the contrast they would have to his rough, weathered hands. He turned away to gain his composure as he spoke.

"Uhh, Angie was going to leave the tickets at will call for us. He is going to leave us field passes as well. We'll be able to go onto the field after the game. The seats are supposed to be good ones- about the 45-yard line on the west side- that's the side of the Broncos. I believe he said they were on the third level."

"From what I understand, there are no bad seats in the stadium," CeCe said.

"This is going to be a good game. I can feel it."

"Anywhere that I can get a good look at those bodies is a good seat for me," Reece said as she smiled and drove on toward Denver. "I wonder if that sideline pass will get me into the locker room. I could do some interviews. I even have my press card with me. Maybe I could go to the office and get a press pass."

"Reece, it doesn't work that way. They had a problem with females in the locker room, so all those interviews are done outside the locker room." Austin could hardly contain his laughter. "Did you bring your camera with you?"

"I'm going to let CeCe take the pictures- she does well on both sides of the camera. She's a real nature bug and sees things in the landscape that most people don't. She will have to show you some of her work."

"Really, CeCe? I didn't know you were inclined to the artistic side, although it doesn't surprise me. Living in such a picturesque place certainly would get those creative juices flowing. Now if its landscape pictures you like to take, wait until you get to Kauai. Just a few miles from my house is the most inspiring place on earth. The mountains seem to just come from nowhere out of the sea. The color of the sky at sunset is unbelievable. It won't be long before you get to see it yourself. Have you set the date?"

"Yes we have. We're going in mid-February. Are you going to be there any time around then? It would be nice to have a guide on the island," CeCe said as she settled back into her seat. She was unaware of the electricity she had set off in Austin.

"Yes. As a matter of fact, as it turns out, Angie will be there then too. He got the selection to the pro-bowl. He will extend his visit and fly over to Kauai when the game is over. We would be glad to show you two around."

"So is Angie free to show us around, or is there a Mrs. Angie?" Reece asked with a smile on her face.

"Oh, no, there isn't a Mrs. Angie. However, there have been many women who have tried to lay claim to the name," Austin joked.

They all laughed and talked until they could see the skyline of Denver coming up in the distance.

Chapter Twelve

Reece pulled the Jeep up to the hotel. The lobby was decorated for the holiday season. The music playing in the background was soft and spirited.

Austin was looking around him as they entered the hotel. "This looks like a nice place. Have you stayed here before?"

"I used to come to the city this time of year with my grandmother when I was young. It has great memories for me. This hotel is one of my favorites and has a great history. A lot of presidents and even the Beatles have stayed here."

"Good day, madam, how can I help you?" The desk clerk asked.

"Hello, we have reservations under the names of Wellington and Carter," CeCe replied

"Oh, yes, here we are, Mr. and Mrs. Carter, and the other room is under Wellington. Is that correct?"

"No, I am Ms. Wellington and this is Mr. Carter. Ms. Landon and I will be sharing a room and Mr. Carter is to have his own room." CeCe was blushing at the thought of them sharing the same room.

Austin could hardly contain his laughter. He was quite amused at the error the desk clerk had made with the room arrangement.

He spoke up. "If there is a problem, we can just make the adjustments and Ms. Wellington and I can share the room."

CeCe jabbed her elbow in his stomach. What was he saying? Wait until she got him away from all these people. This was embarrassing enough, let alone him making matters worse. "Excuse me, but Mr. Carter is wrong about the arrangements. Is there a problem with him having his own room?"

"Not at all Ms. Wellington, it was my error. We have the room arrangements you requested. To correct the mistake, we are upgrading both of the rooms to suites. I hope that will be acceptable to you." The desk clerk handed CeCe the registrar pen. "If I could just have your signature here and initials here, we will have you all set to go."

Austin's side hurt a little from the jab CeCe had landed in his mid-section. He would have to remember not to stand that close to her again if he was going to do something to irritate her. Still, he thought it was funny to watch her squirm a bit. He wouldn't have minded sharing the same room, and bed, for that matter, with her.

Reece was standing off to the side watching the whole incident. She thought it was funny that the desk clerk thought them to be a couple. This was going to be a fun getaway. She was sure that the two were going to make something more of this relationship. Maybe now would be the time for them to start developing it.

"Thank you for your patience and understanding in my error, Ms. Wellington. Do you have your luggage all set? These suites are adjoining. I hope that will be all right?"

The desk clerk handed the keys to CeCe.

"Thank you and the adjoining suites will be just fine. That way, we can help Mr. Carter find his room if he gets lost or has too much to drink."

CeCe laughed and gave Austin a look as if to say, 'two can play this game'. "Thank you again for the upgrade."

"Touche," Austin said as they walked away from the desk.

Reece, who was laughing, greeted them saying; "You two are great together. I think you should have gone with the desk clerk's room reservation. That way I could have maybe found one of those handsome football players to bring back to my room to interview."

"That would be some interview, Reece." CeCe tossed the comment over her shoulder as they approached the elevators.

The suites were wonderful. They had a great view of the museum across the street. The trio had agreed to get settled in and meet down at the Shipwreck Tavern for a late lunch.

CeCe had told them about her friends who tailgated in the parking lot. They had all been invited.

Austin told them that they were invited to the tent that they had set up for friends and family before the game as well. They had all decided that it would be more fun to go to the tailgate party.

CeCe and Reece unpacked their things. Reece was very excited to meet Angie. She had picked up a couple of the sports magazines and read a bit about him, but most of all she had seen pictures of him.

There were the action shots, but the one she found most amusing and appealing was the milk ad that they do with celebrities. She thought he looked like a guilty little boy. If he was half as charming as Austin was, it could be an interesting time.

After the delicious lunch, Austin asked, "What now?"

CeCe said, "I think we have time to shop for about an hour or so if you would like. Our friends said they set up around 3:00pm for the tailgate party. Would you want to do that?"

"3:00 pm! That's four hours before the game. This must be some party."

"It is. They have a whole group of people that come to every game. They even have gourmet food. Not the ordinary hamburgers and hot dogs. They have flags, tablecloths, chairs, and there is even a portable fireplace they bring for cold days like today. They have a full bar that meets everyone's needs."

"Do they play ball?" Austin asked excitedly.

"I bet they do. I'll play against you Austin. That way I can cover you like a blanket. I will show you how those defenders should have done it when playing against you in the NFL." CeCe thought to herself that she should have phrased that better.

"Like a blanket? Why didn't you let the desk clerk keep you to together if you were going to be covering him like a blanket?" Reece laughed as she picked up her jacket and moved quickly away from CeCe in order to dodge her lethal elbow.

They all laughed as they walked out of the restaurant towards the shopping area.

The snow was really beginning to fall hard now. Big fluffy flakes- it appeared as if there were a pillow fight going on from up above them.

"Don't you just love when it snows like this? It takes me back to my childhood every time we have a big snow. I love to make snowmen, but the Colorado snow isn't too good for that," CeCe said as she walked along with her face lifted toward the sky.

"I love the snow, but don't have any memories of it as a child. It never snowed on the West Coast when I was growing up. I did play a few games in it, though. Most of those games were played on the East Coast. The snow is a lot different there. I didn't know you couldn't make snowmen here. Is it because of the lack of moisture in the snow?" Austin asked as he watched CeCe with amazement. She just glided along like she was on skates.

"Haven't you ever heard the term Champagne Powder Austin?" Reece asked. Before he was able to answer she continued. "It is the best snow for skiing. It is so light that when we get a huge dump, it's like floating on top of it. You don't have to work as hard as you do in the east. I've skied that stuff- forget it. I'll take Colorado snow any day, even if it is hard to make snowmen."

"Look!" CeCe grabbed both Reece's and Austin's arm and pulled them to the window she was looking into. "Can we go in? I love bookstores. They have such a wonderful smell to them. All of that paper and leather bound books; it makes you feel like sitting by a fire and reading all day long. We can look for some presents in here. Besides I want to get a travel log on Hawaii. We will need to know what to see and do in Maui anyway. We will leave the Kauai stuff to you and Angie."

CeCe spoke with such enthusiasm that they couldn't deny her the pleasure of going into the bookstore.

"Okay, let's go. I can look for some books for my family. I also want to get a book on fly-fishing. I plan on taking up the sport in the spring."

"Really!" CeCe exclaimed. "I have a good friend who owns a fly shop in the Roaring Fork Valley near Aspen. I wanted to go this fall but never got around to it. We should go in the spring. He owns a place up by the Rudi Damn. It really is the best fishing in the whole state. I love to fly fish."

"Is there anything you don't do, CeCe?" Austin asked as he pulled the door open for them to walk through. Changing the subject, Austin said, "I'm not sure what to buy for my mother and sister, but they both love to read. My sister said something about Oprah's Book Club- do you know anything about that?"

"Oh yes, they are wonderful books. Each month Oprah chooses a book and announces it to her audience. They read it and have an opportunity to write to her and tell her what they felt their connection to the book was. She arranges to have the author along with a group of readers who wrote to her meet and have dinner or lunch. They have a meal that would be indigenous to the area of the country or the world that the book is set in. All of the books are wonderful. I have read most of them myself. There is usually a section set up with all of the books previously chosen. Let's look and see if we can find them."

CeCe hooked her arm through Austin's and guided him over to an area where she thought the books might be displayed. "Oh, yes, here we are. I can highly recommend any of these books. Here, these are a few of my favorites. You know you will never go wrong with Oprah's book selection. She has wonderful taste; I have never been disappointed with any of them. Your problem will be which one to choose. Have a look and I'll come back to find you after I locate the travel section. If you're having a hard time choosing, I will help you. You might want to get a couple for yourself." CeCe walked away toward another part of the store.

"CeCe" Reece called out to her as she walked by. "Look what I found. It looks like the paper that the letters are written on. What do you think? Am I right?"

CeCe walked toward Reece. She was holding a single piece of stationary. It did appear to be the same type of paper.

"Can I see it closer, Reece?" CeCe asked as she reached out for the paper.

Just as Reece handed the paper to CeCe, one of the store clerks came over to them.

"Can I help you with some stationary? Or have you found what you like? Oh that is the most unusual paper I have ever seen. It is hand made by an elderly gentleman in the Southern part of the state. He came in here this summer selling it. It is beautiful paper, isn't it?"

"Yes, it certainly is. My friend here has an admirer who writes her letters on this same sort of paper. We were wondering if it were handmade. Do you happen to have the name of the gentleman who makes it? We would like to contact him directly."

"I'm sure I can get it for you. If you have some browsing to do in the store I will go and look it up for you."

"That would be wonderful," CeCe said.

When the clerk walked away, CeCe spoke softly to Reece. "Maybe this will be a break. Maybe we can find out who buys this stuff in the Yampa Valley. It's worth a shot. Any little bits and pieces we can pick up to help us find out this person's identity will be very helpful."

"I agree, CeCe. It was just so weird finding that here. Let's go over to the travel section and find some wonderful stuff on Hawaii." Reece and CeCe walked arm in arm to find the guidebooks.

CeCe walked up behind Austin. "Well? Have you decided on some books?"

"They all sound good; I could use your help with the selections. I like these four, but could get others if you think they are better."

"Those are great choices. Like I said, you can't go wrong with an Oprah choice. Would you like to go to the childrens section? They have a great childrens area here."

"That would be great. I could get lost in the childrens section. I'll want to buy out the whole store. When I was a kid, I had my nose stuck in a book all the time. It was my way of escaping. Let's go and buy some kids books." Austin led the way. "What is Reece up to?"

"Well, you remember the letters don't you?"

"Yes, of course"

"Well, we think we found the paper they are typed on. The clerk says it is handmade in the southern part of the state. She is looking up the guy's name now so we can contact him and find out if he has sold any to someone in the Yampa Valley."

"Boy what a find that would be. Here we are, the childrens section. I can't wait until I have children and can read to them every night." Austin's mind wandered to a dreamy future, tucking children into bed and reading them a bedtime story. Funny, as he thought about the children, they all looked like CeCe. He really couldn't wait till he was a daddy. And why not have CeCe be the mother of his children? He could have a lot of fun making those kids. There he went again- getting himself all excited, time to concentrate on buying the books.

Reece, Austin, and CeCe all met at the cash register. Each had an arm full of books and things.

"I guess this will take care of the shopping for the afternoon. We should drop the books off at the hotel and get to the stadium. I've never watched a game in the snow before. This will be fun," Reece said as she laid her items on the counter.

"Here is the name of the gentleman who sold the paper to us. Good luck in finding out the information you need." The clerk handed Reece a piece of paper with a name, address, and phone number on it.

"Thank you. I appreciate your help." Reece took the paper and put it in her wallet.

They paid for the purchases and walked out of the store. They had been inside about an hour, and already there was about an inch of snow on the ground.

~ ~ ~

He went about his daily work, but couldn't help wondering if Reece had received the letter he sent to her. He was very excited about her getting it. If only he could be there to watch her. There would be other times. It was just as well that she was away.

He had been very busy as of late, and it was hard for him to be around her as much. Of course, he was not a stranger; they had spent time together. It's just that Reece seemed to be interested in someone else at the moment.

It wouldn't take her very long to realize that he was not right for her. He would be waiting in the wings as he always was. Soon she would recognize them all for what they were.

He wondered if CeCe didn't already suspect who the letters were coming from. She was very bright, and only wanted the best for her friend. She would be sure to put Reece on the right track.

He wanted himself and Reece to be just like CeCe and Austin. Austin had just floated into town and they found each other. Oh, neither one of them knew it yet, but being the romantic that he was enabled him to see it written all over them. Just about everyone in town knew it.

CeCe deserved someone to care about her like he cared about Reece. That Latin Lover had hurt her when they were in college, which is why she was always so cautious.

Reece on the other hand, always had a whole stable of men to choose from. She was as beautiful on the inside as she was on the outside.

Those others thought that she would give them what they wanted, but he knew better. It wasn't what she was after. She wanted to find someone to take care of her and to love her for who she was. That is why he was just waiting for the right time.

Someone was calling out his name. It was time to get back to business; others were depending on him.

~ ~ ~

As CeCe, Reece, and Austin walked back to the hotel, they all talked about the game. This was an important one. There were only two games left in the regular season, and Denver could wrap up home field advantage throughout the play-offs. All they needed to do was to win the game.

When they walked into the hotel, the bellman asked, "May I take your bags for you and deliver them to your room?"

"Thank you, but we need to go up and put on warmer clothes for the game," replied CeCe. "Austin, how long will it take you to change?"

"I'm ready to go. If you ladies need any help, let me know. Otherwise, I'll just sit here in the lobby and wait for you."

Austin took a seat in the lobby and watched CeCe and Reece walk to the elevators.

CeCe turned toward Austin and said, "Austin, don't get into any trouble while we are away. We will be right back to go to the stadium." CeCe spoke with a smile as she turned to walk away.

Austin watched her firm bottom move from side to side. He thought to himself that the workouts she and Reece did everyday sure paid off.

"Mr. Carter?" The bellman brought Austin back from his reverie.

"Yes?" Austin said as he stood to talk to him.

"I just saw you come in and thought I recognized you. You are accompanying the ladies that just went up the elevator, right?"

"Yes, I am. Is there something I can help you with?"

"I was a great fan of yours when you were playing football. I was glad you never played Denver- I would have had to root against you. You were the best in the game. Too bad what happened to you. Anyway, I just received a message that there is some mail for Ms. Landon at the front desk. Would you like to take it, or shall I deliver it to her room?"

"Well thank you for the compliment, I would have liked to play at the Bronco's stadium. If I came here when I was playing, I may have gotten interested more in the state sooner. You have a beautiful state, and the women here aren't half bad either. We are headed to the game now, so you might want to just deliver it to the room. You can probably catch them up there before we leave. If not, I'll tell Ms. Landon that there is mail for her in her room. Hey, where is a good place to go for a cigar after the game?"

"Why, we have one of the best cigar bars around right here in the hotel, Churchill's. It's right over there behind us. They stay open late."

"Do they play any music? I'm looking for a jazz bar or something that plays some music that you can dance to. You know the kind of dance music I am talking about- the kind where you have to hold someone close, not the kind where you say hello to your partner and then wave to them across the room an hour later.

"Yes, I do know the kind of music you are talking about. Here, let me write down a couple of places."

The bellman had been very helpful, and Austin tipped him well. Austin only hoped he could get CeCe to dance with him, he was in the mood for some physical contact tonight, and it wasn't going to come in the form of football.

The doors to the elevator opened and out they walked. Neither of them was aware of the turmoil they caused just by being there. They were both so beautiful.

"Hi ladies, did the bellman catch you?"

CeCe spoke first, "No, I didn't know he was chasing us."

They both laughed. Austin said, "He had some mail for Reece, I told him you were in the room and he might be able to catch you there. Otherwise, he was just going to leave it in the room. Are we all ready? I feel as though I should be in the locker room going through the plays. This is a different feeling for me."

"Austin, what kind of mail was it? I wasn't expecting anything here at the hotel," Reece said, a little concerned.

"He didn't say what kind of mail it was. He just said he had something for you that came in the mail."

CeCe interrupted, "Let's get going, the tailgate party should be in full swing. Austin, we'll let you talk us through the plays that you think they are going to be putting into the game tonight. I still think I could be of some help with the play calling."

CeCe was trying to bring the mood back to the light place it had been. Both Reece and Austin seemed to be a little down. Reece concerned about the mail and what it contained; Austin about the fact that he should be down on the field playing.

"Who wants to put a wager on the score of the game? Loser buys drinks tonight. I say the score will be 28 to 10 Denver. How about you Reece? Austin?

"Okay, but the loser chooses the place of fun. I say the score will be 17 to 13 Denver." Austin felt pretty confident with his choice.

Reece said, "Well you both are going to have to buy drinks 'cause I have the winning score. It will be 5 to 2 Denver."

Austin and CeCe both laughed hysterically.

"Reece, that is a baseball score, teams usually score in 3's or 7's. Although it's not an impossible score, it is very unlikely. Would you like to revise your score?" CeCe guided Reece by the arm out to the waiting Jeep.

"Okay, I say 7 to 3, and still Denver will win. Then I can write about how I got to go into the locker room when they won, what is it they can win tonight, CeCe?" Reece asked innocently.

"They can win the Western Conference title and clinch home field advantage throughout the play-offs." CeCe spoke as they all climbed into the Jeep.

CeCe gave directions to the parking lot that her friends would be in. They didn't have a hard time finding them. The flags were blowing in the wind and snow. The portable fireplace had a welcoming glow. This was the most elaborate outdoor party any of them had ever seen.

Everyone climbed out of the Jeep; Austin was instantly recognized. He didn't seem to mind all the questions he was being asked.

CeCe was surprised to find Shaw and Lisa Corbin there.

"Hello, stranger," Shaw came over to CeCe and gave her a great big bear hug and kiss. "How have you been? I miss seeing you and fishing with you."

"Me too, what are you doing here? I was planning on coming over this fall to pull you away from the shop and go out on the river with me, but time got away. I will come this spring, I promise. Austin wants to learn to fly fish, and I told him about your place," CeCe said as she hugged her arm around Shaw's waist.

"Are you kidding? Do you think I would pass up a chance to see Denver blow this team away? This is my kind of game. I would always get the ball when it was snowing hard. Number 44 scores again. How did you ever become friends with Austin Carter? I was a huge fan of his when he was playing. I can't believe you got Reece to come to the game," Shaw said as he handed CeCe a glass filled with some kind of liquor.

"It's a long story- I'll tell you about it later. He is a really nice guy. This is the first game he has been to since his injury. He really wants to go in there and play. As for Reece, she wants to go in the locker room and interview all the players." CeCe laughed as she spoke.

"What's changed?" Shaw asked jokingly as he hugged CeCe closer.

Austin was talking to several of the guys, but all the time he was watching CeCe and the guy CeCe was hugging. They seemed to be pretty friendly. This guy was all over her.

He hadn't met him when he was introduced to everyone else. Is this why she was so anxious to get to this party? Had she arranged to meet this guy here? Well, he was going to have some competition. Austin thought to himself, I have never thought this way about a woman. It had never bothered him before when other men showed their appreciation to the woman he was with.

CeCe had a different kind of effect on him. Austin excused himself from the group and walked over to where CeCe was standing. Someone handed him a glass of something, and he quickly drank it down. It was warm and burning.

He put his arm around CeCe quite possessively.

CeCe looked up at Austin. She didn't move away; as a matter of fact she moved in closer to his body.

"Hi, I see you have a drink already," Austin said as he stood next to CeCe.

"Hello, I'm Austin Carter." Austin extended his glove-covered hand to Shaw.

"Hello Austin, there was no need to introduce yourself. I have been a big fan of yours since you started playing. My name is Shaw Corbin. I went to school with CeCe and played football in high school, number 44- that was me. Like you, I had an injury that kept me from playing the game. That and a soon to be wife who said "that's it." She wasn't going to let me go out there and get crushed. I did have some promise though. Let me introduce you to my wife, Lisa."

Shaw turned and called Lisa over. "Lisa, I'd like you to meet Austin Carter. He played for the Forty Niners."

Austin felt a little embarrassed at what he had been feeling. This was CeCe's old friend from high school, the one who owned the place over in Aspen. He had a beautiful wife. Austin had just overreacted.

"Hello, it's nice to meet you." Austin regained his composure. "Do you get to come to the games often?"

"No, not really, I just had an opportunity to come to this one and our friends here have this party every time they play in Denver. It's a pretty good set up, wouldn't you say?"

"Yes, I would say. My good friend plays for the Broncos, and I will tell him what kind of support he has out in the parking lot."

"Who is that?" Shaw asked.

"Michael D'Angelo. If you follow Denver, you know him."

"Oh, we know him. He's going to go to the Pro-Bowl this year. He is a big part of where Denver is today. Do you know him from when you two played together in San Francisco?"

"Yes, we were roommates. He's a good guy. We're going to get together with him after the game, would you like to come?"

"That would be great, but I need to check with my better half. We weren't planning on staying, but the weather may change our minds for us. I'll check with Lisa and find out where you are going to be, and if we stay in town then we'll definitely come along. Thanks for the invitation."

Austin removed his arm from around CeCe and looked at his watch, "I did tell Angie I would stop by before the game, and we do need to pick up our tickets. Do you think it would be all right if we leave soon?"

"Sure, just let me say goodbye to the rest of my friends. I'm really excited about going into the stadium anyway. I am anxious to get the game underway," CeCe said as she helped clean up a few of the tables.

They said their goodbyes with promises to come again. Austin was impressed with the camaraderie that they all had. It was if they were a team in their own way.

After they picked up the tickets and found their seats they

headed to the field. They wanted to see if they could catch a glimpse of Angie before he went back into the locker room to get ready for the start of the game.

The teams had just finished warm-ups and were headed back in. Angie was at the back of the group. Austin pointed him out to CeCe and Reece. Reece thought he looked even better in person than in the pictures she saw of him. Of course, all of the players looked good to her.

The game was all that it had promised to be. Because of the weather, it seemed to be a defensive battle.

The score kept going back and forth. It was the fourth quarter and Denver was down by seven points. Oakland had the ball and was driving. On third down and twelve, Oakland threw the ball to the fullback that rushed forward deep into Denver territory.

The fans were very loud. There was lots of hollering and stomping of feet. At times, CeCe wasn't quite sure if it was to keep warm or if it was to confuse the other team.

CeCe turned to Austin and said, "They can't let them score again. It is going to be really hard to come back from that big of a deficit. We need a turnover. A defensive touchdown would be nice right now."

Denver called a safety blitz, the quarterback went back for the pass, and the fullback was right in position. He threw the ball just as the safety flew into him; the ball wobbled out of his hands right into the linebackers. This was the break they needed- the turnover CeCe had wanted. She was jumping up and down and holding on to Austin with all her might.

"Go, Go!" were the cheers coming from the crowd. The field was slippery because of the snow. This slowed the linebacker down enough that the tight end caught him from behind. It wasn't quite the way CeCe had planned it, but Denver did have the ball back. They were on their own forty-yard line.

The crowd silenced a bit so the quarterback could call out the play. It was still pretty loud; it seemed that Oakland had a lot of fans in the Denver area.

Austin said, "Look, Angie is in the game!"

Reece said, "You don't have to tell me that, I have been watching him all night long. These binoculars are pretty good!"

"Here all the time I thought you were learning about the game and watching the plays." CeCe laughed as she turned her attention back to the field.

"They haven't been able to throw the ball all night, but the snow has let up a bit. They need to have some time to get the ball back so if they tie the score and Oakland scores again they can do the same. Both defenses have been incredible." Austin spoke as he absently put his arm around CeCe.

On first down the quarterback dropped back and faked a handoff to the running back. He rolled to his right looking to pass to Angie, but he was covered. He looked to another receiver, but before he could get the ball off the linebacker sacked him for a seven-yard loss.

On the next play, he pitched the ball to the running back. It didn't work. He was dropped with only a one-yard gain.

On third down and sixteen Denver opted for a draw play. Oakland had six men on the line; they were going for a full-on blitz.

The quarterback handed the ball off to the running back, this time it worked. Oakland rushed to hard expecting the pass. The blocking was fantastic from the Denver players. The running back broke a few tackles and gained twenty-two yards in all.

"I could have run through those holes," CeCe said lightheaded. She was enjoying this immensely.

Austin's heart was pounding. He felt as though he were back on the field. He could feel the adrenaline that he felt up on the line waiting for the snap count.

First down on the thirty eight-yard line with the time ticking away, this would be interesting. The quarterback bootlegged to his left, stopped and set his feet; he turned and threw the ball to the opposite sideline to Angie. Angie raced down the field and was stopped at the one, or was he in?

Everyone in the crowd was standing up holding their arms in the air in reference to a touchdown. After sorting through the pile, the officials gathered in conference. The signal had not been given yet. Then the decision: they were on the half-yard line.

The crowd booed the referees and was now yelling 'Angie, Angie, Angie, Angie!' It was riveting. They needed this score to tie the game. Oakland had a fierce goal line stand going.

"Okay, coach what do you call?" Austin turned his head down and spoke in CeCe's ear.

The feeling that came across her when his warm breath whispered in her ear and across her cheek was almost too much with the excitement of the game. CeCe felt dizzy and even shivered a little. She didn't quite hear him and asked, "What did you say?"

Austin bent even closer and moved her over to him as he asked the question again.

This time CeCe heard him and answered.

"I think that I might call a pass or a naked bootleg- oh yeah, the naked bootleg. That will do it. They will key in on the running back." CeCe spoke so confidently. All night long she had called the same plays the coach had called. This wasn't that far off.

"Where do you come up with these things? You need to give the ball to the guys who get paid to pound it in. The offensive line needs to get a good push. Here we go."

Austin put his hands up to his face as if he was warming them, but CeCe knew he just wanted to be out there in the game.

It was a long snap count. Everything moved so slowly. The quarterback back-peddled; Angie went into the corner and was waiting for the ball. It seemed like it took ten minutes for the ball to get to him. He did one of his classic leaps and tipped the ball into his other hand. Now if he could get both feet in bounds they would have the touchdown. He did it! They were only a point away from tying the game.

The crowd was going crazy. Austin and CeCe were clutching at each other and hollering along with the rest of the fans.

Austin could feel the heat between them even with all the clothing they had on. He didn't know if he was more excited about the game or about holding CeCe. He felt that he knew the answer to that by the way his body was reacting.

Reece brought both of them back to the game at hand. "Austin, you should have bet CeCe as to what the play would have been. You would have won."

"How do you know what the play was, Reece?" CeCe asked her with a grin. "I thought you didn't know anything about football? Are you holding back?"

"No, I just got that book about football, you know the one about dummies or something like that. I saw the section on Naked Bootleg, and wanted to know if it had anything to do with the guys being nude, so I read it. And from what I remember, that wasn't a naked bootleg, now was it?"

CeCe and Austin just laughed. Leave it to Reece to find something in a football book about nakedness. Or thought she had.

Denver lined up for the kick. This was important- if they missed the extra point it could be all over. The snap was good and the kick was off right through the middle of the uprights. The game was tied.

There was still time for Oakland to score, so the defense would have to play hard. Denver kicked the ball off to Oakland. It was kicked into the end zone so the ball was not returnable. Oakland started on its own twenty-yard line.

The defense came to play. The crowd was again so loud you almost couldn't hear yourself think.

Reece looked up at the scoreboard and said, "Look! The camera is shaking from all of the stomping. This is great- I don't know if I have ever been in such a loud environment. The fans are certainly showing their support."

CeCe and Austin looked at the scoreboard and agreed with Reece that the camera was shaking from the fans in the stands. They were a part of this, too. CeCe knew that she would be hoarse tomorrow from all the hollering she was doing to support the team.

Denver was playing a zone blitz. If they didn't get there then Oakland would have a good chance to get the ball to the receiver and for him to be able to break away for a long pass play.

The tension was unbelievable. There was a quick snap count, and the quarterback took a short drop and let the ball fly as he got hit. The only person that had a chance at the ball was a Denver player. That play stopped the clock; they had a few moments to call the play. Denver was ready for anything they were going to put on the field.

Again the quarterback stepped back to throw the ball. This time the pass rusher got there and knocked the ball out of his hand. The ball was on the ground; everyone was scrambling to recover the fumble. The ball kept slipping away. First the Oakland player had the ball, then the Denver player, but no one could control it. Finally, an Oakland player fell on it and recovered it at the twenty-two yard line.

It looked as though the game was going to go into overtime. Oakland had time for two more plays; it was third down with two minutes left on the clock.

Austin was standing now hollering with the rest of the crowd. "Denver needs to play prevent defense in order for them not to get away. Here we go again."

CeCe was so nervous she could hardly stand to watch. She wanted Denver to win.

The quarterback stepped back to throw the ball. He avoided the rush and got the ball off to the wide receiver. He broke a few tackles as he ran down the sideline to their own forty-yard line.

The crowd was yelling and screaming. The clock had stopped, but Oakland wouldn't want to leave any time on the clock for Denver to score. The quarterback threw two short passes in-bounds to keep the clock running.

On the last play, Oakland called a time out. They had one left. They were in field goal position.

They were going to try one more play to position the ball in the middle of the field and maybe gain a few more yards.

"This is not good. Oakland is in position to score and Denver won't have any time left to score." CeCe started hollering 'Defense, Defense' along with the rest of the crowd.

Oakland did just as CeCe thought they would. The quarterback handed the ball off to the running back. But wait- the Denver player hit him hard and grabbed at the ball. It was loose. The Denver safety picked it up and started running with it. He was streaking down the sideline. Oakland players were diving at his feet to try and trip him up, but he had too much speed. He was in the end zone and the clock had run out. Denver won!

Austin reached over and hugged and kissed CeCe. The kiss sent electricity through both of their bodies. It was as if they were the only two people in the stadium. All time stood still. Then Reece brought them back.

"Did they just win?"

CeCe turned toward Reece with her faced fully flushed.

"Yes, they won the game. It is a defensive touchdown and time has expired."

"Oh, is that why everybody is so happy? I kind of would have liked to see it go into overtime, with Denver winning of course, that way I could have watched those gorgeous men some more," Reece said laughing and hugging both Austin and CeCe.

"You two must not be cold; you have been hugging each other since the beginning of the game. Maybe I should have sat in the middle seat."

"Reece!" CeCe scolded her. "Now that the Broncos have won the game, we can go onto the field and talk to them. That is better than standing up here watching through the binoculars." CeCe jabbed her in the arm.

"Okay, let's go. I'm ready to talk to them, especially Angie. I can't wait to meet him.

Chapter Thirteen

The three of them waded their way through the crowd. Several of the players were still on the field talking to reporters or other guests. They showed their credentials and walked onto the field.

Austin led the way over to Angie, but before they could get there he was stopped by several players who he had either played with or against during his career.

"Hey, Carter, good to see you man." One of the Denver offensive linemen came over and shook Austin's hand. "We sure would love to have you on the team. You and Angie together, if there were ever a perfect set of bookends it would be you two. You're looking good. Keeping in shape too man, not to mention you still have good taste in ladies. What are you up to anyway? Hey, we're all going out to celebrate tonight, would you and those two beautiful women like to join us?"

"Willy, it is always good to see you. You guys played a hell of a game tonight. That defense would not give up. I haven't been to a pro game since I got injured. Let me tell you, it was not easy sitting up there watching. We're going to go out with Angie. I'm sorry- let me introduce you. This is CeCe Wellington and Reece Landon. CeCe is a huge football fan, and knows just about all there is to know about the game. She can call better plays than half of the coaches in the NFL."

CeCe looked at Austin with a surprised look on her face but then accepted the compliment.

"And Reece here is the owner, editor and writer for our local newspaper"

"Nice to meet you, Willy, is it all right for me to call you Willy?" CeCe extended her hand to shake his.

"Yes ma'am. That is a very big compliment Austin just paid you. He always thought he knew what plays should be called. It's very nice to meet both of you. Maybe you could do a story on me, Ms. Landon. I would gladly sit and talk to you about whatever it is you want to talk about!" Willy shook Reece's hand while he was laughing.

"You said your local newspaper, Austin, just where is it you're hiding yourself these days?"

"I own a cattle ranch and am the football coach for a high school in the Yampa Valley. I spend part of my time in another part of God's country, Kauai. After I was injured that's where I moved. I also fell in love with Colorado and found both the ranch and a job. And that's all she wrote."

"I'd say that isn't all she wrote. Looks to me like there might be a whole bunch more chapters to this story," Willy said grinning. "Why, Ms. Landon here already has her pen and paper out ready to write some more about it."

"That's right, Willy, and please, call me Reece. He doesn't know it yet, but there already is a whole new novel developing. I think it has some romance in it, what do you think?" Reece moved over closer to Willy in order to avoid the inevitable elbow from CeCe.

"Reece, I think you're right about a whole lot of this stuff. Hey, it was nice meeting you both. I hope we can talk more later on. Right now I need to get into the locker room to get in on some of the celebration for winning the division." Willy shook all of their hands again and walked towards the locker room.

Angie came over to them. He hugged Austin and turned toward CeCe and Reece. "What are you waiting for, Austin? Are you going to introduce me to these beautiful women or what?"

"Angie, this is CeCe and Reece. CeCe owns the coffee shop I was telling you about and Reece owns the newspaper. If you don't watch out she'll delve into your background and write a story about you."

Angie reached out and shook both of their hands. "It's a pleasure to meet you two. I have heard a lot about you. I also understand that you are going to make a trip to Hawaii about the time that I'm going to be there with this bum. Can you believe him? He gets injured, goes to Kauai, buys a place in the most beautiful part of the world, then he goes to Colorado to land a great job and buys the ranch of his dreams. Not to mention meeting you two."

Reece couldn't take her eyes off of him. She thought to herself he is gorgeous. He and Austin looked alike. They could be bookends. They were both very handsome and well-developed. It made Reece shiver to think about touching some of those muscles.

CeCe liked him immediately. He was so warm, she felt as if she had known him for a long time. It was the same feeling she got when she first met Austin. They were so much alike, that you would have thought they were brothers.

CeCe spoke first. "Angie, we have heard a lot about you as well. Of course, I follow football and knew what kind of ball player you were before Austin told us about you. I told Austin that you are more subtle with your pushing off than he was. Austin thoroughly denies that he ever did that when he was playing, but we know better don't we?"

CeCe laughed as she patted both of them on their backs.

"We will have to talk about this a little later, CeCe," Angie said reaching out his hand toward Reece. "It looks as though Austin has a date for this evening, would you mind being mine Reece?"

Reece let Angie slip her arm through his as they started walking away.

"Angie, the pleasure will be all mine." Reece turned back and winked at Austin and CeCe.

"You don't think you could get me into that locker room, now do you Angie?" Reece asked as she tossed her head back and laughed.

Austin and CeCe looked at each other and laughed. They walked over to where Angie left Reece with the promise to not be too long before he returned.

"I would like to go back to the hotel and shed some of these layers and freshen up a bit before we go out again. Would that be all right with you?" Reece was asking as they were all climbing into the Jeep.

"I think that would be a great idea," CeCe chimed in.

"Me, too, I'm not used to going out after a game in the same clothes I was in before the game." Austin spoke from the back seat. "It doesn't seem fair that Angie here is the only one to be fresh. Angie, can we valet the car and walk to where it is you want to go?"

"No problem. If you don't want to walk there are always taxi-cabs. But I get to sit in the back seat with the ladies, Austin. You've had the pleasure of their company all evening," Angie said jokingly.

Reece drove the car back to the hotel with the three of them talking about the game. Reece was reliving the game too, but with different visions than the others. She really liked Angie and was hoping she would have an opportunity to get to know him better.

As they walked into the lobby and toward the elevators, the bellman came over to them and welcomed them back.

"Ms. Landon, I tried to deliver some mail to you earlier, but missed you. I left it in the room for you. Is there anything I can get for any of you this evening?"

"Thank you, I don't believe there is anything we need is there, CeCe, Austin?" Reece asked as she entered the elevator.

They both said no. "Thanks again." The elevator rose to their floor.

"How convenient, Austin. All you have to do is stumble next door," Angie said.

CeCe and Reece laughed.

"We'll only need about twenty minutes, if that's all right. We'll come and knock on the door when we're ready. Will that give you enough time, Austin?" CeCe asked him.

"That will be great. See you in a few."

CeCe and Reece walked the few extra steps to their room. When they entered the room they were greeted by the sweet scent of roses. There sat a big vase filled with the most perfect and fragrant roses either of them had ever seen.

"Where did these come from?" asked CeCe.

"There's a card- let's open it!" Reece walked to the table and picked up the card.

"Looks as though they are for you, CeCe."

"For me! It's usually you getting the flowers. I haven't had flowers since Carlos- well, we won't talk about that." CeCe opened the card. It said:

Roses are Red and Violets are Blue
NFL, high school, or any football would be lucky to have you
Thank you for your friendship and helpfulness too
I hope this weekend I will get to know more of you

Enjoy the flowers!
Austin

"Wow! It looks like I was right, CeCe. These are beautiful and the card is really sweet," Reece said, reading it again.

"I don't know what to say. This is really a surprise. I don't know that I ever had anybody do something that nice for me before. Hurry, let's get changed so I can thank him," CeCe said, as she was moving toward the bedroom.

CeCe stopped short of the door. There on the end of the table was sitting the letter the bellman had delivered to the room. It was the same envelope that the other letters had come in.

"Reece, I found the mail that the bellman delivered." CeCe held up the letter.

Reece walked over to CeCe and took the letter. She handled it as though it would burn her fingers.

"How on earth? Who? This is too weird. It's one thing to get them at home. But here, who knew I was here? Obviously this guy does. Do you think he is here, too?"

"I don't know, Reece. Let's open the letter and read it. Do you want me to read it to you?" CeCe asked and held out her hand for Reece to hand her the letter.

"Will you?"

"Of course," CeCe opened the letter. The paper was fragrant as usual. CeCe began reading.

> *My darling Reece,*
>
> *I hope this letter surprises you. I wish I could be with you to watch you read it. The time will come. Soon I am sure of it. For now, just enjoy the words and know they come from my heart.*
>
> *I love you my darling, from the deepest place within me. What is love? For me, it is you and only you. It is the sweet smell of you. The fire in your hair. The sound of your laughter. The spring in your walk. The goodness of you. The total you. You are love, my dear. You take my breath away as if you were the wind itself. Your voice is as sweet as the birds singing in the spring. Look at the mountaintop and see what I see, the pureness of the snow which is the same as our love. Pure, so pure, one could only dream of having this love.*
>
> *Do you miss me and wish to be with me as often as I with you? No need for you to answer, for I can see it in your face when I watch you. Yes, my darling, I do watch you. I am always watching over you. Something is bothering you, but I don't know what it is. I only hope that it will pass and you will be able to concentrate on us. This trip will be good for you; I only wish I could be with you. The time is still not right. I will let you know when it is. For now, feel me with you always, for I am there.*
>
> *Love, Me!*

"He is watching me. And do I love him as much as he loves me? I don't even know who this guy is. Why is he writing me and not telling me who he is? Maybe he is playing a game, but it is getting nerve-wracking."

"Look Reece, we don't have to go out. Let me call Austin and Angie and tell them what's up. They will understand, and they have each other to go out with. They probably won't even miss us. I know this is upsetting you."

"Are you kidding? I am not going to let this ruin my evening. Besides, you don't think I squinted though those binoculars all evening to not to be able to look at and feel the real thing up close and personal, do you? Oh, no. If this guy isn't man enough to let me know who he is, then I am not going to give him another thought. Come on, CeCe, don't just stand there. We only had twenty minutes and we wasted half of them. Let's get changed." Reece walked into the bedroom and began changing her clothes.

A few minutes later they knocked at Austin's door. Angie opened it. He coughed on the jalapeno cornbread he was sampling.

"Wow! You two look great. Not that you didn't before, but wow. What more can a guy say?" Angie opened the door wider to let them enter. "Would you two like some of this awesome cornbread? I guess Ruth made it for Austin to bring along. If she can cook like that, I can't wait to go to the ranch and have a few home cooked meals."

"No, thanks," Reece replied. "I have tasted it, though, and I don't know if there is better anywhere else. She sure can cook. I am ready to go have a little something to eat and maybe a cocktail. How about you?"

"Ah, Austin, are you ready? You might want to take an extra-long deep breath before you come out, 'cause these two ladies will take it away from you," Angie called out to Austin just as he entered the room.

"You aren't kidding, Angie. I guess that is what natural beauty does for you. You don't have to spend hours making yourselves look as great as you do."

Austin was saying the words but his body was reacting as well. CeCe was beautiful. Her blond hair lying against the black blazer she had on looked so inviting. He was remembering when she had hurt her ankle and he had held her close. He could still feel the silkiness of her hair on his fingertips.

"Austin, the flowers are beautiful. Thank you so much. Your poem was great, too. I thought you didn't like my play calling." CeCe's face was radiant as she spoke.

"I thought you would like them. It was the least I could do, since it was you who made all the arrangements."

"Speaking of arrangements and me making them- Reece got another one of these letters I told you about before. So someone else knew about the arrangements." CeCe held out the envelope. Austin took it and began reading it.

"Do you mind if I keep this one, Reece? I would like to read it again and maybe I might be able to remember something someone said."

"What letters?" asked Angie as he looked over Austin's shoulder.

"Come on, we'll tell you all about it on the walk to the restaurant," Reece said as she grabbed Angie's arm.

"I guess that leaves us, Madam," Austin said as he reached over and held CeCe's hand.

They told Angie all about the letters and about finding the unique paper as they walked.

"Have you called the police? There has to be something they could do," Angie said, very concerned.

"Yes, we called them when the letter appeared at my house. They told us that unless there was some sort of threat that there was nothing they could do. So that's why we are looking ourselves. The paper is very unusual, as you saw back at the room. Earlier today when we were out shopping, I found the paper in a bookstore. The store clerk confirmed our belief that it is handmade. She gave us the name of the gentleman that sold it to them. He lives in the southern part of the state. We have a way of contacting him, which is what I plan on doing first thing tomorrow morning. I want to know if he has sold any to anyone in the valley." Reece was concentrating on not falling as they walked their way to the restaurant.

"The words don't sound like they are threatening; however, I can see where you would be concerned. He says that he is watching you; that's the creepy part. Do you have a dog to protect you or something like that?" Angie asked as he helped guide Reece through the snow.

"That's the funny part about all of this- CeCe is staying with me while some repairs are being done on her place, and she has a huge dog named Nitro. Nitro was in the house when the letter got dropped off. So they either know Nitro or they know how to handle him, although he is just a lover. It's just his size that would scare the pants off of you if you didn't know him."

Austin interrupted, "Let me tell you about him later, Angie. He's as big as one of the cattle on my ranch. He jumped on me and almost knocked me over. He is nothing but an over-grown teddy bear. I do think he would protect either CeCe or Reece if he really thought someone was going to hurt them."

Austin remembered the night he met Nitro. He would have loved to stay the night with CeCe that night, but under the circumstances, he hadn't pushed it.

"Ah, here we are. Several of the players come here after a good win, and tonight we have something to celebrate. We still have a few more games ahead of us, though. We can't get too cocky." Angie held the door open for them. As they walked in, several people came over to Angie and congratulated him.

They were seated at a table and made some decisions on a few appetizers. The food was good and the company was better. They talked about many different things.

"Where would you like to go now? We can go down the street- there is a place where you can sing along with the piano player, or we can go to this great little bar that has neon lights and booth seating: the Cruise Room at the Oxford Hotel. Then there is always dancing." Angie was trying to be a good host.

"I would love to go and listen to some music and maybe dance a few dances. That is, if no one is too tired." Austin looked from CeCe and Reece to Angie.

"That would be fine with me. I still have all that adrenaline running around in

me." Angie stood and reached his hand over to help Reece up.

"Sounds good to me! How about you, Reece? Are you up for some more fun?" CeCe asked.

"You bet you I am. I still have some learning to do about this football thing and I think I found the right person to tell me about it." Reece batted her eyelashes at Angie and they all burst out laughing.

Angie hailed a taxi and they rode off to the bar. "I never know what kind of music they are going to have here, but they usually reserve the kind of music that the younger kids like for the weekends. We may just hit it right tonight."

As it was, they did. It was a band that played 'oldies but goodies' (as they billed themselves). They found a table and ordered drinks. Angie brought up their trip to Hawaii.

"Have either of you been there before?"

CeCe answered first. "No, but I have always wanted to go somewhere tropical. I understand that it is beautiful there. Austin has told us a little about Kauai. We will be going to Maui first, and then to Kauai. It will be fun to do some things with you and Austin, if you can find time to take us around."

"Are you kidding? Austin is a great host. I feel like I know the whole island as if I grew up there. Austin had this beautiful local woman, or wahines, as woman are called in Hawaii, who took an immediate liking to him and showed him around. Boy did she show him around. She was very exotic. What was her name, Austin?" Angie asked.

Austin was obviously not in the mood to talk about her.

"I don't remember. CeCe, would you like to dance?" Austin stood and held out his hand before she could answer.

The band was playing a song The Temptations made famous: "My Girl". CeCe loved The Temptations and couldn't resist- she also loved dancing, but she would have liked to hear more about this exotic woman in Kauai. She would have to ask about it at another time. It was more than obvious that Austin didn't want to talk about it.

"I would love to. Are you two going to join us or are you going to just sit here?"

CeCe asked as she took Austin's hand.

"We're right behind you my dear," answered Angie.

Austin loved the way CeCe smelled. As he held her close he could feel the silkiness of her hair and the smell of her shampoo. The smell was wonderful. Did she realize what that smell did to him?

He held her closer dancing to the music. She moved so lightly and allowed him to move her around the dance floor easily. Austin found himself singing along with the band.

"You have a great voice, Austin." CeCe looked up at him and smiled.

"I have a whole lot of talents you don't know about, CeCe. I would like to show you some of them." Austin said grinning.

"Why Mr. Carter, you ought to be ashamed of yourself, propositioning someone that way!"

"Who said I was propositioning you? I was talking about all of my talents. I just learned to brand this year and am pretty good at it. I'm not a half-bad carpenter, either. Lord knows I had to be to fix up the place I bought in Kauai. It was pretty rustic, but I made some nice additions to it."

"Well, I would like to see some of your other talents in that case."

CeCe was trying to recover from the way she was feeling in Austin's arms. She felt as though nothing could happen to her while she was there. His arms encompassed her so warmly and securely. She never wanted to leave the comfort of them.

"CeCe," Austin said

"Hmmm," CeCe answered, still in her dream world.

"May I ask you a question? Don't get mad or get the wrong idea, but I just want to find out more about you."

CeCe answered now, fully aware of where she was and with whom, "Should I be afraid of what you are going to ask?"

"No. I just wanted to ask you about your past. I can't figure out why you haven't gotten married and had a whole brood of kids by now. You seem to have everything going for you. I have heard the name Carlos once or twice mentioned in conjunction with your name before. Is he someone that you're involved with? I wouldn't want to move in on someone else if there is a relationship there."

Move in on. Was he talking about a relationship? CeCe hadn't thought she would ever want a serious relationship again after Carlos. But since the day Austin stepped foot in her shop, she couldn't help but think of him all the time. She didn't know if she was ready to trust another man again. It had been several years and she could still feel the pangs in her heart.

The music stopped, but the band moved right into another slow, sensuous song by Luther Vandross. The music, the excitement of the game, the cocktails, and most of all the company was making her feel euphoric.

She needed to answer Austin but she was afraid that she would start being melancholy and revive some of the anger and hurt. Maybe this is what she needed to do. Reece was the only person she ever talked with about her relationship with Carlos.

"No, Austin, there isn't someone else in my life right now. I did have a relationship with a man named Carlos. Things didn't work out, and it has made me cautious, and to be quite honest, a little burned on the male population. I don't want to bore you with all the details. That was then and this is now. I am happy with the life I am living. I have a great business, the best friend you could ever want in Reece, and of course there is Nitro. He keeps the bed warm for me."

Austin urged CeCe, "Please tell me if you don't mind. I want to know about you and what happened. Besides, I'm enjoying holding you."

"He was from Chile. I met him in college my third year. We were engaged to be married; the wedding was all planned for right after graduation. It was the way I dreamed it would be. The perfect dress, the perfect reception hall, the perfect man, or so I thought." CeCe sighed.

"I told Carlos up front when we first met that I was an old-fashioned girl, that I wouldn't just jump into bed with him. I wanted to be a virgin when I got married. I know that sounds weird this day and age, but I believe in it."

"I don't think it's weird. It's what you believe in and it should be respected."

"Carlos would pressure me every once and awhile, saying that the date was set and that it wouldn't be wrong to have a sneak preview, but I insisted we wait. He agreed and finally stopped urging."

"We had just graduated and it was only one week before the wedding. His family was flying in and we were going to meet them at the airport. Carlos was supposed to be out picking up the bridesmaids' and groomsman's gifts we had selected. I decided it would be a good idea to go to his place and make him a nice lunch before we left for the airport."

CeCe looked off into the distance as she spoke. Her body stiffened. It was very evident that this was painful for her.

"I will never forget: it was a brilliant day in May- one of those days where there isn't a cloud in the sky. I was feeling wonderful. Finally, I was going to meet Carlos's family. I stopped by the store and picked up a few things I needed for lunch. I walked by the card section and found a perfect 'just because' card."

"When I walked up to the apartment Carlos had been sharing with one of our friends, I heard voices and laughter. Carlos told me his roommate had just moved out, so I thought maybe he had just returned to pick up a few items he had left behind.

"I went to knock on the door, but it wasn't shut properly. It opened as I knocked. I stepped in and said, 'knock knock, it's me, CeCe, did you forget something?'"

"I walked toward the bedroom where the door stood open and I saw her. She was a beautiful Scandinavian student who had everything I didn't, and was willing to give what I wasn't."

"It was the most humiliating situation I had ever been in. I wouldn't ever wish it on anyone. Of course, there were all of the usual apologies. Carlos pleaded and begged for me to forgive him. He then had the nerve to tell me it was all my fault. That if I had slept with him this would never have happened that I couldn't expect a perfectly normal male to wait to have sex."

"Well, maybe it was all my fault. But I was not willing to forgive him for what he did. Needless to say I never met his family and the wedding never happened. The whole town knew what happened. I needed something to take my mind off of it, so I delved into the shop. So there you have it, in a not-so-neat nut shell."

"CeCe, I am sorry for what he did to you. We're not all like that, you know. I am also sorry if I made you feel as if you had to tell me the whole horrible story." Austin found himself holding her even closer than before.

"That's all right. I sometimes keep things to myself too much. The only person I have talked to about this is Reece, and she just wants to do awful things to Carlos. Don't get her started on him, or you will hear a whole other side to Reece than you ever thought existed."

Austin gently tipped CeCe's head back and lowered his to hers. He cupped her face with one hand while holding on with the other. His lips gently brushed hers; he was testing at first. The kiss grew with more intensity.

They were both enjoying it when the band announced that they were going to take a break and come back after a short intermission. The lights were turned up as CeCe and Austin parted abruptly.

"I'm sorry, CeCe. I just wanted to take away some of the hurt. I thought I could do that with a kiss. Please don't be offended." Austin reached out for her.

CeCe moved back toward him. "I wasn't offended, it's just that I am not used to kissing in a public place. I feel better telling you about Carlos. It doesn't hurt as much anymore. I guess time has a lot to do with the healing."

They walked back to the table were Angie and Reece were just returning themselves.

"Are you two up for something different or would you like to stay?" Angie asked.

Reece interjected, "Is there a place where we can smoke a cigar? I have always loved the smell of them but have never had an opportunity to try one."

They all laughed and Austin said, "As a matter of fact, I asked the bellman where a good place to have a good cigar was earlier in the evening. He told me that the hotel had a great place called 'Churchill's'. I guess we could go back to the hotel and try it out. What do you think?"

Austin was looking into CeCe's deep blue eyes. He could still see the pain in them over the conversation they just had about her past relationship.

Austin believed that he would be able to help ease that pain. It would take time and he would have to be patient. She was an extraordinary woman and he planned on being in her life.

"I'm up for that, if everyone else is. That way we can just stumble upstairs. Well, that is except for you, Angie. Do you have a curfew or something like that?" CeCe was putting on her jacket as she spoke to them.

"No, I don't have a curfew. We have the day off tomorrow after the win tonight. Austin asked me if I wanted to crash in his room, and it's big enough that I think I will.

It'll save me the trip home- since I've had a few drinks tonight, I would have to call a cab and then pick up my car tomorrow, anyway. This way I can hang out with you all tomorrow before you leave.

"It sounds like a plan then," Austin said, as he guided CeCe by the elbow toward the door. "We'll just go out front and see if we can hail a cab. Don't be too long in coming, though, we wouldn't want to leave you behind." CeCe and Austin laughed as they walked away from the two of them.

"It looks as though Reece and Angie are really hitting it off. I would love to see her find the right man and settle down. She has all of these other guys who are interested, but in what? I don't think any of them have really taken the time to know the real Reece. She is wonderful- so full of life and so giving. She sometimes let's people take advantage of her. I really don't like this Mason guy she is so enthralled by. I met him the day she took me in for my ankle. There is something not right about him. He appears to be too perfect." CeCe was wound up and couldn't keep from talking about Reece.

"CeCe, I think you're right about Angie and Reece, and I hope that they are able to put something together, but right now I want to talk about you, me, us. I really enjoy being with you. You are like the other half of me. So much that you are interested in, I am, too."

Austin put his arm around CeCe to block the wind that was blowing the snow around them. The street was deserted because of the hour and the snowstorm.

"Austin, I'm interested in you too, but you do understand why I'm cautious with my relationships? I wear my emotions on my sleeve, and can't afford them to be damaged much more. I don't want to be a calloused woman. So if I seem cold or uninterested, it isn't so. You just need to be patient with me."

CeCe's face was so beautiful in the light that was reflecting off of the neon sign and the snow falling so heavenly around them that Austin could not resist taking her hands in his and kissing her.

The kiss was slow, sensuous and warming. Austin wanted to erase her memories of that awful afternoon with Carlos.

The wind swirled around them and made CeCe feel as though she was on a flying carpet. She had never felt this way with Carlos. The kisses they had shared were different. She could feel the heat moving from her lips all the way through her body. It felt like warm liquid being poured into her from Austin.

The door behind them opened and Reece and Angie walked out snuggled against each other fighting the wind.

"What are you two doing out here? Come back inside and wait for the cab. There won't be one coming by on its own at this hour and with the weather the way it is, so I called for one. They said it would be about ten minutes," Angie was saying, moving around to keep warm. "We're going back inside to wait."

"We are coming with you." Austin guided CeCe back inside.

Back inside, CeCe turned to Austin and said, "Thank you for understanding. I guess I'm learning more about myself this weekend as well. Maybe it is time for me to put some of those feelings to bed. No pun intended."

They both laughed. Just as Angie and Reece asked what they were talking, about the cab drove up and honked the horn.

Chapter Fourteen

This would be the perfect opportunity for him to get into Reece's office. She would be away until late tomorrow evening, and maybe even longer if this snow kept up. He would wait until the cleaning crew had left the building, that way he would be assured that he wouldn't be interrupted.

The files were there waiting for him to go through. This was something he needed to do. He had only done this that one other time. It had been necessary then, too. This was urgent.

He did a check on the things he needed, flashlight, check. He made sure that he had brought the tiny penlight. It would be sufficient enough to see the lock and look into the desk and files. Gloves check; he didn't want to leave any fingerprints. The instruments he would need to pick the lock check.

He hadn't had to do this for a long time; he might be rusty. He had also brought along a briefcase to put anything into that he would take with him.

He was angry that he was going to have to do this. It was cold outside and snowing hard, too. That was one good thing: the snow would cover his tracks. Why didn't she listen? This wouldn't be necessary if she would just listen to him. But he could tell by the look on her face that she would do what she wanted.

He was afraid this was going to get fouled up. There could be something wonderful between the two of them. He liked her style, and the money wasn't all that bad, either. Maybe this would work. They would just think it was someone breaking in to get some of the equipment in the office. He would have to take some with him to put them off guard.

He sat and waited. The cleaning crew left at about 11:15. He would wait another half-hour or so in order to be safe. He would enter from the back door- it was surrounded by shrubs, so it would be hard to see him with the poor visibility caused by the storm.

The time had come. He walked around the back, and watched to see if he could see any signs of life inside. Everyone was gone. He didn't want to be long, and he also knew that there wasn't any sort of alarm system in the office.

He knelt on one knee and started to work on the lock. He wasn't so rusty after all. It only took a few minutes to pick the lock. The house was Victorian style, and it was in the National Register of Historic Places, or something like that, but you would think they would have a better lock.

He opened the door only to be stopped by a chain. Again a stupid idea, chains were only securities in one's own mind. All this would take was a little push. He put his shoulder against the door and secured his footing, with one good push the chain pulled loose from the door. He was in.

Reece's office was the one up front with a view of the park. He walked in and pulled the shades down in order to hide the beam from the flashlight. He could smell the sweet smell of her. He could see her sitting in her chair with the sunlight glinting off of her hair.

She was so beautiful, and stubborn, too. He needed to take his mind off her and put it to the business at hand.

He had only spent about ten minutes in the office looking for something, anything, when he could see the reflection of the lights and heard the sound of a vehicle. He grabbed a few things and ran out the back.

That was close, he thought to himself. It was one of the cleaning crew coming back. They had forgotten to take the trash bags with them when they left. They hurried back in, grabbed the bags, and left again. He couldn't risk going back; hopefully he got what he came for.

He walked back to the car and drove away. They would definitely know that someone had been in there because of the broken door chain. Oh well, there wasn't anything to link him to it. He hoped.

~ ~ ~

The evening had been wonderful. It had been all that CeCe had hoped it would be. She really enjoyed being with Austin and Angie. The place that he had taken them for dancing was very unique, and the cigar bar was just what they needed to end the perfect evening.

They had all relaxed over a nightcap, and the guys had smoked cigars. Reece insisted on trying it.

She said, "I love the smell. My granddaddy used to smoke cigars and I would just sit at his feet and listen to him talk and puff away. I think that's why I have always wanted to try them."

Well, it wasn't quite the way Reece had thought it was going to be. She took hold of the cigar from Angie and inhaled, before Angie could tell her what to do. Reece coughed and coughed until she had tears streaming from her eyes.

When she had finally recovered, Reece said, "Well, I guess that will end my curiosity over cigars!"

Angie told her that he would teach her the proper way to smoke a cigar, but that they should wait until another time, "Maybe when you guys are in Kauai. Do you think you will be game, CeCe?"

"We'll see. I'm usually game for different things. Maybe we will have a cigar smoking lesson over a glass of scotch."

CeCe felt so at ease as she chatted with the three of them. Everything came so easily. She felt that she had always known Austin. She couldn't believe that she had told him the whole sordid story about Carlos. Austin seemed really interested in her and her life.

CeCe had thought she was really in love with Carlos, but the feelings she was having about Austin were nothing like the feeling she had with Carlos. She didn't feel as though she had to say or do just the right things with Austin. He seemed to be able to read her mind about things she was thinking.

She loved it when Austin put his arm or arms around her. It felt as though she were wrapped in a warm cocoon. CeCe had to know more about him and the woman he was so reluctant to talk about. Maybe Angie would bring her up again. CeCe didn't want to get into a relationship if there were someone else in his life. She had to be careful that this wasn't a rebound sort of relationship. Nothing good could come of it if that were the case.

She really liked this man. He was so different than the other men she had met and dated. They say that there is a soul mate out there for everyone; who knew, maybe they were each others. Time would tell.

"What are you dreaming about, Miss Smiles?" Reece was standing over CeCe with a steaming cup of coffee in her hand. "I took the initiative to order some coffee. I felt after a long evening last night we might need a kick-start. Would you like some? Then you can tell me what you were smiling about." Reece handed the coffee mug to CeCe as she sat up.

"What do you mean, smiling? I was just thinking about our evening last night and how enjoyable it was. You seemed to have a pretty good time yourself last night. I really like Angie, and you two look perfect together. He has a great personality, and the rest is pretty decent, too."

"You won't get any arguments from me on those accounts. He really thinks the world of Austin. He really would like for him to be settled and happy. I think we are going to have a great time with them in Kauai. What do you think?"

"I have no doubts about that. I'm afraid that we won't want to leave. I also would like to know more about this woman that Angie mentioned. I wonder just how much she showed Austin about the island."

"Do I detect a note of jealousy here? I think it's cute, CeCe. We don't often get to see you in this state. Is there something more you aren't telling me? Have you found yourself wondering what it would be like being more than just friends with Austin?"

"Reece, just stop where you are going now, I am very interested in Austin. He is a really good friend. I don't know what's happening to me. I didn't think I would even consider having a relationship with another man for many years to come. Things are still painful for me when I think about my past relationship."

"CeCe, you need to know that Carlos was just a jerk. Austin seems to care a great deal about you. Not all men are like Carlos. Give the guy a chance. You have had a barrier up ever since that time in your life. No one has been able to make a crack in it, until now, that is. I think this is just what you need."

"That's just what Austin said"

"What?"

"That not all men are like Carlos. He was very interested and caring when I told him about that day."

"You mean you told him about Carlos? CeCe, that's great. I never thought you would talk to anyone about it except me. You just keep up the good work, girl. I'm proud of you, breaking out of your shell like this. Now I think we need to get started on this detective work."

"You mean about the paper?"

"Yes. I'm going to get on the phone with this guy now. I'm going to see if he can help me."

"Good idea, Reece. I think I will take a shower and get moving. I would love to go out and run, but I think I would end up on my bum with all the snow that fell last night."

"We can do some more shopping and work out our credit cards if you want."

"That's just what I need to do for my body. I think it would be a good idea for you to make that phone call so we can go and meet the guys for breakfast." CeCe padded off toward the bathroom.

Reece sat down at the phone and dialed the number she was given.

"Hello?" A male voice answered on the other end of the phone

"Hello, I am looking for Mr. Angus Martin."

"This is Angus. What can I do for you?"

"Mr. Martin..."

"Please call me Angus; everyone does."

"Okay, then, Angus, my name is Reece Landon. I live in the Yampa Valley here in Colorado. I was in a book store in Denver and found some of the stationary that I believe you sold to the store."

"Oh yes, I have a hobby of making paper. I love to use the aspen trees- they make such a different kind of paper. The wood grain just jumps right out at you. Did you want to put in a special order for the paper, Miss Landon, is it?"

"Well, I was calling for another reason. I do agree with you that it makes a very different kind of stationary. It's very beautiful, but the reason that I was calling is to find out if you have a particular customer who orders this paper from you that lives in the Yampa Valley. And please, call me Reece."

"Well, Reece, that's a beautiful name. Is it a family name? I love family names. That's where my name came from. My granddaddy and his daddy were both named Angus. You don't find too many of us around. I'm sorry Reece; I get side-tracked easily. I don't get too many phone calls, and certainly not from young women. I assume you are young from your voice. Anyway, I don't usually sell my paper other than at certain stores and at these art shows that I go to."

"Angus, have you been to an art show near the Yampa Valley lately?"

"Yes, I have, Reece, yes I have. I went to a show right before Labor Day. We had a good turnout. I sell other things other than my paper. But I did have a good supply with me there. Seems to me I sold out of it."

"You wouldn't keep any sort of record of who you sold it to would you?"

"You bet your sweet bottom I do. Oh pardon me, I don't mean to be forward. You know you have to be careful with what you say to people nowadays with this sexual harassment stuff. Anyway, I keep very good records."

"Would you look up who you sold this paper to? I have someone who is writing to me on this paper, and I don't know who it is. I would like to find out, and you may be my only link."

"Yes, I can do that, but all my records are at my daughter-in-law's. You see, she is one of these CPA's. She's getting everything in order for me so she can do my taxes. I told you I keep good records. I don't want any IRS coming after me. No siree. I pay enough of those taxes- I don't need to pay any more."

Reece couldn't help giggling to herself. This guy must not get too many phone calls, what with telling her all about his life story.

"Angus, if it would be all right with you I will call you back in a few weeks. Do you think you will have had time to get your records back by then?"

"Yes, I do think that. And if you would ever like to come by and see me and see how I make the paper, I would be glad to have you. We could spend the day together. I don't have a 'Mrs. Martin' to get all huffy and puffy when I spend time with beautiful young women. Not that I didn't have one once upon a time, though. Let me get your number and if I get them back before then I will call you. Does that sound good? I still think you would love it here."

Reece gave him her work number and told him to call her and leave a message if she wasn't around. She told him she was very anxious to find out who this admirer was.

"Goodbye, Angus. It has been a pleasure talking with you. Your operation sounds very interesting, and I may take you up on your offer soon."

"No, the pleasure has been all mine. I hope to meet you in person and put a face to the voice. I am always right about what someone looks like when I see them. Take care, now."

Reece hung up the phone just as CeCe was walking out of the bathroom, her hair wrapped in a towel.

"This guy is a riot. He sounds like he is well into his eighties. He told me all about himself and invited me to see how he makes the paper. It sounds interesting; we might want to go see it sometime."

"Was he able to help you at all?" CeCe asked as she removed the towel from her hair and started towel-drying it.

"He said he sold some of the paper at an art show that he did in August or September. He keeps records, but his daughter-in-law has all of his stuff for tax purposes. He said he will get back to me if he gets them back before I call him again in a few weeks."

"That's just about the time the letters started, isn't it, Reece?"

"Yes it is, and Angus just might be able to help me. Right now I'm starving. Do you think you could get ready in about fifteen minutes?"

"Yes! I'm hungry too. I didn't eat much last night with all the excitement going on. I just need to blow my hair dry, so it doesn't freeze. It still looks like it is snowing hard outside. Isn't it just beautiful out?"

"It certainly is. Now go get dressed."

CeCe walked into the bedroom and choose her clothing carefully; she wanted to look nice this morning.

Chapter Fifteen

Austin hadn't been able to sleep most of the night. He had thought about what CeCe had told him about that creep, Carlos. How could a guy do that to her? If he wanted to sample the other available women, and wasn't willing to wait for her, why ask her to marry him?

Austin could only think about last night. She hadn't resisted when he kissed her, until the lights went up, that is.

CeCe was the perfect size, not like the supermodels you see today. She had all the right curves and kept her body in great shape. Austin needed to keep that in mind, when planning the activities they would do in Kauai. They could do some great hikes, and maybe even some kayaking.

He let his mind wander to the warm tropical breezes and the fresh salt air. Whenever he did this, it brought back certain memories that he didn't want to have, but it was inevitable that they would creep into his mind. It brought him back to that first fall he spent on the island.

He had just had the decision made for him that he was not going to be able to play professional ball again. This was a very painful decision, but the injury was severe enough that he knew as well as the medical experts that it was over.

He hadn't thought about what he was going to do after football until then, and he didn't want to think about it. He had always enjoyed Hawaii when he was going to school there, so it was the logical place for him to go.

After a few weeks of catching up with old friends on Oahu, Austin decided it was time to explore the other islands. He had tired of the metropolitan area and was leaning towards a quieter, more serene setting. He hadn't spent much time on any of the other islands, and a close friend had suggested Kauai.

Austin packed up the few things he had brought with him, and flew into the Garden Island. He was instantly encompassed and overwhelmed by its beauty, the lush green rainforests and beautiful white sands of the non-crowded beaches. Of course, there were the usual tourist spots, but that wasn't what he had come for.

Austin went into the realtor's office and set up some appointments. He wasn't interested in any of the condominium units or anything right on the beach. The realtor told him about several available places she had for him to look at. One in particular sounded very interesting, it was a place up in Kokee. It was small, remote, and very rustic. He would be able to brush up on his carpentry skills. The best part about it was that it was available immediately.

To be fair to the other properties, the realtor suggested he look at them first. Austin was very interested in what he saw right there in the office.

"What's your name?" Austin asked, smiling that toothpaste bright smile.

"It's Poalima. And yours?"

"I'm Austin Carter. I'm not interested in time-shares or crowded areas, just something simple and easy. I have cash today, if there is anything out there I could look at, although the scenery in here is awfully beautiful."

"Thank you, Mr. Carter.

"Please, call me Austin, Poalima."

"Your Hawaiian is very good, Austin. Please call me Friday; everyone else does. My parents weren't very original. I was born on a Friday and that is what they decided to call me."

"I prefer Poalima, if you don't mind. It's a beautiful fit to the beautiful woman it was given to."

"Now you are going to make me blush. Shall we go and look at some properties? We have some up on the North shore as well, so it will take a good part of the day to go from one end of the island to the other. I don't have any other appointments, so I am free to go now. That is, if you are as serious about getting this done as soon as you say you are?"

"Oh, I'm serious, and I can't think of anything better to do with my time than spend it with someone named Poalima." Austin stood and held the door open for her.

They had looked at several properties starting on the North shore. He liked it here very much. There were several places he liked, but he didn't want to spend too much on a place not knowing what he was going to do in the future.

The drive up through the Waimea Canyon was spectacular. The landscape changed dramatically, climbing from sea level to 4200 feet in altitude in a mere 17 miles. It made one think about how awesome Mother Nature really was.

When they drove to the place in Kokee, he knew that it was perfect. The air was cool and crisp. He never thought about needing a fireplace in a place like Kauai, but there was one here. The altitude caused the temperatures to be several degrees cooler than at sea level.

The homes up there were all built very simply. This certainly would allow him to sort through things and think about what he really wanted to do with his life.

Austin purchased the house, and began what he thought was going to be a great relationship with Poalima. .

She was beautiful and exotic. She had been born on the island and had gone to the mainland for her education. She told him, "I just came back here to make a few dollars and have a good time before I leave for a real life."

Poalima taught him several things about the Hawaiian culture and showed him the island. Most of all she taught him how to love. They couldn't keep their hands off of one another. Austin had been on the island and with Poalima for six months and knew that he was ready to settle down. He wanted to marry Poalima and have a family. Poalima wanted a career, but Austin thought that would change after the evening he had planned.

Austin took Poalima out to one of the most romantic restaurants on the island. After a romantic carriage ride, they had a wonderful dinner. Poalima didn't eat much, and neither did Austin, for that matter. Austin was very anxious to tell her why they had come here. He had bought a large engagement ring. He was going to give it to her with dessert.

Poalima looked pale and had been tired lately. Still, it didn't take away from her beauty. She sat across from Austin at the table and twisted her napkin in her lap.

"Austin, I have something to tell you."

"Me too, you go first." Austin felt like a schoolboy not wanting to wait, but he had always been taught 'ladies first'.

"Austin, this is very difficult for me. I have been offered a job in New York. It's an incredible job, and I'm going to take it."

Austin started to talk and she interrupted him. "Let me finish, please. I'm pregnant and I am going to have an abortion. I am not ready for children; there is no time in my life for them now. Please don't argue with me; I have set the appointment and I am going. You can't stop me. I'm leaving for New York in two weeks." Poalima sat back, exhausted from keeping secrets for so long.

Austin was dumbfounded. He had wanted to have a family with Poalima, and she was going to discard it without even asking him.

Austin showed her the engagement ring.

"This was going to be perfect. I want to marry you. I've made all the plans. The only thing left was for you to agree. Poalima, you know I really want a family! Please, listen to me, this will be great. You don't need a job in New York, I'll take care of you right here in paradise."

Poalima wasn't willing to talk about it any further. She had made up her mind.

They left the restaurant still arguing about her decision. Poalima asked him to take her home and they would talk about it the next day. Austin wanted her to spend the night with him. She insisted they spend the night apart so they could think things over.

Austin took her in his arms and asked her to think about how wonderful their lives would be together and with children. Poalima promised she would.

Austin never slept that night, but he was sure he had convinced her to build their future together. He went to the office first thing in the morning. Poalima had come in earlier than usual, and told her boss she was leaving sooner than she thought.

Austin went to the airport only to find that she had left on the first flight out that morning.

He had received a letter from her trying to explain her actions, but she couldn't know how he felt.

Austin threw himself into working on the house. He finally came to a point when he realized that she wasn't coming back and that he needed to move on with his life, as painful a thought that it was, he accepted it. That's when he decided to go to Colorado to find the ranch.

He needed to do something different with his life. Colorado seemed to be the perfect place. He very much enjoyed the mountain atmosphere, and wanted to be in a small place

This is why he felt such pangs when CeCe told him about her relationship. He did know how it felt. Maybe they could build something from these feelings. He definitely did feel comfortable with her.

Angie broke in on his thoughts with a big slap on the back.

"Good morning, Austin. I sure like the company you're keeping these days. Those two ladies are right out of the pages of everything a guy wants."

"I am glad you enjoyed the company. They have become pretty good friends."

"It also appears that CeCe could be more than just a friend."

Austin stood and looked out the window as he spoke. "I am getting to know her better all the time. She is just a little skittish after her last relationship. The guy was a real jerk. Hurt her pretty bad. This will take time, but I am willing to work on it. I like her a lot."

"It's pretty evident. I like her friend quite a bit myself. She is full of energy and great fun. I think we'll have a great time in Hawaii."

"We're going to meet in the lobby to go and get some breakfast in about a half hour, any good ideas?"

"There are plenty of good places around here. We'll ask the ladies what they are up for. I need to go for some treatment on my hamstring later today, but I figure I will do that after you guys leave. Any idea as to what time that will be?"

"No. I know CeCe has some shopping she would like to do. Reece was going to get a hold of the guy with the paper. I wonder if she had any luck."

"That whole thing is pretty weird. Is there anyone you can talk to about watching out for them?"

"Right now they're together, and they make a good pair. They are pretty independent and have good sense about them. I think they are all right for the time being. This guy seems to be non-threatening."

"I hope you're right. He still sounds weird. Hey, did you see the paper this morning? They were talking about you, and you didn't even have to play the game."

"Yeah, I can imagine what they're saying: the old washed up player down on the field wishing to be back in the game."

"Well, isn't it true?"

"Yes, but you don't have to comment on it too. Actually, it felt pretty good to sit in the stands and watch. It feels even better this morning. I don't have all those aches and pains."

"I bet it does. Let's go and meet the ladies, shall we?"

Chapter Sixteen

Ruth and Tucker got the call from the sheriff's department. They were looking for Reece. Ruth told them that she went out of town with CeCe and Austin. They told her that the office was in shambles. They couldn't tell if anything was missing, as of yet, so they needed to contact Reece to do inventory.

Ruth and Tucker talked it over and decided they wanted to wait until the trio came home that evening to tell Reece. It would only upset her and the drive home was going to be challenging enough with all the snow they had gotten. What was going on with Reece, anyway? First she kept getting those letters. Austin and CeCe had told Ruth about them. The bad part was the guy walked right into Reece's house, and had now broken into her office. What would happen if she were there when he came in? Would he be harmful? This latest incident seemed pretty invasive. Now maybe they could do something about it.

Ruth was angry about the whole thing. Reece was a nice young lady, and if someone wanted to court her, why didn't they do it in the usual way? She would have a talk with the sheriff's department herself and see if there was anything she could do to help.

Ruth had closed up the coffee shop later than usual. Tom Dancer had come in and ordered right before she was getting ready to finish up for the morning.

"Can I help you, Tom?" Ruth asked as she walked over to the table he always sat at when he came into the shop.

"I-I-i would like to o-order a sandwich and c-coffee to g-go, please."

"What would you like, Tom? I have some fresh chicken salad I made up this morning. I was going to take it home, but no need for that if you would like it. I also made a fresh batch of cookies about forty five minutes ago."

"That sounds g-good. I'll have the s-sandwich, two cookies, and the c-coffee to go."

"Are you finished with the work that CeCe was having you do on her house? Is that why you came in here, to talk to her? She isn't here. She went into Denver for the game yesterday."

"Yes, I k-know she went away. I am just about f-finished with the work and want her final a-a-approval. I think she will be h-happy with the railing. It is just what s-she wanted."

"Well, I will tell her you came in here today. She is anxious to get back home, not that she doesn't like spending the time with Reece. Those two are quite the pair. I have some bad news for Reece when she gets back."

"W-h-hat's that?" Tom nervously asked Ruth

"Someone went and broke into her office, first the house, now the office."

"When did those two things h-happen?"

"Well the office last night and her house a few weeks back. Well, I guess you couldn't call it a break-in at her house, someone just walked in. Reece has a bad habit of leaving the door unlocked. CeCe thinks she might have scared him off. I think they both got the idea that they need to lock their doors; at least I hope they did, can't be too careful these days."

"When I was at Miss CeCe's h-house with her, she had a k-key hidden in a rock garden. I told her t-then that she needed to be c-careful. What do you think the person is after, that he k-keeps going into p-places of Miss Reece's?"

"I don't know. The police are waiting for Reece to get back to find out what the intruder took. He sure trashed the office, went through all her files. Hopefully, they will be able to find this guy."

"Y-yes, hopefully," Tom answered.

"Let me get that sandwich of yours so you can get on your way and me on mine. I need to get Nitro over to Dr. Baldwin's soon."

Ruth went behind the counter and made the sandwich. She was

thinking the same thing that CeCe had thought about Tom. The drinking seemed to be better under control when he had a good workload. He really did do a great job; Tucker was always pleased with the shodding he did on the horses at the ranch.

Ruth finished up the lunch for Tom and took it to him. She was just about ready to go: she was calculating her time so as not to be late to the vet. Ruth handed the lunch to Tom and said, "Here you go Tom. I threw in the cookies since you got the last of them. I was just going to take them home to Tucker, but he doesn't need them and neither do I. The sandwich and coffee come to $5.19 with the government's part in the deal."

Tom handed Ruth $7.00 saying, "Keep the rest for your t-trouble, Ruth. I appreciate y-your help. You will t-tell Miss CeCe to c-call me, won't you?"

"You bet Tom. Take care, now. Enjoy the sandwich."

Ruth followed Tom to the door and shut it behind him. She finished up the light cleaning she needed to do and left the shop.

Dr. Baldwin wanted to take a look at Nitro's paw and make sure it was healing properly. She had Tucker help her get him into the truck, not that it took much convincing. Nitro loved to ride in the truck. He was a good companion for CeCe, although Ruth would have liked to see her happy with some nice young man.

Austin fit that bill very well. They seemed to like one another well enough; maybe she could help move things along. She would have to invite CeCe over for dinner when they got back.

Tucker would call her a meddling fool, but she didn't give a darn, somebody had to set those two young folks right and she was going to be the one to do it.

Dr. Baldwin had had a full day of appointments. He was very tired; it had been a rough evening the night before and he wasn't his usual happy-go-lucky self.

"Why hello, Nitro, how are you, buddy?" Dr. Baldwin bent down to pat Nitro's head. He handed Nitro a treat.

"You always know I have a special treat for you, don't you, buddy?" Nitro wagged his tail and licked his Dr. Baldwin's face in appreciation of the treat.

"Hi Ruth, don't mean to ignore you." Dr. Baldwin lifted Nitro onto the table.

"Dr. Baldwin, you look tired, rough day?" Ruth asked as she settled her ample bottom in the chair provided in the exam room. She thought he was a good vet. He had such an exceptional way with animals, and they responded to him very well.

"I guess I'm just in need of some time off. Where is CeCe? I really enjoy talking to her and getting the low-down on Reece. Not that I don't enjoy talking to you, Ruth."

"She went to Denver for the football game yesterday. She and Reece went with Austin. I guess it was a good game from what Tucker said. There was a whole lot of hootin' and hollerin' going on in front of the television last night. I told her I would be happy to bring in Nitro for his exam."

"That's right; I knew they were going to the game. Why, I even tried to get CeCe to let me go along as another male companion." As he was saying this, Dr. Baldwin was thinking all along that he knew the three of them had gone away, he was just trying to get some more information from Ruth. It was pretty easy to get her tongue wagging.

"I saw a whole lot of folks poking around over at the newspaper office this morning, all sorts of police cars and all. Do you know anything about that?"

"Yes, some weird man has been writing letters to Reece, and awhile back went into her house, and now broke into her office."

"Did he leave another letter? Doesn't seem right you would break in to leave letters," he said with a worried look on his face.

"Don't know right yet what he did. Messed up the place is all the sheriff's office would say now. They will let Reece tell them what's missing."

"Well, I sure wouldn't want anything to happen to her. I like seeing her around."

"Hopefully they will be able to do something about this crazy person."

"How do you know he's crazy? Could be just a common Joe, people act in different ways you know. Well, this paw looks good, but I still want to put some of this topical ointment on it. Let me give you some to take home. I'll type the instructions on the label." He sat down at the typewriter and typed the prescription out for her.

"Here you go. The directions are on here so if CeCe has any questions just have her give me a call. Tell them both I said hello. I need to come out to the ranch tomorrow to look at one of the mares that Tucker is concerned about, so I guess I will see you then."

Ruth thanked him and set on to home, but not before stopping by Mrs. James place. The Community Garage Sale was this weekend and she wanted to see what needed to be done.

After a cup of tea and some good gossip, Ruth drove to the ranch. She was going to make a nice light dinner for Austin, CeCe, and Reece to have when they got back this evening. They needed to talk to Reece about the office and wanted her to eat something before they did.

Chapter Seventeen

After a good breakfast, the foursome did some shopping. They were all enjoying themselves a great deal. The weather hadn't improved much, so it was a concern as to when they were going to get on the road back home.

"I would love to stay and learn more about football from you Angie, but the drive back could be bit tricky." Reece was loading her packages in the back of the Jeep. "You are welcome to come with us and keep us company."

"That is a very tempting thought, especially since I have an appointment to go get tortured. I will be happy to give you some more of my expertise in the area of football after the season is over, but you know that I have a lot more to offer."

"Well, Angie, we will have to explore those other areas at a later date then. It has been wonderful meeting you. I will be sure to write all kinds of good things about you and the team in the newspaper." Reece had finished loading her things and reached out her hand to shake Angie's.

"I think that we are better friends than that!" Angie wrapped his arm around Reece's waist and hugged her tightly. "I will make sure that I am in Kauai when you are both there. We'll have a great time."

Austin walked over and hugged his friend goodbye.

"Angie, you are a very good player- take that from someone who knows." CeCe looked over at Austin and smiled. "I believe you will help your team win the big one. Thanks for everything! When you come to the valley, we will have to return the hospitality." CeCe hugged him goodbye as well.

The three of them climbed into the Jeep and waved to Angie as they pulled away.

"Would you like me to drive, Reece?" Austin asked her as they eased their way out onto the interstate. "I don't have as much experience in driving in this kind of weather, but I'm willing to drive if you would like for me to."

"No, Austin, it's fine. I just need to take my time. We don't have to be home by any time special, just by tomorrow morning."

CeCe interrupted. "Ruth will be worried sick about us if we aren't there by 7:00. That's when I told her we would be by to pick up Nitro and drop off Austin. I think that's an even trade, don't you?"

"I bet Ruth doesn't think so. She probably would rather have Nitro there. He doesn't sass back, he will eat everything she gives to him, and she doesn't think that he is always trying to get her on his good side." Austin laughed as he talked.

"Now that you think of it, I don't know if it is such a good trade." CeCe grinned devilishly. "What if she won't trade, then what? Will we have to negotiate?"

"Well, now, as I remember Nitro does get to sleep in the bed with you. Would that mean that I would get the same treatment?"

"I don't think so. I do however have a bed that I bought for Nitro that he refuses to use. You would just have to curl up a little to fit on it. Do you think you are up for that?"

"I think I will just have to talk Ruth into letting me back into my own house and bed. I'll charm her and give her the new apron and kitchen gadgets I bought for her. I'm sure she'll make the trade."

They all laughed about the situation and talked about the great time they had. Everyone agreed that it would be wonderful to meet in Kauai. The conversation turned toward the upcoming Community Garage Sale. Austin told them that he was very anxious to help.

"Good, tomorrow morning you can go by Mrs. James's and get a list of the heavy items that need to be moved to the community center." CeCe was wrapping one of the gifts she had bought for Ruth for looking after the shop and Nitro. It brought her mind to Nitro's appointment. "I hope that Dr. Baldwin is happy with Nitro's recovery."

"I'm sure he is; it was looking good to me. But of course, I'm no vet."

"That you aren't, Austin, back to that list. I know there are several large items to be moved. Mrs. James called me and asked if I had an idea as to how to get them picked up. I told her I knew just the right man for the job."

"I suppose you meant me." Austin turned to look at CeCe

Her heart did a leap every time she saw that smile and the dimples that showed. She could remember his warm sweet breath on her face from the night before. "Yes, you were the one I had in mind. You did say that you would help, and I know you have a pick-up truck, so you were the logical person."

"Guess I can't argue with that logic. What time should I go over there? Don't want to wake her up."

"Oh, I don't think that will be a problem," Reece interjected. "This fund raiser is her life. I don't even think she sleeps for a month before the event."

They all laughed as Reece concentrated on driving. She wanted to get them there in one piece.

The trip took longer than they had thought, but overall wasn't too bad. It was just after seven o'clock when they pulled into the drive of Austin's ranch.

Ruth had been anxiously awaiting them and walked out onto the porch to greet them. Nitro was right at her side and wagged his tail and started dancing around on the porch when he recognized Reece's Jeep.

CeCe opened the door almost before Reece could pull the vehicle to a stop.

"Nitro, I missed you!" CeCe let the large dog jump onto her. He was wetting her face with his tongue. "Have you been good for Grandma Ruth? Ruth, what do you say, was he a good boy?"

"Couldn't have been better, never talks back like some folks around here." Ruth grinned at Austin. "How was the game? It sounded like a doozie from the way Tucker was jumping up and down. I swear he acts likes a twelve year old for football, but when it comes to moving something heavy, he holds his back and reminds me as to how old he is."

"I think it's the same with all the male species." Reece glanced at Austin as she opened the back for him to get his bag.

"I have fixed you all a light supper. It will only take a few minutes to put it on the table. It'll give you time to wash up a bit. I'm sure you're tired after that long drive." Ruth opened the door for Austin, but Reece and CeCe stood at the bottom of the stairs.

"I think I would like to go home and finish up an article I started before I left. I didn't get much time to write while I was gone, not that I'm complaining. I had plenty to keep me busy." Angie crept into Reeces thoughts as she rounded the Jeep.

"I insist. You'll just go home and not have anything to eat. I know how you young folks are. Now you just come on in here and wash up. I promise it won't be a long, drawn-out evening." Ruth didn't want them to leave until they had eaten and she had told them about Reece's office. As a matter of fact, they might just want to stay there the night rather than going back into town and staying at Reece's since CeCe's place wasn't quite ready. Ruth was concerned for their safety. No one could tell them if this guy was dangerous or not.

CeCe looked at Reece and they both shrugged their shoulders. CeCe closed the car door and walked over to Ruth.

"I have a few things for you and Tucker for taking care of Nitro and the shop. But I do know that you took care of the shop by yourself. You didn't make anything too incredibly good, did you? I wouldn't want my customers to be disappointed when I go back in tomorrow." CeCe laughed as she hugged Ruth.

"I do have a message for you. Tom Dancer came in and he wants you to contact him. He is just about done with your house and wants your final approval." Ruth walked in the door and headed for the kitchen.

Tucker walked across the big room and shook Austin's hand and hugged both CeCe and Reece. "I'm glad you all made it back all right. Ruth here couldn't rest until she knew you were off the road. Old mother hen, she is. Austin, as you can see everything is the same as it was when you left it. We are still having trouble with that mare and I asked Tom Dancer to come by and look at her. I'm sure that if anyone can take care of her he will be able to do the job. You'll stay for dinner, I take it? I already had mine, but I might be able to talk Ruth into letting me have a bit more. It was delicious, as usual."

"Tucker, how do you stay so slim? I gain weight just by smelling her cooking." CeCe loved the smell of Tucker. It gave her a warm feeling all over. Tucker used to come out to her grandmother's house and help her out with chores she needed doing that neither she nor CeCe could do. CeCe remembered being no bigger than Nitro and trying to help him haul tree limbs and such off the land. Tucker was the only male she felt close to; he was a grandfather figure to her. She loved the peppermint smell, and he always had one for her. It was a treat she knew he would have for her when they finished one of the jobs he would come to do each month.

"I guess it is just good genes. My whole family could eat all day long and not gain an ounce. Good thing too, cause we all seemed to have wonderful cooks in the house."

"It smells wonderful in here, Ruth." Reece walked out of the restroom drying her hands. "Is there anything I can do to help you?"

"Don't be silly! I made some lasagna, salad, and garlic bread. Now just sit yourself right down." Ruth set the steaming bread and lasagna on the table. The salad was already there for them to enjoy.

"What's this? You only have a place set for the three of them. I would be very grateful for some more of that dinner." Tucker wrapped his arms around her tightly.

"Tucker, you just stop that. You already ate dinner, but I do have some fresh peach cobbler and a pot of hot coffee, decaf. You don't need to be up all night since you have to go and help move some of the stuff for the garage sale with Austin tomorrow morning." Ruth steered him toward a chair with the others.

"I guess everyone knew I was moving things tomorrow but me." Austin put on a pouty face. "That's all right. I'm ready to help and I guess you need to leave the heavy stuff for us brawny men."

"Oh my, the stuff is getting thick in here." Reece laughed as she dug into her dinner.

"This is wonderful, Ruth. I don't know how you do it. You are the best cook around. I'm tempted to just steal you away from Austin here. We could make a good pair in the shop." CeCe was really hungry and didn't realize it till she sat down and started eating. She was amazed that she had cleaned her plate and still had room for dessert.

"Better watch out, you once warned me about Ruth's cooking and the weight I would gain, but if you eat like that all the time it will be you who'll have to spend extra time working out." Austin kidded to CeCe across the table from him.

CeCe gave him a swift kick under the table.

"Ouch!" He rubbed his shin.

"You deserved that. I'm just being polite, and yes, I was hungry." CeCe turned to Ruth. "Did Tom say when I should contact him? I am very anxious to get back into the house. I think that Reece will be willing to come and stay with me for a while, too. There was another letter sent to the hotel in Denver. This guy really knows what she is doing and when."

"Ah," Ruth started to speak and Tucker interrupted. "That may not be such a bad plan. We may have all underestimated this person."

"What do you mean underestimated him? He is smart enough to know where I am; enough so he sent the letter directly to the hotel." Reece stood to help clear away the dishes.

"Reece, CeCe, please sit back down. We have to tell you something that is going to be disturbing to you." Tucker was obviously nervous.

"Disturbing? Tucker, you're scaring me. What's going on?" CeCe sat back in the chair, pulling Reece down with her.

"The sheriff came by here yesterday and wanted to know how to get a hold of you, Reece. Ruth and I felt it was best to wait until you got home. Your office was broken into and messed up pretty badly. They don't know if anything was taken, so they need to talk to you. The files were ripped apart and strewn all over the floor. A lamp or two got broken and the desk drawer was pried open. I hate to be the one telling you all this, but I felt it better for it to come from us than someone else."

Shock was written all over their faces. Reece had gone pale. Austin hurried to her side.

"Let's all go into the great room and we can let this settle in and try and make some sense of it." Austin guided the two of them onto the sofa.

"This isn't possible. What does this person want from me? First the letters, him going into the house… now this. The sheriff's office said they couldn't do anything unless there was a threat of a real break-in. I guess this would qualify." Reece was regaining the color back into her face as she spoke. "But what is it they can do? This person knows my every move and now takes advantage of me when I go away. I have never been one to back down from anything and I won't do it now."

"Reece, we did talk about you moving in with me for a while, and it sounds like my place is almost ready. I think we should go with that plan. At least until we get back from Hawaii. Nitro will protect us. I know he let him in last time, but the guy just had to open the door and walk in. We have been very good about keeping the doors locked lately. I'm sure Nitro wouldn't tolerate someone breaking into my house. Let's plan on you moving in this weekend. Would that be okay with you?"

"Yes, I guess so. I've gotten used to the two of you, and it would be a bit lonely by myself. I would like to go by the office tonight. I hate to eat and run, but…"

"Oh, no, you aren't." Austin stood and walked to the door. "You two are staying right here tonight. We have plenty of room. The guest bedroom is vacant and so is one of the other places here. You have your choice. Which will it be?"

"I already put fresh linens on the beds in the guest room in anticipation that you might want to stay." Ruth gestured toward the guest room. "The other places will be a bit musty and will take some time to warm, but I am willing to go out and get one ready for you if you would rather stay in one of them. I would feel more comfortable with you all in the main house, just my own opinion. I know it doesn't go a long way, but there you have it."

CeCe and Reece looked at each other and shrugged. Reece sat back down. "Well, there you have it. CeCe, I think we are out-numbered. Even Nitro seems to have a say in this." Nitro had curled himself up in front of the door. "I guess it wouldn't hurt us to stay the night. I can get up early and meet the sheriff at the newspaper before there are too many people around. I don't want to make more of a circus of this than it already is."

CeCe was nervous about staying in the same house with Austin. She loved being near him, but the thought of staying under the same roof with his room right next to hers was a bit unnerving.

She then berated herself for being silly. It was just last night that she had been under the same roof and his room being adjoined to hers. But that was different. It was a hotel. This was his house.

The last time she had been here in the evening, she didn't know what would have happened if her foot hadn't fallen off of that pillow. Well, Reece would be here tonight, and they didn't know if it was safe to go home. She would stay and try and put her thoughts of him away.

"I agree. We should spend the night here. Has anyone gone by the house to make sure that it wasn't broken into? We may get there and not have a place to stay after all and would have to come back here or stay in the coffee shop."

Tucker walked over and put the teapot on the stove. "The sheriff did say he sent someone by the house to check on it, considering that you already had this guy go into your place. There was no sign of entry there. It looks like he just targeted the office this time."

"Well, that's comforting." CeCe walked toward the door where Austin was standing. "I guess we will need to get out our bags if we are going to stay. Will you help me with them, Austin?"

"Sure. Here, let me get your jacket."

They walked to the Jeep, both deep in thought. "Is Reece going to be all right? She went awfully pale in there."

"Yes, I'm sure she will be. She is pretty determined to not let this get her down. I am hoping the sheriff will take this more seriously now and look into it further. Last time I got the feeling that he thought she should be flattered that someone was writing admiring letters to her."

"I'm sure this will be taken more seriously. I think it's a good idea for you two to stick together for a while longer, too. You can stay here as long as you want, but I do know that you are anxious to get back into your house. It sounds like it has moved right along."

"Yes, even though Reece has a hard shell, she is still vulnerable, and I am ready to move back in. It will do her good to have a change of pace. Hopefully, this will be resolved before we go away to Hawaii."

"Hopefully."

They brought the bags into the house and Austin carried them to the guest bedroom. CeCe, Reece, and Ruth went to clear the table. After they finished, they brought the steaming pot of tea and the warm peach cobbler to the great room.

"I thought we could enjoy this in here." Ruth sat the tray on the coffee table as they began to discuss their thoughts on the recent events.

Chapter Eighteen

He was very anxious to get home and go through the files and things he had taken from Reece's office. It was a busy day for him, and he had a difficult time keeping his mind on his work. The lure of the files was calling him. He drove quickly home and fumbled with his keys. It was dark and his stomach was alerting him to the fact that the only thing he had put into it that day was some very strong coffee. He would just have to ignore it for the time being, he had more important things than eating to think about.

The stack of manila files sat tauntingly on the end of his desk. As he opened the door, he could feel his own excitement and anticipation. What would he find in them? Was it what he was looking for? He hoped that was the case. It would be difficult- that was an understatement; it would be impossible for him to go back and take anything else.

He sat behind the large wooden desk. He picked up a stack of the files and started searching. After an hour of searching the files, he picked them up and started over again. It had to be here, he just knew it, but where was it? He must have missed it. He would go through them more thoroughly. This is where she kept it; he had seen her put things in these files. Now where were they?

It was getting late and he had already gone through the files three times. He was angry with himself and with Reece. Why was he in this position in the first place? Why didn't she listen to him? If she did, they could live the rest of their days out in peace. She was just like the rest of them. He would take a little more time with her to see if he could change her. If not, well, it wasn't time to start thinking about that.

His stomach had gone sour along with his mood. It was time to put something in the empty space just to fill the void. Maybe he could still get the information that he desperately needed. He would just have to wait for another opportune time.

After he filled his stomach, he had to get out of the house. Just sitting there made him frustrated. He would go for a drive and maybe park somewhere, that way he could think more clearly. He grabbed the keys and went out the door. There, he felt better already. A drive was just what he needed. Maybe he would go by Reece's to see if she was home yet.

~ ~ ~

Reece and CeCe finished helping Ruth clean up. She insisted on doing it herself, but the two of them were not going to hear a thing about it. Ruth had told them it was like having two daughters to help her. She loved the company and she felt it was much safer with them there on the ranch. She was secretly hoping that they would stay longer than just the night.

Reece put the dishtowel on the towel rack and stretched like a cat. "I believe it is time for me to hit the sack. I'm sure that I won't be able to sleep much, but at least I can lie down and try to relax."

"I think that's a good idea, Reece," CeCe said. "I think I will do the same. I just want to take Nitro for a short walk before I try out that feather bed in there. It looks very comfortable. I think I will sink right into it and fall off into a deep sleep."

CeCe walked with Reece into the bedroom after they had told Ruth and Tucker goodnight. Reece opened her bag and went in to start the shower. She felt like she needed one after the news about her office.

CeCe pulled the leash off of the hook by the door. It looked as though Nitro had been made right at home. He really didn't miss her when she went away and left him with Tucker and Ruth. This made things easier for her when she did have to leave.

Nitro was ready to go; she could hardly contain him. She grabbed her jacket and hooked the leash onto his collar. Nitro tugged at the leash till she tugged back and he obeyed her silent command. "Let's go, buddy," she kindly spoke to him. "We can't spend all night out here, plus the snow drifts are deep and I don't want to end up with a twisted ankle like the last time I was here. You be good, now let's go!"

CeCe opened the door and bumped right into Austin. "I wasn't expecting anyone to be coming out of the door. I thought everyone had gone to bed. I would ask what you are doing, but that would be a silly question. Would you like some company, besides Nitro, that is?" Austin didn't want her walking around out in the dark. He, too, remembered the last time she was at the ranch.

"Austin, you scared me to death. I wasn't expecting anyone to be out here. So after that kick-start to my heart, I will take you up on your offer." CeCe closed the door behind her and stepped out onto the porch. "Look- the snow has stopped and the sky has cleared."

"Yes, and there is a full moon tonight. It should help light the way for us." Austin guided CeCe down the stairs as he talked. He wasn't taking any chances that she would get hurt again. "I love it when the moon is full and we have such a bright sky out. With all the snow, it almost looks like we have lights out here."

"Yes, it is beautiful isn't it? I even think it would be even more perfect if we could set that skating date for next month this same time. The ice should be good and strong. I think that tomorrow night or the next would be a great night for a cross-country ski trip. What do you think, Austin?"

"I think that sounds great. I never cross-country skied before, but I bet I can learn, especially if I have a good teacher. Are you willing to teach me, CeCe?"

"I bet I will be a better coach than the past receiver coach, who taught you to cheat!" CeCe exclaimed as she tugged on Nitro's leash.

"Oh, that was cold. I thought you were all over that cheating thing. I never cheated. It was just a gentle push. If they weren't man enough to handle it then it was their fault, not mine. I have a couple of appointments tomorrow, but let's say Thursday. Does that work for you?"

"That will be great. It will give me time to get some things in order as well. Remember though, you do have to move that stuff for the community garage sale between tomorrow and Friday. It sounds like Tucker is going to help you move some of it."

"I won't forget. That's one of the things on my list." Austin helped CeCe step through one of the snowdrifts that had formed on the side of the house. "CeCe, I wanted to talk to you about last night when you told me about Carlos. I do know how you feel. Maybe not about the whole thing, but about the hurt that came from your relationship with Carlos. You see, someone hurt me, too. Her name was Poalima. I was all set to marry her and to have a family with her, when she told me she was leaving me and moving to New York, of all places. I had planned for us to have a family together and to live the rest of our lives there on Kauai. Poalima became pregnant, which wasn't the plan, but it just happened. She never even gave a thought to me or to the life she was carrying. She left and I only received a letter from her trying to explain herself. I don't know what became of my unborn child, but I can only guess by her comments before she left and the brief mention of her plans to abort the baby in her letter. I ached at the thought of not being part of that child's life. My own father was not much of a father to me, and I have vowed to be the best example I can be. Do you see how I can relate to your heartache?"

"Austin, I am sorry that happened to you. I can't understand why she would just throw all of that away. It is what I have wanted, always. Carlos was just not the right person for me. I know that now, but it was very painful then."

"I just wanted you to know, not to feel sorry for me, but just so you know that I do understand. I do believe that things happen for the best. Look at me now. I wouldn't have moved to Colorado and met such wonderful people as you and everyone else. I have put the past behind me and only ask that you do the same. Don't let him ruin the rest of your life. You have a lot more to look forward to." Austin put his arm around CeCe as he led her back to the porch.

"You're right, Austin, I do let those feelings put up road blocks for me, and I need to stop doing that."

"CeCe, I really enjoy your company and would love to spend more time with you, do you think that is possible?" Austin reached for her before she could reply and pulled her close to him. He kissed her softly at first, then with growing need.

When Austin pulled CeCe close, she almost stopped him. She couldn't trust herself. The kiss filled her every need. She could feel the warmth growing over her. She felt the crescendo in her body begin to rise. She was helpless under his spell and the full moon shining on them as though they were actors on a stage. CeCe kissed him back fully. She let the leash drop out of her hand and reached up and caressed Austin's thick, curly hair. The stillness of the night added to the intensity. Austin was caressing her softly and moving his kisses down her throat and on her neck.

"Austin," CeCe spoke softly. "I'm losing control, and I can't let that happen. I want you, but I have made a promise that I will save myself for marriage. Please help me to keep that promise, but don't stop what you are doing."

Austin acknowledged her request with a slight hesitation at what he was doing. He would honor her wishes, but there was no harm in making them both feel good at the moment. Austin let his hand explore CeCe's soft breast. As he bushed his thumb over the crest of her breast, her nipple came alive and grew taut.

Austin was the one to pull away. He had to, in order to keep his promise to her. If he let this go any further, they would end up in his own feather bed, and he would be no better than the next guy. He didn't want that sort of relationship with CeCe. He knew this could grow into something special. Something neither one of them had ever experienced before.

Austin's voice was husky with desire as he spoke. "CeCe, I want you, but not like this. It has to be right. I am willing to wait. But I do believe that it is time to retreat back inside where there are other people around who will help keep us in line. I love being with you and hope you feel the same. We will talk in the morning about that cross-country trip, but you might want to have Reece along to keep us honest."

CeCe was embarrassed by her reaction to the kiss they had shared. She was enjoying every moment of it and was letting herself fall into the vortex of it. "Austin, thanks for being understanding and willing to see me for who I am. I think you are going to be one of the best things that ever happened to this valley. I am grateful to have you in my life. I think breakfast will be a good place to discuss the cross-country trip."

Austin opened the door that Nitro had been insistently scratching at to get back inside. Austin took CeCe's coat from her and hung it up on the coat tree. "I am glad that you and Reece are staying here. I feel much more comfortable with you here. You sure you don't want to stay longer?"

"Austin, that won't work. I do think Reece and I are just fine as long as we are together. I know you think that having a male around would be even better, but it isn't going to happen. Goodnight and thank you for being so kind and understanding." CeCe and Nitro disappeared behind the bedroom door.

Austin found himself standing there staring at the door. That was one classy lady, and he was willing to put all the work into it to make sure she stayed in his life.

Chapter Nineteen

He was very anxious to see Reece. He wondered if she got the letter, but he could only hope. He was regretful that he was not able to see her read it as he had watched her before. He would have to go and watch and see if she put the letter with the others.

They hadn't returned last night as he had thought. He sat and waited and watched, but no one was there. The only sign he saw of anyone was when the sheriff's deputy drove up and went around the back of the house. He appeared to be checking the door.

Maybe something happened to Reece. Maybe that was why they weren't home. No, that wasn't the case. CeCe would have been there. He would have heard if anything had happened to the two of them. It was getting late, and he was sure that they would not return home tonight. He would have to take his chances tomorrow and watch to see if Reece did something with the letter that he had sent.

He was sure now that she would not be keeping it at the office. It was a mess. It would take her some time to clean it up. He could be sure of that. He would sit in the park across from her office and watch her some tomorrow. That is, if his schedule allowed him. He had been awfully busy lately. It was good in one sense, but on the other hand, it didn't allow him much time to concentrate on Reece.

There were too many people around tonight for him to sit and wait any longer. He started the truck and drove away slowly. It wouldn't do him much good to get a ticket and the sheriff's department to put two and two together. No, he had to be careful and watch his step.

He would like to write another letter for Reece, though. Maybe there would be an opportunity at the garage sale this weekend to give it to her. First he would have to get inspired and write the letter. It would be ironic if he wrote the letter and gave it to her at the garage sale, since that was where he had gotten the typewriter he loved so dearly. That was just a few years ago. Who would have known the pleasure it would bring him?

Chapter Twenty

After a very restless night for everyone on the ranch, Reece and CeCe packed their things and Nitro's into the Jeep. They thanked Austin, Ruth, and Tucker for being so concerned and assured them that they would be just fine. They refused the offer to stay awhile longer. CeCe was sure that she could not stay and keep herself in control, while Reece just wanted to get her life back to normal.

They drove to Reece's house, dropped off their bags, and got Nitro settled in. Reece was going to drop CeCe off at the coffee shop and head to the office. She was going to meet the sheriff there and try and make some sense out of the mess that awaited her.

CeCe insisted on going with her, if not just to make sure that there was someone else there until the sheriff arrived. CeCe didn't want Reece to be alone too much. They drove to the office and got out. The destruction was visible from the street. This was going to take Reece all day, if not longer, to clean up. She would need to wait to start until she talked with the sheriff, in case they hadn't finished all of their investigation.

The door would need to be replaced in the back. It was a shame that people could be so destructive. There was a white powder all over everything; they guessed this was for fingerprints. Reece started to pick things up and put them in some sort of order. CeCe followed suit.

The sheriff's deputy arrived about fifteen minutes after they had started to clean up.

"Good morning, Ms. Landon, Ms. Wellington. Sorry to have to come and talk to you under these circumstances, but it is something we need to follow up on."

The deputy was a very young man. CeCe thought he was barely old enough to be out of high school.

CeCe stood and pushed some trash into a large plastic bag she was holding. "Do you think this has any connection to the letters that Reece has been receiving? I understand that you didn't find a letter like the last time."

"Well, as you can see, we didn't disturb much. This is the way we found the office when some of the other staff called us and told us about the way it looked. That's why we needed to talk to you, Ms. Landon. We need to ask you to let us know what has been taken. Do you know who or why anyone would do this?"

"I was hoping you could give me some answers to that question. What would they be looking for anyway? I don't keep anything valuable here. I had my laptop computer with me, so that wasn't a lure. I can't help but think the letters and this are related; however, there was no destruction done to my house last time. Although, it could have been that he didn't have time. CeCe thought that she had seen someone leaving the house that day." Reece sat down behind the desk and sorted through the papers that were strewn all over it. "It's going to take some time to pull this all together, and even then I don't know if I will have any answers."

"We have been sending a car by here every hour or so the last couple of evenings. If this guy comes back, maybe we can catch him in the act. You have our number. Please call if you notice anything or can think of anything that will help us in getting this guy." The deputy put his notepad back into his shirt pocket and buttoned it. "I know it doesn't make any sense, but a lot of things folks do nowadays doesn't make sense either. You two take care now and let us know if we can be of any help." He turned around and walked out of the door shaking his head.

"Lot of good he was. I'm surprised they let him carry a gun. He looks no older than some of those kids that Austin coaches." Reece stood as she watched him go to the car. "CeCe, you need to go to the shop and get ready to open. It's going to take me awhile to get this all cleaned up, and I still have an article to write today. I will come by around noon and let you know if I find anything."

CeCe started to protest, but knew that Reece was right. She needed to get in and start some baking or her customers would just have coffee today. "Reece, Austin and I were talking last night, and we thought it would be nice to go cross-country skiing tomorrow night. Are you up for that?"

"Yes, I think it would be great. The moon is full and I know you will make some of that special hot chocolate of yours. We can go up to the cabin and have some goodies, then head back. I think that's a great idea. Too bad we can't call Angie and invite him along." Reece raised her eyebrows and smiled.

"I'm glad that you got along with him so well. I kind of think we will be spending a lot of time with him and Austin in Kauai. I better go now and get started. I'll see you later then. I can come back and help you later this afternoon, so don't do it all yourself."

"Goodbye, CeCe," Reece said as she shoved her out the door.

Reece had been working very hard on clearing her desk and trying to get the article done as well. It was about 11:30 when there was a knock on her door and she looked up to see a large bouquet of flowers covering a man's face.

"Special delivery for Ms. Reece Landon. And a very special delivery it is." The voice spoke behind the arrangement.

"Why, who could be sending me such a large arrangement?"

The flower arrangement was lowered, and behind it was Dr. Mason Albright.

"Mason, how sweet of you, but it isn't my birthday and Christmas is still a week away. I won't argue with you though, you have some of my favorite flowers here." Reece walked to the door and took the arrangement from Mason. "Here, let me find a place to put these. Oh dear, it's still such a mess. Can you believe this?" Reece set the flowers down in the bay window.

"I heard that someone came in here and trashed the place, and thought you could use a pick-me-up. Do you think it was kids?" Mason stepped over some papers Reece had piled on the floor.

"Have you figured out what they were doing? I hope they got what they came for. I have arranged my schedule so that I have a few hours off, and I can help you go through this stuff. Save you some time. What do you say?"

"Absolutely not. I'm the only one who can make any sense of this. It does appear that I am missing a bunch of files. Nothing of importance though. I had my laptop with me and several of the files I have been working on. That is one saving grace. It would take me months to go back and do some of the work if it had been here and was taken or trashed."

"Reece, don't be silly. Two sets of hands are better than one. It would only take us a little while to finish."

"That is sweet of you, but CeCe has already offered to come over this afternoon and help. But I could use a cup of coffee and something light to eat. Would you like to take a walk with me over to her place?"

"I'll walk with you, but if you refuse my help, then I guess I will just go back to the hospital and work. I do have things I can do. How about some dinner tonight?"

"Can I call you later and let you know? I would love to, but it depends on how much work I get done this afternoon."

Mason was miffed- she could tell by the stiffness in his voice. She didn't want him to give up his valuable time to clean up some old files. He was much more needed at the hospital. Besides, she was in a sour mood and didn't want him to see her this way.

"I guess I can't convince you otherwise. I will wait to hear from you later this afternoon. I will walk you over to CeCe's. I won't go in; I do get the distinct feeling that she doesn't like me all that much."

"Don't be silly, Mason, what's there not to like about you? CeCe has just had a lot on her mind lately with the fire and Nitro, and then injuring her foot."

"How is that coming along, anyway? I never did see her after that initial visit. That was a very nasty sprain."

"She has recovered well. We are back into our routine of running or skiing every day. Speaking of which, we are going skiing tomorrow evening. Would you like to come along?"

"I will have to see what my schedule is like, but I would love to go. I have never cross-country skied before, so you will have to give me some pointers."

"Really? I would have thought that you would have done a lot of that being at the ski resort up in Washington. But of course I will give you some pointers. Austin Carter is going with us and he has never skied before either. It will be fun with the full moon and all. Let me get my jacket and we'll walk over to CeCe's." Reece put down the files she was holding and grabbed her jacket.

They walked the short distance. Mason opened the door for Reece.

"I'll wait to hear from you this afternoon. You can't have anything too pressing to get done that you can't have dinner with me?" Mason's cool blue eyes were pleading with her.

"I really do have to finish that article on you and a couple of other things."

"You still aren't bent on doing that stupid article on me, are you?"

"Yes and maybe you will give me the information I need so I can finish it. Mason thanks for the flowers. They really are wonderful and it was sweet of you to think of me and want to help. I am looking forward to tomorrow night, if not this evening. I will call you and let you know how it is shaping up."

Reece reached over and gave him a light kiss on the check. She could tell he was upset with her, but she really needed to get the work done before she could commit to going out this evening.

Reece walked into the shop and waved to CeCe. She was talking with Tom Dancer. Reece went behind the counter and got herself a cup of coffee and a fresh roll CeCe had made that morning. She could overhear the conversation CeCe was having with Tom.

"Tom, that's great, I will go out this afternoon and look at the railing. I'm sure it's perfect. I am anxious to get back into the house. Reece and will be staying with me for awhile."

"I h-heard what happened at her p-place. Seems folks don't give r-respect to other folks p-property these days." Tom absently touched the flask he had in his back pocket. He felt like having a drink now. He knew other people knew about his drinking and they felt sorry for him. There was no need for that. He could control it. He had been very busy lately, and there wasn't a need for drinking. It was just when he was feeling lonely or didn't have things to keep him busy. That wasn't the case now. He had more work than ever. Tom liked keeping busy and working with his hands.

"Yes, I don't know what goes through people's minds. I do know that Reece wanted a railing around her garden before, but she may be interested in something more substantial now. She even may want a gate on the back door to the office, since that is how they got in. I will show her the work you did at my place and I'm sure you will be getting a call from her soon." CeCe picked up the empty plates. Tom had managed to eat all that she had put in front of him. "Tom, do you have a bill for me? I could pay you now."

"I would never take payment until you give m-m-me the final approval. I will come by tomorrow and you can let me know if it is all right. Then I'll give you the b-bill." Tom reached for his wallet.

"That sounds more than fair, but you won't be paying for this, it's on the house." CeCe covered his hand with hers. "Thanks, Tom. I know it is just going to be perfect."

Tom stood to leave. He lifted his jacket and hat off of the coat tree. He walked to the counter and said, "Hello, Ms. R-r-reece. S-sorry to hear about your place. Hope nothing was d-damaged."

"Hello, Tom. Thanks. I haven't gone through everything, but it looks like they just messed up things and took some stuff. It's nice to see you." Reece was surprised at how bright and clear his eyes were, and he didn't even have a hint of alcohol on his breath. "I overheard you and CeCe talking. It looks like we will be moving into her place for awhile. I'd like to talk to you about some ideas you might have for both my house and the office. Give me a call when you have some time to discuss a design. I know you are busy with shodding, but I understand that you really enjoy the other work as well."

"Yes, Ms. Reece, I'll d-do that. I will have some time right after C-Christmas. I'll give you a c-call then and we can t-talk. Thank you, Ms. CeCe, it was w-wonderful as usual. Glad you are b-back." Tom closed the door as he walked out and down the street.

Chapter Twenty-One

Claire had been trying to reach Reece since early Monday morning. She had finally gotten time to do the research on the doctor that Reece had asked her about.

On Monday morning, Claire had left a message on Reece's machine and had tried to call back several times since. The message said that the machine was full and to call back later. Well, she was sure that if Reece needed more information she could call her. Claire was going on a month-long vacation, and she would make a note to call Reece when she got back if she didn't hear from her sooner.

She was regretful that she wasn't able to find anything on him for her. Maybe she got the name wrong. She was able to pull up some information on a Dr. Mason Brighton, but no Dr. Mason Albright.

That had been a terrible tragedy; she remembered doing a story on the fire. It was Wendolyn Bains, wasn't it? She was the socialite that had just gotten married to that promising young doctor. Her father had set them up in a very wealthy neighborhood. They looked as though they had the world by the tail.

If Claire remembered correctly, they had only been married for about six months and Wendolyn had proudly announced the arrival of their first child.

Wendolyn's father had given all of the family jewelry to Wendolyn so she could pass it along to her child when she was old enough. He had made sure that the house he had bought her had a large, secure safe. He had overlooked the fact that it wasn't fireproof. This was discovered only when they went into the rubble of the house to find it melted and no sign that the jewelry survived.

It appeared that the fire started in some faulty wiring in the alarm system he had insisted they have installed. He would never be able to forgive himself. If he hadn't insisted on that system, they would still be alive today. He would have his daughter, son-in-law, and a beautiful grandchild.

It wasn't long after the fire that he died of a sudden heart attack. The whole thing was a terrible tragedy.

They barely had time to start their lives and they were gone before anyone knew it.

Well, that was someone different, because Reece said she was doing an article on a newcomer to the Yampa Valley. This guy had been dead for two years.

Reece always had some interesting project she was working on. She had been a great friend and study partner when they were in college together. Claire would have to make a point of going to see Reece soon. That would be nice. When she talked to Reece she would plan a trip. Maybe next winter; that way she could ski. Lord knows she never found the time to at home.

Chapter Twenty-Two

CeCe finished her clean up, and she and Reece walked back to Reece's office. Reece had made a lot of progress, but most of all CeCe was most impressed with the flower arrangement that almost completely covered the span of the side window. That was the window that faced the park, and Reece loved looking out into it as she worked. She always told CeCe that it gave her inspiration.

"You've made a lot of headway in here, Reece. Where did the flowers come from? They're beautiful, but a bit overwhelming for the space."

"They came from Mason. He heard what happened and thought it would be nice to have something bright and cheerful among all the ugliness. I have made some progress; I didn't realize how much junk I had in here. Some of these files go as far back as when my father ran the paper. He didn't have the luxury of a computer to keep things so neat. Of course, I am a pack rat. I find myself making notes on pieces of paper and keeping them in files even after I have written the article."

"Mason sent the flowers? I didn't think he thought that much of anyone but himself. He sure doesn't strike me as the caring type. About keeping stuff that isn't worth anything, that's all right. I'm the same way; I think it's just human nature. Did you find that anything of importance is missing?"

"It seems only some of the newer files and the stupidest thing, my answering machine is missing. That thing isn't worth a darn. It must have been kids. Who else would break in here and not take other more important things? Why, I even had a cash box with a couple of hundred dollars in it and they missed that!" Reece reached into one of the desk drawers and pulled it out. "I don't think you have given Mason a chance, CeCe. He's a really nice guy. It isn't like you to go and form an opinion about someone you barely know. I think if you give him the chance you'll see he's worth getting to know. I invited him to go with us tomorrow night. If he accepts, maybe then you will get a better chance to see him for who he really is."

"You're right, Reece. I was being too judgmental. It's just that I want you to find the right guy, not one who thinks he's right for you. It'll be fun to have him along. Now let's get this cleaned up so we can go to my place and make plans to move back in there."

"Sounds like a plan."

~ ~ ~

CeCe and Reece went to CeCe's house early that evening. The railing was wonderful- it was just what she had wanted. They had brought a few essentials with them and planned on moving the rest of the stuff in tomorrow afternoon.

Reece really loved CeCe's place and always felt comfortable there. She felt right at home. It wasn't going to be hard for her to live out here for a month or two; Reece rather thought she would really enjoy it.

~ ~ ~

Austin and Tucker worked really hard moving the heavy items into the community center. They had a good chance to talk about the ranch and many other things. One of those topics of conversations was CeCe. Austin had wanted to know just as much he could about her.

Tucker told him about how she was when she was young. "She was a hell of a tomboy, that one was. She would do just about anything anyone else would. She was always tiny but certainly mighty."

That didn't surprise Austin one bit. CeCe seemed determined to do whatever it was she set her mind to. He hoped that she was going to set her mind to spending more time with him, because he certainly planned on it.

One of the places they stopped at was the school. They had several pieces of office equipment. Most of the stuff wasn't any good for anything. It was all too antiquated. But in the very back there were three manual typewriters. They were very old, and should bring a good price. They needed some work, but if you knew anything about these dinosaurs, then you could fix them up and make a pretty good resale price on them.

That was the last load that they needed to pick up and deliver. Austin was sure that he would see CeCe at the center. She had told him that she was going to go over and help sort things out. He had reminded her of the cross-country ski trip she had insisted they do this evening.

CeCe told him that she hadn't forgotten, and she even made up some special treats for him to carry along in his pack.

The afternoon passed quickly, and with all the items having been sorted and priced, CeCe had enough time to move the rest of her and Reece's things back into the house before she had to get ready for the cross-country ski excursion.

It felt very good to be back home. She would have been devastated if she had lost this place. It brought back many memories, and now she and Nitro would be back where they belonged.

CeCe packed a nice light dinner for them to enjoy. She had also made a point of buying some macadamia nuts while she was in Denver. CeCe had made a fresh batch of chocolate chip macadamia nut cookies. She would have to wait and see if they were a hit with Austin. She planned on not telling him that they were in the cookies to see if he would notice.

The hot chocolate with her secret ingredients was ready to be poured into the waiting thermoses.

Nitro always loved going on these trips, and she had made him some of his special treats as well. He did have to carry his own pack, so she prepared that and was just getting ready to get dressed, when Reece came in the door.

"Sorry I'm late, but I just had to finish up things at the office, looks as though you have things under control as usual." Reece sat her computer on the side table as she walked into the kitchen to help with any last minute items that needed to be taken care of.

"You know I don't mind getting this all together. I really enjoy it, besides I get to take along what I want to eat." CeCe wrapped a towel around the fresh loaf of bread she had baked earlier. "Is Mason coming along?"

"Yes, I told him we would meet him out here, since the trail head is just a short distance from your house. I gave him directions. He should be here soon."

"Good; Austin is coming here also and should be here soon as well. He had to get fitted for equipment, since he didn't have any. I love these full moon trips. They are so enchanting." CeCe finished packing the bag and headed into the bedroom to get changed into her ski gear.

The railing just made the room. She was happy that she went with her idea of the aspen leaves. Tom had done a wonderful job. He really was skilled and artistic. CeCe heard a knock on the door and Reece going to answer it.

"Hello Mason! Come in, we're just about ready."

Nitro ran from the bedroom and stood in the open doorway. He was growling and the hair on the back of his neck was standing up. CeCe had never seen him like this before.

"Nitro! What is going on? You know better than to treat our guests like that. I am so sorry Dr. Albright, I don't know what has gotten into him, other than we just moved back into the house and he might be being overprotective." CeCe grabbed hold of Nitro's collar and sat him on the floor. "You behave, now."

"Please, CeCe, call me Mason. I may know the reason he's acting the way he is. I have always had a fear of dogs. I was bitten severely as a child, and from what I understand, they can sense your fear."

"That probably explains it, but he is normally such a teddy bear. Good thing you're a people doctor, under those circumstances." CeCe walked over and grabbed Mason's arm. She walked him over to Nitro. "Reach out your arm very slowly and scratch his ears. He likes that very much."

Nitro sat watching with his big brown eyes. He seemed to pick up on CeCe's calm manner with Mason. He no longer was growling and had settled down.

Mason was leery of the animal. He didn't much like them. But it was time for him to try and make friends with CeCe's best friend, besides Reece, that is.

Mason reached out his arm very slowly and touched Nitro's head very tentatively. The dog just sat there and didn't make any threatening moves toward him.

"Now just rub his ears a little, Mason, and he'll become an instant friend." Reece had walked up behind him and knelt next to Nitro. The dog moved his head toward her touch and washed her face with a large swipe of his tongue.

God, thought Mason. It wouldn't take much for that dog to devour a whole human arm. His mouth appeared to be as big as that of a lion's. *Stop being so childish*, he berated himself. Mason knelt close to Reece. He stared rubbing Nitro's head and the damn dog laid down and rolled over so he could rub its stomach. He made soothing sounds to encourage the dog's good behavior.

"See, that's all it takes. The male population is the same whether it is man or beast. Give a little affection and they always want more." Reece laughed as she rose from her squatting position. "Did you get your skis and poles all right today?"

"Yes, Reece, I even saw Austin there at the same time. Only I rented mine and Austin purchased his. Said he thought he would be using it a lot no sense in renting each and every time. That way he could go out whenever he had the whim. Do you think there might be some used equipment at that Community Garage Sale I keep hearing so much about tomorrow?"

CeCe pulled her equipment out of the closet and set it outside of the door. "Could be- there are some great bargains there. Reece and I will be working the sale both tomorrow and the next day. You should definitely come by and see what you can find. Look, here comes Austin." CeCe stood in the open door way until he was fully in her drive.

The sight of her made him catch his breath. Standing there illuminated in the doorway, she looked like an angel. He was glad there were going to be others around them this evening. With the full moon and all, he didn't know if he would be able to keep himself in line.

He parked his truck next to Mason's and got out. Austin walked around the back of it and pulled out his ski equipment and a basket with a checked cloth over it.

"Looks as though Ruth sent us some of her famous baked goods." CeCe held the door wide for him.

Austin sat the equipment down outside and walked in the door. Before he could get two steps inside, Nitro jumped up and started running toward him. He leaped up and jumped unto Austin's chest wagging his tail and licking his face.

"Nitro! Get down off of Austin," CeCe demanded.

"It's all right, isn't it buddy?" Austin rubbed Nitro's head and he dropped to the floor. "He just wanted to say hello."

"Well, he growled at Mason and almost knocked you into the next county. I don't know what has gotten into him lately." CeCe shut the door behind Austin and took the basket of goodies.

"He's just excited to be back home, that's all. The place sure looks good- not much damage from the fire. Of course, you didn't allow me into the bedroom the first time I was here." Austin grinned as he took a seat on the sofa.

"No, there was no need then, but you could go in and see the new railing that Tom Dancer put in there for me."

"Here, let me do it, CeCe. I was going to give Mason a tour any way." Reece reached for Mason's hand. "Austin, come along. I'm sure you only got as far as this room when you brought CeCe home that evening."

"That'll be great. I would love to see the rest of the place. Then I can imagine all kinds of sordid things." Austin stood to go along with Reece and Mason.

CeCe gave him a warning glare. After the quick tour, they all headed out of the house and put on their equipment. Nitro was all set with his own pack and each of them had one to carry as well.

CeCe believed in being prepared. The moon was bright and full, so it was easy to see the trail. Reece and Mason led the way.

It didn't take either of the men long to catch on to the skiing, although Austin's athletic ability was evident in his first few minutes on the skis. It looked as though he had been born on them.

Mason just took a little longer to get comfortable. They stopped about two miles in to have a hot chocolate break.

CeCe made a special blend with some peppermint schnapps, Irish cream and another special ingredient that she wouldn't tell to anybody, not even Reece.

They just had another mile to get to the cabin. None of them talked much; rather, they were taking in the serenity of everything around them.

Nitro ran ahead the last few feet of the trail. He was waiting there for them when they got there. He had been out often enough with CeCe and Reece that he knew that he would soon get a treat.

The cabin was very rustic and quaint. It had been built in the mid-1800's. This land belonged to Reece's great or even great, great grandparents. CeCe and Reece had been coming here for many years. To them, it was just a stop along the way. They didn't realize the historical implications that it brought with it until they were much older and out of college.

In the summer they would hike up the trail and trim it back and do any repairs on the cabin that needed to be taken care of. Most of the folks that used it respected its historical place in society and took equally good care of it.

Austin was the most impressed. He loved the detail that the cabin had, even though it was more than a century old. He had promised himself that this wouldn't be the last time he used the cabin.

The stream that ran out back of it would probably make for some good fly-fishing in the summer. He made a mental note to ask Reece and CeCe about that.

"Well, here we are. It isn't much, but it's always a welcome sight." Reece reached under a rock and pulled the key out.

"Do you always leave a key for anyone to find?" Mason questioned her.

"It wouldn't take much to get in if you really wanted to. From time to time the high school kids come up here and work their way in. They usually are pretty good about cleaning up after themselves. We'll find a beer can here or there that they missed in their clean up." Reece unlocked the door.

CeCe and Austin were just taking off their skis. CeCe walked by Mason, who was just standing there with skis still attached. "Are you going to keep them on in the cabin? It might make it a bit awkward." She was trying to get him to loosen up. He seemed to be wound tighter than an eight-day clock.

"I was just trying to figure out how to get out of them. They showed me at the rental shop, but I guess I wasn't paying too much attention, or else I would have figured it out by now."

"Here, Mason, let me help you." CeCe bent down and helped him undo the skis. "It can be tricky at first, but it's like riding a bike: once you get the hang of it you never forget. You two did great coming here. Reece and I will probably have to keep a pretty good pace going back to keep up."

Austin had gotten out of his skis and was taking CeCe's pack for her. "I doubt that, CeCe. You two could out-ski both of us even if we were to tie one of each of your legs to the others. This is a wonderful place. How did you find it?"

Reece and CeCe just laughed. CeCe spoke first. "It belongs to Reece's family. We have come up here for as long as we can remember. It is pretty great, though. Do you like it?"

"I love it." Austin had to duck his head as he walked in the door. "They sure made folks shorter back then."

"Hey, don't go bashing short people. It was hard enough to have to listen to that song about short people having no reason to live." CeCe moved over the little fireplace at the end of the room. "I just like to think that I am vertically challenged; besides I see a lot of things in a different perspective down here than the rest of you."

Reece laughed and relayed a story about CeCe being the one who always found the treasures and money, even when they were just kids. "She has a point. Anyone can wear heels and make themselves taller, but it's not as easy for us who have a little more of that vertical height CeCe spoke about to crawl or duck walk to get a closer view of some of the more important things in life, like plants and such."

They all laughed about that and settled in by the fire CeCe had expertly lit.

They enjoyed the meal that CeCe had brought them, a hearty stew. Austin opened the thermos and poured out the stew while CeCe unwrapped the fresh bread that she had made. It was still warm.

They enjoyed the meal and good conversation. Austin was enjoying himself, and wanted to know more about Mason. "Where did you grow up, Mason?"

"Well, I was an army brat and we moved all over the place."

Reece jumped right into the conversation. "I wish I would have known that for my article!"

"Reece, please don't do that article on me. No one is interested in who I am. I have made a few friends here and that's all I really need."

"Too late. The article is done and comes out in the paper tomorrow. I did the best I could with what you would give, and what I observed. Don't worry, I didn't put anything in there that would embarrass you."

Mason groaned. "I'm really a very private person. It is difficult when I have strangers coming up and talking to me like they know me."

Austin spoke up. "I was also concerned about the article that Reece did on me, but it was very good. She is a gifted writer; she even makes some people look better than they are. I should know. You will just have a few of the eligible females probably making an appointment to see you. They'll want to get a better look and check you out for themselves." Everyone laughed at that, even Mason.

CeCe opened up the cookies she had made and offered them to Austin, Mason, and Reece. Nitro couldn't have any, since they contained chocolate, which wasn't good for him. In any case, he was content after having his special treats that CeCe had made for him.

Austin took one of the large cookies and bit into it. "I detect something different here, CeCe. Could it be? Yes, you have nailed the recipe down and the macadamia nuts make them the best in the west and all over the world, for that matter!"

CeCe blushed. "Come on, now. I just wanted to see if you would notice. I bought them when I was in Denver. You really like them?"

"I am telling the truth- these are the best I ever had. If you sold these in your shop, you would have to hire Ruth or someone else full-time to help you. You wouldn't be able to keep up. They are wonderful."

"Thanks, Austin," CeCe said as she nibbled on one of the cookies.

They lingered awhile longer and then cleaned up after themselves and packed every thing back into the backpacks.

Austin and Mason made sure the fire was out and that there were no remaining ashes in the fireplace.

They skied back full and content. The evening was mild and clear. They stopped just at the edge of CeCe's property to look over the edge of the cliff.

The moon shone in the canyon below, making it look surreal. Austin could feel the connection he had with this place to Kokee. It wasn't down into the sea; rather it fell into a river below.

The beauty was breathtaking. The moonlight caused shadows to dance on the mountainous terrain, and gave one a feeling of utopia.

"Isn't this beautiful? I have come by here so many times and have never seen the same view." CeCe kept her distance from the edge as she spoke. "You have to be careful not to get too close. The wind blows up and causes a cornice out there. If you go out too far, you are really just standing on unsupported snow. It gives you a false sense of security."

Mason inched away. "I have no desire to stand out there, then. Heights are not my favorite thing."

Reece started skiing as she turned back and said, "I don't think that any of us has a desire to try out our flying skills without the help of a plane or parachute. And if you do, I don't want to watch. I'm heading back. Anyone else ready to come?"

"I'm right behind you, Reece," Mason said.

"We'll be right there, Reece. Why don't you go in and start the tea pot?" CeCe asked her.

"I can do that," Reece responded.

"CeCe, this is beautiful. I didn't realize this was part of your property. The stream appears to split and go into two directions, is that correct?"

"Yes, it goes off right here as a matter of fact. The stream-bed you saw behind the cabin we were just at is a part of this one. The other drops down and goes into the valley below us. It is pretty spectacular in the summertime when the stream is running. The spring is wonderful. It creates a waterfall just over there." CeCe pointed to the right.

"Thanks for making the cookies. This has been great. We still need to go ice-skating. I think right after Christmas would be good. What do you think?"

"That will be wonderful. I'm glad you liked the cookies." CeCe looked up into Austin's eyes. She could see the tenderness and wanting in them.

Austin tipped her chin up and gently kissed her lips. CeCe yielded to him. Austin wrapped his arms around her and pulled her as close as he could.

She could feel the warmth and desire in him. Austin was right to think that he needed others around them tonight. He wanted CeCe. He would wait. He pulled away and lifted her chin again. She was beautiful. Her lips were inviting him to again pull her close and ultimately, down into the snow.

Nitro came running back and bumped into Austin from behind. Because they were still in their skis, they fell to the ground with their skis entwined.

"CeCe, what is it about every time I kiss you out in nature, you are prone to falling?"

"I won't take the full blame for this one. The skis and Nitro are to blame. Are you all right?"

"Yes, I'm just fine. I think that was perfect timing on Nitro's part."

They lay on their backs and looked up into the sky. The stars were out in abundance. There were so many of them shining down.

Austin broke the silence. "I am in love with this place, this evening, this moment. I could stay here forever."

"We would freeze. Besides, it won't be long before Reece comes back looking for us." CeCe sat up and brushed the snow off of her.

Austin did the same. "I guess we better get back. Thank you for everything."

Austin stood and helped CeCe up. He kissed the tip of her nose, then exclaimed at how cold it was.

"Guess that's our signal to leave."

They skied the short distance back to the house. Reece asked what took them so long, with a smirk on her face. Austin made an excuse that he had fallen and had tripped CeCe at the same time. They explained that while they were on the ground they just looked at the sky and stars for a while.

Chapter Twenty-Three

The full moon was just the thing he needed to be inspired. He was sure that he would have an opportunity to get the letter to Reece this weekend at the garage sale. He eyed the treasure that he had gotten there a few years before. He had the strong desire to make the keys sing. The paper again was calling to him.

> *The moon is shining bright and clear. It reminds me of what I see in your eyes. You know Reece; they say that the eyes are windows to the soul. Your windows are always open and ever so clear. We on the outside are able to see a pure and caring soul. That is what is so attractive about you.*
>
> *Did you know that when there is a full moon, it makes me want to embrace you fully?*
>
> *I love the way you tilt your head back as you laugh. The whole world brightens in your presence. The fire in your hair warms everyone around you. How was so vibrant and beautiful a creature ever created? It is not for me to question that creation, rather it is for me to rejoice.*
>
> *I just want to be the protector and keeper of that creature. Don't get me wrong, Reece, I would never prevent you from doing what you do now. That is what makes you, you. That is what makes me want to be with you.*
>
> *I watch the moonbeams dance off of the snow and feel that they are pronouncing my desire for you.*
>
> *I want you to know that I am always here and willing to accept you when you are ready for me. Don't despair, my darling. I am always close to you.*
>
> *I will be watching and waiting. Accept my love in this form now. It is only for a short time that we will be kept apart.*
>
> *For now, smile your warm smile and laugh your infectious*

laugh, and we and especially me will smile and laugh with you. Stay beautiful and warm for now, Love, Me.

The rubber gloves he was using caused him to be clumsier. He disliked it now that he couldn't feel the sensuous paper between his fingertips. But he had to be careful. After the scene he had witnessed at the newspaper office, he knew that anything Reece received from now on would be carefully examined.

He had no desire to be caught and accused of trying to harm her. But that is what the break-in looked like, an attempt to harm.

The clumsy gloves were necessary. He would be sure and wear gloves when he went to the garage sale too. That way he would not have to touch the envelope and leave any fingerprints on it.

He knew they had very sophisticated ways of getting prints from things now. He would need to be careful.

The letter finished left him with the overwhelming desire to sleep. He did so with the letter close by. It made him feel as though he was next to Reece. He slept and dreamed of the two of them together holding each other, professing their love. The alarm rudely awoke him.

Chapter Twenty-Four

CeCe and Reece got to the Community Center early so they could set up the coffee and baked goods. CeCe was going to donate the profits to the charity that they were working for.

Austin arrived shortly after the ladies. He and Tucker were still moving furniture and such to Mrs. James's liking. That would be their main duty during the sale, and it was certainly enough to keep them busy.

It looked as though the weather was going to cooperate with them. It was a bright and shiny December morning. It was less than a week until Christmas, so everyone in town was in the shopping mood. This was a good time to hold the sale.

CeCe hadn't quite figured out what to give to Austin for Christmas. She had all of her other shopping done. She had seen a painting of the valley behind her house when she was walking by the art gallery earlier in the week; he really did like the view they had seen last night. Maybe that's what she would give him.

The thought of last night sent a chill through her body. As she remembered the long and sensuous kiss, she could feel the growing tightness in her lower abdomen. She had never felt this way with anyone else. He had a strange effect on her, not that she didn't like it.

What was it about Austin that was different than all those other men out there? He certainly didn't have to wait for her. There were plenty of women out there that would jump at a chance to fall into his bed. Was she crazy? No. She had made a commitment to herself and she was going to stick by it. It was a matter of morality.

She had never met anyone before that challenged that commitment. This wasn't going to be easy, but Austin seemed to understand. She really loved being with him. She always felt so safe and secure. A customer brought CeCe back to her duty.

"Hello?"

"Oh, I'm sorry, I was somewhere else. Dr. Baldwin, what can I get for you?"

"CeCe, you looked so peaceful I hated to interrupt. It was almost like I was intruding on a private moment," Dr. Baldwin commented as he tucked his glove-covered hands into his jacket.

"I was just daydreaming. Now, what can I get for you?"

"I understand you have a new ingredient in those famous chocolate chip cookies of yours, how about one of them and a large coffee, please. How is Nitro doing?"

"He's great. Ruth said you told her the paw looked well. I'm still putting the ointment on it. I only have about a dozen of these cookies. Looks like I should have made more of them. Austin said they would go fast."

"CeCe, anything you makes goes fast. It's a good thing I don't visit your shop everyday, or else I would have to buy a whole new wardrobe!"

"I doubt that- you have enough of a work out lifting and wrestling around with the animals you tend to all day."

"That's true." Dr. Baldwin reached into his pocket and paid CeCe. He looked troubled.

"Is there something wrong?"

"I just seemed to have misplaced my money clip is all. It was my grandfather's and I don't want to lose it. I had it the other evening." He looked off, wrinkling his brow. "Oh well, I'm sure I will find it at home or in the office. Keep the change, CeCe, since it all goes to charity. It is awfully nice of you to do this and give your time the rest of the day."

"My pleasure. It benefits the children, and I do know that one hundred percent of it goes to them."

"Thanks, CeCe. I'm going to look around and find some bargains. I will probably end up buying back the same things I donated. You know how that goes." He waved as he walked away.

It didn't take long for CeCe to sell out all of her baked goods and coffee. She then went and helped Reece with the checking out.

Throughout the day CeCe would catch glimpses of Austin. She watched his strong muscles stretch and flex as he moved things. Austin was also keeping an eye on CeCe. He would watch her interact with the customers and flash her bright smile. Everyone who walked away from her was always smiling broadly. CeCe had a way with people. She made them feel good about themselves. He had to turn away when she would bend down to retrieve a shopping bag. The sight of her firm round bottom just made his body jump to attention. This was not the place for these thoughts. He could very easily embarrass himself. Instead, he concentrated on the moving.

Tom Dancer came by the counter with a few items. CeCe thanked him again for the great job he had done.

Mason came, too. He had indeed found some cross-country equipment to purchase. He said that he really enjoyed being outdoors and was going to make a point of trying more sports.

Gino came by and dropped off a copy of his CD that he and the band had produced. He wanted to get CeCe and Reece's opinions. He had also found a guitar. It was painted over, but he was sure that he had found a real treasure. He said if not, it would be good to practice with. He liked the way it sounded.

Gino was gifted; they were sure he could make just about anything sound good.

Mrs. James came by to see how they were doing. She stopped by the office equipment and admired the typewriters. She picked up one and struggled with it. Austin came by to help her.

"I just have to have this. I sold one about two years ago at this sale and could have kicked myself. I missed having it. I know everyone uses computers today, but I'm too old to learn. Besides, this is what I learned on way back when. The keys just move so gracefully. The appearance on paper is much bolder than a printer quality."

Reece got to thinking. "When was it that you sold the typewriter, Mrs. James?"

"Why, I think it was two years ago, or was it three? My son came by and said I needed to get rid of some of the junk in the house."

"You wouldn't know who bought it, would you?" Reece asked her

"Not off the top of my head, but we keep the same kind of records that you are currently keeping now. We recorded what items were purchased, the amount, and by whom. I believe I have those records at home in my attic. Do you need them?"

"Well, I might. I would love to come by and pick them up some time to go through them. That is, if you don't mind. I would be sure to keep them in order."

"Darling, I know you would be very careful with them, but if you are looking for a particular item that was sold, why you could be there until the hereafter. It would be like looking for a needle in a haystack. But I'm not the one to tell you how to spend your time. You come by anytime." Mrs. James paid for her purchases and Austin followed her to her car to load the items.

"Reece, are you thinking what I'm thinking? Maybe the typewriter she donated is the same as the one the letters are being typed on," CeCe said excitedly.

"That's just what I was thinking." Reece said.

~ ~ ~

It hadn't been easy, but he succeeded in getting the letter into Reeces jacket pocket. It was hanging on the coat rack with the rest of the coats from the volunteers.

He was just about ready to put it in the jacket when Austin came by carrying a typewriter for Mrs. James. It almost looked like the one he had gotten at the sale a few years ago.

Austin and Mrs. James said hello. He had to pretend that he was just putting his coat on. He had the hanger in his hand, which should help back up his story if anyone asked.

He hadn't wanted the letter to fall out, so he took Reece's jacket off the hanger and put the envelope in the inside jacket pocket. He felt that it was secure since he had zipped it shut.

He picked up his purchases and walked out to his truck. He had to be more careful.

Chapter Twenty-Five

The sale had been a huge success. Everyone helped clean up, and then went and had some dinner together. Mrs. James was very pleased and felt that they were going to be able to help the children in the community a great deal. She was very much right.

Reece and CeCe had picked up a few great bargains themselves. Reece found a wonderful old cloak that made her look very Gothic. She insisted on wearing it home that evening. Everyone agreed that she looked very dramatic in it.

The rest of the week passed by very quickly, Ruth had insisted that CeCe, Reece, and, of course, Nitro come out to the ranch for Christmas dinner. It had been decided that they would all go to the lake and skate after dinner; that is, if they could move after eating Ruth's wonderful cooking.

CeCe and Reece arrived early in order to help prepare the feast. They had their arms loaded with gifts.

"Where would you like us to put these, Ruth?" CeCe asked.

"Right under the tree, isn't it beautiful? Austin and Tucker went out and got it off the ranch and pulled it back behind the horses."

"It sure is beautiful. It's almost as if it were grown to be a Christmas tree," CeCe said as she put the gifts down along with the others.

"Speaking of the two devils, where are they?" asked CeCe.

"There was a break in the fence and they had to go fix it." Ruth told them. "There's never any rest for the wicked, my mama always used to say. I guess if they had to go out there on Christmas, they must be wicked". They all had a big laugh at that.

"It was very nice to see so many people in church today, wasn't it, Ruth?" Reece asked as she put her apron on.

"I think they are all thinking that if they go on Christmas then they're good for the rest of the year. Maybe they're all right. I do enjoy talking with everyone. Sometimes it's the only place you get to see some of those folks." Ruth was pulling out bowls and pans.

"Now Reece, if I remember correctly, you don't much like cooking." Ruth commented.

Reece protested. "I never said I don't like cooking, it's just that I have such good friends to do most of it for me."

"That's all right. I have other things for you to do. First, you can fix us all a glass of that eggnog. Then the table needs to be set with the good linens and china. I don't let those men eat off of the good china unless it's a special occasion or holiday. They just don't know how to treat the finer things in life." Ruth handed Reece the linens.

Austin and Tucker came in ringing bells and singing carols.

"Sounds like you two hit the eggnog a bit before you went out." CeCe walked into the great room when she heard them coming.

"Who needs eggnog, madam? We are just in the Christmas spirit." Austin came over and moved CeCe under the mistletoe that was hanging in the door. "And look what's above you. We must all comply to the traditions of Christmas." Austin lifted CeCe's chin up and kissed her long and hard.

"Hey, you can't have all the fun!" Tucker chimed in. "It's my turn. Then come Reece and Ruth. Nitro and Austin, you two can be exempt."

While they were waiting for dinner, the group sat in front of the fireplace and exchanged gifts. Austin opened the two things that CeCe had bought for him. The first was the painting she had seen in the gallery.

"CeCe, this is great! It's the valley behind your house. It will go wonderfully in this room here." Austin stood and held it on the wall he was thinking about hanging it on.

"That's what I thought. But I think it'll look much better here above the sofa." CeCe stood and walked Austin over to that wall. "What do you think?" she asked.

"I think you're right." Austin replied.

"Open the other one," Reece urged him. "It's a joint gift from CeCe and me."

Austin opened the package. It was a framed collage of pictures taken at the football game. There was a great picture of Austin and Angie standing together smiling at the camera, another with Austin and Willy. Willy had his huge arm over Austin's shoulder and he was smiling broadly.

The center of the picture had Reece, CeCe, Austin, and Angie all standing there right on the field of Mile High Stadium. The scoreboard was reflected in the back with Denver's winning score.

Austin was overwhelmed. The photography was excellent. He hadn't even realized that CeCe was taking these pictures. He had known she had her camera with her and that they had all had posed for the center picture, but the rest was a surprise.

"Well?" CeCe asked.

"Don't you like it, Austin? CeCe and I thought it would remind you of the great time we had at the game." Reece looked concerned.

"I absolutely love it!" he exclaimed. "It is the most wonderful gift I have ever been given."

Austin reached over and hugged Reece, then CeCe. "Thank you so much. You don't know what this means to me."

Ruth wiped her eyes with her handkerchief. "This is supposed to be a happy time, and look at me. I cry at the drop of a hat."

"That's what makes you Ruth," Tucker said as he came over and hugged her.

Austin gave out his gifts too. He held on to CeCe's until the very end.

CeCe opened it tentatively. It was heavy. Inside the packaging was the most beautiful jewelry box she had ever seen. The wood was exquisite. CeCe lifted it out of the box and carefully examined it. "Where did you ever find such a treasure? And what kind of wood is this, Austin?"

"It's Koa wood. It's a native hard wood of Kauai. I had some of the wood shipped back here so I could make some things out of it. I tinker around with wood, and out came this. When it was finished, I thought it was perfect for you. I know you said you lost the one your grandmother gave you in the fire, so there you have it. Do you like it?"

CeCe was speechless. She had always admired people's ability to create wonderful things out of wood, but she never thought that she would have something like this given to her, let alone made for her.

"Austin, it's beautiful. You are very gifted to be able to make this. I would like to see some of the other things you have made. Thank you very much." CeCe rubbed her hand over the wood and thought to herself that she would treasure it forever.

Ruth was really flustered now. "It's time for dinner everyone. Let's go and eat before I start crying again!"

Austin stood and helped CeCe and Reece up out of their chairs. "I once told you I had other talents, Ms. Wellington. You thought that I was just kidding, didn't you?" Austin laughed.

Dinner was wonderful. They sat around and talked for awhile after they had cleaned up the dishes. CeCe was anxious to go skating.

"Is anybody up for some skating? I would love to go, and we haven't had a chance to get out this year. Besides, we can work off some of those calories we just ate."

"I'll only go if you make some hot chocolate to take along, CeCe," said Reece.

Ruth was adamant that they weren't going to get her out on the ice. "I can just see it now, me all spread over the ice cold and wet; I don't think so. I will go along as moral support. I'll even be the keeper of the thermos."

Everyone thought that would be a great idea.

Tucker stood and said, "I'm going to put on some warmer clothes. It's been awhile since I've been out there and I guarantee you that I will be spending some time on my behind."

CeCe and Reece drove over by themselves, and Austin, Tucker, and Ruth followed behind in Austin's truck.

The ice looked very inviting. Someone had added wood to the perpetual bonfire. Ruth settled herself down right on the bench at the edge of the ice. She had come prepared with a warm blanket to cushion the bench and one to wrap around her already amply clothed body. She wasn't going to get cold.

"Austin, where did you get the skates?" CeCe asked.

"I bought them at the sale. They were barely used, and I figured I could get the blades under me and then see if I needed to bother buying a new pair."

"They look good to me. Now, you did say you have done this before, didn't you?" CeCe teased.

"Yes, but it was a very long time ago." Austin stood and reached out for CeCe's hand. "Would you let me have the honor of your company on the ice?"

CeCe was skating away from him as she turned and hollered, "If you can meet me on the other side of the lake without falling, then I will trust you to guide me around. Deal?"

Austin tested his balance on the skates and was soon feeling very comfortable on them. He glided alongside of CeCe and said, "Well, is this good enough or do I have to do a triple, double toe loop?"

CeCe laughed and was very impressed. "No fair, you were born with natural ability. I had to learn the hard way, with cuts and bruises." She reached out her hand for Austin, but instead he reached his arm around her waist and moved her around with him.

On the third time around, they caught up with Tucker and Reece. Reece was helping steady Tucker. They all skated over to Ruth.

"Let me pour you all some of this hot chocolate." Ruth was ready with the cups in no time.

Reece dripped some of the hot liquid on her glove- she wanted to wipe it away before it seeped through the material. She reached into her pocket to get a tissue, but came up empty. Then she remembered she always carried some extras just in case in her inside jacket pocket.

Reece removed her glove and reached inside the pocket. As she did so, she felt an envelope. What could that be? Had she put a bill or some other important envelope in there and forgotten about it?

Reece pulled it out, but before she even saw the envelope, she knew what it was. She could feel the roughness of the paper between her fingertips.

She was right; it was another letter, just like the rest.

CeCe watched as Reece pulled the letter out. "Reece, where did that come from?"

"I just found it in my jacket. I don't know how it got there," she responded.

Austin, Tucker, and Ruth just stared at it.

Ruth stood up and put her arm around Reece. "Sit right here, dear. What do you want to do? Do you want to open it?"

Reece handed the letter to Ruth. "Here, you read it. Aloud, please."

Ruth opened the letter and began to read. "The moon is shining bright and clear. It reminds me…" She continued on until the end. "Stay beautiful and warm for now. Love, Me."

"How can someone be so destructive and break into the office, yet write something like that?" Reece asked, shaking her head.

Tucker reached for the letter. "Why, he doesn't even mention the office and why he did such a thing."

"Reece, when do you think you got this, and where? I'm guessing it was written between Monday and Friday, just by the mention of the full moon. Think, Reece, when was the last time you wore this jacket?" CeCe urged her.

"I wore it cross-country skiing. Then I wore it to the garage sale.

I wore it the next day to the office; oh wait, I didn't. I bought the cloak at the sale, and I wore it home. I have been wearing it ever since until today. I figured we were going to go skating and I would need it," Reece said.

"Well, I think you can rule out the cross-country skiing trip. It was just you, Mason, Austin, and I. I do remember you wore it to the sale. Where did you hang it?" CeCe asked.

"I hung it just inside the door on the coat rack, along with everyone else's. That means that whoever put it there did so at the sale. They also had to search through the jackets and other coats to find mine. That had to be when it was put there. I had just gotten it back from the cleaner's the day before. I always put tissue in that pocket to have when I need it. I remember putting a package in there the morning of the sale. There was no letter there then, and I haven't worn it again until today." Reece was obviously upset.

Austin took the letter from Tucker. "I think we need to get this to the sheriff's office, Reece. Maybe they can pick something up from it. Would you like for me to take it over?"

"I would just as soon that I don't see any more of these letters. If you would drop it off to the police that would be great." Reece responded appreciatively. "Now, let's go back out and do some more skating. I don't want this to ruin my, nor anybody else's, day. Last one to the other side has to stoke the fire when we get back!" With that, Reece was off like a shot.

Tucker, Austin, and CeCe followed behind. Austin wasn't about to let Tucker be the last one there, so he lagged behind the others.

They all caught up to Reece, and CeCe hugged her. "Reece, this has got to stop. Why, he even says so in his letters. He keeps saying how it isn't the right time, but that it will be soon. That indicates to me that he is getting ready to expose himself."

"Are you nuts, CeCe?" Reece asked her. "The guy broke into my house and office, and actually did some damage at the office. Do you really think he is going to turn himself in? I don't think so. I think he likes stringing me along. Well, I'm tired of it. I may even write an article in the paper about it, and tell him how I feel. That should set him straight. Really, I am just mad now. I don't fear for my life. There is nothing there to make me believe that this guy has enough guts to do anything other than write."

"I guess you're right. Maybe the letter in the paper would be a good thing," CeCe agreed.

"Now, let's play. I'm tired of the whole thing." With that, Reece grabbed Austin's arm and skated away with him.

CeCe and Tucker skated behind them. They were all pretty tired after about an hour and a half. Ruth was waving at them to come back to her.

"I think it's time to pack up and go back. I have some great pie for us to munch on. I always like watching the television on Christmas. They have some of those great movies on, like 'It's a Wonderful Life'. Do you like that movie?" Ruth asked, not to anyone in particular.

It was a resounding yes. They all agreed that it was time to head back.

Chapter Twenty-Six

It had been a festive holiday season, with the exception of the letter Reece had received. Everyone had settled back into his or her normal routine. Reece had decided to have Tom Dancer make her a fence around the back of the house and a gate for the back door to the office.

Tom was thrilled to get the work, and had started on a design right away. As promised, Gino had had his first CD recorded and was giving copies away to all of his friends. CeCe and Reece thought it was very good.

There was something interesting about some of the lyrics that he had in a few of the songs. It made the two of them wonder if he might be the author of the letters. He made references to love and waiting for the right time. Another reference that made them wonder was to the pureness of the snow on the Rocky Mountains.

Was it possible that Gino could be the one? He did seem to have some very strong feelings about Reece. Everything seemed to be going so well for him. CeCe decided that she would confront him and see how he responded.

Reece did publish an editorial in the paper. It was very vague. She never let on that she was being sent letters; she didn't want to start a whole new set of them. Everyone agreed that if she were go public about the letters, she might set off a copycat. That was the last thing she wanted to do. Reece thought that if she let him think that she was enjoying the letters and that she would like to hear from him in person, she might just get him to bite the bait.

The article read:

> *Did you ever have something happen to you or have you ever received something that made you stop and think? I know the answer to that question is an obvious YES. There is always*

that question 'What is this all about'? I have just asked myself that question. I haven't come up with an answer that is satisfactory. I have been the recipient of some beautiful work lately, which has gotten me to thinking. I have never been able to understand why someone would do such a thing and not take credit for it. Oh yes, there is the case for wanting to stay anonymous, but those circumstances are usually left for when large sums of money have been donated. This is not that sort of circumstance. The type of thing I'm talking about when a person should be proud of the work they have produced, and would want the receiver of that work to know from whom it came from and why they were chosen to be the recipient of it.

So, if you have any answers for me or wish to share your experiences with this editor, please e-mail or phone me at the numbers listed below.

I am fascinated by how the creative mind works.

There wasn't a response, but Reece wasn't surprised. She was just hoping, but really thought it nothing more than a shot in the dark.

CeCe and Reece had gone through Mrs. James's records one evening, but they proved to be of no use to them. The records that had names on them were from the people who used credit cards or paid by check. There were many that paid by cash and didn't ask for a receipt.

There were no records of the sale of the typewriter Mrs. James had sold. The only mention was on what date she had donated. It was two years ago. Still, it had been worth a try.

Dr. Baldwin had given Nitro a clean bill of health. Dr. Baldwin still seemed very tired and not quite himself these last few weeks. Ruth thought it was due to the fact that he was working too hard.

CeCe and Reece were very excited. The whole month had passed by so quickly and now they were just a few days away from going on their trip to Hawaii. Austin was leaving just a few days behind them. He couldn't be much help with their stay on Maui, but was all set to show them Kauai.

Finally, the day came. Neither CeCe nor Reece could contain their excitement. This was going to be a wonderful change of pace. Mason came by to see them off. He said, "I wish I could get away. I would love to go with the two of you. I have traveled a lot, but never to the Hawaiian Islands."

Reece was becoming very fond of Mason. He was very sympathetic about the letters and told her he thought that it would be great for her to get away from the valley.

CeCe could see how he could grow on you. Mason hadn't made a good first impression with her, but as she spent more time with him and got to know him better, she felt better about Reece being involved with him. There still was something there, however, that made CeCe think he wasn't Mr. Right for Reece.

Austin drove them to the airport, but not before CeCe gave a whole list of things to Ruth concerning Nitro. "I swear, this must be worse than being a mother. I can't imagine how I would have to go through more instructions with a child that I do with this dog!"

Ruth laughed. "CeCe, this dog is treated as well as most children. Honey, he is your child."

"I guess you're right, Ruth. He's very dependent on me and me on him. Now, are you sure you have all the telephone numbers you need? Promise me you won't work too hard at the coffee shop. I know that Mrs. Thomerson is anxious to work. She has had a tough time of it since she lost her husband last year. As a matter of fact, when she is working, Tom Dancer comes by and sits in the area that she works. I think there may be the makings of a romance there." CeCe smiled as she fussed over Nitro.

"Just get on out of here," Ruth said. "I will make sure not to work too hard, and as far as Nitro goes, he keeps Tucker and me company. I will be sure to let Mrs. Thomerson work as much as she wants. You two just promise to have a good time. I will expect a lei when you come back." She hugged the two of them and shooed them toward the car.

"Aloha!" CeCe hollered to her. "I'll call you when we get in."

"Just remember that there is a three hour time difference, CeCe," Austin told her as he started the car. "Ruth could be real cranky if you wake her up at mid-night."

"I'll remember that," CeCe said as she waved out the window to the diminishing figures of Ruth and Nitro.

Chapter Twenty-Seven

The flight was uneventful, and they were lucky to have a direct connection from Los Angeles into Maui. As they were approaching the islands, the pilot came over the loudspeaker and pointed out the different islands to them. Even from the sky, the landscape and colors were beautiful. They couldn't wait to land and start their tropical holiday.

As CeCe stepped off the plane, the warm tropical breeze surrounded her. They were greeted with leis of fragrant flowers. This truly was heaven. Reece and CeCe were both anxious to get their luggage, rental car, and head for the hotel. It had been a long trip and they were ready to try a tropical cocktail and sit in the sun.

The directions to the hotel were easy, thank goodness, because they were both having a hard time not looking at everything they passed.

The women were staying in a beautiful hotel in West Maui. As they checked in, they were greeted with another lei, then led to their room. The accommodations were exquisite. There was warm dark wood everywhere. It appeared to be the same wood that from which Austin had made the jewelry box. CeCe knew all along that this was how everything would look to her.

Both CeCe and Reece were very anxious to unpack, put their swimsuits on, and enjoy the weather. As they were unpacking, there was a knock on the door. "Bellman," a male voice called out from behind the closed door.

"Just a minute," CeCe answered.

CeCe walked to the door and opened it.

"I have a delivery for you, Ms. Wellington." The bellman was holding a very large tropical flower arrangement. "Where would you like me to put this for you?"

CeCe looked around. "How about on the table there by the

sliding glass door? They are beautiful. Who could they be from?" she wondered aloud.

The bellman held out a card and turned to leave. "Have a wonderful stay."

"Wait just a moment," CeCe said. She walked over the sofa and picked up her handbag. "Thank you for the delivery." She handed the bellman a tip and closed the door behind him.

"What the heck!" Reece had just walked out of the dressing bedroom. "This is a great hotel. The room is so beautiful and big, and then they send you these wonderful flowers." Reece walked over and looked at the arrangement.

CeCe was opening the envelope. She smiled a huge smile as she read the card.

> *'Birds of Paradise, Gardenias and such*
> *I thought these flowers would be a nice touch*
> *Remember to wear sunscreen and enjoy the sun*
> *Although you will enjoy Maui*
> *Kauai is where you will have the real fun*
> *Welcome to Paradise!*
> *See you in a week,*
> *Hugs and kisses, Austin'*

"What are you smiling about, CeCe?" Reece walked over to her and lifted the card out of her hand. "Oh, I see, it isn't from the hotel. I was giving them the credit and not Austin. Wow, that is two times he has sent you flowers. He must know how much you love them."

"I think it was really sweet of him to welcome us to the islands," CeCe said as she walked over and admired the flowers more closely. "Have you ever seen or smelled anything so exotic in your life? These are beautiful."

"I'll say so. The guy really knows how to welcome somebody. I know that flowers have a sort of hypnotic effect on you, but would you like to go and check out the pool and the sun?" Reece was standing by the window looking out onto the pool and the ocean.

"You know, Reece, I really don't feel like wearing this same old swimsuit of mine. Would you mind going with me to that little boutique we walked by on the way to our room? They had some beautiful suits in the window." CeCe was thinking about the new suit for the next leg of her trip, and wanted to have a nice one when she was in Kauai and they all went to the beach together.

"Do you think you really have to ask me if I want to go and buy a new suit, or help you pick one out? I'm game. Let me grab my bag and we'll go." Reece was smiling.

CeCe chose a few suits to try on. The sales clerk handed her two others that she wouldn't have chosen for herself. "Try them, they will go beautifully with you hair and skin tone. The others you chose are nice, but these will really make heads turn," said the salesclerk as she showed CeCe to a dressing room.

CeCe tried one of the two suits the clerk had chosen for her first. It was a bit smaller than she would normally wear, but she was in Hawaii, and they were beautiful tropical prints.

"CeCe, come on out and let me see you in one of those suits," Reece called out to her.

"I'm a little afraid to walk out of here," CeCe replied from behind the door of the dressing room. "I may get arrested for parading around half naked."

CeCe opened the door and walked out. The clerk had been right. The colors made CeCe look as though she had already spent a few weeks in the sun. She was gorgeous.

"Wow!" Reece exclaimed. "If you buy that, CeCe, we'll be surrounded by every eligible man on this island and then some. You look great."

"You don't think it is too much? I mean, too skimpy?" CeCe turned to look in the mirror.

"No way. You're beautiful. It's perfect for you. How about trying the others on and seeing if they look as good," Reece encouraged CeCe.

CeCe went back in and changed into the other suit that the clerk had picked out for her. Reece and the clerk were equally impressed with the second suit.

"I think you should buy them both, CeCe." Reece smiled. "Just wait until Austin gets a look at you in either one of those suits. If he can't keep his eyes off of you now, they will be glued to you when you wear these."

"All right, I will take them both," CeCe surprised herself.

They spent another twenty minutes in the store purchasing some essentials and accessories, and then headed to the pool area.

The grounds were incredible. They led one to believe one was in a tropical rain forest. CeCe and Reece found an area they liked and placed their towels there.

"It's time to try out this pool!" Reece was already lowering her body into the water when CeCe turned around.

"This looks like something from a movie set. We won't even have to get out of the water to get that cocktail, Reece. Look, there is a bar we can swim right up to," CeCe said as she to entered the pool.

"Well, what are we waiting for? I'm thirsty, CeCe, let's go and see what they have."

They swam toward the bar, all the while taking in the incredible scene. They swam past a cascading waterfall with a little hidden grotto behind it. There was a couple sitting behind it, hugging and kissing one another. This gave CeCe a little pang. She could imagine herself and Austin doing the same.

They quickly came to the swim-up cocktail bar, which brought CeCe out of her reverie.

"What looks good, CeCe?" Reece asked her.

"I don't know. What is that drink there, the one with the layer of white and red?" CeCe asked the bartender.

"That's a Lava Flow. It's very good. It contains coconut milk, rum, blended strawberries and some other secret ingredients. They're addictive, I'll warn you." The bartender was scooping ice into the blender as he spoke to them. "Would you like one?"

"Why not?" Was the response from both ladies. The bartender expertly prepared the drink. When the drinks were finished, both CeCe and Reece raised their glasses for a toast.

"Two raffle tickets, good fortune, and most of all great friends!" CeCe raised her glass and clinked it to Reece's as she spoke.

"I'll second that," said Reece.

They both loved the drink. It was cool and refreshing. Reece couldn't believe it had alcohol in it and had to ask the bartender, "Are you sure this has alcohol in it?"

"Yes, it does. I told you they could be addictive, and that is part of the reason. They taste sooo good and you want to have more. But watch out; they'll catch up with you."

CeCe and Reece finished the drink and swam back to where they had set their towels down. They got out and decided that they needed to experience the ocean. CeCe had never seen such blue water. It was every bit as beautiful as the travel logs had described.

It was a short time before several handsome young men surrounded them. One in particular offered to give them some surfing lessons, to which they both agreed. They set up a time to meet him the next day.

Before they knew it, the time was getting late. The sun was slowly moving down in the sky. It was time to go back to the room and get cleaned up and ready to go out for dinner.

"I told you that if you wore that swimsuit we would have men swarming around us, didn't I?" Reece asked.

"Reece, it wasn't only me they were talking to. Everywhere you go, men pay attention to you. I must admit it was fun," CeCe responded with a grin.

"CeCe!" Reece exclaimed. "It must have been the cocktail that loosened you up. I haven't seen you this relaxed and ready to experience new things in a long, long time."

"Cut it out, Reece. I'm having a great time so far, and I just know it is going to get even better. Now, let's get ready for some dinner. I'm starved. I was told about a great restaurant not too far from here where we could sit at the water's edge and watch the sunset. They are supposed to be pretty spectacular, so we should remember to take our camera." CeCe was already walking into the shower as she spoke.

CeCe had been informed correctly. The restaurant was great: the food and atmosphere were just what they needed to convince them that they were not dreaming, but were really there in Hawaii.

The long travel day had begun to catch up to Reece and CeCe. They paid the dinner check and left. It wasn't more than a few minutes before both of them fell fast asleep.

CeCe dreamed of wonderful waterfalls and romance. Funny thing was, Austin was always there. Even after all of the attention they had received today on the beach, Austin still crept into her mind and her dreams.

They both awoke very early, still being on Colorado time.

"CeCe, I think this will be a great time for us to get our daily run in. What do you think?" Reece sat on the edge of the bed stretching.

"I think that's exactly what we should do. We need to try and get on Hawaii time, though. From what I understand, it takes a few days. I don't relish the thought of going back and having to adjust that way."

"Now, don't start that. We have only been here since yesterday. We have a whole week ahead of us here, and another on Kauai."

CeCe was pulling on her jogging clothes as she turned to talk to Reece. "Reece, I find myself thinking about Kauai every few minutes. Why do you think that is? I mean when it is so beautiful here and so much to see."

"Silly. It's because of Austin. I know you aren't ready to admit it, but you are head over heels in love with him and he with you. I am very anxious to get there myself. I'm looking forward to seeing Angie again." Reece finished putting her shoes on.

"But I thought that you were pretty involved with Mason."

"I like Mason, but I don't think it will go any further than that. He does seem to want more from the relationship than I do, but I'm giving myself time to look at all of my options. I like the one with Angie. He and I hit it off just right. We'll see how things go next week. I think I will have a better idea then."

"I like that thought. You two look great together. Your personalities certainly click. I do really like Austin, but I too am giving it time. Now lets get going."

The week passed by very quickly. Both CeCe and Reece enjoyed the surfing. Because they were beginners, they learned in Lahaina Harbor where the waves are very gentle. Neither of them was up for some of the more advanced areas of Maui like Hookipa Beach Park or Honolua Bay. They would stick to the much smaller and safer areas for the rookies.

They really enjoyed the history of the little whaling town of Lahaina. It's history was very interesting and dated back to when it was Hawaii's capital in the 1800's. Front Street was the most interesting part of this town; it put you right back in time.

They really enjoyed the town of Paia. They were able to watch the windsurfers in abundance here. The town made them think of a couple of places in Colorado. It was a town where hippies came in the 60's and became entrepreneurs.

The trip up to Hana was well worth it. They saw many of different views and the further they went the more they felt like they were experiencing the real everyday life of the Hawaiian people.

All in all, the week had passed by much too quickly. Both of them had been told that it would happen, but until the end of their stay they hadn't realized it.

The vacation wasn't over yet; just a portion of it. CeCe and Reece both thought that the best was yet to come.

After reading the travel logs, CeCe had decided that if she had to choose only one island it would have been Kauai. This may have been influenced by Austin's description of the island- CeCe felt that she had somehow already experienced it.

Reece and CeCe packed their things and checked out of the hotel. They did have time to go to one of their favorite restaurants on the island for lunch before getting on the plane.

"Mama's" wasn't too far from the airport. The food was delicious, but they had to have a piece of Mama's famous coconut banana cream pie before leaving.

Full and content, the two of them boarded the plane for the flight to Kauai. CeCe had butterflies in her stomach and she knew they weren't from the flight. The pilot was announcing their approach to Kauai.

As they approached the island, the beauty and splendor was evident even from far above the ground. The beaches were white, while the seas were an unbelievable color of blue. The colors of the foliage were every shade of green imaginable, and then some.

The island appeared to be circular and to rise out of the water into a cone shape. They learned that it was the oldest and most northern of the main Hawaiian Islands.

CeCe was telling Reece about the island. "The island is home of the wettest spot on earth, Mount Waialeale. The name means 'overflowing water'. It's in the central part of the island. There is a rain gauge on one of the trails. Rainfall measurements vary from four hundred and twenty-six to six hundred and twenty-four inches a year. That's more than fifty feet!" CeCe recited what she had read. "Mount Waialeale isn't that far from Austin's place as the crow flies, or in this case a rare tropical bird."

CeCe was anxious to go hiking on some of the trails in the area. From what she understood, it was one of the most recommended places on the island to hike.

The plane was landing now with a light mist coming down. It was typical for it to rain and then the sun to come out and create a rainbow out over the ocean.

CeCe and Reece walked into the terminal to claim their luggage. CeCe was going to go over and get the car while Reece sorted though the luggage. They had expected to meet up with Austin and Angie later in the evening, but they were already waiting for them.

Austin had two leis over his arm, waiting to greet them. "Aloha!" Austin said as he placed the leis over their heads. "Welcome to paradise."

"I thought you two were going to call us later so we could make dinner arrangements," CeCe said happily. "Not that I'm not glad to see you. The island is beautiful from the air- I can't wait to explore it."

"We thought we would come and help you find your way to your hotel, or maybe even talk you into giving up your luxury accommodations and stay with us." Angie smiled mischievously as he took Reece into his arms and hugged her.

Austin was having a hard enough time concentrating on the conversation at hand, let alone Angie throwing him in another direction with his inviting CeCe and Reece to stay with him.

He didn't believe that CeCe could be any more beautiful than she was the first day he had laid eyes on her, but there she was, proving him wrong.

The week on Maui had deepened her skin tone to a golden tan. Her hair had grown lighter as the result of the sun.

CeCe wore a simple little dress with a flower print. It was the same color blue as her eyes and the ocean that lay just beyond the runway. Austin could see that she wore very little under it. That caused him to grow even more excited. CeCe's comment brought him back to safer ground.

"Hey, what am I? Don't I get a hug from the star of the Pro

Bowl?" CeCe walked over to Angie and hugged him. "Or didn't you think we watched the game?"

"CeCe, do you really think I would leave you out? I was coming your way. I, of course, knew that you watched the game. I would expect nothing but that from such a devoted fan, of football, that is." Angie grinned at the two women.

"How did the Quarterback Competition go?" CeCe asked.

"It was great. This is the first year they've had it here on the island. It was very convenient, having it here right after the Pro Bowl. Austin even got to participate a little. I'll wait for it to air this summer so you can be surprised at the results." Angie told them.

"I wish we could have been here to watch the competition. I'm really beginning to like this football thing. I'm sure the players were very relaxed and would have been willing to talk to one very interested female reporter/editor. But on the other hand, I'm glad to see the both of you, for more than one reason. I'm going to get the luggage and CeCe is going to get the car. We both went overboard with the purchases, and our luggage is very heavy." Reece put on a southern drawl to play the part of a helpless female. "I do believe we will have to go to one of those mail places and have some of it shipped home."

Austin agreed that it would be best for CeCe to get the car while the three of them retrieved the luggage. This would also buy him some time to clear his mind. He didn't know how he was going to be able to keep his hands off of CeCe during her stay here, but he had made a promise and he intended to keep it.

After they had collected all of the luggage and loaded it into the car, Austin confirmed the location of their hotel. "You're staying on the South Shore, right?"

CeCe answered him. "Yes we are. How far is it from your place?"

"It's not that far; about an hour's drive or so. But it's a very enjoyable drive. The first time you go there, you want to make sure it is during the daylight hours, so we won't attempt it this evening.

We have made reservations for dinner not too far from your hotel. I hope that is all right. I mean, I hope you don't think we are trying to monopolize your time or anything like that." Austin could think of nothing more enjoyable than spending every minute of every day and night with CeCe.

"Are you kidding? We have been looking forward to this week the whole time. Not that we didn't enjoy Maui, it's just that we knew we were going to have you two here to help us enjoy this place." CeCe smiled, as she did, it created that stir again within Austin.

"Let's get going then, shall we? You two ladies will have time to get changed and cleaned up if you would like. Not that you have to. You look wonderful and the place we are going for dinner is very casual. Isn't that right, Austin?" Angie asked.

"Hmm? Oh yes. You two look great. The week in Maui made you both look like you live on the island full time. The restaurant is very casual. Always Aloha wear." Austin had to keep his mind on the conversation.

"Aloha wear?" Reece asked. "What is that?"

Angie opened the door to the car for her as he answered her. "Just what you and I have on. Now you two can follow us to your hotel. Don't be surprised at how slowly the traffic moves here. It's just the way of life. And I do envy the islanders for being able to live that life."

Chapter Twenty-Eight

The coffee shop had been busy, so Ruth was truly in need of using Mrs. Thomerson's help. Lilly was a very pretty lady. She was tiny with shiny black hair. Her eyes were deep black pools. She had always been thin, but grew even more so after her husband's death. Ruth was determined to change that.

She didn't deserve the treatment she had gotten from that bum of a husband. Everyone knew that he abused her badly. He would come home and take things out on her. Not very often did Ruth think it was a blessing when the good Lord took someone from this earth, but with Lilly's husband it was a relief.

He had gone into one of his rages and had a stroke. Not that Lilly thought it was a blessing, but she did find out that she didn't have to be afraid any more. And she liked working. She wasn't allowed to work or go very many places when her husband had been alive.

This particular morning had been very busy, but as if on cue, Tom Dancer walked in the door. His eyes darted around the room until he spotted Lilly.

Ruth greeted him, "Good morning, Tom. Would you like to sit at the counter this morning?"

"T-thanks, I think I will s-sit at the table. I have some p-papers I need to lay out and l-look at. Is that okay?" He asked Ruth.

"Suit yourself, Tom. I'll send Lilly over to get your order." Ruth went over to the coffee machine and mumbled to herself. "I'll be darned. He does look like he has a little crush on Lilly." It would be good for both of them. They were both so shy; they might need someone to help them out. Well, Ruth thought to herself, she could be that little cupid. She would have to see how things played out.

He walked to the table he usually sat at and waited patiently.

Lilly walked over to the table. "Good morning, Tom. What can

I get for you?"

Tom pretended to study the menu, when all along he knew it by heart. "Did Mrs. Ruth make some of her f-f-famous cinnamon rolls today?"

"She certainly did. Would you like one?"

"Yes, please, and a c-cup of coffee, too. Black, please." Tom answered her.

Lilly filled his order and sat at the table for a few minutes to chat with him. Lilly was very interested in the type of work that he did. Her father had been a farrier, and she used to go out and help him when she was growing up.

That was why it was so hard when she had gotten married and wasn't allowed to do any of those sorts of things any longer. She missed that and would like to be able to get involved in it again.

Lilly had to leave the table and wait on others, but she promised to talk to Tom some more about his work.

Several people had come into the shop to see if Ruth had heard from CeCe and Reece. She had talked to her last night before they left for Kauai.

Ruth was anxious for them to get to Kauai so they could spend some time with Austin and his friend. She still thought he should go by his given name. It was a very good strong name. Michael. Instead, Austin insisted he liked going by Angie. Guess you can't make people do things, but if she ever met him, she would call him Michael- that's what he looked like anyway. She had enjoyed the pictures they had brought back from the football game. Now she would be able to see some pictures of Hawaii.

CeCe and Reece both said they were having a wonderful time, and that the time was just flying by. CeCe said she missed everyone, and especially Nitro.

Ruth assured her that he was being a good boy and was enjoying following Tucker around the ranch. He was getting plenty of exercise.

Ruth warned her not to call again, "Just take lots of pictures and send a postcard."

CeCe agreed not to call, but knew it was going to be difficult. However, she hadn't planned on having such a wonderful time.

Chapter Twenty-Nine

The drive from the airport took about thirty minutes. CeCe thought that she should have let either Austin or Angie drive so that she and Reece could take everything in. This truly was magnificent country.

The mist had stopped and the sun was beginning to shine brightly. A closer look at the ocean didn't change its color or allure.

The morning run would have to be along the beach. CeCe couldn't get enough of the ocean. She guessed she always knew that deep within her there was a strong connection to the sea, she just needed to experience it to bring it to the forefront and to make it a reality for her.

She thought that Austin looked wonderful. He looked extremely relaxed. He, too, had spent some time in the sun. She had never seen him in anything other than his jeans. Not that that was all bad, but he had strong, long legs. He was dressed very causally, which was a good indication that they would not need to dress up for dinner.

When Austin placed the lei on her, she shivered at his touch. His hands were cool against her fully flushed skin. His hand had slid down her back when he pulled her close for a hug. The thin material of her dress wasn't much of a barrier between her body and his. CeCe could think of nothing more than the two of them lying close to one another on a deserted island.

Reece brought CeCe back when she spotted the hotel. "Wow, this is even more spectacular than the hotel we stayed in on Maui. The property sat directly on the ocean. When they got out of the car and stepped onto the grounds they could feel the spray of the ocean against their faces. The memories they would take home with them would last a very long time.

Their accommodations were again nothing short of spectacular. The lanai was spacious and looked out onto the ocean. Austin and

Angie had brought a bottle of champagne with them to start their 'official' vacation in Kauai.

As CeCe and Reece started unpacking their bags, Austin and Angie set the glasses they had brought with along with the champagne on the table on the lanai. Austin expertly opened the bottle and poured them each a glass.

"Ladies you need to come out and have a toast with us welcoming you to the island." Austin called into them. Reece and CeCe walked to the lanai and picked up a glass.

Angie began an obviously rehearsed toast. "Two more beautiful women mankind has never known."

Then it was Austin's turn. "Nor a better time or more fun these beauties will have ever been shown."

"So, to the good times and the better ones, too," Angie recited.

"Let the two of us now show you. Here's to a wonderful week in paradise." Austin raised his glass and they all touched them together.

Reece grimaced. "You must have stayed up all night thinking of that one."

"Are you criticizing our poetic ability?" Angie asked. "Because we could give you some of the others we came up with, but some of them were a little on the tasteless side."

"That's all right, we will refrain from hearing those, at least until another time. Now we only have a few things left to put away, then we will be ready for you to start as our official guides," CeCe said as she set the glass back down on the table and turned to go back into the room.

"Yes, we have plans to show you some things tonight. Would it be okay with you if we use your car? It will be more comfortable than my truck," Austin said.

"Fine with me. Just give us about five more minutes. We'll be ready then." CeCe smiled at them both.

They left the hotel and went a short distance to Spouting Horn.

Both CeCe and Reece had read about the blowhole in the travel log. The water was shooting straight up out of the lava tube making a noise that sounded like a roar. With the sun starting to set, the water spray was making a rainbow, creating a beautiful sight.

Austin explained about the legend of the Spouting Horn. "They say the noise is a howl coming from a sorrowful and enraged mo'o, or lizard. According to legend, the mo'o swam from Ni'ihau to Kauai crying over the loss of two of its sisters. He was crying so hard that he couldn't see where he was going, and he overshot his landing and was carried into the lava tube and was trapped forever. Now every time the horn spouts, we hear him moan."

Reece was totally into the legend theory. "Wow, it really does sound like a moan now that you said that. Is there any way to get him out?"

They all laughed. Angie took her by the arm and led her back to the car. "That is only one of the legends about spouting horn; there are others. I will have to tell you about them, and then maybe you can figure out the real one and help release him; that is if you decide you want to."

They drove to the restaurant and had a wonderful dinner. Austin and Angie walked them back to their room.

CeCe asked, "Would you like to take a walk, or will it get you home too late?"

"I'm game. How about you, Angie?"

"Are you kidding? Sleep never comes between a beautiful woman and me on a moonlit beach. Let's go."

They all walked along the beach and found some hammocks hanging along the way. Reece was the first to climb into one. "Look, it's big enough for two. Come on, Angie, I have always wanted to look at the stars from a hammock in the tropics."

Angie climbed into the hammock with Reece and said, "If I fall asleep here, Austin, just collect me in the morning."

CeCe and Austin laughed and walked off alone. Austin asked

about their stay on Maui, and CeCe told him all of the things they had done. They came upon another hammock and Austin asked if she would like to try it out.

"Sure, why not," CeCe said as she slipped her sandals off and climbed into the hammock. Austin followed behind.

They were there for about an hour talking when the light mist started to get heavier.

Austin moved to get off of the hammock and turned toward CeCe. "I think that's our cue to get out of here." As he turned, he couldn't resist the opportunity to kiss CeCe. She folded into his arms and returned the kiss. "I didn't know how much I missed seeing your smiling face until today when we met you at the airport. You look beautiful and relaxed. I hope you don't mind that I've planned a whole week's worth of activities and that they all include me."

CeCe was feeling very euphoric, but realized if they didn't leave soon she might allow something to happen that she wasn't ready for. "Austin, I don't mind at all. I love your company, and Angie's, for that matter. We just don't want to impose on you and make you think you have to spend all of your time with us. It's your vacation time, too."

"Don't be silly, CeCe. I don't get the opportunity to do these things much when I come here. All I seem to do is work on my place. I do enjoy that, but there needs to be time for play as well. I am anxious for you to see where I live on the island. We can go tomorrow if that's all right with you."

"We are at your mercy. We will let you lead us all around." With that, CeCe kissed Austin and brushed a curl away from his forehead. "Now, we better go before we get soaked. The mist has turned into a steady rain."

They left the hammock and walked back to where they had left Angie and Reece. They were not there. CeCe and Austin hurried now back to the room. That is where they found Angie and Reece.

Reece asked, "Where did you two disappear to? We decided it was going to rain harder and got up and came back here.

"We must have been under a bigger tree. We didn't feel the rain until just a few minutes ago," CeCe said.

"Likely story," Angie laughed.

"Well, ladies, it has been a pleasure, but we do have a little bit of a drive ahead of us, so until tomorrow." Austin hugged Reece, then CeCe. "Get a good night's sleep, and we'll meet you at the Kokee lodge at 9:00 am. We have a great hike to go on."

"Guess that means we'll be out of the morning run routine, then," Reece said.

"I don't think you need to worry about how much physical activity you'll get tomorrow. This is an awesome hike. Bring your camera and wear your hiking boots. See you bright and early." Angie, too, hugged them and the two men left.

Chapter Thirty

It had been about a week now since Reece and CeCe had left on their trip. He hadn't realized just how much he depended on seeing Reece. Even if it was for just a short time, or just to catch a glimpse of her here or there, he really treasured those moments. It allowed him to feel complete in some way, which too was difficult for him to understand.

He had seen the article in the paper that Reece had written; he knew that she was talking about the letters he had sent to her.

He had been right all along; she enjoyed getting them and even said it was beautiful work. Didn't she know that they were merely words without her inspiration? Only because of her, they were more that that. They came alive when he thought of her. She was the one who inspired him to put the words on the paper.

Ah, the paper. It was almost as sensuous as Reece herself. He thought of the paper, and remembering Reece's words made him want to write to her and let her know what she meant to him.

It had been a long time since he sat at the typewriter and wrote the words that crowded his mind. Now the urge was overwhelming. He would sit and let the feelings flow from his mind to his fingertips. The keys were cool and comforting as he began the letter.

Dearest Reece,

I am missing you terribly. I sit here by the fire and though it warms my body outwardly, it can do nothing for my heart or to stoke my internal fire that just the sight of you does for me.

I hope you are resting and enjoying the tropical weather. I am happy for you to get away, but ache at the thought of such a distance between us.

I dream of us being together someday on an island that in-

habits just you and me. The sun would warm your skin and I would protect you from its burning rays.

I can only imagine what it would feel like to carry you in my arms out into the surf and support you there as the waves lap sensuously over your body. Someday we will be able to experience these feelings together.

Things are just not the same here without you. Though the winter is cold, you have the ability to make it feel as though it were eternally spring. You radiate heat with your smile and warmth with your voice.

The days are long and dark without the thought of you in them. I know it won't be long before you are back and warming all of us again with your presence, but I am counting the days.

I am waiting for you to come back to me. I could feel the connection we had when I read your letter in the paper. I now know that you too feel the same, and will accept me when the time is right.

The distance is long between us now, but will soon be shortened when you return. I will wait and wait for however long it takes for me to be sure that it is the perfect time for us. For now, let your mind and body rest. I will see you in my dreams, walking arm in arm with me along that deserted beach with the sun setting at our backs. For though you are there and I am here, I am with you always and ever.

Dream the dream that I write about here, and know it will become a reality some day.

'Til I see you next, my darling Reece.

Love again and ever, Me.

There, he felt better. Whenever he communicated with Reece, whether it be through the typewriter or by just seeing her, it made him feel whole.

He had found that he only needed to wear the cumbersome gloves when he was handling the paper. He needed to take them off when his fingers touched the keys.

This time was better than the last. The feel he got from the keys was diminished when he wore the gloves. It didn't allow him to let his fingers just fly and find the words themselves. He just needed to remember to put them back on before removing the letter and sealing it in the envelope.

This time he felt it would be best if he just mailed the letter. Although he loved putting them in wonderful places for Reece, he just couldn't risk someone seeing him.

It was Valentine's Day, and he could drive to Loveland and have them postmark the letter from there. It was something that a lot of people did with their valentines- sending them to Loveland to have them postmarked.

It was still early enough in the day that if he left soon, he would be able to get there and back before too late. The drive would be worth it to have the letter postmarked from there; it would be very appropriate.

He removed the letter after struggling into the gloves. He rolled the envelope into the typewriter and tapped the keys until the complete address appeared.

He made a few calls to rearrange some appointments. That being taken care of, he placed the sealed letter on the seat next to him. This way he would be able to glance at Reece's name and feel that she was there sitting next to him as he drove down the road.

Chapter Thirty-One

CeCe dreamed of Austin all evening long. It wasn't a surprise to her that she was awake long before the alarm went off. Her dreams took her into a forbidden utopia where she allowed herself to be carried off by Austin and they experienced one another fully.

CeCe's body was flushed and aching when she awoke from her dream. She got up and quietly walked onto the lanai. The trade winds were blowing and cooled her skin. She wrapped her arms around herself only to remember how Austin had encompassed her in his strong arms in her dream.

She could see herself living here quietly with Austin. She wanted some of the same things he wanted. A quiet comfortable life filled with the sweet voices of children.

Did she believe in soul mates? And had she found hers? It felt right. She felt right with Austin.

It was different than the feelings she had had with Carlos. There was just an initial attraction there. Nothing like she felt now. It worried her that Austin might not feel the same. She didn't know if she would be able to take another disappointment in her life. She recognized a long time ago that the thing with Carlos had worked out for the best. And she needed to move away from those feelings and let the new ones take over and finish off the healing. She was sure that was what was happening to her now.

The sun was rising quickly now, and she wanted to swim a couple of laps before she got ready to go to Austin's place.

CeCe quietly walked back into the room. Reece asked her what time it was and CeCe told her to catch a few more minutes of sleep.

"I'm going down to the pool for a couple of laps to clear the cobwebs from my brain. When I come back we can go and have a light breakfast if you would like. Maybe we should make that a hearty breakfast, the way the guys talked about today's hike." CeCe talked to Reece as she wriggled into her swimsuit. "I'll see you in about forty-five minutes. I'll wake you when I get back. Sound good to you, Reece?"

"Great. Swim a couple of laps for me, would you? I just need a few more minutes of beauty rest, and then I'll be raring to go. See you soon." With that, Reece rolled over and appeared to fall back to sleep immediately.

CeCe walked to the pool and slipped into it. She swam effortlessly. It was just what she needed. The exercise energized her and she was glad for it.

The day was perfect: clear and warm. CeCe and Reece loaded a few things into the car. On the way out, they passed a farmer's market. They stopped and purchased a few things to take to Austin and to bring along on their hike.

The local farmers were there with all of their wares. The scent of gardenias was strong in the air as they passed a table of the flowers waiting to fill a room with their perfume. CeCe couldn't resist them and purchased the remaining bunch.

They drove to Waimea with the directions that Austin had given them. It was a beautiful drive, with the ocean alongside of them most of the way. They started their climb up into the canyon, but neither of them was prepared for what they were about to see.

The canyon had been described as the Grand Canyon of the Pacific. The Waimea Canyon was a sight to behold. They were glad that they had left with extra time to spare; they stopped a few times along the way.

The color of the canyon changed by the minute, and the waterfall along the back wall of the canyon was breathtaking. With every minute that went by and the sun peeking in and out of the clouds, shadows were created against the walls. This was unlike anything they had ever seen.

There were hues of the desert; pinks, purples, and reds. Then the tropical greens made one want to be an artist so its beauty could be captured onto the canvas.

The ocean and the island of Niihau were visible well below them as they continued to climb the steep road.

CeCe was sure that the camera lens would not do this beautiful spot justice, even though she continued to snap pictures, as everyone else was doing. She was sure that the memory of that morning drive would be embedded in her mind and she could visit it anytime she wished.

The drive further up the canyon into the Kokee State Park made them feel as though they were in the Rocky Mountains; all this with the exception of the tropical flowers and sounds that surrounded them. The vegetation changed to evergreens and ferns. There were wild fruit trees of many species around them. Austin had told them of how the local islanders came during plum season to gather the treasured fruit.

The weather was much cooler here at the altitude of 4200 feet; enough so that Reece was pulling out her sweater.

"Didn't ever expect that it would be this cool here, did you, CeCe?"

"No, but then again Austin did warn me that it was much cooler here. He even has a wood burner in his place. He uses it often in the winter."

"This should make good hiking weather."

"Have you ever seen anything so beautiful, Reece?"

"I have to say, I'm very impressed."

Both CeCe and Reece were in awe of their surroundings. This was one of the most beautiful and unique places on earth. They were happy to have the opportunity to experience it. CeCe thought to herself that it would be difficult to get much better than this.

The Kokee Lodge came into view just as they rounded the corner. It was in a beautiful setting. The lawn in front was carefully manicured. The car driving into the parking area caused the wild chickens to scatter. There was a whole brood of them running around, little chicks following behind their mother so as not to get lost. Once they got out of the car it was apparent that they were fed and unafraid of humans.

Austin and Angie were leaning against the truck and watched them drive in. There were those butterflies in CeCe's stomach again. Now she was sure they weren't from any plane, or the altitude. It was the sight of Austin and the way his jeans fit him.

CeCe and Reece walked toward them.

"Good morning. Did you enjoy the drive up?" Austin asked as he pushed himself off of the back of the truck.

"It was spectacular." CeCe was surprised that she had found her voice.

"We are ready and raring to go. CeCe got up early and swam some laps for both her and me. Now we are ready to take on the swamp."

"Good. Austin and I got up and chopped some wood this morning. As you can tell, it is a little cooler up here than it is down by the ocean," Angie added to the conservation.

"I think we will leave my truck here and pick it up on the way back. I thought we would have dinner at my place. I'm a simple cook, but with the fresh fish and vegetables available here on the island, it doesn't take an Emeril Lagasse to create a good-tasting dinner." Austin opened the door to CeCe's car.

Angie did the same on the other side for Reece. "I can attest to that, ladies. My coach is never disappointed when I come back from visiting with Austin. He not only cooks a good meal, but it is low in fat as well. Now, how can you beat that?"

"I don't think you can," CeCe said.

"Would you like for me to drive up to where we start the hike?" Austin asked CeCe.

"Sure, Reece and I will climb in the back. Have at it, Austin." CeCe smiled as she got in.

Austin had to avert his eyes away from CeCe's well-toned bottom in order to keep his composure.

They parked the car at the Puu O Kila Lookout. Austin pulled out his own backpack and put it on. The other three followed suit.

The hike up to the overlook was not far, and CeCe and Reece were anxious to look out over it. Austin wanted them to go a few feet further up on the trail to afford them a better look.

The beauty that awaited them was unbelievable.

"This is my favorite place on earth. The view from up here down to the ocean makes everything seem right," Austin explained as he looked out thoughtfully.

CeCe was breathless. The view could not be real. The lush green rugged mountains created by lava plunged directly into the ocean below. The contrast of the beautiful blue to the many shades of green was amazing. Mother Nature had given them a break in the weather to allow them to see the rugged Na Pali Coast.

The birds seemed to be suspended in space as they barely fluttered their wings to change their direction.

CeCe was mesmerized and could see why Austin spoke of this view so passionately. She had never seen anything so beautiful in her life.

"Mauna join the Kai," Austin whispered.

CeCe barely heard the words Austin spoke, but the beauty commanded silence that overtook visitors at this spot.

"Mauna join the Kai. What does it mean?" CeCe asked as quietly as Austin had spoken the words.

"It means Mountains join the Sea. It is where I have always been meant to be. It will live on in my soul long after I leave this good earth." Austin just kept staring down into the Kalalau Valley far below them.

"It's beautiful. The words are beautiful as well. I take it they are Hawaiian," CeCe said.

"Yes. I knew the minute I saw this place it was for me. Kind of like when I drove down off of Rabbit Ears Pass. This place joins the two things in nature that I enjoy the most, the mountains and the sea." Austin turned toward CeCe as he spoke. He could see that she was very taken with the view. This pleased him greatly.

Austin stepped away from the edge and started to walk. "We get to see this view for awhile more before we turn away from it. If we are lucky, when we get to the end of the trail, the clouds will move away long enough for us to get a view down into the town of Haena on the North Shore."

Everyone followed behind Austin. Angie stayed at the rear to help. The first part of the hike was fairly muddy. It required climbing down over the red dirt-covered rock. With the help of the men and the excellent shape they kept themselves in, CeCe and Reece had no trouble negotiating this part of the trail.

The trail flattened out as they began walking on the boardwalk that had been built to allow hikers to enjoy the hike and not fall into the swampy ground below them. They were walking deeper and deeper into the caldera of the long ago burnt-out volcano.

The vegetation here was very different from any place else on the island. All of the trees seemed to be stunted. Soon they walked into an area that was truly a rain forest. The logs were covered with several different species of moss. Some of them brought the fallen limbs to life in the form of animals. Rare birds chattered just beyond them further into the lushness of the trail.

A very elaborate set of steps carried them down to the deepest area and then back up and into an open space. Here the clouds moved in, creating a misty dream world around them. With the clouds came a light mist. The atmosphere made CeCe think about fog machines and the eerie feeling of it all.

They walked along the trail until they came to the lookout. The mist was coming and going, providing small glimpses of the North Shore below. They all sat on a bench while CeCe pulled out her camera and some of the fruit she purchased at the farmer's market that morning.

"Let me just set the camera up on this rock, and then we can all huddle together and get a good picture." Just as CeCe set the camera up and was ready to click the timer button, the mist across the valley cleared, which provided her a great background.

"Here we go," CeCe said as she ran to the group and wiggled between Austin and Reece. Once the picture was snapped, she had everyone turn around to look at the view without the mist. They were only given a glimpse before the mist moved over them again.

"This place is awesome," Reece said.

"I love how the mist moves in and out," Angie said as he got up and brushed off some dirt from the seat of his pants.

"Thanks for the fruit, CeCe," Austin said. "Are you guys ready to head back, or would you like to linger here longer?"

"I'm ready," CeCe said.

"Me, too," said Reece.

"Well, Austin, I guess we can start back. Remember ladies, we have to climb up all those stairs we walked down," Angie said.

"Great. It's a natural stair machine!" Reece exclaimed.

They all followed behind Austin again. As they crossed the walkway again, the mist got heavier and made the walkway slippery. Angie stepped right off the edge and landed in mud up to his knees. Everyone rushed back to help him get out and back up onto the walkway.

"Angie, are you okay?" Austin ran back to him and reached out an arm into the thick fog. The mist lightened up to reveal a mud-covered Angie just standing there. "I've done the same thing myself. It was the first time I came up here. I know of a stream with a little pool not too far from here that you can clean up in."

"The only thing hurt is my pride," Angie said while shaking mud off of himself. "This stuff gets a pretty good grip on you and won't let go. I think I am going to need some help getting out of it."

Austin, CeCe and Reece all grabbed hold of his forearms. They gently tugged on him until he was able to crawl back onto the walkway.

"Thanks, I could have been there all night if you guys let me fend for myself. I think it would have been a long cold evening. Now where is that little pool?"

"It's just up here a ways. It looks as though all of us could climb in with all the mud you got all over us." Austin said as he picked up his pack and continued on the trail.

They walked awhile before they came to the stream.

"Here it is", Austin said. "The pool is just up around that corner. I think I will jump in and cool off, and clean up as well."

"It sounds like fun", Reece chimed in, "but I didn't bring a swim suit. Guess CeCe and I will have to wait for the two of you."

Angie pulled out a pocketknife and cut off several substantial ferns and handed them to both CeCe and Reece. "Don't be silly. You have plenty of nature to cover yourself with. Austin and I promise not to look, right Austin?"

Austin wasn't sure if he could handle the sight of CeCe with just a few ferns covering her body but didn't say that. "Sure, I won't deny you two the pleasure of the cool pool. You can even go in first."

"What do you say, CeCe?" Reece asked her.

"Sure, why not? It isn't any different than having some of those tiny swim suits on," CeCe said out loud, while all the time her mind was spinning. She only thought that the cool water would help lower the body temperature that rose from the thought of sitting next to Austin naked.

Reece and CeCe rounded the bend in the stream and came upon the beautiful little pool that was fed by the stream. There were hanging vines and different species of flowers growing all around it.

Reece squealed in delight. "Look how beautiful it is. It's like something out of a fairy tale."

Austin and Angie heard Reece squeal. Austin called out, "Are you two all right?"

They both hollered out simultaneously, "It's so beautiful."

CeCe and Reece both removed their clothing and donned the ferns. They were stepping into the pool when the guys came into view.

"It's a bit cooler than what I was expecting." CeCe said, making a face.

"Just dip yourself in all at once- it will be easier," Austin said as he started removing his shoes.

Angie said, "Look! I cleaned off my boots and legs in the stream. It wasn't that cold."

Austin tried not to let his eyes stray toward CeCe as she gingerly entered the pool, but it was difficult. As CeCe slipped into the pool, the ferns fell away, revealing her beautifully tanned skin. He had to concentrate on the task on hand; otherwise he would be the one who would need that fern to cover his excitement.

CeCe was trying to do the same, not to stare at the two men's beautiful bodies. Reece, on the other hand, did not avert her eyes. Instead, she commented on the scar that Austin had on his knee.

"Did that hurt?"

Austin was confused. "Did what hurt?" he asked as he slipped into the pool.

"That scar on your knee."

Angie said, "You weren't supposed to look."

"Oh, I looked alright. You were the ones who promised, not me. I don't have a problem with it, do you?"

"No, I guess I don't." Angie smiled and splashed water at Reece.

"Back to my question. Did it hurt, Austin?"

"It was painful. It's the injury that forced me into retirement. But I don't have to endure any of that physical punishment any longer. The only punishment I endure are the things that I choose to do to myself."

CeCe was quiet. She was marveling at how great it all felt. She thought she would feel awkward, but instead she felt wonderful and content.

CeCe raised a leg out of the water and stretched it. "This feels so good. I thought it would be too cool to sit here very long. It's just what you need in the middle of a hike, someplace to cool off your hot tired feet and let your mind absorb all of the beautiful things you just encountered."

Austin wanted to push her leg back down and tell her to stop. He was having a difficult enough time being in the same body of water with her in such close quarters, let alone revealing her shapely legs. God, she was beautiful. She looked as though she belonged here. What was he thinking? She looked as though she belonged everywhere she went.

Reece was talking about Valentine's Day. "I brought you both something for Valentine's Day. I'll give it to you when we get to Austin's place."

"That's right. It is Valentine's Day." Angie said with a smile. "Will you be my Valentine?"

"Yes, but not until we get out of the pool and get some clothes on," Reece said. "Which brings me to the conclusion that I better get out or I will become a prune"

"I'll second that," CeCe said as she pulled the ferns in front of her and started to climb out. "No peeking, gentlemen."

"It's not fair," Angie said frowning, "Reece peeked."

"That was Reece and not me. Although I did notice a couple of war wounds on you, Angie," CeCe said as she climbed out laughing.

"Well, in that case, there is no sense in us waiting for you to get out and dressed before we do. Looks as though you two have already seen everything." As he spoke, Angie pulled himself up out of the pool. Austin followed him out. They all were laughing at the situation.

They finished the hike and returned to the starting point. CeCe wanted to have a picture with them all together with the Kalalau valley in the background. She was looking for a place to set the camera down, when along came another couple.

"Would you mind snapping a picture of us?" CeCe asked.

"Of course not, if you will do the same for us. We are on our honeymoon. We love the view from here," the man said as he looked down sweetly at his wife.

"Sure, but you go first. I want to get the best possible shot for you." CeCe arranged them together as if she were a professional photographer. "Ready?" She snapped a few pictures with their camera then handed it back.

They all stood arm in arm smiling into the camera. CeCe asked them to take one more. She arranged Reece and Angie together and directed the man as to what direction she wanted him to take the picture. She grabbed hold of Austin's hands and said, "Go ahead."

Little did she know this would be one of her favorite pictures of them all together. None of them were dressed up, but it was perfect. It captured the energy and the beauty of that day.

They drove thoughtfully back to the lodge to pick up Austin's truck.

"I'll lead the way, you can follow me," he stated as he got out of CeCe's vehicle. "It's just about a mile from here. The road gets a bit bumpy, but then again you're not going too fast."

CeCe climbed out of the back and into the driver's seat. Austin closed the door behind her.

They drove out of the parking lot and up the road a bit and turned onto a road on the right. CeCe thought to herself that she would have missed it if it hadn't been for Austin in front of her.

The drive only took a few minutes. CeCe and Reece felt as though they were driving right through the middle of a rain forest. After a few turns here and there, they came out into a clearing. On the right hand side of the road stood a very quaint cabin. It reminded CeCe of her own place in Colorado.

Austin drove to the gate and opened it for them. He gestured for them to drive through. The lawn was beautiful and the tropical flowers were all in full bloom, many of which CeCe had never even seen before.

CeCe drove the car up the long drive and parked off to the side in order to let Austin pull his truck alongside of her car.

CeCe opened the door and walked over to the stairs. "Austin, is this all yours?"

"Sure is. Headaches and all."

"It is beautiful. I can't wait to see inside," CeCe said as she walked around the house.

It was picture perfect. There was a covered lanai in front and an uncovered one in the back. It looked perfect for sun-bathing. The windows were paned and covered with blue gingham checked cloth. There were French doors that opened onto the front lanai. CeCe could tell just by looking at the detail in the railing that Austin cared about the place very much.

"Well, would you like to see the inside?" Austin asked.

"I don't know about you, CeCe, but I'm ready to look into the soul of the house," Reece said as she climbed the stairs and waited for Austin to open the door.

When Reece and CeCe entered, they were both very impressed. The wide-open room reminded CeCe of the great room at Austin's ranch. The room had been decorated in colors that they had seen in the canyon that morning. They were accented with cool blues and greens. The room was decidedly masculine, but nonetheless appeasing to her.

The floors were gleaming with the rich glow of the Koa wood that CeCe recognized from the jewelry box that Austin had made her.

"Wow," was all Reece said.

"This is the main area of the house. Off to the right is the bath, up over here is a small guest room and upstairs is the loft." Angie sounded like he might have been trying to sell the house to a perspective buyer.

"Can we see the rest?" Reece asked.

"Go for it. I'm going to fire up the grill. You might want to light a few lamps while you're upstairs. It gets dark quickly when the sun fades." Austin spoke as he opened the grill lid on the lanai.

"Light lamps?" Reece asked.

"Oh yeah, didn't we tell you? There's no electricity here. Austin uses gas for just about everything. What doesn't run on gas, he has batteries for… like the stereo. Before I take you up, I'll put some music on." Angie walked over to the stereo and put Jackson Browne on the CD player.

They climbed the rustic stairs into the loft, and were greeted with another beautifully decorated room.

The bed in the middle of the floor was massive. CeCe thought that it had to be bigger than a king bed. That's what she had at home and this thing was much bigger. Of course, it may have been because of the beautiful bed frame that encompassed it. It appeared to be made of bamboo. It was very unique and beautiful.

The room had a few other things in it. In the corner stood a huge wardrobe made of the same bamboo and some of the dark Koa wood adorned it.

The loft had a sliding panel across the front to afford the occupant privacy from anyone who might be below. The panels were too made of bamboo and folded in an accordion fashion.

"All of this work with the bamboo; it is gorgeous! How did you ever get these things hauled up here?" CeCe yelled down to Austin.

A laugh drifted up from down below when Austin came into view. "Well, I didn't."

"What do you mean, you didn't? Was it here when you bought the place?" CeCe asked.

"No," was the reply.

"Then how did…" CeCe stopped in mid-sentence. "Did you do this, Austin? Did you create this beautiful work?"

Austin blushed. "It was nothing, really, once I got the materials. That was the hard part. I told you that I was handy. This is just a bit of my work."

CeCe and Reece looked around and saw many things that they could only guess that Austin had made. The woodwork was amazing. She would love to come back to Hawaii sometime and stay here. Only she would want Austin to be with her. With that thought, CeCe felt it was time to leave Austin's bedroom.

They climbed back down and familiarized themselves with the rest of the house. CeCe went to the car and got the cooler that they had filled with the things from the farmer's market that morning.

The fragrance of gardenia's filled the room the minute she opened the cooler.

"Do you have a vase, Austin?" CeCe asked, holding the delicate flowers in her hand.

"Yes, right under the sink there."

CeCe reached under the sink and found the vase. There was a card attached to it by a ribbon. CeCe turned it over and looked at the obviously feminine handwriting. She didn't read the content of the card, but she looked to the bottom where the signature was. She was sure that what she was going to see was Poalima's signature. Sure enough, it was. CeCe felt a pang of jealousy.

Poalima had been here before, Austin had even told her as much. She was the one who sold him the place. She had spent time with Austin here. The bed upstairs was possibly where their child had been conceived.

"Did you find one?" Austin asked.

CeCe almost dropped the vase as she was startled by his voice. She placed the vase with the card attached back into the cupboard. She felt for another and retrieved it.

"Ah, yes. Here's one." CeCe brought up a vase and rinsed it in the sink. How stupid was she to think that he didn't still have things of Poalima's around? Of course he did. He still had feelings for her.

CeCe filled the vase and placed it on the table. There sat two packages: one with her name on it and another with Reece's. The envelope underneath was drawn with a heart asking 'Will you be my Valentine?'

"Hey, Reece, guess we better get the Valentine's out of the car to give to these two gentlemen," CeCe said as she handed the box and card to Reece. "Looks like they beat us to it."

Reece went to the car and brought in two envelopes. She handed one each to Austin and Angie.

They all opened the envelopes and read the card. Inside Austin and Angie's were certificates to the spa where they were staying for a massage.

"We figured after all the running around we're going to do that you two may want to relax and be pampered for a change," Reece said.

CeCe unwrapped the package and found a beautiful hair ornament made of the Koa wood, adorned with tiny polished seashells. "Austin, did you make this?"

"I cannot tell a lie. Yes, but Angie made yours, Reece," Austin said.

"But not without Austin's expert help. The massage is a great idea. Thanks ladies, but I would have settled for one from you two right here on the deck."

Reece tossed the box lid at him. "I bet you would have. It's not bad enough we go skinny dipping with you. Now you want us to be your own personal geisha girls. Besides, I don't think my hands are strong enough to massage your muscles."

"I wouldn't be so sure of that. Maybe after dinner we can try to work out a few of the aches and pains that I have." Angie rubbed Reece's neck from behind as he spoke.

CeCe pulled her hair up into a bun on top of her head and secured it with the ornament Austin had made for her. She turned and modeled her head as she said, "What do you think?"

"It's beautiful. The color of the wood in contrast to your hair is stunning. I like your hair up like that," Austin said blushing.

"Well, shall we help you with something?" CeCe asked.

"Yes, let's start the salad. Angie, would you light the torches outside?"

"I'll light the candles and lamps. I'm not very good in the kitchen," Reece volunteered.

CeCe started preparing the salad makings that she had brought fresh that morning. The vegetables were very crisp. Austin was keeping himself busy with the grill and preparing the fish.

"One of the guys I know here on the island goes out and catches the fish fresh. Whenever I'm around, he lets me to buy some of it from him before he sells it to the markets. This is as fresh as it gets. Have you ever had Ahi?"

"We had our first taste of it in Maui, and it was wonderful. Every time we went anywhere, I asked if they had fresh Ahi. Of course, the answer was yes most of the time. How do you fix it?" CeCe asked as she finished up the salad.

"I either like to blacken and sear it just for a second, or I love it on the grill. That's how I am going to fix it tonight. How do you like yours? Rare, medium rare- please don't tell me you like it done any more than medium."

"I love mine rare. I also know that Reece likes it that way. Isn't that right, Reece?"

"Isn't what right?"

"Don't you like your Ahi rare?"

"I love it that way. How did you know that was my new favorite, Austin?"

Austin picked up the fish he had been working on and carried it to the door as he spoke over his shoulder. "I guess I can read your mind. That makes it unanimous, then. Everyone likes it rare."

"I really hope you're kidding about reading my mind. I wouldn't want you to know what I was thinking all the time. But some of the time I guess it wouldn't be hard to read." Reece raised her eyebrows a few times in jest.

Everyone laughed at her comment and agreed that it was probably best if everyone had to just think they could read your mind.

Austin had prepared the fish perfectly. The dinner was a complete success. Everyone got up and helped clean up the dishes.

Austin stood with his hands on his hips. "I have never had so much help before. This is great. It will allow us time to go out on the lanai and look at the stars while the coffee finishes perking."

They all headed out to the back lanai and stood gazing out into the star-strewn sky. The clouds had moved out with the trade winds, allowing them the full view. Everything was so quiet. There was only an occasional croak of a nearby frog or a passing insect.

"I thought it was quiet at my place in Colorado, but this is incredible. There is barely a sound. Not even the sound of a far-off plane or car. At this moment the air is so still that you don't even hear that," CeCe said as she hugged her arms to herself.

"CeCe, are you cold?" Austin asked as he was opening the door. Before she had a chance to answer, he returned with two fleece jackets that were his own. He handed one to Reece and the other to CeCe "Here, put these on." CeCe tried to protest, but he insisted.

"I did bring a sweater, but I left it in the car."

"Thanks, Austin," Reece said. "Do you think we could take a little walk, Angie?"

"Sure, let me grab one of the lanterns. We wouldn't want to step in a hole and hurt ourselves. It might change the whole rest of your vacation, although I would take care of you if you were laid up in bed. I would just have to take up vigil at your bedside." Angie quickly retreated from Reece's playful shove.

CeCe and Austin stayed out on the lanai. Austin pulled over the chaise lounge and offered it to CeCe.

"I think we should both lie in it and look up at the stars. Would you object to that?" CeCe asked quietly.

"No objections from me." Austin climbed on to the chaise and patted the space next to him.

No objections from me, Austin thought to himself. I should have said I've seen enough stars from that same chaise lounge, but no, I had to agree to the suggestion. Now I'm lying here holding this beautiful woman who I can't take my mind off of.

Austin unconsciously held CeCe closer as he let his mind wander. He had done this before with Poalima, but that was just pure sexual attraction. This was different. Austin felt something else. He couldn't describe it. He thought that he had all the right feelings with Poalima, but there was something different in the way he felt about CeCe.

Austin buried his nose deep into CeCe's hair. It was fragrant and soft. He could smell the shampoo she used. The rain that had dampened it and the sweet smell of the gardenia she had playfully placed behind her ear.

CeCe looked up at him and asked, "What are you thinking? You seem to be so content."

"I am content. I'm full, tired, and very comfortable holding you."

Austin couldn't resist. The moonlight reflected in her eyes and danced off of her full, ripe lips. He let his lips slowly caress hers. Then the kiss deepened. Austin felt like he was up in the sky with all the other stars. CeCe tasted so sweet and wonderful. She kissed him back fully.

Austin let his arms encompass CeCe. He pulled her on top of him and allowed his hands to slide down her body. As his hands reached her firm bottom, he moved them cautiously across it. He squeezed and released. He moved his hands away from that dangerous area and back to her face. He brushed her hair out of her face.

"CeCe, you're so beautiful and perfect. I wanted to share this special place with you. I could see how you were affected by the view today. That valley is so unique- just like you. Do you think that you will come back here one day?"

"Austin, you, like the valley, take my breath away. I'm glad you want to share these things with me. I enjoy being in your company very much. Just because I want to save myself for marriage, doesn't mean that I'm not alive and don't enjoy your touch. I do very much. Don't worry so much, I'll let you know when things are going too far." CeCe kissed him softly and then more intensely. She raised her head when she heard Reece and Angie's footsteps on the stairs out front. "Yes, I will come back and I hope you are here when I do. Now, I think we should go in so Reece and I can head home."

CeCe rose, and as she did so Austin touched her softly. He groaned but got up from the lounge.

Angie hung the jackets on the rack. "Would you ladies like to stay this evening? I would be more than happy to sleep out here on the sofa. It folds out into a queen-sized bed."

Austin jumped in. "It really is a long way down in the dark back to your place. We could stop by there on the way to the North Shore in the morning, so you could pick up anything you need, like fresh clothes and a swimsuit. I think it would be a good idea myself."

CeCe didn't relish the thought of driving in the dark, and she hadn't gotten much sleep the night before. "What do you say, Reece? I'm easy; I don't care one way or the other."

"Sounds great to me. I could have another glass of wine in that case."

"Great, it's settled then. I'll get the clean sheets for the bed. You don't know how many times Angie has climbed into the bed with all of his clothes on. You're liable to find a whole beach in there."

Austin joked as he walked to the linen closet.

After the bed had been remade, they all sat around and talked until it fell silent in the room. Everyone had dosed off except Austin. He just sat there with CeCe's head lying on his chest reflecting on the day and the time they spent together on the lanai. He was reluctant to move, but felt it was necessary since they needed to get an early start tomorrow morning. He woke everyone up and they all retreated to their own beds.

The fresh mountain air mixed with the sea salt and the long hike made for a great sedative. CeCe woke early and refreshed. She didn't want to wake the others yet; instead she wanted to take a brisk walk.

CeCe headed out to the car. She had thrown in her running shoes at the last minute. She would put them on and head out for about an hour. If nothing else, she decided she could head back toward the lodge and then back again.

She was sitting on the steps when she heard the door close softly behind her.

"Good morning, Sunshine," Austin said. He was standing there dressed in a T-shirt and some running shorts. "I didn't think I would see you for another hour or so. I love to get up early and take a quick run. What were your plans, CeCe?"

"Good morning, Austin. I was thinking the same - that it would be another hour or so before you woke up. I'm sorry if I woke you; I tried to be quiet. I wanted to take a walk or run this morning. It gets my blood flowing. Any suggestions?"

"Do you mind if I come along?"

"Not at all. It would be good to have someone along so I don't get lost in the rain forest."

"Great. Let me get my hat." Austin went back inside and thought to himself, she looks great even just after she gets out of bed. Not many women can make that claim. He grabbed the hat and headed back out the door.

"Let's go, my lady."

They walked to a trail-head very close to his house. It was a gentle slope and curved smack dab in the middle of a forest. The plant life was beautiful and the songs the birds were singing were a symphony of the island. Suddenly, the terrain changed. The sun seemed to be blocked out by the tall cedar trees. It was cooler in here. The aroma was of cedar and wild ginger. It was different than anything CeCe had seen or smelled in Colorado.

"What happened to all the plant life we saw on the beginning of the trail?"

"The cedar trees are so acidic and they grow so big that they block out the sun, so very little grows beneath them. The trees are pretty old. How are you doing?"

"Good. This is a great trail; I wouldn't have taken it just because I didn't know how long it was. I was going to run along the road."

They both fell silent and picked up the pace a bit. They came out onto a road and headed back to the house.

"Austin thanks for going with me this morning and showing me this trail. It was beautiful. I'm sure you have lots in store for us today."

"We're going to go to the North Shore. It will take a while to get there so we need to get going soon. I thought we could do the first part of the Kalalau Trail hike. It is breathtaking and close to the area where we're going to snorkel. Do you have snorkel gear?"

"Yes. We bought some when we got to Maui. We decided we didn't want to rent it there and here again. It's not the best, but it works. We're really excited to snorkel. I read about the Kalalau Trail and the snorkeling on the North Shore. I guess we better get back then and get going."

They had reached the road that Austin's house was on and the CeCe's competitive streak kicked in. "Race you to the house. Last one there has to massage the others feet at the end of the day." With that, she took off running. Austin took off behind her, but liked the view he had. He felt confident that he could stay where he was for a while and turn on the speed at the end.

They neared the gate to Austin's, and he realized that he had underestimated the speed that CeCe had. She turned it up as he pulled alongside of her. Before he realized what was happening, she ran ahead and touched the gate. "Looks as though you have some foot massaging to do tonight, Mr. Carter."

"Guess you're right. I didn't think those short legs could carry you that fast."

"You would be surprised at what these legs can do."

They both strolled toward the house where the aroma of fresh coffee wafted out.

Angie opened the door with two steaming cups in his hands. He handed one to each of them. "Not that you need this to kick start your morning, but I thought you might like some just the same."

"Thanks, Angie," CeCe said as she sat on the step and pulled the laces on her shoes. "I would love a quick shower and then I will be ready to stop by our place and get our gear."

"Ladies first," Austin said with an exaggerated bow.

"I won't be long." CeCe stood and went to the door as she spoke.

"That's what they all say." Austin stood and watched her.

"The shower is big enough for two; too bad I took mine already, CeCe, I could have helped you wash your back," Angie called out to her.

"Angie, you can wash your own back. I can reach mine just fine," CeCe hollered out the door.

Chapter Thirty-Two

Reece's absence caused him to ponder his future here in the Yampa Valley. He wondered if he would be able to stay and live the life he had dreamed about for himself, or if his past would haunt him.

The demon that he thought he had buried was again resurrected. This time its target was Reece. The only way he knew how to get peace was to follow along and do what was expected of him by the demon.

He felt drawn to Reece; it was as though he were playing a game. Would she be able to detect the secret he had hidden or was she just another pretty brainless woman? He felt that he knew the answer. She was bright enough all right, but could she feel what he really wanted?

Reece had been distracted by the trip that she had gone on with CeCe. He found out that Austin had a place there on one of the islands they were visiting and that football player friend of his was going to be there.

What did that guy think… that he could move in on the good thing he had planned for himself? Reece was a beautiful woman and she had plenty of money to go along with it. He had thought that he was over this after the last time, but it had become a game to him. He felt the need to do it again. He would continue to try and get her to love him and to trust him. Then it was easy from there.

The valley had many a place where one could lose their footing and go tumbling down into the brush below. It could be weeks before anyone would find them.

It wasn't time to get all excited about that part now. There were still lots of work to be done. He had to get Reece to love and trust him first. It would be a shame to leave the valley. He had really become very attached.

He couldn't wait for her return. He would have to work really hard on getting her to see that he was the right man for her. He also didn't lack the confidence that he would be able to accomplish his goal.

The telephone rang and brought him back to reality. He let the answering machine pick it up. He could hear his own voice announcing that he was not available. He recited it in his head along with the machine. 'Hello, you have reached …'.

The doorbell was ringing at the same time. He rose to look out and see who was there.

Chapter Thirty-Three

The drive to the North Shore was beautiful. They arrived early enough to be one of the first on the trail. They put on their packs and started hiking up. It wasn't long before they were treated to the spectacular view. They walked along the ridge and had a full view of the ocean below them. The trade winds were blowing to keep them cool as they continued along the trail.

Again, they were treated to views that they never imagined existed. The coral in the ocean made the water a vibrant turquoise color. They could see the reef they would be snorkeling in after they finished with the hike.

They viewed the rugged Na Pali Coast with its volcanic cliffs covered with the emerald plant life from the trail.

All too soon, they came to an area where they turned away from the ocean and its view.

"Don't worry, we will come out at a beautiful beach," Austin assured them.

A cool stream stood before them and made them decide how to cross.

"I don't know about you, but I'm going to just take off my hiking boots and wade across," CeCe said decisively as she sat on a rock.

"I think that's the best way to maneuver through here. I've tried walking across the rocks and ended up on my, well, you get the picture," Austin said as he sat next to CeCe.

"This is beautiful. I wonder how many times I will utter that word while I'm here on this island." CeCe looked around her in amazement.

"I don't know about you, but I find new things every time I go somewhere that makes me awestruck." Austin held out his hand to help CeCe up.

CeCe walked over and picked up a piece of bamboo and declared it her walking stick. They crossed the stream and continued to the beach. They played for a short time and decided it was time to get back and snorkel.

On the hike back, they stopped and took several pictures. At one point the trade winds blowing off of the ocean blew Angie's hat off his head. CeCe continued to snap pictures in succession of the tumbling hat evading Angie's grasp.

They laughed so hard that their sides hurt.

The drive to Tunnel's beach was just a short distance. They would not be disappointed. The weather was cooperating, as were the ocean conditions. The water was fairly flat.

They chose a place a few feet from the water's edge and hurried into their snorkel gear. Angie was the first one into the water. The underwater kaleidoscope of sea life was incredible. As they swam along, the fish wove in and out and all around them.

Reece was so totally engrossed in a large colorful school of fish that she almost didn't notice the sea turtle that swam right in front of her. Reece turned to see if the others were close enough to see the turtle.

CeCe did indeed and was able to snap a great picture of the two of them side by side.

They retreated back to shore where the all they could talk about was the wide variety and the number of fish they had encountered. They lay on their towels and warmed their bodies in the sun.

Austin's eyes had been on CeCe the whole time. The brightly colored bikini she wore contrasted with the warm glow of her tanned skin. He kept envisioning the scene at the pond from the day before when the ferns fell away from her body. CeCe's triangles of material couldn't keep that vision from his mind.

Reece handed the sunscreen to Angie. "Angie, would you mind putting this on my back?"

"Not at all. Do you need some on your front?"

"I think I can take care of that. You just concentrate on covering the places I can't reach. I don't want to look like an abstract painting. That's what happens when I try and get it on myself."

"Oh, alright. Turn over. Not that this isn't enjoyable in its own way." Angie carefully covered Reece's fair skin with the coconut scented lotion.

"How about you, CeCe?" Austin asked.

"Sure, but I don't use the same lotion that Reece uses. I'm lucky and have darker skin. The sun doesn't take as much as a toll on me as it does her. I still use sunscreen, though. Got to protect from those nasty UV rays." CeCe rolled over onto her stomach.

Austin squeezed the sunscreen out in a design of a happy face on her back. "There, I think I'll just let it stay like that. It could become a new thing. A sun tattoo. Hey that's a great idea. No ink or needles involved, and over time it will disappear."

"I don't think that's a great idea. Anyway, I won't let you experiment on me. You can try it on your own skin. Let's see, we could put a heart with the word 'mom' in it if you like. Besides, that's what henna tattoos are for. There are temporary and don't expose the rest of your skin to the sun. So just go ahead and rub all that sunscreen in, please." CeCe settled back down on her towel and smiled at the thought of a sun tattoo.

"Okay, go ahead and be a party pooper." Austin rubbed the lotion into CeCe's smooth skin. He thought that he could go on all day, but that others might notice that the lotion wasn't the reason for his continuing to touch CeCe.

"Mmm, you can continue that if you like. I'll just fall asleep while you massage my shoulders. Hey, by the way, don't you owe me a foot massage?"

"Yes, but I think I that you had an unfair advantage this morning." Austin moved over to his own towel.

"And how is that?" CeCe asked.

"You didn't tell me that you could run that fast. I thought that I could just catch up to you and that we would finish the race together."

"Yeah right. That's why you pushed off in the NFL. You wanted to finish in a tie every time you went out onto the field. I watched you and could see how competitive you were. So don't give me any story about how you would have called it a tie. You would have been the one lying here asking for your massage." CeCe raised herself up on her elbows as she talked to Austin.

Austin's eyes fell to the deep crevasse CeCe's breasts made and quickly looked away. How was he ever going to be able to spend the rest of this vacation with her? Seeing her in her bathing suit was almost too much for him. She didn't have a clue as to how beautiful she was.

A golden strand of her hair came loose and fell across her cheek. Austin reached over and swept it back for her. He had to get his mind off of the feel of her so he picked up on her comment about his playing style.

"I don't think you will ever give me a break from that pushing off thing. I was just playing the game the best I knew how. Just because I burnt one of your Denver defensive backs a few times. I still contend that I played every game fair and square."

"Oh, no, Austin. I wish I had a mirror so you could see how much your nose is growing. It is huge from the tales you are telling." CeCe pretended that she had to back away to let it continue to grow.

"Very funny. Now just relax a bit, and if you're good, I'll consider buying you some shaved ice and dinner in Hanalei."

"You know that I'm easy when it comes to food. That's not fair. There you go again, not playing fair. But that won't keep me from accepting your offer. Now you've made me hungry." CeCe lay back down on her towel.

The beach at Ha'ena had a shower that allowed them to rinse the salt water from themselves and clean up a bit. They drove back into Hanalei where Austin fulfilled his promise of shaved ice and dinner.

They drove back to the hotel in comfortable silence. The hike, sun, snorkeling, and good dinner made for a tired group.

When they arrived at CeCe and Reece's hotel it was late. The room was big enough to accommodate all of them. The living area had two sofas that made into beds, so CeCe felt that it would be only appropriate to offer for Austin and Angie to stay the night.

"I think the tables are turned tonight, gentlemen. We stayed at your place last night because it was too late to drive home; well it is even later tonight. We have plenty of room. What do you say?" CeCe offered to the two men.

Angie rubbed his chin deep in thought. "Well, we do have a change of clothes and a swimsuit. What more does a guy need?"

"Sounds good to me," Austin said with a renewed energy. "There is a good nightclub that I know we can go to. I don't get there often because of the drive up to my place. But, with staying right here we could go there if that sounds good to you."

"I know the place he is talking about, we can watch people make fools of themselves with karaoke. A few drinks and watch out! It's enough entertainment for a month. Why, even Austin and I have indulged on occasion, isn't that right, Austin?"

"I'll take the fifth on that one, Angie. Are you ladies sure you don't mind the intrusion and maybe the tarnishing of your reputation?"

"Keep them guessing has always been my motto," Reece said.

"It's settled then. You'll stay with us. We can get an early start tomorrow again. What's on the agenda, Mr. Travel Guide?" CeCe sat back, content with the arrangements. She thought to herself that she was getting used to sleeping under the same roof as Austin. She didn't want to make a habit of it. It was pretty enticing.

They took turns with the shower. When CeCe finished, the guys had made drinks for her and Reece. They enjoyed it on the lanai. The surf was strong, making an alluring sound.

Austin broke the silence. "If we are going out we should go now.

But it isn't necessary. Anybody want to stay here?"

"Are you crazy? We'll miss all the fun. We can think about our beauty rest when we get home." Reece was already at the door holding her sweater in her hand. "Let's go- I've got my second wind."

They all walked out into the warm tropical breeze and climbed into the car.

"We probably could walk the short distance, but I'm sure it will just drain all the rest of our energy," Austin said as he closed the door.

The club was packed. Just as Austin and Angie had predicted, patrons were waiting in line for their chance at karaoke. It was fun; some of the participants had some talent, while others only had the liquid courage from the glasses they were holding in their hands.

They sat at a table off to the right of the stage area and ordered drinks. Several people came over to Austin and said hello. Most said that it had been a long time since they had seen him here. A few offered a story or two about their adventures together.

"This is too much fun, Austin. Now where is the ladies room?" CeCe rose out of her chair.

"It's over there to the left, but be careful- you have to pass in front of the stage to get there and someone might pull you in front of the microphone."

"They would have a serious problem. I don't think anyone would want to hear me sing anything."

CeCe and Reece walked toward the ladies room. Just as they passed the stage, a very exotic woman took the stage and began singing in a beautiful voice. She was singing a Hawaiian song in her native language.

"She has a beautiful voice with the face and body to match!" Reece exclaimed as they walked by.

The woman smiled and her eyes followed them around the corner.

Just as Austin sat back down he heard the familiar voice singing. Before he turned around he knew to whom the voice belonged. It reopened the wound he thought he left in Kauai.

Poalima was standing there, just as beautiful as ever. She was singing the song that they had heard the first night they went out together. She was looking straight toward the table where Austin and Angie sat.

"Holy shi…," Angie started to say but was interrupted by Austin.

"Don't start. I saw her, and she has certainly has seen me. I don't think this is going to turn out very well. Maybe we can get out of here before she comes over. That's wishful thinking. She is just about finished with the song." Austin had turned away from her.

She finished and walked away to a thunderous applause. She smiled sweetly and touched a few shoulders and cheeks on her way over to the table.

"You're right, Austin. This isn't going to very good. She's headed right toward us."

Poalima walked over and put her hand on Angie's shoulder. "Hello, Angie, long time, no see. You're looking good as ever." She leaned over and kissed him on the cheek.

"Austin." She breathed the word out sensuously. She sat on his knee and wrapped her arm around him. As she did so, she pulled him close into her chest so that he would have a full view of the breasts that were well exposed by the flimsy top she wore.

"I've missed you so much. I've sent you letters, but they keep coming back- return to sender. You're not still mad at me, are you?"

"What do you think, Poalima? I thought that you were in New York, with this wonderful job and life. I wouldn't think that you would bother yourself with coming back to this place."

"Austin, you are still mad. I am in New York, but I needed to come back here to get a few things and my father's health is failing. I didn't expect to see you here. This is an added bonus. I saw you two walk in with those women. I see that you guys still have it. Just walk into any resort and find yourselves someone to hook up with for the evening."

Austin pulled Poalima's arm off of his neck and guided her to a standing position. As he did so, she wrapped her arms around his neck and shamelessly hooked her leg behind his as to bring them into a full body contact. Poalima could feel the warmth of his body, but wasn't getting the reaction she had always gotten before and was hoping to get this time.

It was just at that moment that CeCe and Reece walked out of the ladies room. They were laughing and talking when they looked toward the table. CeCe saw the woman who had been at the microphone when they passed by entwined with Austin.

"Wow, that didn't take long. That woman works fast," Reece said.

CeCe knew instantly who she was. She had felt something when they walked by and their eyes locked. This was Poalima, and from the looks of it Austin was just as happy to see her as she was to see him.

Austin was unaware of the scene that CeCe was witnessing. He was just angry with Poalima. He put his hand on her leg and unhooked it from himself. When he did this, he bent forward which afforded Poalima the opportunity to close her mouth over his. She was trying to invade his mouth with her tongue. Austin quickly pulled away.

"Poalima. What is wrong with you? You're acting like some cheap… Never mind, you know what I mean!"

"I thought you would be happy to see me, but I can see that you're not. Since I did get the chance to see you while I'm here, I thought maybe we could make up for some lost time."

"Are you crazy? You destroyed any chance of us getting back together when you flew out on that plane and followed through with your appointment."

"Oh, that. It was really not bad. I felt a little regret, but the new job and life took all my time and left none for me to ponder what would have been."

"I don't really want to talk to you about this right now, Poalima. Just go back to your life in New York and leave me be! I know now that I never really knew you. Not if you could do what you did." Austin sat back down, exhausted from his anger.

CeCe pulled Reece's arm and held her back. "That's Poalima, Austin's old friend from here. He told me she had moved to New York, but she must be back." Just then CeCe saw Austin slide his hand along Poalima's leg that was practically wrapped around his waist. Poalima dropped her leg and kissed him fully.

CeCe didn't understand. Austin had told her that things were over with them. She had hurt him and did some unforgivable things, but there they were locked in each others arms.

Reece pulled CeCe along back to the table. As they approached Angie stood up abruptly, which caused Austin to stand and turn around facing CeCe.

"Well, gentleman, aren't you going to introduce us?" Poalima tossed her glossy hair back as she spoke.

Angie interrupted. "Poalima, this is Reece and CeCe. They are from Colorado where Austin lives. They won a trip to Hawaii and we're showing them around."

Poalima thrust out her hand toward CeCe. She had seen them walk in together. Austin had his arm around her shoulder and Angie had hold of the redhead's arm. This brought her to the conclusion that this is how they were paired. She didn't care about Angie's date, but Austin's was a different story.

Poalima sized up CeCe. She had beautiful eyes and her skin wasn't pale like most blondes she would see on the beaches. She had a beautiful body. She wondered how close of a relationship she and Austin had.

"Hi, nice to meet you," Poalima said as she shook CeCe's hand. She then shook Reece's hand as well. "Are you enjoying the island?

These two certainly can show you all the sights."

"Yes, we are having a wonderful time, but I am exhausted and have a pretty good rum headache going on." Reece walked over to Angie. "Do you think it would be okay if we left? It has been an exhausting day."

Austin quickly took the opportunity that Reece had afforded them. "I'm pretty tired myself. Poalima, it was nice to see you again. Good luck in New York and tell your family I said hello." He picked up CeCe's sweater and put it over her shoulders.

CeCe followed along with the rest of the gang. "It was nice to meet you. Sorry we didn't have a chance to talk more."

They all walked out to the car. Austin had left in a hurry and had forgotten to pay the bill. "I'll be right back. I need to go pay our tab." He shut the door and walked back inside. Everyone in the car was quiet and deep in thought.

Reece broke the silence. "I was having a hard time taking that display in there. Poalima certainly thinks she owns Austin."

"I think it was more a ploy to see what reaction she would get from everyone, including Austin. She just came back to the island for a visit and then she is headed back to New York." Angie turned in the seat as he spoke to CeCe and Reece.

CeCe was watching out the window as she spoke out loud. "She certainly is beautiful. She had everyone's attention in the club when she was singing. I can see why she captured Austin's eye. I could see the pain in his eyes tonight. It will be interesting to see if he is able to talk her out of going back to New York."

"CeCe, you have it all wrong. He is over her. She just can't stand the thought that he doesn't care anymore," Angie said, as he tried to explain to her.

"Well, it doesn't look that way to me. Look at them at the door." CeCe motioned at Austin and Poalima.

When Austin went back inside, Poalima came over to him and slid in front of him, wedging herself between him and the bar. Austin pulled back immediately; he motioned to the bartender who understood that he wanted to pay the bill.

"You came back without your little friends, Austin. I knew you would," Poalima said.

"I came back to pay the bill. I think you have had too much to drink by the way you're acting, Poalima."

"I have not had too much to drink; on the contrary, I was hoping to sit and have some more with you, Austin. We could have a good time getting to know each other again."

"I told you, you lost all opportunity when you went through with your plans. I admit I was hurt, but I'm over that now. I have built a new life for myself. I enjoy Colorado and coming back here. I won't let you spoil that for me. And as for my little friends, they're much better people to be around than you. Enjoy your life, Poalima."

With that, Austin paid the bill and walked to the door with Poalima close behind. Austin opened the door, and as he did so Poalima threw her arms around his neck.

"Austin, you can put on this act, but I know how you feel. I will keep in touch, but for now I will leave you with this." Poalima bent his head down and kissed him hard. With her free hand, she grabbed Austin's hand and brought it to her round firm bottom. She held it there until Austin broke free.

"Poalima, stop trying to create something that isn't there. You don't need me; you made that very clear when you left. Goodbye and good luck." With that, Austin turned and walked back to the car.

This is the scene that CeCe, Reece, and Angie witnessed.

"It does look as though he still has feelings for her," Reece said.

"I guarantee you he doesn't. I have known him a long time and that isn't how Austin reacts to situations that he likes being in. It was all her. I believe it was just a show for all of us."

Austin's long strides got him to the car in just a few steps. He got in and turned around and faced CeCe. "I'm sorry you all had to witness that. Poalima has had a bit too much to drink and isn't thinking straight."

"She is very beautiful, Austin," CeCe said, still staring out the window. "I think we were all very tired anyway. Besides, Reece has a headache, and we don't want her to feel bad for the rest of the adventures." CeCe was putting on a good show. She didn't realize that she could feel such jealousy.

They drove back to the hotel and walked to the door. Reece unlocked it and entered. Austin didn't feel like going in just yet.

"Do you think I could borrow your key for a little while? I want to take a walk and clear my head," Austin said.

"Sure, Austin." Reece handed him her key. "Would you like company?"

"No, thanks." Austin took the key and walked away toward the beach.

CeCe wanted to walk with him, but she knew he was thinking about Poalima and maybe wondering what he was going to do.

She thought it would be a shame if the football team were to lose him as a coach. He really cared about the kids and the team had never played better. That wasn't the only thing she was concerned about. She had gotten very close to Austin. She was sure that she was falling in love with him, but she couldn't interfere with his feelings for Poalima.

CeCe had known all along that there was a chance that Austin was on the rebound. She should have protected her feelings better and not let her guard down. That was too late now, but still, she would not interfere.

"What a conniving bitch!" Angie exclaimed. "She was always that way- Austin just couldn't see it. He has now. I've never seen him so angry with a woman than he was with her tonight."

Reece walked over to CeCe who was standing on the lanai. "She was all over him. Was that a ploy to get him to succumb to her?"

"Poalima could never stand the fact that she couldn't have anything she wanted. The thought that Austin would not come running back to her has to just be killing her. She just wants to make him her puppet. She has chosen the wrong guy to screw with. Austin is finished with her."

CeCe was taking in the conversation, but didn't believe it all. She could see the pain in Austin's eyes when he had told her about Poalima and her leaving him. You don't get over that easily. She watched Austin walk along the path that led to the beach and could see him in the faint moonlight. He sat on one of the chairs left on the sand. He was tossing pieces of driftwood out into the ocean. Part of her wanted to go running to him; the other part reasoned that he needed to be alone.

"CeCe, you're awfully quiet. Are you alright?" Reece asked as she put her arm around CeCe.

"I'm just exhausted. I think I will go to bed. We're going to need our strength for tomorrow since we are kayaking. I'll want to get up and run in the morning before we go, so I'm going to go to bed. Goodnight, you two." CeCe hugged Reece and kissed Angie on the cheek before she headed out of the room.

"I think she's right about getting some rest," Angie said.

"Yes, she is. Goodnight, Angie." Reece hugged him and followed CeCe into the bedroom.

Austin sat for about an hour fuming at Poalima. How dare she think he would let her back into his life after what she did? What was done was done and it was for the best. The only regret he had was for the lost life of the child he never would know.

How could he have been so stupid as to think that Poalima wasn't anything more than what she was? He had known the minute he met CeCe that there was something special about her. He wasn't interested in anybody else but her. CeCe was everything that Poalima wasn't. She carried her beauty so much more gracefully; the fact that she didn't know how beautiful she was made her even more so. What was he doing comparing the two of them? There wasn't a comparison. He should have known before that Poalima wasn't what he was looking for in life. CeCe was what he wanted, so he just had to put Poalima out of his mind and move on.

Feeling better and knowing that he was through with Poalima forever, Austin got up and walked back to the room. He was suddenly exhausted. When he walked in, everyone was sleeping. He fell onto the sofa and fell asleep almost as soon as his head hit the pillow.

CeCe woke up very early and dressed in her running clothes. She walked quietly out of the bedroom. It was dark in the rest of the room since the drapes had been drawn across the large window. She walked straight to the door and ran right into Austin. CeCe let out a little yelp.

"I didn't expect anyone else to be up. You scared the hell out of me."

Austin had grabbed hold of her wrist as she raised it to fend him off. "I was waiting for you to get up. I knew you were going to run this morning and I thought I would go with you. Is that alright?"

"Sure, but warn somebody next time, will you?"

They walked out of the room quietly. CeCe walked to a bench and started stretching.

Austin wanted to just watch her, but he couldn't do that, so he stretched as well. CeCe was beautiful even this early in the morning. She had her hair pulled up on her head, secured with the hair ornament he had made for her. The spandex shorts and jogging top did nothing to conceal her perfectly toned body. He had to quickly avert his attention to something else to control his growing excitement.

"CeCe, about last night…"

"Austin, it was great fun. I'm just sorry we didn't get to hear you and Angie sing." CeCe didn't want to get into a conversation about

Poalima and she knew that was what he wanted to talk about.

"I just want you to know that I had no control over Poalima. She was just acting out and trying to get back at me for returning all of her letters and not taking her calls."

"You don't have to explain anything to me. I'm just here to have a good time. Are you ready?"

They ran hard on the beach and along the path back to the hotel. Austin stayed abreast of CeCe. He felt that this was the way to go this morning. Even though the view from behind was better, it made it hard for him to concentrate.

After everyone showered and had breakfast, they drove to the river that they were going to kayak. The mood seemed to be light and carefree. Austin thought to himself that he overreacted to Poalima's behavior last night and that it was over.

CeCe didn't want to let on that she felt that she had been a fool to think that Austin was over Poalima and that they had a future together. She would just enjoy the rest of her vacation and deal with her feelings when she returned home.

Chapter Thirty-Four

He had gone by the house and walked the familiar path around the back of the lot. It was dark and Reece wasn't home now, but somehow he felt closer to her by being there. He would walk to the door and look in. He might sit in the garden for a while and dream about her being there with him.

The letter would be waiting for her when she returned. She would be happy to know that he had missed her when she was gone. He knew that she would get a kick out of the postmark too.

When would he be able to hold her in his arms? Not for a while yet. She needed some time to realize that he was right for her. He couldn't risk her finding out his true feelings toward her until then. But, oh how sweet it would be. He would shower her lovely body with kisses and hold her until neither could stand it any longer. Then he would make love to her all night long. It wouldn't be like those others who just wanted to violate her. He truly wanted to love her, to take her to a pleasure place she had never been to before.

The sky was dark with threatening snow clouds. He would wait awhile longer before moving into the yard, just to be sure no one was watching. He was grateful that Reece had such a large lot with very few neighbors. Why, they could even lie out on the beautiful lawn summer evenings and make love with no one ever interrupting them.

The first large snowflakes drifted down. He would want to go now so that the snowfall would cover his footsteps. It was only a few more days until Reece returned, and then he could watch her, rather than just dreaming about her.

He crept slowly and quietly toward the garden. It was all covered with snow now, but was beautiful in full bloom in the summer. He sat on the cold wrought iron bench for just a short time. The last time he had been here, he had had the dog to contend with, and then CeCe had come home. Neither of those would be a problem this time.

He walked slowly toward the door. He knew before he got there that it would be locked. He tried it anyway. It was locked. He was glad Reece had heeded everyone's advice to lock her door.

He looked longingly into the warmth of the kitchen. He knew that Reece's bedroom was just off to the left. He could almost smell her fragrance; it hung in the air when he went into the house to place the letter there. He would love to go in, but that wouldn't be right. He would be no better than the rest of them, invading her privacy. Everyone should have privacy.

It would be easy to get in, though. He looked over to the cellar doors that were locked with the padlock. It would be easy to remove the clasp with a few quick turns of a screwdriver.

He hurried down the steps toward the cellar. He slipped but caught himself before he fell fully. "Slow down," he told himself. "You won't do yourself any good if you knock yourself out and they find you sprawled out here in the morning." He listened to himself and moved more cautiously.

He moved close to the lock, pulling out the tiny penlight he had in his pocket. No, it would not be a good idea to turn it on; someone might see the light. He put the penlight back in his pocket, but didn't notice that he had missed. It rolled out onto the ground next to the evergreens. He allowed his eyes to adjust in order for him to examine the lock. It was stronger than he thought which made him feel better. She would be safe from some intruder.

He allowed himself a few minutes more, and then regretfully rose. It was snowing harder now and the cold was seeping into his bones. It was time to leave. Soon, very soon, he would not have to worry about someone seeing him here. Reece would want him here with her.

He then moved quickly and quietly back into the darkness of the grove of trees. He could now wait until Reece returned. He felt closer to her now and it would last until he was able to see her again.

Chapter Thirty-Five

The kayaking had been wonderful. The weather was warm and sunny. The kayaks were made for two. CeCe and Reece sat in the front of the kayaks while Austin and Angie sat in the backs, so that they could better control the kayaks. That was fine with the both of the women, since they didn't have to work as hard. At one point, CeCe and Austin tipped their kayak. They struggled to right it and get back in.

The day had been a good one. They ended up on the beach walking until the sun set.

CeCe struggled to keep the thoughts about Austin and Poalima together out of her mind. Some of the time she was successful, but mostly it was all she was able to think about.

Time was winding down and their stay on the island was drawing to a close. Tomorrow they would head home and back to their everyday lives. Not that CeCe minded- she missed Nitro, Ruth and Tucker. She missed seeing her customers, too. It would be good to get home; but then again, she would have to deal with her feelings about Austin.

Austin and Angie insisted on meeting them at the hotel in the morning in order to help them with their luggage. They were leaving on a later flight the same day, so it wouldn't be a problem for them.

CeCe took one last opportunity to run along the beach in the morning. The air was heavy and humid, but not too hot. Her skin was going to miss the warm humidity when she went back to Colorado. She liked running in the rain; it was as soothing to her as the waves crashing on the shore.

This was a very unique place. She had never felt so relaxed. The beauty here would last her a lifetime. Austin played a big part in how she felt about Kauai. He had shown her things that she might not have seen if the island weren't so special to him as well. She was grateful for him sharing and hoped that she would be able to return here again.

CeCe ran back to the hotel and showered. When she came out of the bathroom, Austin and Angie were waiting. Reece greeted her with a steaming cup of coffee.

"This smells great, Reece. Thanks. How did you know that I needed this?"

"I just knew."

"Good morning, gentlemen. Did you get a good night's rest? I don't think I was awake for more than five seconds after my head hit the pillow," CeCe said as she sat on the sofa.

Austin sat his empty cup on the table in front of him. "Us, too. Did you enjoy your run? I would have liked to have gone with you this morning. Looks as though you got almost as wet as when we were kayaking."

CeCe laughed and said, "Not that wet. It was a good thing we had a dry bag, or all of our stuff would have been ruined."

"That's for sure," piped in Reece. "I've looked in every drawer, nook, and cranny, CeCe. I think we've gotten everything. Thanks for taking me with you, and thanks guys for the fun time."

"It was our pleasure ladies." Angie bowed at the waist. "Shall we go? Your chariot awaits you."

They followed the guys to the airport and pulled into the car return area. CeCe returned the keys to the rental car. She turned around to go back and gather her luggage, and bumped right into Austin. He was standing very close to her.

"Excuse me. I didn't know you were there. I could handle the luggage myself."

"No need to when you have us around," Austin told her.

They went through the agriculture checkpoint and moved to the counter to check in. There was a long line. Austin excused himself and came back and told them to follow him. He had a special card that allowed him to check into the first class counter. He would just check in now with Angie and get their seat assignments and allow CeCe and Reece to check in as well.

They walked to the gate and waited about fifteen minutes before their flight was called.

CeCe rose and hugged Austin and Angie both. She didn't want to let go of Austin, but knew that she must.

"Thanks again for everything. I will come back here someday. I promised myself," CeCe said.

"Great. Hopefully, we can arrange to all come together again." Angie moved alongside of them.

"Well, guess we'll see you guys later," Reece said. "Don't forget to keep in touch, Angie. I'm sure Austin would love for you to come to his ranch. If that's the case, we'll all go out to dinner. I would offer to cook, but it wouldn't be the neighborly thing to do, since I'm not much of a cook," Reece joked.

"I'll take you up on that, Reece. I'll have some time on my hands until mini-camp starts, so I'm sure you'll see me. Take care, and CeCe, you make sure you keep this guy in line."

"Who…me?" Austin asked, looking shocked. "I'm always good."

CeCe pretended to choke. "Yes, that's why you always seem to be in trouble with Ruth. Angie, you'll definitely see me at some more of your games. I loved being there in the middle of all the excitement. See if you can't get that coach of yours to teach you how to catch the ball without pushing off."

"We won't get into that now, CeCe."

They were beginning to load the plane, so Reece and CeCe had to gather up their stuff and move on with the other passengers. Austin absently put his arm around CeCe's waist and walked with her. When they neared the ticket agent, Austin removed his arm and tipped CeCe's chin upward. He kissed her lightly and said goodbye. CeCe and Reece moved through the gate and looked back to wave.

They found their seats on the plane and prepared themselves for take-off. CeCe was in a daze. She had thought that she had her emotions under control until Austin kissed her. It was just a light kiss, but she felt that he might as well have ravaged her right there in the terminal. Her skin was flushed and she couldn't concentrate on what it was Reece was saying. Finally, she brought herself back.

"I'm sorry, what were you saying?"

"I said, I had a wonderful time. I hope that I can return the favor to you sometime; that is, take you somewhere with me. I really got to know Angie, and I like him a lot."

"We did have a good time. What about Mason? I thought you were beginning to build a relationship with him."

"Well, I do like him, but you know how it is." Reece batted her eyelashes at CeCe.

They both laughed and settled in. CeCe watched as the plane lifted off, leaving the island behind in the clouds.

Chapter Thirty-Six

The trip back was good. CeCe was anxious to see Nitro. As they drove up into Austin's drive, Ruth opened the door and Nitro ran out onto the porch. He waited there until CeCe got out. Nitro tilted his head sideways and his ear rose. When he heard CeCe's familiar voice, he came running off the porch and jumped onto her.

"Nitro! I missed you, boy. Were you good for Ruth and Tucker?"

Nitro licked CeCe's face all over. She lifted his paws off of her and bent down to hug and pet him.

"You don't look as though you lost any weight while I was gone. Ruth, was he good? Did you stick to his diet?"

"Heavens, yes, he was good. I'll miss him now that you're back. Tucker will miss him even more. We did pretty well with the diet. He does tend to beg a bit, and you know me- I'm a softy."

CeCe and Reece filled Ruth in about their trip and told her they would have pictures for her soon. Lots and lots of pictures, they assured her. They gave Ruth the gifts they had bought for her and Tucker.

CeCe gathered up Nitro's things and headed home. It was wonderful in Hawaii, but it was nice to be back home in Colorado, too.

It didn't take long to get back into their routines. Reece spent most of the next morning reviewing her phone messages. There were the usual calls; she had gotten a call from Mason welcoming her back, as well as from Dr. Baldwin. She was very interested in the one that was going to give her an opportunity to work on a new series of articles for the paper. The articles were about football, of all things. She was up for the challenge and knew where she could get some good information.

The mail was another thing however; it was piled high on her desk. It was late afternoon by the time she got around to sorting through it.

The junk mail pile was quickly gaining ground on the other mail. She lifted a magazine off the pile and was ready to drop it into the junk mail when she spotted the envelope.

There was no mistaking the letter. She lifted the envelope and looked at the postmark. Loveland! Who did she know in Loveland? Then it dawned on her that it was postmarked on the 14th - Valentines Day! Did this person know someone in Loveland, or did they drive all the way there?

Reece opened the envelope and the fragrance of the paper filtered past her. She began to read the letter.

Dearest Reece,
I am missing you terribly. I sit here by the warmth of the fire and though it warms my body outwardly, it can do nothing for my heart or to stoke my internal fire that just the sight of you does for me.

Reece reached for her jacket and headed over to CeCe's. She would just be finishing up now.

CeCe spent a little extra time at the shop getting things in order again. Ruth had done a great job, but CeCe just wanted to linger. She had missed the conversations with her customers. She was brought up to date on all the things that happened while she was away.

Dr. Baldwin came in and asked how the trip was. He said that he was sorry that he didn't get the opportunity to go with them. He asked all about Reece and said that he had counted on CeCe to make sure she hadn't found some surfer dude who would steal her heart. CeCe reassured him that that didn't happen. Dr. Baldwin reminded CeCe of the appointment she had later in the week to do a final check on Nitro's paw. CeCe told him she hadn't forgotten.

Tom came in and looked as though he wanted to talk to her, but she was very busy at the time. Austin came in looking better than ever. The sun made him look even more handsome.

CeCe couldn't help think about the time they had spent together. It had been so easy and comfortable, the four of them spending so much time together. She didn't want to think about Austin every waking minute, but that was difficult.

When Austin came in, he looked as though he wanted to talk. She was right in the middle of a rush. She couldn't help wondering if he had seen Poalima, or if he had heard from her. It was evident to CeCe that Poalima was still interested. CeCe would have to decide if she could continue to get involved with Austin under those circumstances.

The bell rang as Reece opened the door. She struggled to shut it behind her with the wind and snow blowing.

"What a difference from just two days ago. It seems like longer than that, doesn't it Reece?" CeCe asked as she came around the front of the counter.

Reece reached in her pocket and produced the letter.

"Looks as though whoever is writing these knows a whole lot about me. They knew I was in Hawaii. They either know someone in Loveland or they drove there to have this letter postmarked."

"Oh, Reece. I was hoping that this was going to be behind you. What do you mean, postmarked Loveland?"

Reece handed her the letter.

It looked like the same envelope and it was typed, CeCe thought to herself as she took the letter from Reece.

"Oh, I see. It was postmarked on Valentine's Day. That's a pretty long drive to have it postmarked if he lives here."

CeCe read the letter. "All I can say is that this guy has a way with words. I think we need to give it to the sheriff. Maybe they can pick up on something from this one."

"Yes, I agree. I'm not getting anywhere with them. But that doesn't mean I'm going to quit trying. Sooner or later, I'll figure this out. Now, how about a cup of coffee or tea for your travel buddy?"

Chapter Thirty-Seven

CeCe drove home and picked up Nitro to take him to see Dr. Baldwin. The weather had cleared a bit for the time being, but was still threatening to snow at any minute. CeCe was longing for the warmth she had experienced while in Kauai.

Nitro was happy to see her and jumped right into the car. CeCe tried to keep her mind in Colorado and not in the past in Kauai. That was a difficult task.

Dr. Baldwin's waiting room was almost empty when they arrived. His assistant showed them to the exam room. CeCe would be glad to have all memory of the fire over with. That would come when Nitro got a clean bill of health.

Dr. Baldwin came in to the exam room with a huge smile on his face. "CeCe, it is always a pleasure to see you."

"Hello, Dr. Baldwin. Hopefully, this will be the last time we will have to come here until Nitro is due for his annual exam. His paw seems to be doing very well, but he keeps scratching at his left ear. I might as well have you check it out while we're here."

Dr. Baldwin lifted Nitro up onto the table. "Let's have a look here, boy. Yes, that paw is just fine. No need to worry about it any longer. Now, let's look in that ear."

Dr. Baldwin patted his lab coat looking for his light. He reached into his pockets but came up empty there as well.

"I seem to have lost my light. I'll just go into the other exam room and find another. I don't know what I could have done with it. You know how it is- you have a favorite. I'll be right back."

Dr. Baldwin was back very quickly. He looked into Nitro's ear and saw a burr buried in there. He had CeCe help hold Nitro still and reached in and pulled it out.

"There, I don't think that will be bothering you anymore. It looks clean in there, CeCe, other than that little irritant. I think you probably will have your wish to not see me here again until his annual exam is due. Maybe we can get together some evening; you, Reece and myself, to look at those pictures you took in Hawaii. Let's try and set something up."

"Sure, but I'll have the pictures at the coffee shop for a while. I promised everyone I would bring them in so they could see all the fun we had. It is such an incredible place. You should go sometime."

"I tried, remember? You said you thought you would do just fine without me."

"Sorry to say, we did."

They chatted a while longer and CeCe left to take Nitro home. She was glad to have that final exam over with. Now maybe she could forget about the fire and almost losing Nitro.

Reece was really driving herself with the series of articles on football. "I'm learning so much, CeCe. Next year when we go to games, you'll be surprised at how much I know," was what she would say whenever the subject came up.

The rest of the winter flew by. Reece was relieved to not have any new letters or intrusions into her personal life. She was enjoying correspondence with Angie.

CeCe had kept herself busy with the shop and working on community projects. She never stopped thinking about Austin and wondered what happened in his relationship with Poalima. She saw him often in the coffee shop, but avoided spending time with him alone. She felt that if she gave it time and if it were meant to be, then things would work out with him.

On an occasion or two their hands would touch in the exchange of an order or payment. The spark was still there, if not more so than before. CeCe had to hide the shiver it would send through her body. The way Austin looked at her left no doubt that the desire within him was stronger than ever.

Austin didn't know how to get through to CeCe. Poalima had tried to get in touch with him, but he refused to talk to her. He didn't want to have anything to do with her.

He could have wrung her neck for messing up what he had going with CeCe. He couldn't stand the thought of not holding her and touching her. Once the weather got warmer, and things settled in he was sure that they could get back on the right track.

Austin was thinking about going back to Kauai, but wanted to hold off until CeCe knew that everything with Poalima was over. He couldn't risk her thinking that he was going back there to start up the relationship again.

. As promised, Angie did come and visit. He came in late April just before the first mini-camp would start. This was the opportunity that Austin had been waiting for. He was sure that CeCe would agree to go out with him if Angie and Reece were along.

Austin opened the door to the coffee shop. It was after the rush and CeCe was in there by herself. She turned as she heard the bell ring.

Austin could feel the excitement rush through his body at the sight of her. The time that they spent apart did nothing but make him want her even more. Her skin still held the color she had gotten on the island. That made him think of the hike and the pond and he quickly put it out of his mind in order to control his excitement.

"Hello, stranger," Austin said as he slid onto a seat at the counter. "How have you been?"

"Hello, Austin." CeCe smiled as she dried her hands on the towel. "Would you like a cup of coffee?"

"That would be wonderful. I came by to ask if you were going to be free a couple of nights this week. Angie is coming to town today and I thought we all might be able to renew the good time we had in Kauai right here in Colorado."

"That's wonderful. How's the old boy doing? He must be getting ready for mini-camp."

"He's great. That's why he is coming now. He'll be too busy to do much of anything once he starts back in to camp. That's why I came in here, to let you know that Angie will be here and that both of us thought it would be fun if we could all go out."

CeCe hesitated, she wanted to go out with Austin but she was afraid of what of what might happen. What could it hurt? "Sure, Austin that would be great. Have you spoken with Reece yet?"

"No, I haven't, but Angie did. He talked with her this morning to find out what her plans were. She said she would make time for him anytime."

"Great. Any ideas as to where you would like to go? I mean, if you like, I wouldn't mind fixing dinner at my place."

"CeCe, I couldn't ask you to do that. That's not why I came in here. I don't want to make more work for you. You already work too hard as it is. No, we could just go to the Chalet, they have good food."

"What, are you afraid of my cooking? I would really enjoy fixing dinner and having company. It gets lonely out there all by myself."

"What about Nitro?"

"Well, he isn't much of a conversationalist. I think it's settled. We'll have dinner at my house. Any requests?"

"I heard you make a mean lasagna. I'll bring the wine and dessert."

"No thanks to the dessert, but you can bring the wine. Dinner at 8:00 at my house. Do you remember how to get there?"

"Does a bear ... never mind. Of course I know how to get there. We'll be there at 8:00, then. Thanks, CeCe, it will be nice to sit across the table from you again and have a real conversation."

"Now go on and get out of here. I have work to do."

Austin stood and reached his hand in his pocket to retrieve money. CeCe stopped him.

"The coffee is on me. Just bring some good music to put on the CD player- we seem to have similar tastes."

Austin leaned across the counter and brushed some flour off of CeCe's cheek. "Thanks again, CeCe."

CeCe watched him walk out the door and across the street to his waiting truck. She never got tired of watching his muscular body move.

She shook her head and thought about what to make for dessert.

~ ~ ~

Reece arrived ahead of the guys. She looked gorgeous in white wool slacks and brown silk blouse. CeCe looked equally as beautiful. She wore black Capri slacks and a powder blue cashmere sweater. The blue made her eyes stand out.

Nitro announced Austin and Angie's arrival even before they knocked.

"I'll get it," Reece called out as she opened the door.

"Aloha, howdy, good evening, or however you say it. Nice to see you again, Reece." Angie stepped inside and hugged Reece. "This place is wonderful. The view is just as beautiful as it is in Hawaii."

CeCe walked over to the three of them. "Welcome to my humble abode. It ain't much, but it's all I have."

"I love it," Angie said as he reached down and hugged CeCe. "Any predictions for my team this year?"

"No, but I do have one for Austin's team. If he will let me help him call the plays, they will be state champions."

"Is that so?" Austin said, amused. "Well, even though you are critical of my play calling and how I used to play ball, I did want to bring you some flowers." Austin held out a beautiful bouquet of tropical flowers.

"Austin, they are beautiful. Where did you get them?" CeCe exclaimed.

"I have my connections. Where shall I put them?"

CeCe took them from Austin. "Thanks."

Austin held her hand and then kissed her briefly. "I'll help you.

Just show me the way."

CeCe was caught off guard. She recovered quickly and said, "This way, Austin."

When CeCe was looking for the vase, she remembered how she felt when she found the one with Poalima's handwriting on it. She remembered the pangs of jealously she had felt. But now it was different. Austin had brought her flowers.

With the flowers arranged in the vase and the table set, Austin opened the wine. They had a few minutes to sit and talk before CeCe served dinner. The conversation revolved mostly around Angie and the upcoming season.

Nitro was right in the middle of things. He kept bringing his ball for Angie to throw for him. CeCe commented that maybe Nitro could be the team mascot. That way she would have to escort him to all of the games.

They sat down for dinner and enjoyed a wonderful salad, and then the lasagna. It was every bit as good as Austin had heard, and maybe even better.

Angie was going for a third helping. "My grandmother would be envious of this dish. She is full-blooded Italian and she loves a good lasagna. Where did you get the recipe, anyway, CeCe?"

"I got the original recipe from a friend of my grandmother's, and then I've added a few touches myself through the years. So it's changed, but now I have it up here." CeCe pointed to her head. "I'm glad you like it. I like to make it when I have company so they can take the leftovers home; otherwise, I find myself eating too much of it. You know a girl has to watch her figure."

They all laughed at CeCe's comment. Austin just watched her in amazement. The candlelight was reflecting off of her hair and made her eyes deepen to a dark blue. He wanted to walk over and kiss her full mouth right then and there, but of course he knew he couldn't. The dinner she had prepared was wonderful.

"Austin, hello, earth to Austin," Reece was saying to him.

"Yes, Reece?" he answered, embarrassed by his thoughts.

"I was just saying, you brought the perfect wine to go with this dinner. I didn't know you were such a wine connoisseur."

"Well, it's easy when you have such a wonderful cook." Austin held up his glass and gestured toward CeCe in a toast fashion. "To you, CeCe, and the wonderful meal you've prepared for us."

"Here, here!" Reece and Angie chimed in.

CeCe and Austin's eyes locked- they could both feel the excitement across the table. CeCe rose to break the spell. "I have a simple but not understated dessert. I think we will have coffee and dessert in the living room, if that is alright with everyone else."

Reece stood to clear the table. Angie stood as well. "Let us clean up the dishes since you made this wonderful dinner." CeCe protested, but in the end lost her argument. CeCe and Austin went out into the living room where Austin put one of the CD's he had brought on the player. Angie hollered out from the kitchen to turn it up. Austin did as he was told.

After a few minutes, Angie came out of the kitchen holding an imaginary microphone, mouthing the words. He twirled around the room and held out his hand to CeCe. CeCe stood and took hold of his outstretched hand and started dancing with him. Austin grabbed hold of Reece. They were all dancing and laughing. Austin tapped Angie on the shoulder. "Mind if I cut in, partner?"

Angie replied, "Be my guest, Mr. Carter."

At that, Austin wrapped his arms around CeCe and swayed to the music. It felt so good to both of them. It was like nothing had ever come between them. CeCe rolled her head back and looked up into Austin's eyes. The look she saw there was unmistakable. His eyes were smoky and pleading. CeCe knew the way he was looking at her meant that he had wanted to take her in his arms long ago. She had been so determined to not make the mistake of coming between him and Poalima that she had missed all the other signals he had been sending.

Austin was glad for the opportunity to hold CeCe. He was going to make sure that she knew how he felt about her tonight before he left. This was the opening he had been waiting for. He missed holding her and touching her. His thoughts were consumed with her during most of his waking moments, and many of hidden sleeping ones.

The music stopped and CeCe said, "I'll get dessert and bring it in here."

Austin grabbed her hand. "Here, let me help you. I can at least bring the coffee in."

CeCe agreed to let him help. "You two behave yourselves, now. I can hear everything that goes on in here."

Angie wrestled Reece to the sofa and said, "I promise not to let her seduce me."

Reece hit him on his arm, "What makes you think that I want to seduce you?"

At that, CeCe and Austin walked into the kitchen smiling. They kept the conversation light while preparing the dessert. CeCe had made an old family recipe: Crunch Cake. She explained, "You crush vanilla wafers and chopped walnuts, add some butter, and place it in the bottom of a bread pan. Make the pound cake and pour it over top, and an hour or so later you have Crunch Cake."

"This is awesome!" exclaimed Austin. "You could make a mint and three-quarters of the town fat with this."

"Thanks, I like it quite a bit myself," CeCe said as she broke off a tiny piece and put it into her mouth.

Angie broke off a piece and fed it to Reece who in turn did the same for him. Everything seemed so right.

~ ~ ~

He stood outside the door and watched through the window. He had come to talk to CeCe, but hadn't expected to see Reece there.

She was standing there with the warmth of the room glowing on her face.

There was that football player again, moving in on his territory. He would have to do something to make sure he didn't get in the way. His plans were well thought out, and he couldn't afford for someone to mess them up.

He had stood at the door with his hand raised to knock when he heard them all laughing. He moved over to the window. The light was shining out into the yard so it made it easy for him to see where he was stepping. In order to get close enough, he had to step into the flowerbed where the fresh young shoots were just beginning to rear their heads. Too bad they might not make it after the abuse he was about to put them through.

He would have to make sure he took control of this situation. He was being forced into moving too fast. He needed more time for his plan to work properly. Reece still didn't trust and love him the way he needed her to. In order for this to work, he needed her to make him part of her life. Once he had access to do what he wished with her money, well then, Reece was no longer any use to him. She was just another pretty face, and Lord knew he had been through many of those in his lifetime.

Damn, he didn't like being forced into moving quicker than he wanted to. That's what had happened the last time. He would just have to grin and bear it.

He watched for a while longer. This guy was way too friendly with Reece. Look at how he was putting his hands all over her, like she belonged to him. Reece wasn't too quick to fend him off, either.

Nitro lifted his head and sniffed the air. He started to grow more agitated. He moved from the floor to the window and started barking.

"What is it, boy?" Austin stood and went to him. "Is there some critter out there you want to get? That's all I need- to let you out to get sprayed by a skunk or porcupine. CeCe would never forgive me."

"No, she wouldn't," CeCe said. "Come on, buddy I'll take you out on the leash." CeCe hooked the leash to Nitro's collar. "Anyone want to come?'

Everyone agreed it was nice enough of an evening that they would like to take a little walk. They all grabbed a sweater and headed for the door.

That dog. He didn't seem to like him. He could sense that he was out there, now it looked as if everyone was coming out. He needed to get away. He quickly ran back to the car and started it. He left the lights off until he was down the road a ways. Hopefully, they wouldn't see him leaving.

Austin opened the door to see the distant lights on the vehicle. "Looks like someone was looking for you, CeCe."

"No, they always make the wrong turn at the intersection. Once they get on the road there they realize that this isn't where they want to be. You can see the place up in the road there where they all turn around. I've been thinking about asking the county about putting in one of those roundabouts. You know the kind they have in Europe. It would make it easier for folks." She laughed as she let Nitro lead the way.

Nitro went directly to the flowerbed. He kept sniffing around as if he were going to find something. "I bet it was the deer again, CeCe," Reece said as she hugged herself. "They keep coming and eating all of the garden CeCe plants," Reece said to the rest of them.

"You could be right."

Nitro finished sniffing and took them on a short stroll. When they returned, Angie and Austin decided it was time to get going.

"Angie, are you going to come with Austin to the Charity Ball on Friday?" Reece was gathering her things to leave as well.

"Oh yeah, Austin told me all about it. I guess you and CeCe are bachelorettes. They auction you off or something like that."

"Something like that," CeCe explained. "Every year the genders take turns to either be the prize or the buyers. You go on a date with the highest bidder and all the money goes to the charity. This time, it's the females turn; otherwise, we would have you and Austin up for bids."

"It sounds like fun." Angie turned toward the door. "You can count me in. See you there, ladies."

Austin and Angie headed out the door. Reece followed close behind. CeCe watched the cars retreat as she reflected on the evening. She liked the way things had turned out. Even though they hadn't talked about it, CeCe was sure that things were over between Austin and Poalima. Now it was a matter as to which way things would go with them and if she was willing to let events take what seemed to be a natural progression.

Chapter Thirty-Eight

It had been a long time since he had written to Reece. He knew he was going to see her this evening. It would be an opportunity to get another letter to her.

Things had changed a bit. He didn't quite understand his feelings. For a time, Reece had been all that he could think about, but now he wasn't quite as obsessive over her. There was a distraction in his life that made him wonder if he really was doing the right thing. But the feeling to write to her was overwhelming today.

He sat at the typewriter and removed the gloves. He liked the feel of the keys under his bare fingertips too much to wear them while he typed.

Darling Reece,

I am still here watching and admiring you. I haven't forgotten about you; I have just found myself distracted.

No matter the season, you are as fresh as the mountain spring air or the first fallen snow. I watch you in amazement and wonder if you feel the same about me.

Now that spring is here, I will be able to watch your well-toned body as you venture out each day.

The flowers are pale in comparison to you. Their beautiful bright colors can't compete with the creamy white skin that you so carefully tan to a beautiful healthy glow.

The smell of the new grass and budding trees are overpowered by the fresh natural scent that fills the air as you pass by.

You, Reece, are the most beautiful creature on this earth. Not only outwardly, but the inner you. You will make me proud tonight along with the rest of the people there.

I have missed you and am sorry for the distractions that have kept me from you.

Did you miss me and wonder what had happened to me? I have seen your interaction with others. I thought you were becoming involved with another, but now I know you are just waiting for me.

I have been tempted to move on. I don't know if the distance between us is too far. I am willing to continue to wait and try. I know that you will eventually see that we are right together.

Watch whom you let into your life and whom you trust. Not all of us are are what we seem.

There is danger in the air- be cautious. I will be waiting and watching over you.

Until we can be together, Reece, Love, Me.

He carefully removed the paper with his glove-covered hands. He held it close to his nose so he could smell the fragrance that emitted from it. Now he would have to think about how he would get the letter to her. He would be excited for her to receive it. He would wait until the evening was almost over. Then he would make sure she saw it. He loved watching her reaction to the letters. Tonight would be no different.

~ ~ ~

CeCe and Reece arrived early at the conference center to help set up. There wasn't much to be done, but they were there if someone needed them. The evening had a bit of a nip in the air, which made all the guests' faces glow.

Austin and Angie arrived fairly early. They pulled in front of the entrance where several valets were waiting to take cars. Austin spotted Tom as he came around to open the door for him.

"Good evening, Tom, I thought you might be attending tonight and join in on the bidding process."

"G-good evening, Mr. Carter. I t-thought I might be of b-better service here. It l-looks as though it will be a g-good fundraiser, though."

Austin handed the keys to Tom. "Let me introduce you to my friend, Angie. Tom Dancer, this is Angie D'Angelo. I've known Angie for a long time, we played together for awhile."

Tom stuck out his hand to shake Angie's. "I've s-seen you on TV- you play football for the D-Denver Broncos, nice to m-meet you, Mr. D'Angelo."

Angie shook Tom's hand and said, "Nice to meet you, Tom. I hope you like the Bronco's. I've been told you are very good at your trade."

"Yes, s-sir. I do like to watch f-football. D-don't know if I would want to be out there getting k-knocked around, though. I've b-been k-kicked around a few times by some horses. I don't like t-that feeling. I imagine it m-might feel about the same."

"That it does, Tom. Nice meeting you." Angie waited for Austin to come around so they could go in.

Tom got into the car and drove it to the parking area.

CeCe and Reece were standing near the front putting the finishing touches on the makeshift stage. Austin walked in and the sight of CeCe made him catch his breath.

She was wearing a blue satin evening gown that was the exact color of the ocean.

Her hair was piled high on her head, which gave her the appearance of being taller. There were loose strands of hair trailing down her slender neck. Austin couldn't believe how beautiful she was. He wanted to embed this picture in his mind and was sure that it would be there forever.

CeCe felt Austin's presence the minute he walked into the room. It was as though there were a magnetic field that connected them. She raised her head and smiled as the two men walked toward her. There were those butterflies in her stomach again.

Austin reached down and took CeCe's hand and raised it to his lips. "Good evening, princess. You will fetch a fair price in the bidding tonight. I have a feeling I will walk away from here with my wallet much lighter. I don't intend for anyone else to out-bid me."

CeCe blushed at the compliment. "I feel like a princess."

"You look like a princess."

Angie and Reece were standing off to the side watching the interaction between their two good friends. Angie had his arm around Reece when CeCe and Austin turned to them.

"Hey, I didn't think you were able to touch the goods before the auction," a voice said from behind them all.

Everyone turned to see who made the comment. It was Dr. Baldwin.

"Good evening, ladies and gentlemen. I take it you are going to be bidding on these lovely women. May the best man win." Dr. Baldwin walked over and shook both Austin and Angie's hands. He reached for Reece's hand and raised it to his lips. He did the same with CeCe. "This is my favorite charity. I believe I am sitting at the same table as you all."

Reece introduced Angie and they chatted awhile. Mason came over to the table and proclaimed that he too was going to be sitting with them.

The evening progressed well. Everyone was enjoying themselves immensely. The time was nearing for the auction, so CeCe and Reece excused themselves from the table to go and join the other women near the stage.

He had loved seeing and being near her this evening. He hadn't quite figured out how to get the letter to her. Then it came to him. There were the envelopes filled with the information as to where the winners of the bidding would go on their date. This would be the perfect place to put the letter.

He found an opportunity to steal away and find the packet with Reece's name on it. He handled it carefully and slipped the letter in between the other envelopes. This would be the perfect opportunity for him to be able to watch her read the letter.

He moved through the darkened stage area back to his seat and sat back down. He raised the glass to his lips and felt the warm liquid move through his body. It was just a matter of time now before Reece would hold the letter he had written to her.

~ ~ ~

CeCe and Reece were the last to go. CeCe told Reece she wanted her to be last. She knew that Reece would have brought in a good bid. CeCe was surprised at the amount of bidding she created. Austin and Dr. Baldwin were the last to hold out. Austin was determined to be the winner. Austin raised his bid to five thousand dollars, which brought Dr. Baldwin to a halt.

"Guess you win, Austin. I need to save some bidding power for Reece."

CeCe was amazed. She took her packet and waited for Austin to come to the stage to claim her. He held her hand and helped her off the stage. When they returned to the table, she looked at him.

"That was awfully generous of you, Austin."

"My dear, I would have paid twice that amount to have the evening with you." Austin smiled into her eyes.

CeCe could feel herself melting away.

The bidding began on Reece. As expected, the bidding was spread all around the room. At the table where CeCe and Austin sat, Mason and Dr. Baldwin kept raising the bid. It was quickly apparent that the bidding would continue between just the two of them.

Mason was determined that he would win the bidding on Reece. When they reached the five thousand dollar mark, Mason was getting angry. He was fiercely competitive and didn't want to give up, but he hated to put out that kind of money out for some charity that he really didn't care for.

The auctioneer was at fifty-five hundred dollars and was about to award the final bid to Dr. Baldwin, when a wave of a hand in the back of the room caught his eye. "Six thousand is the bid from the back of the room. Do I have sixty-five hundred?" Everyone turned around to see who had bid the six thousand dollars. It was Angie. He had gotten up from the table before the bidding began and didn't want to disturb the process. He just stood there leaning against the door, looking over to the table to see if anyone would up the ante.

Mason was furious now. He was sure he had the bid won before since that is where Dr. Baldwin had stopped with CeCe. Now he had to contend with this arrogant football player.

Reece stood on the stage, smiling at the scene that was playing out before her. She was glad that she was able to raise such a large amount of money for the charity.

Dr. Baldwin took the bid of sixty-five hundred. Mason went to seven thousand. All eyes turned to the back of the room. Angie mumbled under his breath, "This ought to end this little game," and more loudly announced, "Ten thousand dollars."

A murmur rumbled through the crowd. The auctioneer asked for ten five, and when no one bid he said, "Ten thousand going once, going twice, sold to the generous gentleman in the back"

Everyone got up to leave the room, since Reece had been the last to be auctioned off.

Angie walked to the front and pulled out his checkbook. Reece took the packet of envelopes and stepped down with Angie's help.

"Angie, I would have gone on a date with you for a lot less than that," she teased, and then said more seriously, "The charity will be very grateful to you."

"I think it was fun, and it was for a good cause. Besides, those two guys were going to kill each other," Angie said as he wrote out the check.

CeCe and Austin stayed at the table and waited until Reece and Angie returned.

They walked back to the table as Reece untied the ribbon that held everything together. "Let's see what all that money bought you, Angie. Here, why don't you open it? It belongs to you."

Reece handed over the packet to him. Angie finished opening the packet. He looked at the front of the envelopes that told him where they were going. He came to the envelope with Reece's name typed on it. "I believe this one belongs to you, Reece." He handed her the envelope.

Reece and CeCe recognized it immediately. Reece's hands shook slightly as she opened the letter.

"Is there something wrong, Reece?" Angie asked.

"It's the same as the other letters. It's been awhile. I thought maybe they had stopped for good." Reece looked around to see who was near. There were groups of people standing and talking, but no one looked to be interested in her. Reece read the letter.

He knew he would be able to see her read it. She was so beautiful. Her long elegant fingers opened the letter as his heart beat loudly. He stood behind the curtain where he was sure that he wouldn't be seen. He could see the blush in her cheeks deepen as she read the words he wrote to her. If things had gone his way, he would be sitting with her there. He would leave now with the satisfaction of watching her open the letter. Sleep would come easy tonight with just the thought of her.

Reece handed the letter to Angie, who read it along with Austin. "How long has it been since you received a letter like this?" Angie asked.

"It's been awhile, I think it was right after we came back from Hawaii."

The banquet crew was starting to clear the tables. CeCe got

up and gathered her things. "Let's go somewhere and have some coffee, shall we?"

Everyone got up and moved toward the door. Austin and Angie went and got their coats. Angie suggested they go to Austin's place. They all agreed.

Tom had brought both of the cars around. He opened the door for CeCe and Reece. "Did you b-both enjoy the evening?"

"Yes, Tom it was great," CeCe answered him. "Thank you for helping out with the valet parking. Did you get to have dinner?"

"Yes, I d-did, thank you. Everyone seemed to be h-happy tonight, y-you d-drive safely, now." Tom closed the door behind them and walked to the men. "H-here are your k-keys, Mr. Carter. I t-take it your evening was good as w-well?"

Austin took the keys. "Thanks, Tom; we did have a good time. Both Angie and I here got the winning bids for dates with CeCe and Reece. We were happy to donate the money and it was a fun way to do it. I will be giving you a call soon to check on your schedule for shodding. Tucker said that some of the horses need to be done soon.

"I'll w-wait to hear from you, then, d-drive safely." Tom closed the door behind them.

CeCe and Reece were just getting out of the car when Angie and Austin drove up.

"Just one cup of coffee for me, I need to get home and to bed," Reece spoke as she entered into the house.

"I agree. I'm pretty tired myself," CeCe said.

"Reece, do you want to talk about the letter?" Angie asked.

"No, I don't think there is anything to worry about. It sounds as though the guy is harmless. It just was creepy when he showed up at my house and then when the office got broken into. If the letters come by mail, or the way this one came, it's all right. Hey, how about that coffee?"

They spent the next hour talking about the date that they would take from the auction. CeCe and Austin were headed over to Aspen. They were going to ride and fish. This was perfect for them. CeCe had wanted to go over to the Roaring Fork Valley to fly-fish, and now she would have the opportunity.

Reece and Angie were going to a Mystery Dinner theater and an overnight pack trip. Angie was thrilled. The times were planned, and CeCe and Reece drove away from the ranch contently.

It was interesting to him the reaction that he witnessed. Reece seemed to be frowning when she opened the letter rather than joyous. He was glad that Mr. Carter's friend won out the bidding. If he were not able to take Reece on the trip, then he wanted someone he could trust. He didn't know him very well, but he seemed like a nice guy. He had seen him play football and watched him on the television after the games. He was sure that this guy would treat Reece well until it was his turn to take over.

Chapter Thirty-Nine

The weekend they had chosen to go on the trip was a beauty. The weather was perfect. CeCe and Austin drove over to the Roaring Fork Valley, with CeCe talking most of the way. She was so excited about this weekend; they were set to stay in Snowmass Village. They were going to go horseback riding somewhere near Maroon Bells. Austin had never seen the Roaring Fork Valley before; he was in awe of the rugged mountain peaks and the greenness of the landscape.

"Is it always this quiet here?" he asked.

"Heavens, no," CeCe replied. "In the winter it's one of the most popular places to be. If you think the slopes and the town are busy in the Yampa Valley, you should see it here. Some of the country's most elite gather here to party and ski."

"Well, I like it like this. We seem to have the place to ourselves. I hope the weather holds; although, I do understand that when it rains it's a good time to fish."

"That's what my friend Shaw said. I called him and told him we would be over here this weekend and he and Lisa invited us to come to their place. He said that he would take us out on the river and extend our fishing lesson. He claims that he has the prime piece of property; it's where the Roaring Fork River and the Frying Pan River meet. It's supposed to be the ultimate in fly-fishing. I have fished before, but never here. Tucker took me out a few times and I loved it. I could use a refresher though. "CeCe sat back, content with the conversation and the company.

Austin looked over at CeCe. He could see the excitement in her eyes. What more could any man want in a woman than what CeCe had to offer? She was beautiful and didn't spend hours making herself look that way. Her body was perfect. She did work on keeping it firm and attractive, but she wasn't obsessive about it.

Austin's thoughts were making him excited. He found himself often thinking about a future with CeCe. He knew that she was cautious about getting involved in a relationship after that scum Carlos had hurt her so badly, but Austin could feel her reserve slipping away. She had opened up to him again. It took some time to convince her that Poalima was not what he wanted, but he thought that he might have finally gotten through to her.

This weekend was going to be good for both of them. It could be the break- through point in the relationship that Austin was waiting for so anxiously.

CeCe sat and looked out the window as they passed along the road. She never tired of Colorado's beauty, although she did love it in Hawaii. Austin's place in Hawaii was the perfect compliment to his ranch here in Colorado.

Her thoughts of the trip to Hawaii evoked mixed emotions in CeCe. She had felt close to Austin there, yet she was convinced that at the time he still had feelings for Poalima. Austin had worked pretty hard to explain to her that the relationship between he and Poalima only still existed in Poalima's mind. He told CeCe that the Poalima's beauty and manipulative manner had blinded him. He only thought that he loved her, and the only regret he had was for the loss of the child.

CeCe thought that she would love to go back to Hawaii with Austin. The picture that played out in her head was of the two of them making slow, sensuous love in his large bed. The sounds of the tropical birds singing and the sweet, pungent scent of ginger wafting in the windows would surround them. CeCe shivered at the thoughts she was having and forced herself to think about something else.

Austin saw the shiver and watched as CeCe wrapped her arms around herself. "Are you cold? I can turn on the heat."

"Excuse me?" CeCe answered.

"I saw you shiver. I asked if you were cold."

"No, on the contrary. I was just thinking how nice the weather is and what a great weekend we choose." CeCe blushed. She thought to herself *If only you knew what I was thinking.*

The fund raising committee had thought ahead enough to make sure that they arranged separate accommodations for the two of them. The condominium complex they chose was beautiful. It sat up on the mountainside and would be an easy walk to the slopes during the winter.

Austin left CeCe to unpack and walked next door to his place. They agreed to meet at Austin's at 6:00 for a cocktail before they headed into town for dinner. CeCe felt she needed that time in order to gain her composure. She didn't know what had gotten in to her on the way there.

Austin unpacked and left the condo. He went to a liquor store and to a little deli.

At exactly 6:00, CeCe knocked on the door of Austin's room. Austin opened the door and gestured for CeCe to come in.

Austin was always amazed at the effect just the sight of her had on him. As she walked in, he caught the familiar scent she always wore. It made Austin want to pull her toward him. And that was just the way she smelled; the way she looked was a whole other story.

No one ever did clothes justice the way that CeCe did. She could wear a potato sack and make it look like a Hollywood designer had made it just for her.

CeCe wore a light blue sweater that made her eyes even bluer. The slim black pants she was wearing emphasized her firm body. Austin thought it was going to be hard to keep his hands off of her tonight. She was beautiful.

"I thought we would have a cocktail here before we left for dinner. I decided we would have dinner here in the village rather than going into Aspen. I heard there is a great place here where they serve seafood. They have a grilled lobster on the menu, which sounds interesting to me. Is that alright with you, CeCe?"

"Sounds wonderful, I'm starved, but it looks like you have that situation taken care of. You did a nice job of putting this all together."

"My pleasure, a glass of wine, CeCe?"

"Sure. Can I help?"

"You already have. Your presence has made the evening better already."

Austin handed CeCe a glass of wine and they chatted about the next day's events. Austin was anxious to go riding. He had really come to enjoy it since he bought the ranch. CeCe missed the activity. She didn't get much opportunity to ride horses, but really loved it.

Austin looked at his watch and announced that it was time to go. He stood and retrieved CeCe's jacket. He let his hands linger on her shoulders once he had helped her into it.

CeCe noticed his hands there, but didn't mind. She liked the feel of them there and the security she felt when she was around Austin.

The walk was pleasant and helped them to work up even a bigger appetite. By the time they reached the restaurant, CeCe and Austin were both more than ready to eat.

When they walked into the restaurant, Austin was aware of how many men watched CeCe as she walked by. She was unaware of it; however, Austin felt a sense of pride just being with her.

Dinner was wonderful, CeCe thought to herself. She couldn't keep from saying something to Austin about how the cocktail waitress and the hostess were falling all over themselves to stand next to Austin.

"Don't be silly, CeCe. They're just doing their jobs."

"Well, if their job is to touch every man that comes in here, then I guess you're right."

Austin laughed, but had to raise his eyebrows at CeCe's comment.

The walk back was well needed, and caused them both to be ready for a good night's rest. Austin unlocked CeCe's door with the key she handed over to him.

"I could just come in with you. It would save the housekeeper from having to make my bed in the morning."

"I have an idea," CeCe said with a huge smile on her face. "Why don't you just get up in the morning and make the bed yourself-that way you will save her from having to do it anyway. Goodnight, Austin." CeCe reached up and kissed him lightly as she shut the door on him.

"Damn," Austin mumbled as he walked the few steps to his room.

The next morning was just as spectacular as the day before. CeCe had set the alarm for five-thirty in the morning. She had brought supplies so she could make them a hearty breakfast before they went out on their adventure today.

CeCe called Austin's room at six-thirty. "Rise and shine! Breakfast will be ready in fifteen minutes. Don't be late, or I might have to eat yours." CeCe hung up the phone before Austin had a chance to respond.

Fifteen minutes later Austin appeared at the door. He could smell the wonderful aroma before CeCe even opened the door.

"Good morning," CeCe said opening the door to him.

Austin didn't know which was better: The sight of CeCe in her jeans or the spread she had put on the table. Well, he did know which, but his stomach was growling so hard that he had to take care of that first.

CeCe had prepared apple oatmeal pancakes, fresh slab bacon, breakfast fries, and steaming coffee.

Austin didn't waste any time. He cleaned the last of the breakfast off of his plate and said, "CeCe, you're amazing! The looks of an angel and the ability to make a meal into a masterpiece."

"Thanks, Austin. I have about an hour before we're supposed to be at the stables."

"Let me clean up. It's the least I can do after the magic you worked in the kitchen this morning." Austin stood and reached for the plates.

"No. This will be a two-person effort- we'll do it together."

They cleared the table and washed the dishes. Austin was thinking that he could get used to this. He liked the domestic feel. Problem was, it was with CeCe and only her that he could see himself doing these sorts of things with. He didn't want to rush things, but he felt that he might be breaking through her reserve. Time would tell, and he wasn't about to give up.

They drove the short distance to the stables and were greeted by a tall young man dressed in jeans, boots, and cowboy hat.

"Good morning. You must be Mr. Carter and Ms. Wellington. My name is Dillon," the young man said as he removed his hat. He stuck out his hand to Austin, and then CeCe.

"Good morning," CeCe answered. "That's us; nice to meet you, Dillon."

Austin shook Dillon's hand while under his scrutiny. "Hello, Dillon. Will you be going with us?"

Dillon kept staring at Austin. He snapped his fingers and said, "Now I know where I've seen you before. You played football. I never liked the way you pushed off from your defender, but you always got the job done!" Dillon was obviously excited to have Austin here at the stables with him.

CeCe couldn't help but laugh at Dillon's comment. Austin, too, found it funny that Dillon would have the same opinion of his play as CeCe.

Austin put his hand on Dillon's back as they walked toward the horses. "Dillon, I think it's time to choose our horses. Both CeCe and I are accomplished riders. Which horses do you suggest for us?"

"I have just the horse for each of you. I am obligated to take you out to the turn-around point, but then I can leave you to come back on your own if you'd like."

"I think that would be great, Dillon," Austin said, as he thought of being alone with CeCe in the beautiful surroundings.

They mounted the horses and started down the trail. Dillon was a very informative guide. He pointed out different things along the way. When they got to the halfway point, Dillon asked if they would like to ride back on their own.

Austin looked at CeCe and acknowledged her nod. "Sure Dillon, we would like that. It will give us time to linger at lunch if we like, and it will allow you to get back and take out another ride. You will stay for lunch with us, I hope?"

"No, sir. I've brought along the lunch here and it is for the two of you. I will help you set up, and then I'll be on my way." Dillon got off his horse and removed the basket from his saddle. "There's a nice place right here next to the stream."

Austin got off the horse and helped CeCe off. He walked over to Dillon and handed him a generous tip. "Dillon, that won't be necessary. I can set everything up. Thanks for being our guide."

"Thanks! It was my pleasure, Mr. Carter. You're the first professional football player I've met. I hope you'll come back again soon." Dillon got back on his horse and turned around. "Ms. CeCe, I didn't mean to leave you out. You sure do know a lot about football. I wish my girlfriend loved the game the way you do. It was a pleasure to meet you. If I ever get over to the Yampa Valley, I will stop in your shop."

CeCe walked over to Dillon and reached up to hug him. "You are a special young man, Dillon. Keep up the good work and follow your dreams."

"Thanks- I will." Dillon turned the horse around and rode away.

CeCe and Austin unloaded the picnic basket and laid the food out on the blanket Dillon had left for them. They shared a bottle of red wine, fresh fruit, and crispy sourdough bread.

The sounds of the stream and the birds were the only sounds other than their own voices. Austin thought that it couldn't be any more perfect.

CeCe was transported to another time. She kept thinking about the hikes they had taken in Kauai. This was as tranquil and wonderful as those times had been.

They packed the basket with the exception of the last of the wine and the blanket. CeCe laid back and let the effects take over. She was talking to Austin about the cloud formations. "Look! I see a dragon in that one."

Austin lay back on the blanket next to CeCe. "A dragon, no way. It's an angel. See- there is the head and her dress and the wings."

Austin looked over a CeCe and couldn't resist kissing her. He leaned over and traced her lip with his finger. Her lips were full and inviting. When his lips met hers, they tasted deliciously of the wine she had just finished. The kiss was light at first, but then grew deeper and deeper. CeCe responded and moved closer to him. She wrapped her arms around him and moved her hands through his hair.

They lay there for several minutes embraced together. The electricity between them was almost tangible. Austin could feel himself growing with excitement. He let his hands wander over CeCe's body and felt her response to him. She seemed to be much more relaxed with him than she had been previously.

The passion was heating up, when off in the distance they heard a crack of thunder. Then the first fat raindrops started to fall around them.

CeCe sat up quickly and straightened out her clothes. "Colorado afternoon showers. We better head back before we get stuck in this storm. I noticed that the horses have ponchos on the back of the saddle."

Austin stood and folded the blanket. He smiled and said, "Mother Nature's timing wasn't too hot."

CeCe stood and walked to the horses. She turned back to Austin and said, "Austin, I really love being alone with you. I think I'm ready to put those things in the past behind us."

Austin walked over and wrapped his arms around her. He lifted her chin and kissed her deeply. "CeCe, you need to know I will never hurt you. I can't believe my luck in finding you." He kissed her again, and the thunder cracked, this time sounding closer. "Let's get out of here before we get fried."

They packed the horses and rode off toward the stables. By the time they arrived, the rain was coming down steadily.

Dillon came out and grabbed the reins. "Did you have a good lunch before the rain started?"

"Yes," Austin answered. "Thanks for the great food and taking us to the beautiful spot. We'll have to return sometime and try again."

"You're welcome. Please come back. I really did enjoy watching you play pro ball. Well, I guess I better go and take care of these horses. See you again soon." Dillon waved as he walked back to the stables.

CeCe and Austin had given back the ponchos, so they were getting soaked. They grabbed each others hands and ran back to the car.

They laughed and shook the rain out of their hair. Austin looked over at CeCe and couldn't resist. He wiped a stream of rain that was running down her face and onto her neck. CeCe shivered. Austin leaned over and kissed her. "CeCe, I have fallen in love with you."

CeCe pulled back and looked into his eyes. "Austin, I know I love you, and it scares me. But I am willing to give it a go and see where it takes us."

"CeCe, you don't know how happy that makes me. I have never felt like this about anyone else in my life. I promise to make you happy." Austin pulled CeCe close and they just sat there for a few minutes. Austin started the car and drove them back to their lodge.

That evening they had a quiet evening. They walked to a nearby restaurant and had a wonderful dinner. On the way back, they talked of many things, including their fly-fishing expedition the next day. When they arrived at CeCe's door, Austin pulled her close and kissed her. "CeCe, this has been the best day ever. I can't imagine what each and every day will bring us now." He kissed her again turned and walked to his door.

CeCe couldn't believe the way she felt. She had closed herself off for so long since Carlos that she now felt like she was being reborn.

The butterflies were there again, and this time they were dancing up a storm. She felt as though she were sixteen again and had just discovered boys.

Austin was everything she had wanted. He respected her commitment to her morals, yet he made her feel as if she were the only woman in the world.

CeCe thought that she was never going to get any sleep tonight, but that it was a good reason to be awake.

She undressed and climbed into the bed thinking all along about Austin and their future together.

The next morning brought sunshine. CeCe had replayed the whole day over and over again. She was ready to go and see if she had just dreamed some of it, or if it were all reality.

Austin found himself whistling and anxious for the time to come when he would see CeCe's beautiful face. He couldn't have planned a better day than yesterday or a better ending. He was excited for this one to begin so that he and CeCe could begin their future together.

Austin knocked on the door and waited for CeCe to open it. He held the bouquet of flowers behind his back. When she opened the door, he quickly thrust them forward to her.

"Austin, a girl could get used to this!" She reached for his arm and pulled him in. When she did so, he caught her up in his arms and kissed her. CeCe kissed him back and then pulled away to close the door.

"I called Shaw and he's going to meet us at his shop in an hour. I figured it would take us about that long to drive there. I packed a lunch for us."

Austin started to open the basket.

"Stop that." CeCe slapped his hand away. "It's a surprise."

"You know I can't wait for surprises."

"Well, you'll just have to wait. You can carry all that stuff down to the car if you want something to do."

Austin loaded the car and they drove down the valley to CeCe's friends' fly-fishing shop. Shaw came out of the door as soon as he saw them drive up.

CeCe opened the door and walked into Shaw's open arms. He hugged her long and hard and kissed her cheek. Austin stood and watched, all the while cautioning himself not to be jealous. This was just her long-time friend; besides, he had a beautiful wife that he had been with for a long time.

Shaw released CeCe and came over to shake Austin's hand. "Nice to see you again, Austin."

"This time I'm on unfamiliar territory. I've wanted to do this for a long time and now I'm here. I understand that CeCe has done this before."

"Yeah, she used to go out with Tucker when she was younger, and Gino and I used to talk her into tying our flies. She was the best at tying flies that I ever ran across. The best part was that she liked doing it."

CeCe walked over and said, "What tales are you telling about me now?"

Shaw put his arm around CeCe and took the picnic basket from her. "It's all good my darlin', all good.

They went out to the river and put on their waders. Shaw showed them a few things and they waded into the water. Austin loved it: the water rushing by and an occasional bird swooping down toward the water. They had been fishing for about and hour and a half when Shaw said that he was going back to have lunch with Lisa.

CeCe walked out of the water with him. "Here, I brought a lunch for the two of you as well. I didn't know if she would be able to join us, so I put it in a smaller basket inside the larger one. I made some of those cream puffs that you love so much and Mandarin Orange salad. You two enjoy and we'll see you a little later."

"Thanks, CeCe, you didn't have to do that. I'm sure we'll enjoy it. That's a pretty good catch you have there."

CeCe looked over to where Shaw was looking. "You mean Austin?"

"Yes, I mean Austin. He can't take his eyes off of you. Now go back and show him all that I taught you."

CeCe smiled and watched him walk away. When she turned back, Austin was watching her.

"Would you like some lunch or do you want to fish longer?"

"I've been wondering what you have in that basket all morning. Not to mention I'm starved."

CeCe watched as he moved his long legs out of the water and walked toward her. He laid down his fishing rod and wrapped his arms around her. He kissed her lightly and then released. "What are you waiting for? Show me what you brought for us. My mind has been racing all day, and it's just been making me more and more hungry."

"It isn't fancy, just a salad and some wine. Dessert is light. I think you will like it all."

"There isn't any doubt about that. We can sit right over here at the edge of the river. Here, let me set up."

Austin took the basket and blanket from CeCe. They laid out all of the food and dug in. It didn't take long for them to finish up.

"CeCe, you will never cease to amaze me. You make a picnic

lunch better than a gourmet six-course meal." Austin was finishing the last of the brownies.

"Thank you, Mr. Carter. I'll take that as a compliment." CeCe stood and brushed off the crumbs.

Austin put the remains of the lunch back in the basket. "Well, are you up for some more fishing? I say we have a contest to see who catches the first fish. The winner gets to choose his or her prize."

"Deal. But you better be prepared to pay. I can have pretty expensive taste."

"Better yet, the loser gets to choose the prize for the winner. It does have to meet with their approval."

"Austin, what do you have up your sleeve? I can think of lots of things that would please you, but I'm afraid of what you would do to please me."

"Come on, CeCe, I told you that it would need to meet your approval."

"That you did. All right. Let's get back in there and see who wins."

They both picked up their rods and waded out into the middle of the river. The water was more forceful now.

They stood close enough to one another that they could talk without yelling, yet far enough away to not get their lines tangled.

CeCe squealed as she got a bite. Austin watched as she pulled on the line. He was just about to put his rod on the bank when CeCe lost her balance and fell into the water. The current was strong enough that it kept pulling CeCe further downstream. Her rod was jammed between two rocks. It was apparent to Austin that CeCe was in trouble.

Austin reacted quickly and followed her downstream on the bank. He got about fifty yards in front of her and grabbed a large low tree limb. He worked his way into the stream and reached out for CeCe. She had gotten turned around and was headed toward some rocks. Austin reached out with one arm while holding onto the limb just as CeCe was passing by. He kept her from running into the rocks. CeCe pulled herself up on Austin's arm as he pulled them both safely to the bank.

"That was a wild ride. I didn't think I was going to be able to get out of the middle of that stuff." CeCe stood, rubbing her legs and arms.

"Are you okay?" Austin asked, full of concern as he wrapped his arms around her. "I couldn't just stand there and watch you float away. That current is really strong."

Austin couldn't resist. He lifted CeCe's chin and kissed her mouth. CeCe responded fully. "I don't know what I would do without you around, Austin. This isn't the first time you've rescued me."

"No need to thank me. I think we need to get the fishing rods and head on back to the hot tub. Guess we'll have to have that contest some other time."

"Guess so. Thanks again, Austin. You really did save me this time."

Austin put his arm around CeCe, and they walked to where she had fallen into the water. Austin walked over to retrieve CeCe's rod that had wedged between the rocks. He smiled and picked it up. "Look what I found," he shouted over the noise of the stream. He raised the rod with a fish still attached. "So, who gets the credit for the fish?"

"Why, of course I do. It was my fly rod and my fish," CeCe said

"I don't think so. I'm the one who pulled it out of the water. I think it's mine. Tell you what. I'll give you the credit, but I get a prize, too. Plus, you did say I saved your life. So, I guess you have to go with what I say."

CeCe pondered the situation. "Okay, Austin, you win, but I caution you that if you choose anything kinky I can refuse the prize."

"That's fair. Okay, here it goes: my prize for you is a trip to Kauai at my expense."

"Austin, that is too much for you to do."

"No, it isn't! I have airline miles I can use. Aren't you going to ask what my prize is?"

"Yes. What is your prize?"

Austin came closer to CeCe. He picked up both of her hands in his and bent down on one knee. "CeCe, I love you more than I ever knew I could love anyone. Please know that I have never meant anything more in my life when I say that. The other part of your prize, or should I say my prize, is that I want you to be my wife. I want to spend the rest of my life with you. Will you marry me? In Kauai at the overlook?"

CeCe looked down at him in amazement. She was speechless.

Austin squeezed her hands. "Well, what do you say?"

CeCe wet her lips nervously. "Austin, I don't know what to say. I mean, I love you, too. Yes, I will marry you. Yes, Yes, Yes!"

Austin stood up and picked her up in his arms. They were laughing and crying and kissing each other. Austin swung CeCe around and put her on her feet. He reached in his pocket and pulled out a box. He handed it to CeCe.

"What?" she stammered. "When did you plan this?"

"I've been carrying this around with me for a while now, waiting for the right moment. Did I hear you say yes?"

CeCe opened the box. Inside was a beautiful band with three sparkling diamonds.

"Austin, this is unbelievable. I did say yes. When do you want to do this?"

"As soon as possible, I would like for Angie and Reece to be there with us. Is that alright with you?"

"I wouldn't have it any other way. Are you sure that you don't want to have it here so that your family can attend?"

"Oh, we'll have one here. I figured we could have it in December or January. But I can't wait to love you fully. We will have two weddings, one in Kauai, where I have always wanted to give my love to someone special, and the other in this beautiful state with all of our friends and family in attendance."

"Austin, I can't believe how happy I am! Thank you for loving me. Can we go now and call Reece, Angie, Tucker, Ruth, Shaw and Nitro?"

"Anything you say, my princess."

Chapter Forty

Everyone was so happy for CeCe and Austin. Ruth said that she always knew that they would get together. She offered to watch Nitro while they went to Kauai to get married. She understood the urgency that Austin felt. She was thrilled that she would be part of the wedding that they planned to have in Colorado in January. Tucker would walk CeCe down the aisle of the little Chapel right in the center of town. Ruth had already planned the menu and couldn't wait to get started on the cooking.

CeCe and Reece had gone shopping for a dress for CeCe to wear. She didn't want a frilly wedding gown. Instead, she settled on a replica of a nineteen-forties style. The dress was ankle length with soft cotton antique lace covering a simple silk slip underneath. Reece's eyes welled with tears as CeCe walked out of the dressing room with it on. She couldn't have been more beautiful. It was perfect for her.

Angie and Reece accompanied CeCe and Austin to Kauai for the ceremony they had planned at the overlook. CeCe and Reece drove up through the canyon on the brilliantly sunny day. Austin and Angie were already there. Austin could see his bride-to-be coming up the walkway to the overlook. The sight of her took his breath away. She was a vision out of a fairy book. The dress fit her body perfectly, and she wore a crown of gardenias and bluebells on her head. The blue in the flowers accentuated the color of her eyes. They were both the color of the sea below them. She looked as though she was floating up to him. Austin was overcome with emotion.

CeCe walked the short distance to where Austin stood waiting for her. She grinned as she walked to him and said, "You really are my knight in shining armor. I love you, Austin Carter."

Austin took CeCe's hand and squeezed it tight. He didn't need to say anything just the look in his eyes told her that this was what she had been waiting for all of her life.

The sound of the birds and the rustling leaves were the only music that was needed. The love between the two of them filled the air. Reece thought to herself that she had never experienced such a beautiful wedding. She had never seen her long-time friend so happy. She was thrilled for them.

The minister asked them if they wanted to say something to one another. Austin went first. "CeCe, I never knew I could love someone as much as I do you. You are my life. I promise to love and cherish you and to grow old and gray with you. Thank you for loving me. Thank you for being you. Thank you for being my wife."

CeCe wiped a tear away that had rolled down her cheek. "Austin, I love you with all of my heart, body and soul. I am thankful for the day that you walked into my life. You are my strength, my darling. Let us walk through life together hand in hand and face all the adversities together and conquer each and every one of them. Together we can do anything and create anything, and with you, I am ready to start our life together. Thank you for being you and letting me be me. I love you, Austin, from here to eternity.

Even the minister's voice cracked as he finished the ceremony. Reece and Angie stood side by side watching the openly raw exchange of love between their two friends. Reece wept out of happiness for CeCe.

When the minister pronounced them husband and wife, Austin reached down and kissed CeCe with so much passion that it felt like the world stopped turning. They turned to their two friends and hugged and kissed them as well.

Reece wiped the tear off of CeCe's cheek and said, "That was more than beautiful. Look at the surroundings and the two of you. I am so happy for you both. We have some champagne in the car chilling, and then we will be on our way down to the hotel."

Angie cleared his throat and said, "I took all my gear out this morning, CeCe, so you won't be tripping over it. Reece and I brought a few things up to the cabin. I brought them with me yesterday and laid them out for you both before we left today. I will only be staying another day, so I won't see you for a while. I need to get back to work- the season starts next week. Reece has agreed to fly back with me."

Angie hugged CeCe and his good friend Austin. "You have a hell of a prize there, my friend. I know that you know that, but I just thought I would tell you anyway. Take care, you two. I love you both."

Angie and Reece walked back to the car, and CeCe and Austin stood and looked out into the valley and the ocean beyond.

They stayed for a while, and finally Austin took CeCe's hand and helped her walk back to the car. They drove the few short miles to Austin's cabin. He stopped the car and walked around to her door. He opened it and reached in to lift CeCe off of her seat. He carried her up the stairs and opened the door. Before he walked through the door he gave her a long, deep kiss. "I love you, CeCe. Thank you for loving me back." He walked the rest of the way into the doorway. The room was fragrant with the smell of fresh flowers. There on the table sat a chilling bottle of champagne and a tray of cheese and crackers. There was a note attached.

Thought you might need some nourishment. There is some fresh sashimi in the fridge. Enjoy you two- you deserve this happiness.
Love, Reece and Angie.

Austin sat CeCe on her feet and took her chin in his hand. "CeCe, know that I will never hurt you. All I want to do is love you. This is just the beginning."

Austin kissed her softly, and then more deeply. He let his hands slide down her arms and then back up again. He settled them on her full breasts.

CeCe responded. She never knew she could feel this way. Her voice was husky with desire when she said, "Let's go to the loft. I have thought about your bed there often." Austin took her hand and walked her to the stairs. "After you, Mrs. Carter. And oh, one more thing: it's our bed you were referring to."

CeCe climbed the stairs and removed her headpiece. Austin came behind her and kissed the back of her neck. CeCe shivered, "Austin, will you unbutton the buttons for me?" Austin's fingers were cool on her skin. His hands trembled a bit as he started unbuttoning the tiny buttons. When he reached her waist, he let them linger there and pulled her against him.

CeCe could feel the excitement in him. He was hot and hard. Austin slowly turned CeCe to face him and she could see the desire in his eyes. He slid the sleeve of the dress down her arms and trailed his fingers ever so lightly. CeCe threw her head back with desire as Austin reached around and slid the zipper down and pulled the slip off of CeCe's shoulder. Both pieces of the dress fell to the floor and there before him she stood like a goddess. The thin lace cups of her bra barely contained the fullness of her breasts. The thin triangle of sheer material that covered her only brought more excitement for Austin.

Austin pulled her close and kissed the tops of her breasts. He slowly slid the bra strap over her shoulder and exposed the rosy peak. He kissed her softly and she gave a low moan. Austin moved to the other breast and made it rise to meet his waiting lips.

CeCe moved her hands through Austin's thick dark hair. She was ready to love him fully. Austin slid his hands down to her waist and removed the barrier there so that he could see his beautiful wife completely. He could barely contain his excitement.

Austin picked CeCe up and laid her on the bed. The sheets were cool against her hot skin. She waited and watched as Austin removed his own clothing as quickly as he could.

CeCe watched him. *God he is beautiful*, CeCe thought to herself. *And he is my husband.* She reached out and touched his firm stomach and moved her hand down until she heard him gasp.

Austin slid close to CeCe on the bed. He kissed her with the fever of desire. He worked his way down her body. The desire was too much; he had to be inside her.

Austin supported his weight and slowly entered CeCe. She was wet and ready for him. CeCe raised her hips to blend with the tempo Austin had set. It didn't take long for CeCe to experience her first crescendo. She shuddered and a moan of desire escaped her mouth. Austin kissed her and continued his motion. It wasn't long before they were matched in rhythm again. This time they both reached the point of no return together. Their bodies shuddered and released their desire. CeCe felt the fire throughout her whole body. She never knew she could feel like this.

CeCe's voice was thick with desire and love, "Austin, I hope we just made a baby."

Austin moved closer and looked into her deep blue eyes. "CeCe, are you serious? You know that I have wanted a child for a long time."

"You bet I am. I can't think of anything more exciting than having a whole bunch of little Austin's running around under foot."

"CeCe, I love you so much. I promise to be the best dad and husband ever."

"I know you will, Austin. Now, would you like to ensure that we are making those little ones?"

Austin didn't answer; he just kissed his beautiful wife and began making slow sensuous love to her.

In the early hours of the morning, Austin lay next to CeCe, holding her in the crook of his arm. CeCe lightly traced her fingers over his chest. "Austin, do you think you could go and get some of that food Reece and Angie left us? I'm starving. This making love thing makes you hungry. It's as though I ran a marathon." A wicked little smile slowly curved at her lips. "After I get some nourishment, I think I'll be ready to exercise again."

Austin laughed and hugged her closer. "What have I created here? I will be happy to get you some food, but not until you show me how much you love me."

CeCe rolled on top of Austin and kissed him. She could feel the desire starting to rise in him again. She really didn't care about the food; she was more interested in making love to her husband.

Chapter Forty-One

Throughout the summer and fall things began to change for him. His desire for Reece had been lessened. He began to realize that he loved her, but not as fully as he had once thought. She was not out of danger yet. He could feel the evil around her and he hoped that Angie would be there to protect her. He had found another to love. It had taken him some time to realize that she in turn loved him. That he didn't need to express his words on paper; instead, he was able to express them to her openly. He did feel the need to tell her why he hadn't written to her, or better yet, why he had.

She was still one of the most beautiful creatures on earth. He would write to her and deliver one last letter. There was no need for her to know who he was, just that he would not need to communicate with her through the letters any longer.

The keys and the sound of the typewriter still held an allure for him. He sat to write to her one last time.

> *My dearest Reece,*
>
> *I am writing to tell that this will be the last time you will hear from me. I have found that I am capable of loving another. You are still the wonderful woman I have thought of so often these last couple of years. I see now that you have someone by your side to protect and love you. However, I will still caution you as to the dangers that surround you. Don't let your guard down. Sometimes you don't recognize the danger, but it is there just waiting for you.*
>
> *Someday I will tell you how I felt and feel now about you in person. For now, you will just have to settle for the words I write. I am happy with the path my life has taken. I have found someone who loves me and who I love in return. I'm sorry if I made you feel uncomfortable in my letters. They were never*

meant to be anything but flattering. I can see now how you may have felt differently about them. My desire for you was nothing but admiration for the beautiful person that you are.

I hope that you are as happy as you look. Yes, I do still see you. You do seem to be happy. I believe that Mr. D'Angelo is the perfect match for you. Don't push him away let him protect and love you the way he feels that he needs to.

It was me who left the letter at your house, but I never went into your office. I wouldn't have destroyed your personal things. It was someone else. Please believe me.

Take care, Reece, and be happy in your life. That is all I have ever wished for you.

For now I will sign this the same "Me". Someday you will know my real identity, but only when it is necessary for me to tell you.

Loving you always, Me.

He pulled the paper from the machine, not caring if his prints would be on the paper. He felt satisfied that he had completed this chapter in his life. He had time to fold it and put it in its envelope and go and meet her.

Tom's speech had improved greatly since he had allowed himself to fall in love with Lilly. She needed him and he needed her. She had never been treated so well or felt so loved until Tom had come into her life.

Tom realized that Reece wasn't what he needed. She was a beautiful person inside and out, but his speech never allowed him to express his feelings for her. Lilly helped him through his shyness. He had quit drinking all together. He had other things to do to fill his time, mainly loving Lilly. It all began when she was so kind to him at CeCe's coffee shop. She, too, had changed. She became the vibrant young woman she had been before she was married to her abusive husband.

Tom would never forgive that bastard of a husband she had had. He could have ruined her. She was tough, though, and came through her awful experience with flying colors. Tom didn't realize how much he cared for Lilly until Dr. Baldwin started showing her attention.

Poor Dr. Baldwin, he seemed to come in last these past couple of years. Oh well, he still was a ladies' man and hopefully, he would find one who would be able to tame him.

Tom would need to get the letter to Reece one last time. He would hold onto it until he knew the time was right.

Right now he was going to meet Lilly to go to Reece's house for a Christmas celebration. He would not take it with him now. He didn't want anyone to find it and get the wrong idea. Next week would be soon enough.

~ ~ ~

Reece had planned the little get-together at her house. Claire had flown in from Seattle as she had said she would. She was staying at CeCe's house since she and Austin were living at the ranch.

CeCe was just beginning to show. She was about twelve weeks pregnant. Both she and Austin were ecstatic, and Reece couldn't wait to be the indulgent aunt.

The guests were just beginning to arrive. CeCe opened the door. Mason was the first to arrive- he had a beautiful young lady on his arm. He introduced her as his fiancee He had met her in the emergency room when she had torn the ligaments in her knee.

"He didn't waste any time with her, did he?" CeCe whispered to Reece. "She's pretty young, don't you think?"

"Shh, CeCe, he'll hear you. She is young; however, I hear she's loaded as well. Her father has some dot-com company. Rumor has it that they will be moving to Beverly Hills next month. They have a huge wedding planned. I wish them the best of luck." Reece walked back to the kitchen.

Claire came in with her arms full of gifts. "I just had to pick these up and bring them for you all. Everyone has been so kind. I have had such a wonderful trip. I don't know why I didn't do this before."

"Here, let me take those from you." Austin removed the packages and placed them under the tree.

The room was full of guests. Reece introduced Claire around the room. Claire looked over to the corner of the room and asked, "Who is that handsome couple over there? They look vaguely familiar to me."

Reece explained, "You may have seen her picture somewhere, they're 'new money', so to speak. The guy is Mason. That may be where you saw him before. I was trying to get some information about him for an article in the newspaper. He practiced in Washington and I thought you might be able to help me with some information. I may have sent you a picture."

"Yes, that must be it. I remember now. They make a handsome couple."

"Here, let me introduce you." Reece walked Claire over to the two of them.

"Mason, I want to introduce you to my friend, Claire. Claire, Mason."

Mason stood and took her hand "My pleasure. I haven't seen you before. Are you new to the area?"

Claire laughed, "Heavens, no, although I wouldn't mind living here. I went to school with Reece. I live in the Seattle area. I understand you lived in Washington yourself."

Mason dropped Claire's hand, "Why, yes, I did practice there for awhile. It was a very small town."

"You look familiar to me, but Reece reminded me that she had been looking for some background on you and had sent me a picture. I'm sure you don't mind the move here. It is so beautiful- I wouldn't mind living here myself."

"Yes, it is beautiful. If you don't mind, I promised to bring some refreshments to my fiancee Nice meeting you, Claire." Mason walked away toward the table.

"He's kind of strange, isn't he?" Claire said. "One minute he's Mr. Charm, and the next he's standoffish. Was he afraid I was going to jump his bones or something?"

"No, Claire. Mason can just be weird. He had the hots for me for a while, but he didn't like the competition. Just as well. CeCe never liked him. She was glad when someone else came into my life."

"I can see where CeCe is coming from. From what I understand, this Angie guy is something else. Where is he, anyway?"

"He'll be here in a little while. He had to drive up from Denver. You know it's right in the middle of the season. The Broncos are doing very well. They're headed for the playoffs again."

"Since when did you get so interested in football, Reece?" Claire asked.

Reece laughed. "It's a long story, but I have really become quite knowledgeable about the game. Come on over, I want to introduce you to more of the guests."

Dr. Baldwin took an immediate liking to Claire. He offered to fill her in on anything she needed to know. The last Reece saw of Claire, she was firmly attached to his arm.

Austin and CeCe were standing talking with Tom and Lilly. Austin had his arms around his wife's slightly swollen stomach. CeCe was amazed at Tom's speech. He still stuttered, but it was much less than before. Lilly had flourished as well. She had gained some weight and muscle. Rumor had it that she was working with her father and Tom. They seemed to be good together. Tom was telling CeCe about the new work he was doing.

"It all has to do from the work I d-did on your place, Ms. CeCe.

Mrs. James said she had seen the work and was impressed. Thank you for recommending me to her. I really enjoy the work with the horses, but the iron fencing work allows the creative side in m-me to come out."

"Tom, it isn't anything I did. It was your work that she was impressed with. I am pleased for you. Lilly, can I depend on you to help out during this next few months at the shop and right after I have the baby? I know Ruth is dead-set on taking over, but once this little one comes she will want to be with me some helping out."

"CeCe, don't you worry. I would love to help out. I am spending most of my time between your shop and my dad's business. Tom has become a sort of partner with him. Dad has taught Tom some things that he learned way back when from his granddaddy." Lilly looked up at Tom, and he squeezed her close.

"I sure have learned a lot from him. He is a t-tough bird, though. Lilly, can I get you something?"

"Sure, let's get a plate. I'm starved, if you will excuse us?"

Lilly and Tom walked away hand and hand. CeCe smiled to herself. "I guess Ruth was right. She seems to always be right."

Chapter Forty-Two

The plans were in full swing for the wedding that CeCe and Austin had promised to have for everyone to attend. CeCe, Reece, and Ruth had sent out all the invitations. Ruth helped to alter CeCe's dress since she had grown a bit since the first time she had worn it.

Austin invited his football team to the wedding. They had won the state championship just like CeCe had said they would. With a lot of hard work from the players, a little luck, their coaches' knowledge, and the secret weapon of CeCe's plays they had pulled it off.

They had all attended the championship game. CeCe sat on the edge of her seat, wanting this so badly for her husband and the team. Reece had learned a tremendous amount about football, and was no longer attending to get a glimpse at the buffed bodies. She wrote about the game as if she had written about it all her life.

Reece was getting offers to move on to the Denver area from one of the large newspapers. She was considering it, but didn't know if she wanted to leave her business in someone else's hands. That was a decision she would make later.

Austin wouldn't let CeCe into his workshop. He was working on "something special", as he would say whenever she asked. He told her she would get to see it on their wedding day.

CeCe said, "We are already married, so we have already had our wedding day."

"You know what I mean. Now go on and get out of here. You are not allowed in here. Besides, there isn't anything in here that you can help with."

Tucker came over and put his arm under CeCe's elbow. "I think we should leave him alone. He's being pretty secretive about this. All I know is that it involves wood, I hear the saw and he got out the router the other day. We'll know soon enough."

"You're right, Tucker. The suspense is just killing me. I do need to run into town to talk to Reece. I guess I'll leave him to his secret."

Tucker helped CeCe into the car. "You drive safely, now."

"I will, Tucker. Ruth gave me a list of things to pick up for the wedding, so I'll be awhile." CeCe drove down the drive and into town.

~ ~ ~

Reece had just gotten home and turned on some lights. She put the teapot on the stove to heat some water. She was ready to sit and relax.

CeCe had come by and they had gotten some of the essentials for the wedding this weekend.

Reece fixed her tea and had just sat down when the doorbell rang. Reece groaned and got up to see who was there. Mason was standing there under the light. *What was he doing here?* Reece thought to herself. She opened the door and said, "Hello, Mason, this is a surprise. To what do I owe this pleasure?"

"Hi Reece, I just finished up at the hospital and thought I would come by and say hello. Is this a bad time?"

"No, not at all, I just got home and was having some tea. Would you like some?" Reece opened the door wider for him to enter.

Mason walked in and took a seat. "Tea would be nice, if it's not too much of a problem."

"Not at all," Reece rose and went into the kitchen.

Mason stood and walked over to the table where Reece had her mail piled up, waiting to be opened. He filed through it, watching the kitchen to make sure Reece didn't appear. He quickly sat back down when he heard her finish making the tea.

"Connie and I had a wonderful time at your little get together, and she wanted me to make sure I stopped by and told you so."

"I got a thank you from her in the mail. How are things progressing there? I understand you will be leaving soon to move to

California."

"Yes, I'm just trying to wrap up things here. I have everything set there to start my new practice." Mason shifted his weight and the subject. "I enjoyed meeting all of you friends. That Claire was great- she's a real character. She had everyone in stitches all night long."

"Yes, Claire. She is a great one to have at a party. As a matter of fact, she's planning on coming out in March. She had such a good time."

"Where did she say she was from?"

"Washington State."

"Yeah, she said she thought she knew me, but I think I would have remembered her."

"At first she did, but then she remembered that it was from when I was trying to write the article on you when you first arrived here."

"Funny how people think…" Mason stopped talking when the shrill ring of the telephone cut into their conversation. He was sitting right next to it and looked at the caller ID. He immediately recognized it as familiar area code. "Would you like me to pick it up?"

"No, I'll get it." Reece rose to answer the phone. "Hello?"

"Reece, I'm so glad I reached you. I tried all afternoon at work and had no luck."

"Claire, it's nice to hear from you. I was just talking about you to Mason. He stopped by tonight and we were talking about how funny you are at a party."

"He's there? Listen to me, Reece. You need to get rid of him now. I knew I saw him before."

Reece wrinkled her forehead in concern. "What do you mean?"

Mason was watching her closely. This was what he was afraid of. Now he was going to have to go through with his plan and then head to Washington to take care of this other bitch. Why hadn't she left things alone?

"Reece, remember I told you about a Mason Brighton, the guy that was married to the wealthy socialite. Well, when I got back I started to remember more. You hadn't sent me a picture of him. You just asked me to get some information about him. I went through all my files and found the tragic story about the couple who seemed to have everything going for them. They were killed in the fire in their home. Her father blamed himself because he had insisted on the safe and it had been determined it was faulty wiring. Well, Reece, Mason Brighton didn't die in that fire. It's him, all right. He now has dark hair and it in the picture it was blond and longer. I'm going to fax it to you, so you can see for yourself."

Reece nervously turned away from Mason. She interrupted Claire. "Not here, send it to CeCe's, you have the number. I'll get it later." If it was him, she didn't want him to see photograph.

"Reece, you be careful now. I'll fax this to CeCe's right away. Get rid of him." Claire broke the connection; however, Reece stayed on the line. "Yes, CeCe will be glad you are sending her the copy of that poem she wanted for me to read at her reception. Yes, it was so good seeing you, too. Listen, Claire, I should really go now. Mason is just sitting here alone having to listen to me gab to someone else, and I need to go to the store to pick up something for dinner. I'll call you next week after the wedding. You take care now. Love you, too. Bye." Reece spoke into the dead phone.

"If you didn't get it from the conversation that was Claire, she just called to say what a great time she had. She really enjoyed meeting everyone here. She would just go on and on if I let her." Reece nervously picked at an imaginary thread on the chair she stood by.

"I thought you said you got a letter from her?" Mason asked.

"I did. She always did like to go on about things. Listen, Mason, I hate to end our conversation, but I need to go to the store and pick up a few things for dinner."

"Why don't you let me take you out?"

"Thanks, but I don't feel like it. I think I will pick up some soup and then hit the bed."

"Okay, then, guess I will be on my way. Take care, Reece. I enjoy our friendship very much." Mason walked to the door and lingered there for a second. "Sure I can't pick up some dinner for you and bring it back here?"

"I'm sure you have better things to do than baby-sit me. Connie probably would love to have you call her. Thanks for stopping by, Mason. Tell Connie I said hello and good luck with the wedding plans."

"I'll do that. Goodbye, Reece."

Reece shut the door and leaned against it. Could it be possible? Reece had seen some signs that Mason had a temper. CeCe had never liked him, and she liked everybody. She said right from the beginning that there was something about him that bothered her.

Reece looked out the window to be sure that he was gone. When she was sure, she grabbed her coat and keys to drive to CeCe's place. She would go and get the fax. If it were true, she would have to call the sheriff. Had it been him who was sending the letters and had broken into her office? It would make sense. Files were missing that had articles about other newcomers she had written about. But the letters were written differently. They had not been threatening and the words were loving. She would go and see what Claire was sending her.

~ ~ ~

He had decided this would be a good time to deliver the last letter to Reece. He sat in the truck waiting until she had gotten settled in and the darkness helped to conceal him. He was going to put it in the door, so that when she left in the morning she would find it.

He waited until he thought the time was right, and was just reaching to open the truck door when he saw Mason standing at the door. Now he would have to wait awhile longer.

The time ticked by slowly until he saw the door open and Mason leave. He didn't like that guy. There was something about him. This was the danger he felt for Reece and was warning her about in his letters. He was sure of it.

Tom was glad when Mason had found someone else to hang around instead of Reece; only what was he doing back here? He was supposed to get married to that lady he had brought to the party.

Now Mason was walking to his car. He started it and drove away. Good, he felt better now that he had left her alone. Shortly afterward, Reece came out of the house and got in her car. Tom saw Mason's car return around the block but his headlights weren't on. He pulled over to the side of the road, waited, and then followed Reece's car.

Tom was curious now. He had to know what was going on. He, too, followed the pair. It looked as though they were headed out to CeCe's. Tom knew that CeCe was living out on the ranch with Austin.

Reece approached the house and got out the keys to open the door. She got out of the car and looked around her to make sure she was alone. When she got in, she locked the door behind her.

When Mason was sure where she was going, he backed off and passed the road to CeCe's. He waited until he could see the lights come on in the house before he shut off his headlights and drove down the road in darkness.

Tom, too, watched from a distance. He shut off the light in the cab and got out at the beginning of the road. He quickly moved through the trees on a path that led to the back of the house. It was a cross-country ski path that led to the ridge on the other side of CeCe's house. He got there just in time to see Mason lifting the key out of the garden in fake rock CeCe had hidden it in.

Tom was angry; he had told CeCe not to leave that there when he had come to the house to make the railing for her! He had warned CeCe then.

Mason walked slowly to the back door and fit the key into the lock. It turned quietly. He stepped into the warmth of the house. He could see the glow coming from the little room that CeCe had made into an office.

Reece walked over to the fax machine. It was just starting to print out the papers. She sat in the chair and anxiously waited for it to finish. When it had, she lifted the paper out and began to read. The face that smiled out at her from the article was certainly that of Mason's. She continued to read as her nerves warned her to place the call.

"She was beautiful, wasn't she?" Mason stood in the doorway, filling it fully with his outstretched arms.

Reece jumped. "Mason, what are you doing here?"

"Now, that is a silly question, isn't it, Reece? I knew that Claire was going to be a problem. She ruined everything. You were supposed to be my next wife. I think I would have been content here. There would have been no need to get rid of you. Not like Wendolyn. She was stupid and had to go and get pregnant. I knew I couldn't ever get anything from the relationship after she made me sign that prenuptial." Mason shook his head as he talked.

"The whole thing was pretty elaborate. Of course, she wasn't still alive when I started the fire. I drugged her drink. She said that a glass of wine here and there wouldn't hurt the child. I was able to find a cadaver to put in the house in my place. There was no need for them to compare dental records; who else would be found holding his loving wife in their bed?"

"Of course, I took all the jewelry out of the safe, but there wasn't as much cash as I had hoped. I wouldn't be able to hock the jewels until later. I had the old man's safe combo and had gone in there to get some of the stash that he had at his own house. Problem was, he walked in on me and thought he had seen a ghost. He had a bad heart and reached for the pills. I was quicker than he was and was able to secure them before he could. He was gasping for air the whole time while I told him the truth about what had happened that night."

"Pity you had to get involved. And your friend, Claire. Now I have to make a trip back there. She will be missed at the television station. CeCe, of course, will miss you a great deal. I guess the wedding won't be happening."

Reece couldn't believe what she was hearing. He was going to kill her. He had killed those other two innocent people. He was a madman.

"You see, Reece, there was no need for you to get involved. Once I saw that I wasn't going to be able to convince you to sign away your fortune to me, I moved on to another."

Reece didn't recognize the face that stood there before her. It had changed somehow; evil and ugly. She could feel herself begin to shake. She couldn't let him know she was afraid.

"No need to be afraid, Reece. Yes- I can smell the fear." Mason was moving away from the door closer to her.

Reece had to get out. She saw the collection of snow globes sitting on the edge of the desk and thought she might be able to use one of them to stun him. She would have to wait until he got a little closer.

Mason moved around the side of the desk, and Reece needed to react now. She lunged forward and grabbed the large globe she had bought CeCe two Christmas's ago. Mason, too, lunged forward, but Reece got a good hold on it. He grabbed her arm as she swung it forward and connected with the side of his head. An ugly gash opened and blood spilled down his cheek and into one eye.

Mason swore as she struck him, but was able to stop her from hitting him full force. It stunned him, but not enough. He was able to keep hold of her. He pulled her arm back and behind her back.

Outside, Tom realized that he needed to do something. He needed to stop Mason before he hurt Reece. Tom quickly moved to the back door, but Mason was now dragging Reece by her hair through the front of the house and out of the front door.

It was snowing big flakes now, and the wind was starting to howl.

Tom ran through the house just in time to see Mason standing at the edge of the ravine. Tom yelled to him, "Mason! It's me, Tom. Wait! I want to help you. Reece has ignored me for a l-long time. It's time she learns a l-lesson."

Both Mason and Reece looked at him in surprise. Reece couldn't believe what she was seeing. Tom was a good man. He had really cleaned up his act since he had met Lilly. What was he saying?

"I've been writing letters to her forever, but do you think she would give me a chance? No!"

It was Tom who had been writing those letters. But he never wrote anything threatening. Why didn't she see it? He had been there at the auction.

"You don't think I knew it was you writing the letters? You provided a smoke screen for me when I broke into Reece's office. I tried to find any information Reece had gotten on me. Tom, now you've really complicated things. I don't leave any witnesses."

Tom looked over Mason's shoulder to distract him. "Is there someone at the little cabin up there, Reece?"

Mason looked over his shoulder toward the path. When he did so, this allowed Tom to signal to Reece that he was there to help her. He mouthed the words 'I'm here to help.' Mason tugged on Reece's hair and said, "Well, is there anyone up there?"

Reece understood what Tom was doing- trying to distract Mason. Tom was there to help her. Could they do it? Could they overcome him?

Tom moved closer. Mason inched closer, not realizing he was moving out onto the cornice that had formed. "Watch it, Tom, don't get too close. I'll throw her over the edge and write a letter saying that you were the one writing to her and couldn't live without her."

Tom had to be careful. That cornice could give way any minute. Tom would distract him again. This time he turned around and looked the other way. "Damn. It must be CeCe coming back to pick up something. I thought I heard a car door and Nitro."

"Not that mangy dog. He doesn't like me." Reece let out a scream and Mason let go of her hair to try and muffle her. When he did so, it allowed her enough time to twist away from him and to connect her leg with his shin.

Reece squirmed away just as Tom ran in. Tom yelled out to her, "Run to the house and call the sheriff. Hurry, Reece!"

Reece ran and looked back- the last she saw was the two of them wrestling on the ground. Reece ran into the house and called nine-one-one. She locked the doors, grabbed a knife, and locked herself into the bathroom.

Reece heard two faint screams; she was worried that Mason would hurt Tom. Tom was there to help her, but why was he there? Reece stayed where she was until she heard footsteps walking toward the bathroom.

Reece sat on the edge of the tub with the knife in hand. She wasn't going to give up without a fight. The doorknob began to turn. Reece huddled closer to the corner of the room. She screamed out, "Go away! I won't give up without a fight!"

"Reece open the door- it's the sheriff. I'm here to help, it's okay."

Reece recognized the voice and stood to open the door. She fumbled with the lock. "Tom, you need to help Tom. He came here to help me. Is he all right? I heard them struggling and screams."

"My men are investigating what happened out there. Are you all right?"

"I guess, but you need to help them. If they fell into the ravine, they could be hurt."

"Reece, the cornice gave way and we can see two bodies in the ravine. They both fell onto a ledge, so the fall wasn't all the way down. We can see movement in one of them, but don't know who is who. Maybe you can come help and tell us what happened here tonight."

"There's a fax in the office that will explain who Mason really is. He killed innocent people for their money. He came here and was trying to work his way into my life so he could do the same to me." Reece wrapped her arms around herself to stop the shivering and the thought that she had almost died.

"Would you like us to call someone?"

"Yes, please call Austin and CeCe- they're staying at the ranch."

"Why was Tom here? Do you know, Reece?"

"No, all I know is that he was there, standing in the snow, distracting Mason. He told him that he was the one writing the letters. Mason said he knew that and used it to his advantage to break into my office. Mason was afraid I was getting too much information on him and would uncover his real identity."

One of the officers came in the door. "Sheriff, you might want to come out here. They're bringing the men out of the ravine now."

"Reece, I'll be right back."

Reece grabbed his arm and said, "No, I'm coming with you. If they're alive, I want to say something to both of them." Reece shrugged into her jacket.

Reece recognized the jacket that Mason had on earlier, but she didn't recognize the sounds he was making.

He was obviously in pain. They stayed their distance from the cornice and waited as the rescue team brought him up. One of the team came over to the Sheriff.

"What's his condition?"

"He has a mangled leg and some good lacerations, but nothing life-threatening."

They brought Mason over to the waiting ambulance. Reece went to the stretcher. Mason stopped his groaning long enough to spout obscenities at Reece. "Bitch! You think you can play with people's lives. Look where it got Tom. Stupid fool, he really thought he was in love with you."

Reece took a step back, "Mason, I don't get it. You had everything. You had a good career. Why?"

"You'll never get it. It was all a facade. I stole the whole thing, the identity- everything. I never went to school. I bluffed my way through everything I did. It always worked until you came along." Mason grimaced in pain.

"That will be enough from him. Take him to the hospital and make sure he is under tight security. This guy is going away for a long time." The sheriff directed the paramedics to the waiting ambulance.

"What about Tom?" Reece asked.

"They're just bringing him up now. I don't know his condition. It sounds like he is the hero here, Reece. Who would have thought it? Mason a fraud and Tom a hero. Should make for some good reading in your paper." The sheriff pointed his finger to the area where Tom and Mason fell. "I'll go see how he is."

Reece stood as the snow swirled around her feet. She felt helpless. She jumped as someone touched her shoulder. It was Austin.

"I came as fast as I could. CeCe is right behind me. Reece, are you all right?" Austin engulfed her in his warm arms.

Austin could feel her shaking. "Come on, let's go inside."

Reece pulled away. "No, not yet Austin. I want to see how Tom is. He saved me. He was the one writing the letters. He distracted Mason long enough for me to get away. They both fell into the ravine. Tom isn't moving, Austin. He has to be all right. He has a good future ahead of him with Lilly."

The sheriff walked back to where Reece and Austin stood.

"How is he?" Reece asked, as tears started to roll down her check.

"He's going to be all right. He has some cuts and bruises. He was able to grab hold of one of the roots to that big tree. It broke his fall. He came out of it better than Mason."

"Please let me talk to him."

"They're bringing him over to the ambulance now."

Reece walked over to Tom. "Tom, are you going to be okay?"

Tom blinked and looked at Reece, "Yes, Reece, t-thank you for worrying about me. I have a letter for you in my truck. It was g-going to be the l-last one. It will explain things. I could never s-say the words, so I wrote them to you. They came out smooth and uncluttered. I d-don't stutter when I write. You know I said those t-things to distract M-mason."

"Yes, Tom. I know that you were here to help me. If you hadn't been here I would be gone now. Thank you for saving me."

Tom pulled his arm out from under the blanket. "Reece, he was the danger I was warning you about. I always just got a terrible feeling of evil when he was around you. I'm glad he will finally get what he deserves. Can you do me a favor and c-call Lilly? S-she will be worried. I was s-supposed to be there for dinner. I don't like when she w-worries."

Reece squeezed his hand. "Anything you want, Tom. By the way, I meant it when I said that the words you wrote were beautiful. You should try your hand at writing. Anytime you want a space in the paper, it's yours. Your words are eloquent and beautiful any way you put them."

Tom smiled as the paramedics moved him along.

Reece was exhausted, but she wanted to get the whole thing over with. "Let's go, Sheriff. I'll finish telling you the rest."

A deputy brought the letter in that Tom had told them was in the truck. Reece opened the letter and recognized the words. She didn't know why she never put the connection together before. Tom was an artist with his hands and his words.

Tom and Mason were going to be all right. Mason would get

what he deserved. They would be able to find out the whole truth about him.

Austin and CeCe took Reece back to the ranch and spent the night sitting with her. As usual, Reece wasn't going to let this get her down.

"We need to move on from this and work on something more important: the wedding."

There was no stopping her now.

Chapter Forty-Three

The day finally approached. Both Austin and CeCe were excited to repeat their vows in front of all the people who mattered so much to them.

It was a brilliant day for a wedding. It had just snowed two inches the night before. The January day was like those Austin had dreamed of. He loved the cold, crisp air and the way the sun shone on the snow, sparkling like a field of diamonds.

CeCe had slept at Reece's the night before; she wanted this to be like the first time when they were married at the overlook. It had only been a few months, but it had taken that long to put together this storybook wedding.

CeCe and Reece arrived at the church in the horse-drawn sleigh. The entire town was there. The church was overflowing with people. Right up front sat Tucker and Ruth. They were part of the family and Austin insisted they take their rightful seats.

Tom and Lilly sat just behind them. Tom had his arm in a sling and a bandage on his head. It reminded them of the awful scene from earlier in the week.

The whole football team was there as well; they were all wearing their State Champions jackets in honor of their coach.

It was just past noon and the wedding was to have begun, but where was Austin? Austin was always on time. He had been there once already; his friends had talked to him.

"I was barely able to control him. He was like a kid in a candy shop," Angie said looking at his watch. "He should have been here. He went back to the ranch to get the gift he had made for CeCe. I'm sure he will be here soon."

In the background there was the faint sound of a siren.

~ ~ ~

Austin couldn't believe that he had forgotten to bring the gift that he had made for CeCe. What was he thinking? He guessed he wasn't thinking in all the excitement. Austin pulled into the ranch and grabbed the gift. He was going to be late if he didn't hurry.

All he could think about was the cradle that he had made for the child that his most beautiful wife was carrying.

He had already had the Koa wood shipped in from Kauai so he would be able to make CeCe something special from the wood. When CeCe told him that she was pregnant, he knew exactly what to do with it.

Austin placed the cradle in the back of the truck and secured it tightly. He jumped in and started to make his way back to the church.

Austin came around the corner of the lake that he and CeCe had skated on last January. Was it really just a year ago? The sun was brilliant, and he almost didn't see the woman standing there in the road.

Austin had to slam on the brakes and swerve to the side to keep from hitting her. The woman was frantic. "Help, you have to help me! My son fell into the lake. We were all here skating, and he got too far out and fell in when the ice cracked."

Austin didn't hesitate. He needed to help. CeCe would understand. They would just be late. Austin grabbed a few things from the truck and raced to the ice.

The boy was trying to pull himself up, but the ice broke beneath him. He disappeared under the water.

Austin watched anxiously, and the boy reappeared. "Wait! I'm going to help you!"

The boy continued to struggle. He went under the water again. This time he didn't come back up.

The boys' mother was hysterically screaming "Do something! He's drowning!"

Austin lay on the ice and dropped the rope into the water in hopes the boy would grab hold of it. Nothing, Austin stood to get a better view. The sun was shining brightly into the hole in the water. Austin could see the helpless boy floating there below the surface.

He knew if he went into the water he would have difficulty getting out, but what else could he do? Austin shouted to the woman, "Go to my truck and call for help. There's a cell phone there. Go, go now!"

The woman ran, falling on the ice and picking herself back up. Austin couldn't wait any longer. He took off his shoes and jacket and jumped in. He had to dive down to reach the boy. How long had it been? Did he wait too long? He couldn't think of that now; just getting the boy out of the water.

The woman came running back with the phone in her hand. She screamed again when Austin raised the lifeless child out of the water. He had to get him out of there, but each time he tried to get out the ice broke more. It was so cold that he was beginning to lose control of his muscles. If he wasn't careful, he would have the woman in there with them.

Austin shouted out orders to the woman to grab hold of the rope that he had lying on the ice. She did as she was told. It was awkward, but he was able to hold the child up while tying the rope onto him. The boy sputtered and convulsed, and almost fell out of his arms. The boy was struggling now, half-conscious and not understanding what was going on. Austin spoke calmly to him, "Just hold on buddy, we're going to get you out of here." The boy stopped struggling, but couldn't control his shaking from the cold and fear.

After what seemed like an eternity, Austin was able to secure the rope and help the boy lay flat on the ice. With the help of his mother, the child made it out of the water. She wrapped the blankets around him that Austin had brought from the truck.

Austin knew he wouldn't be able to get himself up on to the ice without the aid of the rope and someone strong holding onto the other end. Yet he had to try.

His legs were like dead weights now and were hard to keep moving. Austin had exhausted himself trying to get out. He would have to just wait until more help arrived. He hoped it was soon- he didn't know how long he could hold on.

The sun shone on the ice and made it a beautiful blue- the color of CeCe's eyes and the color of the ocean that had stretched out forever before them as they were married in Kauai.

The cold was seeping in deeper now, and was making it difficult for Austin to keep his head out of the water. He had long ago let go of the edge of the thin ice.

He was tired and just wanted to rest a little longer. Thoughts of CeCe came to mind as he did this. Who would the child look like? Would he have her beautiful mouth and eyes, the color of the sea in Kauai?

Austin wrapped his arms around himself to try and keep what little warmth that was in him there, at the same time vainly attempting to tread water. The tightness of his arms around himself reminded him of the short and wonderful time that he and CeCe had spent together. She was the best thing that could have happened to him. He knew that the minute he saw her.

As he started to slip under the water, the last thing Austin thought of was the sweetness of her kisses. That would stay with him always. He could feel the warmth of CeCe there in the cold blue water. He could feel her holding him; she was there with him. It was comforting as he felt himself float away.

~ ~ ~

Everyone knew that something was wrong. A few of the volunteer fireman's pagers went off and they left the church to attend to the emergency.

CeCe was worried. Surely Austin was just hung up by whatever emergency it was that was calling the firemen away.

Austin probably got out to help. He knew that she would understand. That was the way he was. She could feel the nagging worry at the base of her neck. Something was wrong; she could feel it.

Angie said he was going to get in the car and go and see what was taking Austin so long. He insisted that Reece and CeCe wait for him there.

Angie drove out toward the ranch. When he came around the bend in the road, he saw all of the emergency equipment. That's when he saw Austin's truck. Angie got out- he was sure his buddy would be able to leave whatever the emergency it was now that other help had arrived.

Angie walked over toward the crowd. He could see the shoes and jacket lying on the ice. His stomach sank.

An officer came over and pushed everyone back. "Come on, folks we don't need someone else to fall in the ice. Please back up."

Angie pushed his way in. "Officer, where is Austin Carter? That's his jacket there. He was supposed to be at the church."

"I know, son. He stopped to help. A young boy fell into the ice and Austin was able to get him out."

"Where is he?"

"Well, it doesn't look good. They're in there trying to recover him from the water now."

Angie was devastated. He watched and waited while they finally pulled Austin from the water. He was blue and lifeless. The paramedics began to work on him immediately. Angie couldn't wait any longer. He had to go and get CeCe.

Chapter Forty-Four

It had been a long trip and CeCe was exhausted, but she couldn't rest until she went to the overlook. The time difference was three hours from Kauai to Colorado, which gave CeCe a few hours before the sun would be setting.

They drove the beautiful drive up through the Waimea Canyon and into Kokee' state park, the overlook wasn't too far now.

They stopped the car. CeCe walked up the walkway with Reece right behind her. She stood in the same spot where just a few months before she and Austin gave themselves to each other as man and wife.

The sun was just beginning to set. It always made the ocean seem to take on another life. The colors were brilliant: blue, orange, pink, and purple. A light mist had just begun to spray in the wind. Watching the sun set on the sea with the rays creating prisms of color across the water reminded her of that beautiful day they had given themselves to one another.

Tears began to run down CeCe's cheeks. She could only think of all the good times they had spent together. When she shivered, she felt his warm arms come around her swollen stomach.

CeCe turned and touched Austin's face. "Darling, I thought I had lost you. I want you to know that I will always be with you and you will live on in my heart forever, after we're both gone. I knew this is where we needed to come to renew you. Promise me you will be here with me for a long time."

Austin kissed his wife and hugged her to him tightly as he looked out over the beautiful landscape. "This is where I have always been meant to be with you, my darling: 'Where the Mountains Join the Sea.' Yes, CeCe, I will be with you for a very long time. Now, I think it's time we got you off your feet." Austin picked CeCe up and carried her back to the car.

Made in the USA
Las Vegas, NV
23 January 2021